Interstellar Medic:
THE LONG RUN

C000282594

BAEN BOOKS by PATRICK CHILES

ECCENTRIC ORBITS
Frozen Orbit
Escape Orbit

INTERSTELLAR MEDIC
Interstellar Medic: The Long Run

Frontier

To purchase these titles in e-book form, please go to www.baen.com.

Interstellar Medic:
THE LONG RUN

PATRICK CHILES

This is a work of fiction. All the characters and events portrayed in this book are fictional, and any resemblance to real people or incidents is purely coincidental.

Copyright © 2024 by Patrick Chiles

All rights reserved, including the right to reproduce this book or portions thereof in any form.

A Baen Books Original

Baen Publishing Enterprises
P.O. Box 1403
Riverdale, NY 10471
www.baen.com

ISBN: 978-1-9821-9328-7

Cover art by Marianne Plumridge Eggleton

First printing, March 2024

Distributed by Simon & Schuster
1230 Avenue of the Americas
New York, NY 10020

Library of Congress Cataloging-in-Publication Data

Names: Chiles, Patrick, author.
Title: Interstellar medic : the long run / Patrick Chiles.
Other titles: Long run
Description: Riverdale, NY : Baen Publishing Enterprises, 2024. | Series:
  Interstellar medic ; 1
Identifiers: LCCN 2023048255 (print) | LCCN 2023048256 (ebook) | ISBN
  9781982193287 (paperback) | ISBN 9781625799531 (e-book)
Subjects: LCGFT: Science fiction. | Novels.
Classification: LCC PS3603.H5644 I58 2024 (print) | LCC PS3603.H5644
  (ebook) | DDC 813/.6—dc23/eng/20231127
LC record available at https://lccn.loc.gov/2023048255
LC ebook record available at https://lccn.loc.gov/2023048256

Printed in the United States of America

10 9 8 7 6 5 4 3 2 1

Dedication

To medics, firefighters, police, and ER staff everywhere.

Acknowledgments

My understanding of emergency medicine and human/animal/alien anatomy is purely superficial. I could not have written this book without the help of some wonderful subject matter experts, to whom I am forever grateful:

Many thanks are due to Assistant Battalion Chief Chas Adams and the men and women of the Madison Township, Ohio, fire department. Most everything I learned about emergency medical services comes from the time I spent with them on runs and in the firehouse. They have a difficult job and were extremely patient and accommodating with my many questions.

Thanks are also due to Sarah Adams, MD (no relation to Chas), a science fiction fan and great source of understanding regarding human physiology and response to medications.

Finally, to my wife, Melissa, a nurse and former EMT who began my education in emergency medicine. Any resemblance to Melanie Mooney is purely intentional.

1

Delivering babies is the highlight of a paramedic's career, a welcome respite from the daily parade of illness, injury and death that otherwise defines our existence. Bringing a new life into the world is transcendent, a near-magical affirmation of our profession's essential goodness, a welcome reminder that we are more than mere escorts for the dying into whatever afterlife awaits them.

All of that happy horseshit goes out the window when the baby has tentacles and fangs dripping with toxic goo.

It's nothing personal, mind you. The kid can't control itself, and I certainly can't expect much from the parent at this point. She (or he; with this species it's interchangeable) is strapped to a gurney in the back of our bus, with her tentacles pinned beneath a makeshift concoction of restraints and her fangs safely concealed behind a breathing mask. Childbirth can drive a human mother half crazy, but a hextopus in labor is like wrestling snakes and there's no referee to call foul when the teeth come out.

At this point I should mention "hextopus" isn't what they call themselves, but it's the best English classification I can think of for a species with six elongated, retractile limbs: If an octopus has eight tentacles, then six makes for a hextopus. If I'd paid better attention to Latin in college I could probably come up with a more scientific-sounding taxonomy, but at this point I'm just trying to get the baby out alive.

Hextopods are technically amphibious, but they strongly prefer water. Our immediate problem is that we're in a standard atmosphere of oxygen and nitrogen, which is what most Union races breathe, but I'll save the exobiology lesson for later. This species normally gives birth underwater, and I'm told it goes a lot more smoothly in their natural environment. That makes sense, and it also explains why the mom-to-be is damned near out of her mind right now, to the point of being dangerous.

I take my eye off the job at hand for a split second to check the cat's cradle of cargo straps holding her back. Each of her tentacles is a couple meters' worth of pure muscle and could tear me in half like prying apart a mollusk. The oxygenated fluid we're pumping through her mask calmed her down enough for us to get her into our cobbled-together restraints, so at least I don't have those appendages to worry about.

The baby is another matter. It won't be nearly as strong as a full-grown hextopus, but it's absolutely complicating things. Thankfully our scanners show the head is coming first, because I don't want to reach up into Mom's birth canal to wrestle with a writhing mass of tentacles, much less have to deal with the fangs. Our anatomy instructor warned us that these things come out instinctively snapping at whatever's close, which in this case is me. And while they're not venomous, their saliva is toxic to most other races, including humans.

The normal reflex would be to close my eyes as I reach into the birth canal, but that's something I learned to control a long time ago on the farm. I tell myself this is no different than delivering a calf, while the carbon-flex protective sleeves I'm wearing ought to shield me from the pointy parts and their poisonous slime.

I find the head, and here's where I have to be extra careful. The birthing process is a lot less complicated underwater, where Mom naturally spits the baby out when the time comes. Here, they have to work at it because they're averse to delivering in open air. That means going elbow-deep up her birth canal, finding the baby, and pulling it out. It's almost all head but for those flailing tentacles, and my hands quickly find something about the size and shape of a football. I start massaging it toward me, gently coaxing it along with my fingertips.

Thing is, you have to be cautious with the head because these creatures are smart. And I don't mean "smart" like trained horses or dolphins; hextopods are fiercely intelligent. Beyond human intelligence, in fact beyond a lot of other Union species. Their method of communication is so subtle as to have been overlooked for centuries, at least by my notion of time. It wasn't until they'd built vehicles to finally leave the confines of their underwater homes that the powers-that-be realized these beings were deserving of membership in the Galactic Union.

The Union's not quite sold on humans yet, which is why I'm here, but that's another story.

I feel my way forward until my fingers move past the crown and the first baby tentacle wraps itself around my hand. This is not a pleasant sensation, and I fight the urge to recoil in fear and disgust. Before long both of my hands have these wormy little appendages wound tightly around them, and I'm safe to start applying some force. I take a deep breath, my translator tells Mom to do the same in a burbling speech I can't begin to understand, and I pull back in one smooth, continuous motion.

In my hands is a writhing infant hextopus, its skin frantically changing colors as it reacts to the shock of its new environment. This kaleidoscope of hues is the baby's silent cry as it emerges into its new world. Mom begins changing colors in rhythm with her baby; this is how they communicate. There's no time for me to marvel at their strange symbiosis, so I place the baby in a makeshift tank and am immediately rewarded by its tiny tentacles releasing their death grip on me. The newborn is now in its natural environment and I watch its colors settle into calmer shades of pink and blue as it breathes for the first time. I realize I've been holding my breath as well and collapse onto the floor with an exhausted groan. I've been on shift for barely an hour.

Back home, this would've earned me a stork pin for my EMS uniform. I don't know what the Union awards for delivering an alien squid baby.

My name is Melanie Mooney, and on Earth I was a paramedic. That's also what I do here, though the job is equal parts medic and veterinarian. I realize that sounds either contrary or redundant, but stay with me. The Union tapped me for this job because I'm something of a unique asset in their view.

In case you haven't already figured this out, the answer to the longstanding question of whether there's other intelligent life in the universe is unequivocally *yes*. Lots of it, in fact. At present there are over two dozen different intelligent species in the Union, with many more lingering on the outskirts who've yet to be selected for admission.

Ours is one of them. I mentioned they weren't entirely sold on humans yet. There are a lot of criteria the big brains in charge (and some are literally just that—big brains) have for judging a species' readiness, but the main one is culture. If they don't believe your species is prepared for the shock (and trust me, it's shocking) then they'll keep their distance and quietly observe until they think you're ready.

That doesn't always work out as planned, which is how I got here. They might be smart, but they're not infallible. That should offer our own species some encouragement.

The reason I'm a "unique asset" is because I have an ability that is considered rare in the Union: that is, I'm able and willing to care for a wide range of species. For being so technologically and culturally advanced, when it comes to medicine a lot of the various Union species can be surprisingly provincial. Very few are willing to provide medical care to anyone outside of their own kind. They have reasons, sometimes not particularly good ones, but it's heartening to know that civilizations more advanced than ours aren't perfect either.

I don't know if this is a quality all humans share—many surely don't—but if it's widespread enough then that's a big check in humanity's "plus" column, so I'd better not screw up this gig. I attribute my own flexibility to growing up on a farm and being a veterinary student before switching gears to become a medic. Being able to diagnose and treat creatures who can't tell you what's wrong with them turns out to be a valuable skill in the rest of the galaxy.

The "bus" I referred to earlier is our ambulance. On Earth we'd also call it a "squad." Cops usually called it a "meat wagon," but we hardly ever use "ambulance." Too many syllables.

In its former life it was a Union Class III executive transport, with the comfy interior stripped out and replaced with an adjustable gurney and every type of life support we might need. Air ambulance services on Earth would do the same thing, equipping old private jets for rapid patient transport.

As the name implies, an interplanetary transport can do a lot more than a boring old jet. And I've learned "interplanetary" doesn't do it justice either. It'd be like calling that Earth jet a puddle jumper. I'm no rocket scientist, but these things can zip around in ways that would make actual rocket scientists need to change their shorts.

I understand enough to know that the distances between worlds are almost beyond comprehension, and the technology used to bridge that gulf is even more so. I never paid much attention to this kind of thing before, but I've learned the reason it takes our puny space probes years to reach other planets is because our methods are antiquated by Union reckoning. It was explained to me that our probes are passively coasting between worlds, whereas Union pilots can keep their feet on the gas, so traveling across a solar system can be done in a matter of hours. I've been able to grasp that much.

Getting to planets in other star systems is a whole other feat which I don't begin to understand. Translated into English, they said it's best described as creating a bubble in space that lets a ship move almost instantaneously between stars. However it works, they don't even describe the technology as an engine; it's a "drive." After it was described to me, I asked, "Like warp drive?" and they said that's essentially correct. I may not have paid much attention to the actual science before, but I have watched a few sci-fi movies.

If I'd taken more physics in college I might understand it better, but I'd been in veterinary school, so biology it was. My Union mentors assured me that even if I'd done better in freshman calculus it still wouldn't be fully explainable. But thank goodness I had at least that much, because I've learned that math is the true universal language. The symbology may vary, but in the end two plus two equals four and the first derivative of any whole number is zero, no matter which star system you're from.

It kind of has to be. I remember my old math professor said that calculus is the key to understanding nature, which I didn't fully grasp until much later. It's been used to do everything from determining that the speed of light is a universal constant, down to setting the ideal price for a bag of chips at Walmart.

He also said there was some debate as to whether Newton invented calculus or discovered it, since it can model pretty much everything in nature. The longer I'm out here, the more I'm convinced he discovered it. It's just too perfect.

My hosts patiently explained our transport's basic functions in a way I could comprehend. Knowing that is kind of essential to the job, for the same reason a flight medic needs to understand how the aircraft she's riding in works. Doesn't mean I can fly the thing, but when the pilot tells me why we have to do certain things in a certain way, I get it. For the same reason a flight medic knows that taking a helicopter into severe icing is suicide, I know that certain phenomena in space are off-limits to us even though I'm not able to pilot the ship. Black holes would be the most obvious example, but there's more ways to get yourself killed out here than I thought possible. Of course vacuum is bad; that's what space suits are for. What I didn't know was how dangerous the radiation environment can be—there are limits here despite the Union's advanced technology, and where we can go depends a lot on what our little ship is equipped to withstand. Just as you can't use a fishing boat as an icebreaker in the Arctic, we can't take a Class III transport anywhere near a pulsar: the radiation would overwhelm our plasma shields and cook us in our own skin. That's one of many no-no's.

I've been doing this going on six months now, but I was an earthbound medic long before that. Ten years seems to be the point when most of us get burned out and either move on to other work or stay on as jaded losers. I hadn't reached that point yet, but had sure felt it coming. Getting tapped by the Union might have moved the timeline further out for me, but it's on my mind as we clean up the back of the squad from our messy hextopod delivery.

Cleanup after a big run is never pleasant, but this one's even more difficult thanks to the cumbersome hazmat suit I'm wearing. Among all of the water and alien bodily fluids is the creature's toxic slime. It's nothing personal on their part, it's a natural secretion that helps them digest their food. Like stomach acid, just highly concentrated, and it happens to come out of their mouths which are uncomfortably close to their birth canals. I try not to imagine the prospect of having my mouth that close to my privates as I mop up the mess, wipe down every surface, and sweep a glowing decon boom over the remaining nooks and crannies to finish the job.

As I strip off the hazmat suit and stuff it into the recycler—nearly everything's recycled on a spaceship—I take a look around. The bay is all gleaming silver and pristine white composites, lit by ceiling panels that hold some type of organic illumination I don't understand. It looks like something out of a science fiction movie, which is kind of my life now.

It didn't start out this way.

2

I was headed home after the end of my three-to-midnight shift, driving down an empty country road to our farm. I inherited the property a couple of years earlier, but have never been able to think of it as mine. It still feels like my father's, while I'm only the caretaker until I figure out what to do with it.

After coming around a bend in the road, I noticed a glow off in the woods. The forest here is dense, and the treetops had been sheared off in a path leading straight to those lights. My heart sank—this looked like a plane crash, and those flickering lights could've been a fire.

I'd been off duty for almost an hour, but the medic switch in my brain flipped itself back on right away. We're legally bound to assist in any emergency we might come across, on duty or otherwise. I was spent, but the adrenaline surge woke me up as if I'd pounded a half-dozen espresso shots.

This area had always been a well-known dead zone, and sure enough my phone was useless. I kept an emergency-band radio in my pickup, but when I tried to call in there was nothing but static. That was strange, but I couldn't lose time fussing over things out of my control. I hopped out and grabbed my personal first-aid gear from the tailgate, and pulled a headlamp from one of the outside pouches. I put it on and began picking my way through the woods, toward what I hoped wasn't a burning aircraft.

It was a rough couple hundred yards of crashing through underbrush. My feet kept getting tangled in vines and I stumbled, falling flat on my face. I reached up to feel the fresh cut on my right cheek—wet, but not too bad. So long as I wasn't dripping my own blood onto the patient, I would deal with it later.

I made it to the crash site, which had pummeled a clearing out of the trees. Thankfully there was no fire, but there was an awful lot of smoke. The lights which had looked like fire from a distance were coming from the aircraft itself, some steady, some pulsing intermittently. Planes have running lights so this wasn't particularly surprising, but these weren't the familiar red and green strobes. There was a persistent yellow glow coming from one end, which I assumed were the engines. If those things were still turning then I'd give them a wide berth. Getting scorched by jet exhaust or sucked down an intake were things to avoid.

The plane's fuselage was pretty banged up but still mostly intact, with skin as lustrous as polished silver despite the damage. It was shaped like a flattened cigar, so I assumed the wings had been torn off on impact. No tail, either. Maybe it was military?

Hopefully none of the passengers had been thrown clear, but even more so I hoped none were trapped inside. If I needed the Jaws of Life to pry anyone free, they'd be screwed until more help arrived. Airplanes have emergency locator beacons that automatically go off in a crash, so even if I couldn't get through to anyone, somebody would be on their way soon.

That part I was right about. Exactly who "somebody" was would come as a surprise, though much later.

For now, I had to concentrate on doing first things first. That meant finishing my survey of the scene to make sure it was safe to get to work, though "safe" is an elusive term when it involves wrecked machinery and there's no one else on scene. All bets would be off once I crawled inside this thing.

I didn't see any bodies around the crash site, which made sense as there were no obvious breaches. No windows, for that matter, which made it really odd. Was it a drone? This thing seemed awfully big to be one of those. I called out, announcing EMS on the scene, but nobody answered. They had to be inside. It would've helped if there was a door somewhere. Eventually I found a section that had been torn open, and I could see partway inside.

I pulled on a pair of tough work gloves from my trauma bag and started prying away at the damaged section. It was very light stuff, but strong. The crumpled parts gave way as easily as tin foil, but the intact sections wouldn't budge no matter how much weight I put into it.

Not that I had a lot of weight to begin with, being barely five feet tall and a hundred pounds soaking wet. The younger firefighters nicknamed me "Tiny," but my size also made me a prime candidate for confined-space rescues. Think caves, collapsed buildings, mangled-up car wrecks. I can wheedle my way into most anything, which shuts the big guys up when I'm able to get into places they can't.

I didn't know much about airplanes other than what we learned in heavy rescue school, in particular what to look out for. One this size would have two pilots, maybe a flight attendant ("stewardess" had long since fallen out of favor). Probably passengers, but not always, so I was looking for at least two victims inside. I pulled aside a section of crushed metal and got a peek into what was left of the cabin. It was all white, or at least parts of it used to be. There'd been a fire, that much I could tell from the partially scorched interior.

That's when I saw an arm sticking out from beneath a panel. It was thin, with unusually long fingers. I didn't think much about this, as blunt force trauma can do awful things to a body. It appeared ashen under my headlamp, and gray skin is never a good sign. If this guy was already in pallor, he could have been dead anywhere from fifteen minutes up to a couple of hours.

I reached for his wrist to search for a pulse, but found nothing. I could move the arm, so rigor hadn't set in yet. That meant they'd been here about two hours at most.

That was when the arm moved.

I recoiled in shock and banged my head on a dislodged panel. Postmortem muscle contractions are a thing, but it was nothing I'd ever experienced firsthand. What was most unnerving was when the hand opened up to grasp mine. Dead bodies can do some weird stuff, but they don't do *that*.

Holy hell, this guy was still alive! I unwrapped his unusually elongated fingers from around mine and reached for his wrist again. It took a while to find it, but there was a pulse now. Thready, which explained the pallor. Something I couldn't yet see had to be pressing against him and restricting blood flow.

It was decision time. Should I wait for heavy rescue to arrive, or keep making my way inside? A crashed aircraft is by definition of dubious structural integrity. I'm no engineer, but those are the kinds of questions we're trained to ask ourselves before climbing into wrecked vehicles: namely, is this thing likely to come down on top of me?

I pushed against the side panels with my foot and braced my back against the bare metal behind me. Nothing gave way, and I didn't hear any telltale creaks or groans that might signal impending collapse. It wasn't much to go on, but it was all I had at the moment.

Besides the headlamp, there was a flashlight on my belt. I took it out and shined the beam into the small opening near my patient's arm. It looked like there was enough space to work in, but it would be close quarters.

I shoved the trauma bag in ahead of me before crawling in up to my shoulders. If I could do that comfortably, then the rest of me could make it all the way through. "Hang tight, I'm coming in," I announced to whoever was inside.

It turned out I didn't have to worry about space. This machine had plenty of it after I got past all that crumpled metal. This part of the cabin was mostly intact, lined with soft paneling in varying shades of white mounted within a thin metallic framework. I made another quick assessment of the scene, looking both for victims and any signs of immediate danger. Smoke and fire would be the big ones, which were blessedly absent. No petroleum smells, either. Had it simply run out of fuel?

Searching the cabin with my headlamp and flashlight I counted three patients; two were in matching light gray skintight jumpsuits. One of them was the guy with the pinned arm. The third was up front, a long-haired blond fellow dressed in white. He sat in a sleekly curved seat, slumped over what I assumed were the controls. The instrument panel was devoid of any actual instruments, but I knew enough to recall that the latest jets had what they call "glass cockpits" which replace all of the dials and gauges with computer screens. I still had no idea what kind this was, but it was definitely new and very high-tech.

I turned to my first patient, the one with the trapped arm. I wasn't looking at his face yet; my first impression was that he wore an odd kind of bug-eyed helmet. Again, this was unusual but not a complete surprise. This had to be a military jet, and who knew what sort of funky gear they wore?

He was pinned, but not badly. One of those interior panels was pressed against him. When I moved it I found it was as light as the metal skin outside, but its frame wouldn't give way easily. It didn't look like it was keeping anything from falling, so I put my shoulder against it and shoved off with my feet. There were scraping and groaning noises as it finally began to move, hopefully enough to pry this fellow loose.

His arm was free now. I could feel his pulse beneath my fingertips, much stronger with the blood flow unrestricted. A good sign. I began checking the rest of him for any signs of trauma—limbs out of place, bleeding, the obvious stuff. Now that there was a pulse, I pulled out my stethoscope and began listening for heart and respiratory activity. It took a while to find it, and when I finally landed on a good spot there still wasn't much to speak of. His heart rate was weak and irregular and his breathing was shallow. This guy could crash any minute.

I checked my watch—twelve minutes since I arrived on scene. There still weren't any sirens, and it's not like I carried a defibrillator in my go bag. If this guy coded and I had to give CPR, that meant the others would be left to fend for themselves. This was not a good situation, but I could only assess one person at a time, so I had to quickly finish this guy and move on to the others. I began exploring with my fingertips, looking for more signs of trauma. I needed to check his pupils for response, so I reached for that strange bug-eyed helmet visor.

It wasn't a helmet. It was hard to imagine how I missed that; maybe it would've been more obvious in daylight. That was his actual head, egg-shaped and of the same gray pallor, with glistening almond-shaped eyes, big and black as night.

My mind began racing. Already amped-up from the rush of being first on scene, now my heart was about to burst out of my chest like a creature from one of those space alien movies . . .

Space alien.

The words tried to escape my mouth but I was dumbstruck. My attention was drawn away from my patient—which should *never* happen—for another look around this wrecked whatever-it-was.

It hadn't resembled any airplane I'd ever seen in the first place, and now it looked even less so. To begin with, there were only a few seats. The rest of the cabin was empty, nothing but those spongy white wall panels. Where did everyone sit? It reminded me of a padded cell, of the kind sometimes used for mental patients. Maybe that's where I needed to be myself, because this was all too crazy. For being in a crash, the interior was remarkably intact. There were a few things that looked like they might be out of place, but then I had no reference to judge against. It looked like nearly all of the damage was absorbed by the outer hull or airframe or whatever it was called. Just this one area I'd been able to crawl into got crunched, but the occupants had obviously been knocked around hard.

I turned back to my patient. He turned his head to face me, but I couldn't tell if there was any recognition in those jet-black eyes. The adrenaline was really pumping now; my hands were shaking and my stomach felt like it was doing backflips. I wiped my palms on my pants, suddenly aware that I was sweating profusely.

I heard movement. Something was shuffling behind me. A hand gripped my shoulder, firm but not in a threatening way. There was a voice but I couldn't tell what it was saying. I felt a pinprick on my right temple.

The cabin swirled around me before everything went dark.

I woke up the next morning in my bed. Everything was normal, which wouldn't have seemed odd except that I was on my back with my grandmother's old quilt draped over me. I never slept this way— I'm almost always on my stomach with the quilt and sheets in a tangle around my legs.

I must have totally zonked out, but that didn't make any sense either. I was as alert as if I'd been up for hours and finished off the day's first pot of coffee. My blue utility pants were draped over the back of a chair by the window, and my go bag was tucked away in a corner.

I never do that. The bag stays in the garage when it's not in my truck bed, and the uniform gets stripped off in the mud room before I go in the house. There's a good reason for this: we're exposed to all manner of biological nastiness on the job, so every medic with half a brain strips down before coming inside. It's basic decontamination. I was also still wearing my uniform T-shirt from the night before, so out of caution I'd have to strip the bed and spray the mattress down with Lysol.

I was never this careless. Maybe I was more wiped out than I thought, because this was not what my normal routine looked like. It was almost like I'd been led home and put to bed after staying too late at the bar after work.

What did I do after work last night, for that matter? I was on the late shift, so hitting the bar at midnight with the guys would've been a definite possibility. I felt a jolt of panic, that I somehow got blackout drunk and *oh god I'm an alcoholic.*

No. I was confident that wasn't the case. Two drinks were my usual limit; it's been that way since college because I don't like losing control. It's not fun anymore if I can't drive myself home.

Did some sleazeball slip something into my beer? Did I get roofied? If so, they'd been awfully polite about it, what with tucking me into my own bed and putting my stuff away nice and neat.

That couldn't be it either, but I couldn't shake the feeling that I hadn't made it home on my own. Somebody had helped me, maybe one of the other medics who responded to that last run . . .

The last run. That was it. I hadn't been on duty, just passing by on my way home. It had been a plane crash, that much I remembered. It was all such a whirlwind, almost too much to handle. Good thing those other guys showed up . . .

Who, though? I couldn't recall which house responded, and I'd have remembered if it were one of our own. Maybe they'd come from the next county over; we're spread far enough apart that jurisdictions get blurry. Ultimately it comes down to who can get on scene first.

I reached for my phone and saw it was dead. I must have forgotten to plug it in, because the battery was completely drained. The clock on my nightstand said it was almost noon. I wasn't due at the station for another couple of hours, so I flicked on the TV. A plane crash would be all over the news.

I made a quick run to the bathroom, then impatiently sat through the last few minutes of *The Price Is Right*, waiting for the local news. I endured the flashy graphics and earnest music, impatient for them to get to last night's big story.

At ten past noon, I was still waiting after nothing but weather and farm reports and human-interest nonsense about some old lady who lost her cat. The only halfway interesting bit was another report of some farmer's missing cattle, but not one word about a plane crash. Odd, but I couldn't dwell on it. It was time to get ready for work.

3

It started to become obvious that something was off when I pulled up behind the station. The parking lot was almost full, but it wasn't the usual collection of obnoxiously large pickups. It still held a lot of obnoxiously large pickups, just not the ones I was used to seeing. A bunch of guys must have traded shifts today. I parked my equally large F-150—I had an excuse, what with living on an actual farm—and made my way into the firehouse.

Most of the guys were still pulling gear from their lockers, and a couple were eyeing me funny, like I wasn't supposed to be there. I found one of my fellow medics, Kyle, who was also looking at me funny. He was a redheaded, wiry little snake in the grass, but he happened to be the first person who talked to me.

"What's going on?" I asked. "You guys aren't supposed to be on until tomorrow."

"Check your watch there, Tiny. You're the one who's off. Really off."

Kyle could be a tiresome prankster. I glanced at my watch and wondered why I was taking him seriously. "What are you talking about? I'm on time for—"

I noticed the date: the fourteenth. What the hell?

He was staring now. "Yeah."

"I don't understand."

"Neither does the chief, and he's got questions. Word is you never clocked in, didn't call in either. He had to call me in to cover your shift."

17

I decided this was more of his juvenile mischief. Had to be. I was running out of patience. "Don't bullshit me. It's Wednesday. I'm on mids this week."

He gave me a quizzical look, as if I'd lost my mind and he wasn't sure what to say next. "It's Thursday, and you're off until Saturday," he said, with the kind of exaggerated calm we used for disoriented patients. "Maybe longer once the chief decides what to do with you."

I was at a loss. I'd somehow slept through an entire day and the guy I get along with the least had been called in to ride for me. I was in for an epic ass-chewing.

"Chief's in his office," Kyle said over his shoulder as he climbed into the rig. "He said to send you in if you decided to show up today."

Without a clue of what else to say, I replied with a nervous nod and headed down the hall to whatever fate awaited me. None of this made sense. I was a good medic, damn it. I never left my partners hanging like this. And if this was a setup, then that meant Kyle or somebody wanted to get me in serious trouble. I wondered what I could've done to make myself a target, and how anyone could've engineered such a malicious prank.

Understand that some of the younger guys can be real meatheads. They've bought into the whole first responder mythos and would love nothing more than for the firehouse to be their own personal He-Man Woman-Hater's Club, where they can belch and fart and scratch their balls while telling raunchy jokes without judgment. What they fail to understand is we girls can be even worse when they're not looking.

I decided my offense was simply possessing XX chromosomes. These were the thoughts swirling through my bewildered brain as I knocked on the battalion chief's door. They might've been ridiculous, even delusional, but right then they were all I had.

"Enter."

"You wanted to see me, Chief?" Of course he did, but what else was I supposed to say? I stood in front of his desk with my hands clasped behind my back in the customary stance of someone who's about to have their ass handed to them. He didn't motion for me to sit down.

He was a large man who looked older than his years, with a jowly face and the traditional fireman's handlebar mustache, flecked with gray. He leaned back in his chair and stared me down for several agonizing seconds. "What happened yesterday, Mooney?"

Where to start? I was going home and got detoured by a run I could barely remember? I realized if it actually had happened the day before yesterday, that would explain why it hadn't been on the news.

Honesty was always the best policy, especially when you didn't know what was happening. "I don't have an answer for you, Chief. I don't even know myself."

His lips twisted into a scowl. "You understand that's not going to cut it, of course."

"I understand. I thought I was on time for my shift today."

"Twenty-four hours ago, you would've been. But you weren't, so I had to pull someone from his day off to cover your shift. And you can't tell me what you were doing yesterday. I expect this kind of behavior from the younger guys, but not you." That last part stung. He might not have meant it as such, but it was a sideways jab at my utter lack of anything resembling a social life.

I was at a loss. It would've been nice if I'd been able to remember where the last day went. My mouth was dry, and I swallowed hard. "I got off shift last night . . . I mean Tuesday night . . . and was almost home when I came on that plane crash off 900 North. I stopped to render aid and—"

He held up a hand to interrupt me. "Plane crash? What the hell are you talking about?"

"The one in the woods outside Walnut Ridge. You guys didn't get the call?"

"Nobody did. We'd for sure have heard about something like that."

"Well, *somebody* responded. Maybe one of the nearby counties—"

"You live out towards Carthage, right?"

"Yes sir."

"I'll reach out to the other chiefs, but I can tell you there hasn't been a word about any plane crash. That sort of thing gets around. What kind of plane?"

I searched my memory, which still felt frighteningly thin. "Couldn't tell for certain. Wasn't a light plane, that's for sure. Some kind of jet, but no markings. It was all polished metal. Wings and tail must've snapped off in the crash because I never saw them. I assumed it was military."

The chief stroked his chin as he studied me from the corners of his eyes. In his shoes, I'd have been skeptical too. "How many victims?"

Good question. "Three, I think."

"You *think*? You didn't fully assess the scene before jumping right in? We've had conversations about your freelancing before, Mooney."

No kidding. He'd already held up my last promotion after lecturing me on being too eager for my own good, charging into scenes before they were secure. In my defense, sometimes the right thing to do doesn't fit into our standard operating procedures.

"No sir, I determined the site was secure." At least I thought so. The more I tried to recall, the fuzzier it all became.

"What mystifies me is why you didn't call this in yourself, if you were the first on scene."

Another good question. I had a vague memory of not being able to raise anyone. "Like you said, I was headed toward Carthage. There's a lot of dead zones out there and my handheld was out of range."

"And you went home after that?"

I hesitated to answer that one. "I guess so, since that's where I woke up this morning. But I don't remember going home."

He lifted a bushy eyebrow and drummed meaty fingers atop his desk before huffing out a deep sigh. "You know what? I believe you. You happened onto a scene that rattled your cage. Between that and exhaustion, maybe you found your way home from habit and zoned out." He leaned forward and clasped his hands together. "But that still leaves some questions which bother me. If you found a wrecked airplane, worked the scene alone, and nobody else got the call, then we've still got potential casualties out there." He picked up the phone and called his cohort over in the neighboring county.

I spent the next hour in his office waiting for word on my mystery crash scene, to no avail. Nobody in the surrounding counties got the call, and the FAA didn't have any records of an emergency beacon going off. The military, of course, didn't acknowledge anything. The chief docked me a day's pay—fair enough since I hadn't shown up yesterday—and it seemed like he was getting ready for more when he was cut off by the station alarm's warbling tone of an ambulance call. "Looks like you've got a run, Mooney."

I glanced past him at the shift calendar on a whiteboard behind his desk. "Aren't I supposed to be off today?"

"You were. But Jennings is behind on his CE training and here you are, rested and ready. We'll finish this later." He dismissed me with a wave, and I was happy to follow his cue. I ran out to the bay and climbed into the already idling squad. Kyle was behind the wheel, waiting impatiently.

"You're my partner today?" He shook his head. "Try and keep up, Tiny." I could never be sure if he was serious; it paid to keep my guard up with him.

A laptop mounted between our seats displayed every active call in the county. Ours was highlighted in green, which told dispatch we were responding. It was a slip-and-fall, which could land anywhere in the range between nothing or a broken pelvis. We never assumed anything, though I recognized the address right away. "Frequent flyer," I sighed. "He's turning into a weekly event."

"Maybe for you. Never been there."

I smiled to myself. "You're in for a treat." He reached up to flick on the lights and sirens, and we were on our way.

Ten minutes later we let ourselves into a dingy apartment. I'd been here enough to know where the key was hidden, beneath a cracked flowerpot beside the front door. We were greeted with the overwhelming stench of cigarettes, musty carpet, and human waste. I knew what to expect, and it was satisfying to see Kyle's freckled nose wrinkle at the odor.

"Code brown," he said with disgust.

"Back here," a voice wailed. We made our way to the single bedroom at the end of a short hallway and found a portly man on the floor, wedged between his bed and a motorized wheelchair. An oxygen cannula hung loosely around his neck, away from his nostrils. The first thing I did was put it back in place; he needed the O_2. One of his legs was bent out at an awkward angle, which would've looked painful if I'd not already known what was up. I could see Kyle was expecting a badly wrenched knee and was taken by surprise when he found our patient's leg ended at the thigh.

No matter how disquieting the scene—and we'd both experienced much worse than this—it's always important to project calm. "What's going on, dear?" I asked lightly as I began checking his vitals.

He rolled his eyes and theatrically waved his hands. "Ain't it obvious? I fell outta my damned bed!"

"Yes sir, you certainly did." By now I had a BP cuff on one arm and a pulse oximeter on his finger. His O_2 sats were in the low nineties and heading up thanks to having his cannula back in place. His blood pressure was uncomfortably high though, one sixty-five over ninety-eight. That could be chalked up to the pain and stress of his current awkward condition, but we'd need to keep an eye on it. I knew from prior history that he was diabetic (thus the missing leg) and high blood pressure could indicate any number of bad things about to happen. "Have you checked your blood sugar recently?"

He waved angrily at a glucose meter on the floor, as if it were the cause of his problem. "That's what I was reaching for when I fell!" He was mad at himself, but it was easier to be pissed off at inanimate objects. His breath didn't smell unusual, which can be an indicator of high blood sugar. I took his meter instead of digging one out of our kit and pressed it against his finger. He wailed like a banshee, all out of proportion to the pinprick that he had to administer himself regularly. Overreactions like that can be annoying, but they're also common when somebody is hurting for other reasons, and this guy was definitely in a pickle.

Kyle stood with his hands on his hips and shot an exasperated look at me, as if this were somehow my fault. I'd forgotten all about missing my last shift until then. Let your buddies down and you'll pay for it one way or another.

"Let's get this chair out of the way first, give ourselves some room," I said, purposefully ignoring my partner's attitude. Kyle tapped the chair's joystick and moved it clear, at which point our patient rolled over onto his back like a helpless turtle, uncovering a mess which is best left unmentioned. Suffice to say we found where the smell was coming from.

Lovely.

"You get the lift," I muttered. "I'll get him cleaned up," and proceeded to use a whole package of wet wipes on our hapless victim. "You hang on, sir, and we'll get you situated."

Kyle returned and unfolded a nylon tarp with carrying straps on either end. From there it was a simple matter of getting the patient sitting upright, but heaving him up into his chair wasn't. I stay fit, but this job required real muscle and I'm not proud to say my already annoyed partner had to do most of the lifting. I just didn't want to make matters worse and lose this guy on my end.

With our patient cleaned up and mostly comfortable in his chair, we still had business. "We need to get a few more vitals on you, okay?" I adjusted the loosened BP cuff and slipped the pulse ox back onto his index finger while Kyle attached ECG leads. After a few minutes his blood pressure had settled down, O_2 sats were back in the high nineties, and the twelve-lead showed normal sinus rhythm. Our assessment didn't reveal any signs of broken bones or other trauma, other than a severely wounded ego.

The next part was routine. We already knew the answer, but had to ask. "Would you like us to take you to the hospital? We think you should go."

He looked at me like I had a third eyeball in my forehead. "Hell no! They'll keep me up all night doing more tests and I'll come out sicker than when I went in!"

Kyle and I exchanged a look: *Couldn't argue with that.* We lingered a few minutes to complete the "against medical advice" paperwork, collected our gear, and left. Back at the station, we wiped down the squad and hosed off our boots.

That run was the highlight of my shift. There weren't many calls that night, and nearly every one of them was another slip-and-fall. Our single hospital transport came from a minor car accident. It was obvious the guy who got rear-ended was looking to milk the other guy's insurance for all it was worth, but we never take chances when someone's complaining of a neck injury.

If that sounds jaded, so be it. After a day like this one, you end up pleasantly surprised when someone's in actual distress.

It was after midnight when my shift ended, and I was in no mood to go home and sulk. It's better to do that at a bar, and there's a little dive along the river that I liked to hit on my way home after a rough day. The beer is always cold and Mac serves the best burgers in this part of Indiana. It was a nice night, so I took a table on the deck overlooking the river to lose myself in the sound of water caressing the rocks.

I must have been really lost in thought, because it was almost two hours later when Mac tapped me on the shoulder: I didn't have to go home, but I couldn't stay here. He seemed concerned. Following his eyes, I looked down at the table to find a single bite taken out of my burger and maybe one or two pulls from the longneck sitting by my plate.

I tossed a twenty on the table to clear my tab, which was way more than I owed, but then he'd let me hang out long after closing time. I didn't have to check my watch to know it had to be well past 3:00 A.M. when I finally climbed back into my truck to drive home.

Taking a turn that led back through the woods, I saw something completely unexpected, but still strangely familiar: a yellow glow off in the trees. I'd finally put all of yesterday's—or the day before yesterday's—events out of my mind and here I was, looking at what appeared to be the exact same scene. Did no one actually report this? Or maybe the crash investigators had finally arrived. Air Force, probably. In my gut, I knew that wasn't a civilian jet.

Against my better judgment, I pulled off onto the shoulder and followed the trail of snapped-off trees into the same clearing.

That's when I blacked out. Again.

☤ 4 ☤

I woke up on the worn-out floral pattern sofa in my living room, a leftover piece of my parents' furniture from years ago which I could never bring myself to replace. I felt bleary-eyed and slightly nauseated, like from a hangover, except that I'd barely had half a beer.

I couldn't remember how I got home either, which would seem like déjà vu except for the two people standing in front of me.

That woke me right the hell up.

My first reaction was to lunge for the side table, where I kept a loaded .38 revolver in the drawer. I was groggy enough that my hands fumbled at the knob, while something was telling me to relax. Like I could hear them in my head.

"That won't be necessary," one of them said with a slight wave of his hand, like I'd been Jedi-mind-tricked. "Please don't be alarmed."

I stared at them like an idiot for what felt like an eternity. They could have been twins: both tall and thin, with shoulder-length blond hair so light that it could've been spun gold. I self-consciously fluffed my own hair. Whoever their stylist was, I could've used a referral. They wore identical pale two-piece suits with silver piping, which I assumed was some kind of uniform. The only difference between the two was the color of their eyes, which shone like jewels. One was sapphire blue, the other emerald green. Whoever these guys were, they were definitely not from around here.

"A-alarmed?" I stuttered. "I wake up in my living room, with no idea how I got here, with a couple of guys that look like Nordic gods standing in front of me. And I swear I just heard one of you in my head. So yeah, I'm alarmed."

They exchanged looks; Green Eyes gave Blue Eyes a nod like he was answering some unspoken question. "May we sit?" Blue Eyes asked.

I got the sense this was to put me at ease more than it was for their own comfort. I waved them to a pair of wingback chairs across from me. What else was I going to do? "You'll have to excuse the mess. I wasn't expecting company." Sarcasm felt like my best defense.

"You're wondering why we're here."

"I'm wondering a lot of things right now."

"Not long ago, you came across one of our survey vehicles which had experienced mechanical difficulties. It was what you might call a 'forced landing.'"

"You mean it crashed." I knew that, but why did it feel like it had happened ages ago?

"Yes, though the situation was rather more complex than that. It is also somewhat beside the point. You stopped and rendered aid to its occupants. Why?"

For the first time, I felt like I was looking at them in the same way they seemed to be looking at me. That is, like a specimen under a microscope. Their question was so obvious as to be ridiculous. I pointed at the blue six-pointed emblem on my shirt. "I'm a medic. It's what I do."

"You no doubt noticed they were not your typical patients. Yet you showed remarkable composure."

Why did that feel like a distant memory too? They had for sure been unlike any accident victims I'd ever come across. I remember thinking they were children, which wouldn't make sense if that had been a military jet . . .

I was being interrogated, which made me impatient and not a little pissed off. "Are you with the Air Force?" I kind of knew the answer already; they were dressed alike but not in any uniforms I recognized.

"No."

"Space Force?" It was a stretch which later turned out to be not too far off the mark. At least not in astronomical terms, which I would also learn later.

"We are not part of your military, or any other arm of your government." There was a slight emphasis on *your*.

"Independent, nongovernmental agency..." I trailed off midsentence. "United Nations, then?"

"We are quite outside of any such organization. They are completely unaware of our presence, by design."

Presence seemed like an awfully loaded word in this context. "You're, um, not from around here. Like *really* not from around here. Are you?" I couldn't bring myself to finish the thought yet because the answer was terrifying. "So when are the guys in sunglasses and black suits going to show up? Or has that already happened and they brain-zapped me?" It would explain how I'd managed to skip a whole day of my life.

Green-eyed guy and blue-eyed guy exchanged another look. They seemed amused. "We can assure you that is purely fiction. Now, if you don't mind, we still have many questions. We are particularly curious about your ability to render aid to those who may seem... unfamiliar."

"Training," I shrugged. "Reflexes. You come on an accident scene like that one, the training takes over and you just go. Everybody thinks they'll turn into Superman in a crisis, but the reality is you fall back on your training. If you haven't practiced to the point where it's second nature, you'll freeze. Or worse, screw up. Our job is to get the patient stabilized and take them to an ER where they can be fixed."

Blue-eyed guy seemed especially interested. "Yet you encountered beings which were completely outside of your experience."

I was so in the moment that his choice of words—*beings*—went right over my head. "Not entirely." I stood and smoothed down my wrinkled uniform. "Look, guys, this is all getting weird and I need coffee. Can I have a moment?"

Green Eyes stood in what seemed like an imitation of human manners. "Of course. This is your home, after all."

My home. Damned skippy it was. As I headed for the kitchen and turned on the tap, the smell of well water brought another rush of memories.

I was in the barn with Dad, tending to Snookie, a Jersey cow we'd had since I was barely old enough to milk her. She'd provided us with the key ingredient for a lot of homemade ice cream over the years and was getting up in age. She was still in remarkably good health for being over twenty years old, which I mentioned to Dad.

"It's because she's spoiled rotten," he said while injecting a syringe of antibiotics into her mouth. "You made her into a house pet."

I dug my boot into the dirt. "I can't help that she acted like one."

"Because you treated her like one of the dogs!" he said, mock-complaining as he finished off her injection and gave her a scratch behind the ears.

"She liked to climb up on the back porch with us in the evening," I remembered fondly. "You have to admit that was kind of funny."

"What about letting her into the kitchen? That wasn't so funny."

"She was still a calf," I protested.

"And a calf can leave almost as much manure. *In the house*, Mel. In. The. House."

I'd remembered that lesson well, after he forced me to clean up the pile from the kitchen floor before Mom found it. It didn't stop me from letting Snookie in again; I only got smarter about it.

He studied me, no doubt catching the amused look I had to be wearing. I've never been very good at hiding my expressions. "Vet school teaching you any different?"

Where to begin with that? "Well, it's definitely more clinical. Learning to assess and diagnose a sick animal is a lot different."

He conveyed his understanding with a grunt. "You get to know these creatures pretty well on a farm. Spend enough time around them and you figure things out quick. It's different when you're not around them every day."

"It is," I agreed. "Every animal I see, it's the first time for them. Even if I've seen the same breed before. And it's not like they can tell me what's wrong with them."

"Empathy," he said, giving Snookie another rub behind the ears as she nuzzled him. "It has to become like a sixth sense, getting to know an unfamiliar animal so quickly."

Dad had of course known what I was talking about; he'd been the county extension's vet for decades. He hadn't steered me into veterinary medicine on purpose, but growing up in that environment, in his shadow, had made it a foregone conclusion. I'd come to love animals and had a fascination with medicine; it seemed like a natural progression.

"And then your father died," Green Eyes said. "That changed your path in life."

I could only answer him with a blank stare. I hadn't voiced any of those memories. "How would you know that?" I demanded, alarm bells ringing in my head. This was rapidly becoming too much to process. I had instinctively known something was wildly different about this pair, but still couldn't bring myself to speak it out loud. "You're reading my mind."

"In a sense. Yes."

"How?"

"Empathy is a more important quality than you may imagine," he said coolly. "There are some species who have it as part of their essential biology. A 'sixth sense,' as your father explained."

I slammed the coffee pot back into its cradle, hard enough to crack it. "It's your turn to explain. Who the hell are you people, and what do you want with me?"

His face projected a serenity which seemed natural, but was no doubt intended to keep me from losing my shit. He was choosing his words carefully. "We are emissaries, from a civilization which you have had direct exposure to through your actions. Normally, we would have taken more concrete measures to ensure this did not leave a lasting impression."

"You mean wiping my memory."

"It is more delicate than that, but you are in essence correct." He paused as I sipped at my coffee, noticing my trembling hands. "Rest assured you are in no danger whatsoever. Whatever transpires from here is entirely up to you."

"Why? What makes me so special?"

"You have demonstrated an ability which our society, for all of its qualities, does not have in abundance. That is, the ability to render aid to species quite different from your own."

"*Species*?" I could feel my heart begin to race. "That wasn't a human I was treating, was it?"

"It was not," he said. "It was from another star system, far beyond your own. As are we."

I stumbled back into the living room and collapsed onto the sofa. "I knew it!" Or at least I remembered now. Almost breathless, I struggled to get the words out. "You're space aliens!"

Blue Eyes answered for them. "That is not how we think of ourselves, but it is understandable from your perspective."

Green Eyes elaborated. "What we call our 'union' is a collective of different races from across the galaxy. We don't consider any of them to be 'alien' any more than you might consider a particular variety of plant or animal to be alien. We are what we are, as you might say."

"And you are . . . ?"

"As we explained, emissaries."

"I get that's your job. What's your species? Where are you from?"

"It is something more than our job, and the specific designation of our kind is difficult to pronounce in any language you may be familiar with," Blue Eyes said. "Our home world no longer exists. Our race was forced to spread out into the galaxy."

"You were scattered among the stars?" It sounded a lot more poetic than I felt.

"Our home world was the second planet of a white dwarf star in proximity to the open cluster your astronomers call the Pleiades. When our star began the end of its life cycle, it first expanded to eventually consume our planet before collapsing in on itself. Our civilization was fortunate to have been advanced enough to embark on what we called the Great Diaspora. We scoured our region of the galaxy, searching for other systems to settle. We were unsuccessful, though we managed to form allegiances with many of the species we encountered."

"Is that where the 'emissary' part comes in?"

"That is correct," Green Eyes said. "As we encountered other races, we came to realize that ours possessed a unique empathic ability. We are able to connect with and understand others in ways that are uncommon."

"You mean read their minds? Like you've been doing with me?"

"It is more nuanced than that," Green Eyes explained. "With certain races, we can sense precisely what they're thinking. With others, we can gain more of a general understanding. It largely depends on the emotional state of the subject. Your kind tends to become rather anxious, which from our perspective means you are telegraphing your own thoughts."

"So it's something I can control?"

"In time, yes. That will depend on your comfort level with us."

"I'm mighty uncomfortable right now," I grumbled. "But I get what you're trying to explain. It's kind of like working with sick animals. They can't tell a human what they're feeling, and blood tests or X-rays don't always paint the full picture. Sometimes you're left with gut instinct."

Green and Blue exchanged looks again, like they were impressed that I grasped whatever they were talking about, though it seemed like a first grader realizing there was more to math besides addition and subtraction. The kid might not be capable of understanding it, but she knows it's there.

Blue Eyes leaned forward. It was remarkable, and not a little unsettling, how he could command my attention. "What you call 'instinct' is the reason we sought you. As we mentioned, you possess a trait which is important to our collective civilization."

"How so? I don't have anything close to your abilities."

"While that may be true, it is not in the way you think. You have shown competence, and a willingness to not allow the unexpected— even shocking—to deter you. You would be surprised at how uncommon that is within the Galactic Union."

Now I was even more confused. That didn't make sense. "How so? I can't imagine you get to be a galaxy-spanning civilization without being smart."

A thin smile crossed his face, probably more from my human naïveté than amusement. "Intellectual ability isn't the limiting factor. It is the general reluctance of many of our member species to provide medical assistance to anyone outside of their own kind."

"Intergalactic racism? And here I assumed it's one big happy, harmonious United Federation of Planets."

"It is not like your televised entertainments, I am afraid." Green Eyes actually looked saddened by this. "It is also not as crude as you suggest. Our member civilizations are not hostile to each other, but very few are comfortable with providing care for species they are not intimately familiar with. It is a cultural limitation, not an intellectual one."

"I'm still having a hard time with this. I hear what you're saying, but it sounds comparable to veterinary medicine. You take what you know and apply it using your best judgment."

"A valid comparison, if somewhat superficial." He must have caught the look on my face. "Do not take that as an insult. If we didn't think you were capable of learning, we would have left you alone with no memory of your encounter."

Blue Eyes jumped in to elaborate. "Imagine if one of your animal species could speak to you. A canine, perhaps. Would that make it easier for you to treat it?"

I was reminded of the *Dr. Dolittle* books I'd read growing up. "Of course. If they could tell me what they felt, I wouldn't have to rely so much on instinct."

"Which makes perfect sense, from your point of view. Now, imagine your patient was part of a greater civilization of intelligent canines. How might you feel as an 'outsider' in that context?"

I had to think about that one a minute. "Like I didn't belong there? Like they should be able to take better care of themselves than I could?" I was of course ignoring the part about them not having opposable thumbs; I had the feeling it was irrelevant to the point he was trying to make.

"That is an apt approximation of the difficulty we face. We have a comparatively small number of individuals within the Union who can look past their own kind and are not intimidated by the prospect of rendering aid to others."

"So they're afraid of making mistakes?"

"In a sense. There is a different appreciation for animal species within the Union. All but the simplest organisms are assumed to have their own form of intelligence. Pets and livestock are not generally a feature of our civilization."

"So you wouldn't have people—or whatever you call them—with my kind of background."

"Very few." He pulled a small rectangular crystal from his tunic and placed it on the table before me. It contained text in a language I couldn't recognize, which began translating itself into English the moment I picked it up. "Which is why we are offering to add you to their number."

5

The human female known as Melanie Elizabeth Mooney, inhabitant of Sol 3, locally known as "Terra" or "Earth," is hereby offered legal residence and employment within the Medical Corps of the Galactic Union. This arrangement is conditioned upon her agreement to:

1. provide appropriate and expedient care as required for any Union citizen, regardless of species;

2. complete all necessary training required to provide such care;

3. demonstrate the ability to assimilate, and be able to conduct herself accordingly, within the variety of cultures which comprise the Union.

Successful completion of a probationary period, equivalent to eighteen months as measured by her species, will qualify her for full recognition as a Citizen of the Union.

The contract went on from there, with more terms and conditions reduced to language I could understand. Compensation wasn't mentioned in any currency, only that all my needs would be met and that I would have the freedom to do pretty much whatever I felt like when I wasn't on duty.

I was given twenty-four hours to consider their offer. Rejecting it would result in a complete mind-wipe of everything I'd seen and heard since that night in the woods. Breathing a word of it to anyone while I was considering their offer would result in a mind-wipe for me and whoever I mentioned it to. At the end of the contract was a place for my handprint, which amounted to my signature. Press my hand against the crystal, and I was in. Leave it alone for the next

33

twenty-four hours, and I'd forget the whole thing ever happened. Red pill, blue pill. Which hole do you want to go down, Alice?

And boy, did I have questions. How long was the training going to take? Human anatomy and physiology alone was a full semester, and they'd mentioned something like a dozen different species. That sounded like a couple years' worth of schooling.

Where was I going to live? How would I get around, learn the language? Or languages, for that matter. Back to the dozen different species . . .

When I looked up, ready to pepper them with questions, Green Eyes and Blue Eyes were gone. I went to the front porch and there was no mysterious car pulling away, no fresh tire tracks heading off into the distance, no flying saucer zipping into the sky. It was as if they'd never been here. The crack in my coffee pot had even disappeared, somehow fixed. That had been nice of them.

The crystal had gone blank. When I reached for it, the text reappeared in glowing golden letters. I pulled my hand back and the words disappeared. I assumed that meant it was for my eyes only, and would only be readable when I reached for it, but I wasn't taking any chances. It was coming time to get ready for my shift, and I wasn't about to leave this thing lying around. Not that I had roommates that might get into my stuff, but it still felt like leaving the house with a stack of cash on the kitchen table. I went to the sideboard and pulled out an old velvet jewelry pouch—like most everything else in the house, it was one more thing of my parents that I couldn't part with. I carefully picked up the crystal by its edges, not wanting to accidentally activate it with my handprint, dropped it into the pouch, and slipped it into my backpack before heading off for work. Just another day, with an employment contract from an alien civilization sitting among the random junk of daily life.

At the station, I was back on rotation with my normal shift and caught more than a few questioning side-eyes. I ignored them and headed straight for my locker to place my pack and its unmentionable contents safely under lock and key until I could think things through.

Not that there'd be much time for any of that. The hourglass had been turned the moment I finished reading their offer, and my workday was barely getting started. By the time I got home early tomorrow morning, I'd only have a few hours left to activate it.

Was that what I was going to do? If I didn't accept, I'd never know the difference. The thought lingered as I inspected my trauma bag and the rest of our equipment while my partner gave the truck a once-over outside. Twenty minutes later we were satisfied we were ready for the day, and sent word to dispatch.

Before I even had a chance to step down from the cab, an alarm blared overhead: the long, monotone signal for a fire and ambulance run. An amber line appeared on the center console's laptop: MMVA, multiple motor vehicle accident. Cops were on scene, the highway was blocked, and two more squads were already on the way. This sounded ugly.

When a call like that comes, adrenaline takes over. Time slows down and you get tunnel vision, tuning out the rest of the world while every sense in your body goes on high alert. By the time we flicked on the lights and siren and barreled out of the squad bay, the magic alien crystal hidden in my locker was the last thing on my mind.

"Good God."

If you ever hear that from a crusty old medic rolling up on scene, you know it's bad. Russ Finley had been with the department almost literally since I'd been born and was on his way to retirement. He'd been running squads for so long, and become so jaded, that it had made him wholly unsuited for promotions. If that sounds counterintuitive, you don't know fire departments.

Here Russ was, well into his fifties, still doing ambulance runs, and utterly aghast at the situation playing out before us.

What had once been a sparkling new BMW had gone left of center. Judging by the mess in the opposite lane, the driver had tried to avoid a deer or some other decent-sized animal. Probably jumped out of the cornfield adjacent to the highway; that was a persistent danger here in farm country.

The Beemer had crossed into oncoming traffic and got creamed by a semi. The semi won, but not without taking its lumps. Its driver was sitting cross-legged by the side of the highway, trying to chain-smoke the trauma away. We were a good hundred feet distant and could see his hands trembling from inside the squad. "He looks shocky," Russ said. "Need to keep an eye on him."

True, but the mess wasn't limited to Peterbilt vs. BMW. The Beemer got hit so hard that it knocked the engine clean out of its compartment, the finest German engineering transformed into a three-foot aluminum boulder dropped smack into the middle of Highway 40. This in turn was plowed into by an old Corolla which had been trailing behind the semi. The Toyota practically exploded around the Beemer's engine block, ejecting both driver and passenger. Honestly I don't know if safety belts would've done them a bit of good in this case. They would've been crushed if they'd stayed in the vehicle.

The problem was finding the Corolla's occupants. There were two human-sized holes in what was left of the windshield, but only one body. The first was easy enough to find, having hit the pavement at about sixty miles an hour. I'll spare the details, but he was at the bottom of our rapidly growing triage roster.

I stood up in the doorway of our cab, still scanning the scene while Russ grabbed the trauma bag from his side of the truck. "Where's the other passenger?"

He shrugged as he came around the front, but I saw him eyeing the adjacent cornfield.

"Oh man," I muttered, and waved at one of the mass of state troopers to get his attention. I pointed at the field, in the general direction of where I thought the other human projectile went. "Anybody searching over that way? We may have somebody in that corn."

"Got two on it now." He keyed the mic clipped on his epaulet to check in with his troopers working in the maze of corn. He had three stripes on his sleeve.

"You in charge here?" I glanced at the name badge over his right pocket. "Sergeant Lopez?"

"I am. You're gonna have your hands full. If you're right about the cornfield, then we've got four victims so far. Two from the Corolla, one in the Beemer. The other one . . ." He nodded across the highway, where the BMW had jumped the median.

That hadn't been a deer. I started searching in anticipation for the other squads, as heavy rescue and hazmat should've been here by now. A train whistle wailed in the distance, and I knew why. *Damn.* "Hang on." I had tuned out the radio chatter while we were assessing the scene, missing the news that both squads had been blocked at two different railroad crossings. In big, congested cities like New York, first responders had to fight perpetually clogged traffic. Here in farm country, we had to contend with miles-long freight trains and monstrous combines blocking our way. I called them and learned both were presently hauling ass in the opposite direction, headed for the nearest open crossing.

I turned back to the trooper and jerked my head toward the distant whistle. "Heavy rescue's on the way; they got blocked by that train. We're it for now." I studied the scene once more. "Where's the BMW's driver?"

The trooper pointed to the semi's undercarriage, at the twisted wreck of what used to be a silver 330i. "Keep looking for our missing person in the field," I barked, and ran for the semi. I waved for Russ, who was tending to its trembling, chain-smoking driver. He had draped a space blanket over him and was taking his vitals. The cab and trailer were sitting upright, no apparent risk of the rig tipping over, so I began belly-crawling underneath it toward the destroyed Beemer. "EMS," I shouted. "Can anyone hear me?"

A pained moan barely registered above the background noise. I scrambled back out and practically screamed at Russ over my shoulder. "We've got a live one, under the trailer!"

I began worming my way back under. I was probably being too impatient; Russ was much older, and much larger, than me. But time was not on our side, and my size was the reason I'd become the go-to for confined-space work. I crept forward, finally reaching what was left of the Beemer and its driver pinned inside, deflated airbags draped around him. I couldn't believe this guy was still in one piece. I reached for his neck, and have to admit to being more than a little surprised at finding a decent pulse. "Can you talk?"

"Yes." His voice was weak but clear.

"Can you tell me your name, sir?"

"Andrew," he groaned.

I kept one eye on him as I opened my trauma bag and snapped on a pair of gloves. First things first: get a C-spine collar around his neck. There was no getting him out of this tangled mess yet, but I had to make sure any damage to his neck wasn't made worse by my futzing around.

His face was a maze of contusions, cuts and gouges. Head wounds bleed like crazy, all out of proportion to their severity. His glasses had been slammed into his face by the airbag, leaving gashes around his eyes. There was a nasty laceration across his forehead, not too deep but from what I could see it was responsible for most of the bleeding. I wrapped it with a four-by-four and gauze. This injury wasn't life-threatening, and the pressure would keep the blood out of his face for now.

I stuck my head into the twisted compartment for a better look. "Andrew," I said. "You go by Andy?"

"Drew."

Of course he did. The guy was driving a BMW through the middle of farm country. Probably a lawyer or banker from Indianapolis. The more prosperous folk around here avoided being that ostentatious, though they'd spend as much money on a truck or SUV.

"Can you tell me your age, Drew?"

"Thirty-eight," he said through gritted teeth.

His left arm was free, hanging out of where the driver's window used to be. The car's roof had been sheared off and he was damned lucky his head hadn't gone with it. Judging by the unnatural peak beneath the shirtsleeve, his forearm was broken. Airbags might keep you from getting killed but there was no guarantee you wouldn't end up with some broken bones. So there was my next task. I pulled an IV bag and air splint from my bag and got to work. "Looks like you've got a broken arm, Drew. I can't set it yet, but this'll protect it while we get to work. Okay?"

"Okay," he groaned. "It hurts."

No doubt, I was thinking as I searched for a good vein in his hand. "What's your pain level, on a scale of one to ten?"

"T-ten." It came out as a mumble.

Thought so. "All right. First I'm going to give you something for that pain." I inserted the intravenous needle and taped the port in place as Russ crawled up alongside. He held the IV bag while I snatched a syringe of Dilaudid and pushed it into the port. It's powerful stuff, comparable to morphine. Drew settled down right away and we got to work, first getting the air splint in place around his arm.

The rest of him was pinned good; his right arm was jammed under the empty passenger seat which now occupied the space where the center console used to be. His shoulder was at an unnatural angle. I winced, imagining the pain he must have felt before the Dilaudid got to work. For all of the nasty stuff we have to deal with, there's always something that makes your skin crawl no matter how often you see it. For me, it's dislocated joints. Broken bones may hurt like hell but they're a temporary kind of pain; that is, until they're set back in place. Dislocations are horribly painful from start to finish, and resetting them is no walk in the park either.

Thankfully the meds were doing their job; our patient didn't flinch as Russ cut the airbag free from around his out-of-place shoulder. I wished we could've reset it right there, but this wasn't the time. We couldn't have gotten any leverage from here anyway.

This might seem like small potatoes, given the mess he was in, but you're essentially working your way down a ladder of bad stuff. If the patient is conscious and breathing, the next thing you look for is bleeding. Bandaging his forehead took care of that. I was going to have to crawl past his arm to get to the rest of him, and protecting that with the air splint ensured we wouldn't make matters worse while we worked.

Russ cut away the seat belt and forward airbag, while I cut our patient's shirt open to begin assessing his chest and abdomen. He winced as I palpated his chest. Broken ribs, most likely, and nothing we could do about them now.

His abdomen was a mass of bruises. One in particular felt hard to the touch, which meant internal bleeding. I glanced down past his abdomen, trying to get a look at his legs. They were somewhere behind the steering wheel and the twisted instrument panel, and that's where the real trauma was going to be. That exquisite German engineering had kept his upper body mostly intact, but could only do so much with the engine compartment pushed up into the driver's seat.

No way we'd be able to get him out of this on our own. There were sirens in the distance; hopefully that was the heavy rescue crew. They were about to get a workout.

I reached for the radio mic clipped to my collar. "This is Mooney, squad 183. We're underneath the truck. Patient is semiconscious with multiple crush injuries. I can't assess his legs. We're going to need the jaws."

The radio squawked and I heard the sirens stop. "Copy that, Mel. Heavy rescue is on scene now. Be there in a sec."

"Copy." I looked down at where his legs should be. If this went the way I thought, he'd start bleeding like a gusher as soon as we pulled that console free. "We're also gonna need LifeFlight."

They answered with two rapid mic clicks, shorthand for saying they heard me.

I looked back toward the highway as the heavy rescue truck pulled up alongside. From beneath the semi, I saw pairs of blue-clad legs running all over the place. One trailed a heavy, black hydraulic hose. That would be the Jaws of Life.

We were soon joined by two medics from station 185, the heavy rescue crew. "Helo's on the way, Mel. What've we got here?" one shouted.

I repeated my assessment for them and moved closer to our patient as Russ draped a heavy canvas tarp over us. "They're getting ready to pry the dashboard free. This will protect you from debris. It's about to get noisy, but I'm going to be right here with you, okay?"

Drew nodded silently, his eyelids droopy. I spotted his wallet, wedged inside a cupholder. I shoved it into my chest pocket; the LifeFlight crew would need his ID.

From the corner of one eye I saw the Heavy guys wedging the scuffed yellow scissor blades of the jaws into the driver's compartment, between the floorboard and console. Another dragged a rolly—a flexible stretcher for confined spaces—beneath the trailer. He set it up alongside the driver and waited.

"Clear!" one of them shouted. With a grinding whine, the jaws slowly opened and began to spread the crushed Beemer apart. We were careful to stay clear of the machine, but also had to be close enough to catch the driver and ease him onto the stretcher.

Drew's right arm dropped free as the passenger seat moved

enough for it to fall loose. All that leather must have cushioned the impact because it looked fine, other than his dislocated shoulder.

I'd been right about his legs. Even if he was lucky enough to have avoided a spinal injury—which looked doubtful—it was hard to see how they'd work again. They emerged from under the console as two pulpy masses of tissue, as if there were no bones left inside to keep them in place. A stream of blood began squirting from his right thigh.

"*Shit*," Russ muttered. "There goes his femoral."

I was ready for that, but it didn't make things easier. The patient might have been freed, but we were still in tight quarters and a sliced femoral artery wouldn't wait for us to drag him clear. I snatched a pair of clamps and forceps from a pouch on my hip. Finding the source was easy: his right leg was shredded into hamburger, and now that the pressure was relieved the artery was gushing like a damned garden hose. If we couldn't get it clamped off quickly, he'd bleed out before LifeFlight could get here.

Knowing the source of the bleed isn't the same as getting to it. The human body responds to blunt-force trauma in some bizarre ways; stuff gets moved around to places where it shouldn't be. Working underneath a wrecked semi didn't help; the lack of direct sunlight left us with headlamps and handheld flashlights. Russ held a light on the area while I began fishing around inside of our patient's thigh. Blood was pooling up and I couldn't see. "Can you give me some suction?"

That was when we heard a shout from the firefighter with the jaws, right about the time gasoline fumes attacked my nose. "Gas line broke!"

He pulled the jaws free and scrambled out from under the trailer just as I felt my coveralls getting soaked in flammable liquids. He wasn't running away, he was going for the spill kit stowed in their truck. I could hear him shouting for the hazmat gear. Two more of the guys started unrolling a pig around the area, a big burlap-wrapped roll of absorbent material to contain the spill. Another came up from behind us and started scattering what amounted to cat litter over the expanding pool of gasoline.

All of this was happening in my peripheral vision. As they worked to contain the spill, I was still trying to stave off the gusher from my patient's leg. With his free hand, Russ began moving a small hose around the area where I was working, suctioning away excess blood. I was still working mostly by feel, but now I could see a little better. *There.*

"Got it!" I kept one hand on the sliced artery and clamped it shut with the other. We watched the wound area to see if any more blood escaped, but it looked like we had it. I had no illusions that he'd be able to keep that leg, but at least he wasn't going to bleed out underneath this truck. *Not on my watch* sounds melodramatic, but that's how it feels being the only one standing between your patient and certain death.

I noticed Drew trembling about the same time Russ called it: "He's going into shock." He'd already pulled out a space blanket and O₂ mask.

"Bag him." As Russ put the mask in place, I reached back for my trauma bag and slammed my head against the trailer's undercarriage. I cursed myself for not putting on a helmet before crawling up in here, once again in too much of a hurry for my own good. I started pushing fluids through the IV while Russ rhythmically squeezed the pouch to force air into the patient's lungs. We needed to get this guy out from under the truck, but first we had to get him stable or it wouldn't matter. The heavy *thump thump thump* of an approaching helicopter grew louder and the air began to swirl around us.

I made one last assessment of our patient, now secure in the rolly, before we pulled him out from underneath the trailer. Between the blood loss and pain meds, he was out. The bruising around his abdomen was an ugly, deep violet blotch we called the "seat belt" sign. Chances were good that his spleen was ruptured, but that would be left to the ER docs.

We dragged him out onto the highway and two more medics came running up in black jumpsuits and bulky helmets; they'd be the LifeFlight crew. A squat red-and-black helicopter sat on the pavement nearby with its rotors turning, behind the trailer and as close as the pilot could safely land. They lifted their earpieces back and I shouted at them over the whining engines as we carried him to the waiting chopper. "Patient's name is Andrew Larsen, thirty-eight years old. Pulse one twenty-five and thready, BP ninety over fifty-two. Hypovolemic shock, likely broken ribs and internal bleeding. Lacerated right femoral, we clamped it off."

The flight nurse was typing this into a tablet as one of the heavy rescue guys helped her partner load our patient into the chopper. She looked at the patient, then back at me. I could tell we were both thinking the same thing: he'd probably never be able to use those legs again if he kept them at all. Finally, I handed her the wallet I'd removed from the BMW's shattered console. She read his driver's license and did a double take. "Andrew Larsen?" she asked over the helicopter's roar. A sardonic grin creased her face.

I didn't see much to smile about here. "What's funny about that?"

"He's a big-shot lawyer from Indy," she said as she climbed into the cabin. Once again, my gut had proven right. "Specializes in truck accidents." With that, she motioned for us to get clear and slid the chopper's door shut. I could see her giving the pilot a thumbs-up, and their engines began to whine.

I turned and covered my face with my arms as the chopper spun up and away. Irony could sure be ironic sometimes.

6

The LifeFlight helicopter had become a noisy speck in the distance. I wiped my brow and turned back to the scene to find Russ by the cornfield with one of the state troopers. His bushy eyebrows lifted as he got his first good look at me since crawling out from under the truck. My coveralls were coated with a mix of road grime, fuel, and blood. I reeked of gasoline and oxygenated iron.

"You look like shit, Mel."

Not that he looked much better. "Nice to see you too." I leaned forward, resting my hands against my knees, and took a deep breath. "They find our missing passenger?"

The grim look on his face told the story. "Nothing we could do for her. One in a million shot. Landed headfirst against a big rock in that field," he said, holding his hands a couple of feet apart. "Caved in her head like a rotten melon." He blew out an exasperated breath. "Otherwise she'd have probably made it. All that corn cushioned the impact."

"We need to go in and recover?"

He shook his head. "Coroner's on the way. Troopers are marking off the scene, getting pictures and all before they take her." The protocols changed dramatically, turning into a full-blown investigation whenever fatalities were involved. He nodded toward the semi. "How's our guy?"

I looked back in the direction the chopper had gone. "Stable for now but there was internal bleeding. If he lives, it'll be without his legs."

"Damn shame," Russ said.

There wasn't much left to say. We both turned silently, taking stock of the scene. Troopers had already marked off the spot where this cascade of calamities had begun and were getting photos of what was left of the first victim, smeared across the opposite side of Highway 40. The fire battalion chief was coming from there, headed in our direction. At a scene this big, the chief always shows up.

Our work was mostly done at this point; another squad was looking after the truck driver, who was mostly just shaken up. He'd had a front row seat to the whole horrific mess, and the troopers were going to have a lot of questions once he'd settled down.

"You two all right?" the chief asked. Any lingering displeasure from our earlier talk about missing my shift was lost in the chaos around us.

"Highway Patrol's got one a hell of a mess to sort out, but for our part we're good," I answered for both of us. I nodded toward the scene across the highway. "What's their thinking?" Not that it mattered to us, but we were curious as to how this catastrophe started.

"Cops think the BMW driver was speeding, but the guy he hit shouldn't have been walking along the highway either. Driver drifted onto the shoulder at the wrong time. Probably on his phone."

"That'll be interesting," I said. "Flight nurse said he's a big accident lawyer out of Indy."

Chief's eyes widened. "You're shitting me." He turned back to where the troopers were working. "I don't think they know that. None of their guys have been under the trailer to tag the vehicle yet, not until hazmat's cleaned it up." He pointed toward the trooper I'd spoken with when we first arrived. "Be sure you let the on-scene commander know the driver's ID," he said, and placed a hand on my shoulder. "Good work today, Tiny." The chief acted like he wanted to say more, but instead left me with a pained look that didn't quite register in the moment. I'd find out why later.

Back at the station, I shucked off my utilities and threw them into a biohazard bag. There'd be no cleaning them. I stood under a steaming shower for what felt like hours, washing away the grime and gore and general tension. I could feel my body go slack under the steady stream of hot water, the adrenaline flushing out of my system with the dull *woosh* of each heartbeat. I wanted nothing more now than to curl up under a blanket and sleep. If things stayed quiet for a while, I might be able to do just that.

It was after I got out of the shower and opened up my locker when I learned what the battalion chief's odd look had been about earlier. An envelope had been slipped inside, which I opened with more than a little trepidation.

My heart pounded as I unfolded the contents, a single page on department letterhead. That was rarely good, and this wasn't an exception:

Disciplinary Action: 1) Failure to report for duty, 2) Failure to wait for secure scene (third offense).

It's not worth recounting the specifics. I crumpled onto a bench, still wrapped in a towel. They were suspending me without pay for a solid month, signed off by the battalion chief and the union rep.

I knew it was bullshit, but what could I say? *Sorry, Chief, but that plane crash I told you about? Totally not an airplane. And then I had these visitors . . .*

There was no arguing my way out of this.

I pulled on a fresh pair of coveralls and looked up and down the empty women's locker room. Being the only chick on shift, I had the place to myself. I opened my backpack and fingered the velvet bag inside, pondering its contents.

I'd been with the department long enough to where burnout was becoming a threat. Everyone reaches that point eventually. You either move on to something else, or stay with it and become part of the furniture. Like Russ.

A burned-out medic can be as dangerous as a rookie; sometimes more so. I'd known for a while that the time for a change was coming; the question had always been what that would look like. Going back to finish vet school would take a lot of work and even more money, and I'd been out of it for so long that it'd be like starting over. Likewise, selling the farmhouse was an option that I couldn't bring myself to consider, even though Mom and Dad had been gone for years. And though I'd sought a promotion, that desire had always been tempered with a healthy skepticism of moving up into management. This letter put the nail in that coffin.

I reached into the pouch and pulled out the blank crystal, again being careful to grip it by its edges and not accidentally set off a chain of events that couldn't be undone. Whatever came next, I knew I didn't want *this* anymore.

For the last several years my life had been consumed by work, either tending to what was left of the farm or rolling with the rescue squad. First-responder life isn't very conducive to dating, what with the overnight hours and constantly rotating shifts. Think it's hard to stay in a relationship that way? Try starting one in the first place. Eligible men tend to find other ways to amuse themselves after a few consecutive weekends of their dates not showing up.

I had no family ties left, no real relationships outside of the firehouse, and now even that was being taken away. This was a chance for a clean slate, a way to get out from under the battalion chief's thumb, maybe for good.

"I'm too young to feel this old," I muttered. Did that come from desire, or desperation? Did it matter?

I checked the clock on the wall. Less than six hours to deadline. Oh, what the hell . . .

I touched the crystal's face and the silhouette of a blank handprint appeared. I pressed my palm against the glass.

It was all I could do to keep my composure and finish my shift. It was a quiet night, not a single run after the carnage on 40. I'd have welcomed another mass casualty event; it would've kept my mind off of the whole unjustified mess. I was mad at the station, the union, and myself.

This is what I got for doing the right thing? I could've passed the scene right by and no one would've been the wiser, including me. If anyone had come asking questions later, it would've been easy to chalk it up to fatigue.

Part of me was equally angry with my extraterrestrial visitors, which sounds peevish but it's the truth. Of all the places they could've been, why'd they have to cross *my* path? What was so special about Nowhere, Indiana? It brought to mind the folklore of missing and/or mutilated cattle associated with strange lights in the sky. Most of the cows around here were of the dairy variety, so unless there was a galactic shortage of fresh milk, that didn't explain their presence.

Of course it had been an accident; same as the one we'd just cleaned up. That lawyer hadn't wanted to hit that hapless vagrant on the side of the road, but a moment's inattention had set off a gruesome chain of events. What might have happened to the ship I'd come across? Clearly they hadn't intended to crash-land in the woods near my house, but here we were.

Serendipity, a fifty-dollar word for random events that play out in beneficial ways, like hitting the lottery with a ticket you found on the sidewalk. Was this going to be beneficial?

It was hard to see how it couldn't be. I didn't feel all that special, but these "emissaries" thought differently. They'd invited me to join a rather exclusive club. Would I be the only human in it? That was a little intimidating, though the two who'd contacted me would've been impossible to distinguish from humans if they hadn't told me.

I spent the remaining hours of my shift on a La-Z-Boy in the common area, zoning out on TV with the rest of the crew. Hilariously enough, one of the guys put on *Men in Black*. I had to leave the room after the first ten minutes, and no doubt everyone thought they knew what was up. I'd just been suspended and they must have figured I didn't want to talk about it. They were only half right. Not a one of them could've suspected this might be the last time they'd ever see me.

How would they handle my disappearance? I wondered as I pulled up to the darkened farmhouse. Other than my truck's headlamps, a single light on the porch was the only source of illumination. I was halfway expecting to find a flying saucer parked in the front yard, and was kind of disappointed to find both it and the house were empty.

Inside, I flipped on every light as I made my way upstairs. Having the place all to myself now, I'd taken to leaving most everything on. Funny how we humans can be about what might be lurking in the dark. I didn't know when my visitors would return, only that they would. The crystal slate was blinking steadily like a homing beacon, a reminder that I'd put something irreversible into motion.

Not knowing what else to do, I began packing for an extended trip. With no idea of what kind of climate to expect, and no clue as to what clothing might be culturally appropriate, I grabbed whatever would feel comfortable and began shoving it all into a duffel bag.

I moved on to my parents' room and opened the small safe in their closet. After all this time, that remained the only reason I'd ever set foot in their space and it still felt like I was violating their privacy.

The deed to their—my—property sat in a fat legal envelope on top of an old cigar box. I removed them both from the safe and sat on the edge of the bed. I hadn't opened that box since Dad died. Almost six years gone, why did I still feel the need to compartmentalize?

I brushed aside a thin layer of dust and lifted the lid. Inside was filled with pictures going back to my childhood, the small mementos of daily life that had been the most important to Mom. She'd passed a few years before Dad, and putting together this collection had been one of her final acts.

"A house is only a house," she'd once said, "filled with stuff that won't mean anything after we're gone. Experiences are what matters. That's what you keep with you, that can't be taken away." And this frayed old cigar box held the physical record of her most treasured experiences.

A few trinkets were loosely arranged around the edges. My first baby tooth, in a tiny silver jar. An engagement ring which had belonged to my great-grandmother. A cheap plastic bead necklace we had made together when I was in kindergarten. I pushed them aside and lifted out a handful of yellowed photos. Vacations to Florida, high school and college graduations, an epically miserable road trip to Yellowstone (to be fair, I was only twelve), and a bunch of pictures she must have taken when I wasn't looking. It was mundane stuff, mainly of me and Dad doing things like trying to cook for her (I wasn't great, but he was worse), working in the barn, feeding the cattle, riding in his lap on the tractor, and one of me tending to an injured bird I'd found on our doorstep. All highlights from the millions of little moments that make up a life together.

And here I sat, about to leave it all for who knew what. It felt like I owed her and Dad an apology. My first instinct had been to take Mom's memory box with me, but it was hers, not mine. I placed it back in the safe, locking it away for an unknown future.

I shouldered my bag, took the big legal envelope that held my last official connection to home, and headed downstairs. As I rounded the base of the stairway, I stumbled and dropped everything to the floor.

There they stood in the living room, like a pair of alabaster sculptures. Ol' Blue Eyes and Green Eyes. I grabbed at my chest and caught my breath. "Don't you two know how to use the doorbell?"

Green answered. "We apologize for causing you any discomfort. We assumed that you understood we mean you no harm. Quite the opposite, in fact."

"Is this what I can expect in the future? Aliens appearing out of thin air at random?"

"There may be some who do that, but over time they will adapt to your particular social customs," Blue Eyes said, "like ringing the doorbell."

I could feel my pulse throbbing in my neck. Expected or not, their sudden presence was unnerving. "How is it you two keep appearing in my house? Do you beam in with some kind of transporter, like *Star Trek*?"

Green Eyes turned to the foyer, somewhat puzzled. "We opened the door."

"Next time use that doorbell. It's the little plastic button on the right." I moved past them to the picture window in the living room and peered into the front yard. The porch light didn't offer much, but it was enough to see there was nothing parked outside. "How'd you get here? You didn't just walk in from the woods."

"Our vehicle is in your yard, out by the tree line," Blue said. "It is cloaked to avoid any undesired attention."

That was more like *Trek* than they could know. "Undesired attention..." I muttered while searching for signs of it. "So it's invisible?"

"For now," Green said. "At idle power, there is more than enough energy in the system to enable the electromagnetic camouflage."

I whistled. "Guess I shouldn't be surprised."

"It is not as fantastic as you suppose. Your own military is working on similar technology. Theirs is still quite crude in comparison, but they are on the right track, as you might say."

"So what do we do from here? Is this the part where you lower your shields, or whatever, and take me aboard your flying saucer?"

Green Eyes smiled disarmingly. They were indeed good at this emissary stuff. "The next steps are going to seem rather mundane. We have been researching your local property statutes, and it will be necessary to 'take care of business,' as you might say. It appears you have been thinking about this as well." He nodded at the envelope on the floor by my duffel bag.

"Not nearly enough," I said. What to do about the house? I couldn't simply abandon it. "I can't let the farm go to seed. The house needs looked after, lawn needs mowed, brush will need clearing." I was thinking it through on the fly. "It's not like I can ask the neighbors to look after the place for a few years."

"It is not," Blue Eyes agreed. He pointed to my old iPad on a side table. "We took the liberty of making some preliminary arrangements on your behalf."

I picked up the tablet, which showed a directory of property management firms. I shouldn't have been surprised that they could do an internet search as well as anyone else. One of the selections was highlighted. "What kind of arrangements?"

"There is an establishment which can take care of your property during your absence, for however long you require. You simply allow for regular charges to your bank account. As part of your compensation, we will ensure that you maintain sufficient funds."

"We'll need to do the same for property taxes," I said. They weren't kidding about this part feeling mundane, but it was important. "If I don't keep up with those, the county will take over the farm. I'd like to have a home to come back to," I said, assuming I eventually could and having no idea if that would be the case.

Another smile from Green Eyes. "That was somewhat easier. We have taken care of your property tax obligations for the foreseeable future."

"Taken care of? How? They're billed retroactively." Not to mention the damned rates went up all the time.

"While property management requires physical interaction and timely payment," he explained, "government tax obligations are easier for us to manipulate."

"Manipulate," I repeated. "In what way?"

"They are managed within a computerized recordkeeping system that is rather crude, even by the most advanced human standards. Your property has been removed from their records, and will remain transparent to the authorities until such time as you may elect to return."

So I did have that option, but at the moment I was more impressed with their hacking skills. "What about other government databases?" I'd already sent my resignation letter to the firehouse, but it was only one of many official loose ends to tie up.

"Completely removed," Green Eyes said with a certain satisfaction. He seemed to get a kick out of pulling one over on the establishment. "If you decide to return, your existence will be restored as if nothing occurred."

I was warming up to him. "Okay, you've convinced me. And just let me say that if you ever wanted to set up shop here on Earth, you could become a very wealthy man."

"Wealth is a concept which you'll find to be somewhat malleable in our culture," Blue Eyes said.

"So people—or whoever—in the Union don't care about money?"

"Most do not. Some do. One or two in particular." They traded a look that told me there was much more to that story. I had the feeling there'd be a steep learning curve. In time I'd eventually learn how right, and how wrong, I was.

7

The last thing to tend to was my trusty old F-150. I parked it in the equipment barn next to Dad's old John Deere and popped the hood to disconnect the battery. I pulled a heavy tarp over the truck and wondered how long it'd be before I saw it again.

I locked up the barn and took one last look around the property. The keys in my hand felt heavy, a reminder of everything I was about to leave behind. I placed them in a magnetic box hidden under the back porch and took a deep breath. "That's it," I sighed. "I'm ready to go." Not really, but it seemed like the thing to say.

"Very well." Green Eyes took out one of those crystal slates and swept the area in a circular motion, then held it up to the sky. "We are clear of ground and atmospheric-based detection. There are no satellites transiting our departure cone."

Without a word, Blue Eyes headed for the front yard. Green Eyes slipped the crystal into a pocket and gestured for me to follow. "If you please. We will not be detected, but we must move quickly."

I nodded and followed them around the house, toward the tree line. As we rounded the front, I stopped dead in my tracks. Where there had once been nothing but grass and woods beyond, now sat a silvery machine that looked like it could've been a giant blob of liquid mercury. It was shaped like a teardrop, with a flattened base. There were no lights, no doors or windows. Suddenly an opening appeared near the pointy end of the teardrop. I assumed this was the front.

Their ship wasn't that big, maybe twenty feet end to end. "Seems small for such a long trip."

"This is a trans-atmospheric shuttle," Green Eyes explained patiently. "You'll find our home ship to be much more spacious."

"Home ship?" I wondered. "Like a 'mothership'?"

"That would be an accurate analogy, yes."

"And where is it?"

"In orbit at what your astronomers refer to as a 'Lagrange point' near your moon. It is advantageous for a number of reasons, but for our purposes its greatest advantage is for avoiding detection."

I knew almost nothing of astronomy, another gap in my understanding that was likely to be filled in soon. "Can't it be cloaked, like this ship?"

"At lower power settings, yes. Once we activate the drive, it will become visible in the electromagnetic spectrum, which is why we have to carefully time our movements."

"That's what you were scanning for earlier. So there's nothing up there near the Moon?"

"At present, your space agencies have nothing at Lagrange point two. That will inevitably change in the future, but for now that deficit serves our purposes quite well." He waved me toward the open portal, which was almost at ground level.

I stepped inside and found it identical to the wrecked ship I'd found a few days ago, except of course everything seemed to be in place. It felt sterile, all soft off-white walls with metallic highlights. A sphere of dark metal sat atop a pedestal near the back of the cabin, behind a transparent screen.

There were a handful of contoured couches, with one mounted forward in front of a semicircular panel. Blue Eyes sat in this one, and the panel lit up with what I guessed were instrument displays. Ahead of him, the blank wall transformed into a wide oval window. "How is it we're able to see through the wall?"

"Synthetic vision," Green Eyes explained. "There are sensors embedded in the outer skin that can create a virtual window wherever you need it." He pointed at the sidewall next to the seat I'd taken. "You are welcome to try it for yourself."

I tapped the wall and a similar, if smaller, oval appeared. As luck would have it, I was looking straight at my house. "Why not put in windows? Seems simpler."

"It is not from an engineering perspective, even with transparent alloys." I had no idea that was a thing. "Windows create structural weaknesses in the pressure vessel." He could tell I was skeptical. No matter how advanced they were, devices can break. "I can assure you this solution has proven most reliable."

Looking around the small cabin, it still seemed like tight quarters for going most of the way to the Moon. "How long will it take us to get there?"

"A little less than one hour, by your measure of time."

Time was another complicated subject I was going to learn much more about, though I didn't realize it at that moment. "An hour? It took our astronauts a week to get there."

"Three days, actually. They were using a primitive mode of propulsion."

Primitive. A crash program that had dominated American culture for the better part of a decade, and in their eyes it might as well have been Vikings crossing the ocean in wooden longboats.

As Blue Eyes' hands danced around the control panel, a subtle vibration began to build up around us. A barely audible buzz emanated from the floor. I felt a slight pull toward the rear of the craft, and I turned to stare at that odd metallic sphere on its pedestal. Whatever was happening, I could sense it was somehow at the center of it all. It left me a little queasy.

"We are lifting off," Green Eyes said with a gesture toward my synthetic window. The house, the barn, the farm all fell away into the darkness. Beyond were lights from surrounding farms and scattered neighborhoods, with Indianapolis glittering in the distance as we gained altitude.

An amber light flashed above us and my heart about stopped. Were we in trouble?

"Acceleration warning," my companion said. "Please remain confined to your couch until it disappears."

My entire body lay in this strange, semispherical couch. There were no rests for my head, arms, or legs, just one continuous cushion, like a high-tech beanbag. Its pliable padding seemed to absorb me as we zipped through the clouds into the night sky. I could tell we were going incredibly fast, but barely felt the acceleration. "Shouldn't we be feeling g-forces or something?" I didn't have to be a pilot or Indy racer to understand what those were.

Every car accident I'd ever worked had been a firsthand demonstration of the effects of sudden acceleration—or rather, deceleration.

"This is what the couches are for," he explained. "The cushions are made of an acceleration gel, a safety feature which augments the inertial dampening field."

Inertial dampening . . . I had only the vaguest idea of what that could mean and it seemed impossible. How could they get around basic physics? Again, I suspected the answer to my question had to do with that sphere in back.

The sky ahead had become impossibly clear and black. Looking to my side, more lights from dozens of cities receded behind us as the horizon curved away beneath a faint greenish-yellow glow. I was seeing the Earth's curvature and its thin sheath of atmosphere for the first time. We were already in space, after barely a minute's travel.

"How fast are we going?"

"At present, thirty thousand kilometers per hour. Now that we are above the atmosphere, we will continue accelerating until we reach our home ship."

"So how does this thing work?" I guessed that rockets weren't involved, judging by their moon landing comment.

Green Eyes swiveled in his couch to face me. The amber light was still glowing overhead, and he was careful to keep his head and limbs inside the gel cushion. "What is your understanding of physics?"

"Thin," I said. "I understand acceleration and inertia in principle, mainly from dealing with accident victims. I know that it's impossible to go faster than light, that speed has an effect on time, and that quantum physics is supposed to be as bizarre as it sounds. That's about it."

"It is enough to start," he said with another disarming smile. "While you don't necessarily need to know precisely how all of this works, it will be useful if you have some basic comprehension."

"Like knowing how my truck works, even though I take it to someone else when it needs service?"

He nodded appreciatively. "A fair analogy." His eyes turned to the pedestal behind us. "That sphere is the basis of our propulsive force and the source of our inertial dampening field. Those forces are inextricably linked. The sphere is a stable isotope of an element your scientists call moscovium. Its atomic number is 115 on your periodic table—which is an excellent method for categorizing elements, by the way. 115's basic form is highly energetic, with a half-life of milliseconds. Synthesizing a stable isotope is currently beyond human abilities, though we don't believe it will remain out of your reach for long."

"How long is 'long' by your standards?"

"By your time reference, less than a century."

I blinked, hard. There was one more mental adjustment I would have to make. Human perceptions of time were nothing on a cosmic scale.

Green Eyes ignored my double-take and continued. "It won't be possible to grasp the potential of element 115 until your scientists arrive at what they term a 'unified theory.' It is the ultimate pursuit in their understanding of physics."

I tried to recall the concepts our "Physics for Physicians" professor had tried to get across to us during my second year of vet school. It was an elective, mostly to teach us the effects of radiation on living things, but we couldn't get there without first going over some fundamentals. "I've heard of that, but I still don't know what it means. All I remember is there are a couple different competing theories of physics which don't work together."

"That is mostly correct, by current human understanding," he said. "Independent of each other they are perfectly adequate, though there are certain aspects of each theory which are in conflict. What you call 'relativity' explains the behavior of gravity and its relationship to time and space, but it cannot fully explain behavior at the subatomic level. Likewise, your 'quantum' physics explains atomic and subatomic actions quite well, but it does not work at larger scales. A unified theory would explain how these two conflicting theories remain correct in isolation, while filling in the gaps of understanding between them. This is essential for manipulating gravity, which is the key enabling technology for interstellar travel."

I felt my eyebrows jump. "You can manipulate gravity?"

"We are doing so right now. This ability also enables a number of safety features, such as inertial dampeners. This is why you do not feel our acceleration, which would be fatal without a dampening field."

That didn't make me feel any better. No matter how marvelous their technology, sometimes things don't work the way they're supposed to. If they did, these guys wouldn't need a medical corps. People, and I assumed aliens, got sick, had accidents, got injured by malfunctioning equipment. "So we're utterly dependent on that gravity ball back there to push us along. What happens if it breaks?"

"It is not pushing us so much as it is bending the gravity fields around us, in essence moving local space out of our way until we reach our desired location. The vehicle you encountered experienced an anomaly with its gravity drive system. It is rare, but when it occurs the results can be catastrophic."

I didn't need any convincing, and tried not to think about what would happen if the magic space ball suddenly decided to stop working.

There were too many questions boiling inside me and I couldn't focus long enough to express them in anything resembling organized thoughts. When they fired that ball up, it seemed to mess with both my gut and my head. "How do you 'move space out of the way'? There's nothing there."

"There is much more than you realize. While space may seem physically empty, a vacuum, it has a structure that you cannot perceive. Your scientist Einstein realized that space and time are inextricably linked in a continuum defined by gravity. There are certain races in the Union who are capable of sensing this continuum."

"You mean they can see gravity?"

"Not in the way you might suppose, but close enough."

I took an educated guess. "Like seasonal bird migrations. They know where they're going over thousands of miles by sensing changes in Earth's magnetic field. Some are amazingly accurate, returning to the exact same location at the same time every year."

"That is an excellent analogy. The race I spoke of were among the first to harness 115's potential; the beings you encountered at the accident site."

"The little gray men. Does their species have a name?" They'd only spoken of these varied alien species in general terms. "Or is that not a thing in the Union?"

"It is," he said, "and they do. You can think of them as Reticulans. It is derived from Zeta Reticuli, your name for their star system."

"Reticulans. Got it." And since we were on the subject, if we were going to be traveling halfway across the galaxy together, I needed to know my escorts by something other than eye color. "I still never got your proper names."

Green seemed amused. "You should be warned, our names confer somewhat more information than you are used to. They trace family lineage back several generations, to the beginning of our Diaspora." He held a hand to his chest, as if we were meeting for the first time. "I am Byyruumn-Kchajkk-Urtserr-aan-Tykkggetta. A mouthful, as you might say."

He wasn't kidding. "Yeah, we'll have to shorten that into something I can remember. How about Bjorn?" Simple and Scandinavian, which given his appearance made it a no-brainer. It also kind of fit with the first syllables of his name.

"Bjorn." He seemed satisfied with my suggestion. "Yes. I wholeheartedly approve."

I jerked a thumb at Blue Eyes up in the cockpit. "What about your partner? I'd ask him myself, but he seems kind of busy right now."

"He is. I don't think he will mind my speaking for him. You may call him Savvuun-Jkaech-Yrsuun-aan-Kvallbara."

I couldn't help but snicker. "I could try calling him that, but it would be embarrassing. Think he'd mind 'Sven'?"

"I do not," Sven called from over his shoulder.

I rubbed my hands together. "Glad we could get that out of the way. Now, about translations. If your language is this hard, what will the others be like? I need to be able to talk to my patients." Not to mention get along in the Union in general.

"You will have that ability, once you've been fitted with a translation wafer."

"A wafer? Like an implant?"

"Yes, but do not be alarmed. It is a commonly used tool among our citizens. While the Union does not strictly require it, you will find it to be essential. It allows your brain's auditory region to process foreign speech and translate it into your native tongue. The only limitation is the translator's ability to learn your language, which will improve with time."

"How long should I expect that to take?"

"Not long at all," Bjorn said. "The wafers already contain basic English grammar and syntax. It will need only to master your local dialect. The more you utilize it, the higher fidelity of translation."

I assumed the basic foundations of our language—and who knew how many other human languages—had come from their observations of us. Maybe they'd had more direct interaction with us than they let on.

Maybe I wasn't the first human to be admitted to the Union?

⚕ 8 ⚕

My question and answer session with Bjorn lasted for most of the trip, and left me with even more questions. The distance we'd covered, almost two hundred thousand miles, in such a short time was only the least startling aspect. The sky ahead didn't change, until I could see what appeared to be a steadily growing hole in space. I hadn't given much thought to the Moon before; there had been times when it was prettier than others, but it had always been part of the background of life on the night shift. Now it commanded my attention. It was "new," in Earth's shadow and almost completely dark. Over time it developed a faint bluish glow, which I realized was a reflection of earthlight.

The only clue that we had slowed down came from the sudden sensation of weightlessness. I felt my arms lifting away from the gel cushion and spotted my duffel bag floating in midair nearby. I gave it a gentle push and it bounced off the sidewall. "What happened to the artificial gravity?"

"It's not artificial," Bjorn said. "Gravity is being manipulated for our needs. We are approaching our home ship, so the drive's output must be reduced to allow for a safe approach. Otherwise our distortion field would push the ship away. What you are feeling now is more akin to your kind's typical experience with spaceflight."

"Am I safe to get out of this couch, then?"

He waved. "Of course. Push against the frame and the gel will release you."

I pushed away too hard, flew up, and bounced off the ceiling. It

63

was a lesson in why the interior was coated with soft paneling. I ricocheted toward the floor at the same rate, and reached for the empty seat to steady myself. Once I got over the disorientation, I couldn't stop laughing. No wonder people paid big money for this kind of experience.

"Be careful not to do too much," Bjorn cautioned. "Nausea is a common reaction to microgravity."

He wasn't kidding. My head and my guts were struggling to find equilibrium; good thing I'd only had a light supper the night before. In fact, I was getting hungry. It was nearly time for breakfast, which made me wonder what they did for food. Hopefully they'd thought of that.

Looking past Sven in the pilot's seat, I realized something was missing outside. "If we're close to your home ship, where is it?"

"Directly in front of us," Sven said. "It will remain masked until we activate its gravity drive."

Oh yeah. Back to the energy thing. So they didn't have unlimited power. I wondered what their mothership looked like. Was it a bigger version of this teardrop contraption?

As if reading my mind—and maybe he was—Sven tapped an icon on his panel and a 3D image appeared above it. "This is our home ship."

With no idea what to expect, I was both amazed and disappointed. Expecting to see something out of a movie, I instead saw a silvery dumbbell, a fat cigar-shaped body set within a pair of rings at either end. It was impossible for me to tell which end was which, and maybe it didn't matter.

"How big is it?"

Bjorn floated up beside me. "By your measure, one hundred and twelve feet long. The center hull contains our living accommodations and working spaces."

"What are those rings for?"

"Those are field projectors for the gravity drive. It is considerably more powerful than the one powering this shuttle."

"Are all of your ships like this?"

"Not at all," he said. "You'll find a variety of design philosophies, though their functions demand certain forms. It is similar to the way your seagoing ships all have the same basic features."

"So there are bigger ones than this out there?"

"Oh yes. This is a Class II interstellar cruiser, ship number 803."

"No endearing names then? Just the number?"

"That is our custom. Other races are more emotionally attached to their vessels. More creative, you could say."

Emotional attachment did not seem to be part of their nature. If that's what worked for them, fine, but it seemed like something this slick needed a name. Then again, this was my first starship, so I was easily impressed.

Studying the image, I pointed to a teardrop-shaped depression in the middle of the big cigar. I hazarded a guess at what it might be. "Is that where we land . . . dock, whatever?"

"Correct. Our fuselage will nest within the primary hull." I noticed him glancing at one of the panel displays. "In fact, we are almost there."

I felt us come to a stop, if only because I was now drifting back up to the ceiling. An oval outline appeared along the opposite side wall; it was the door that had blended in so seamlessly before. I couldn't perceive much beyond that, other than to see that there seemed to be a lot more room.

Beyond that doorway, the aliens' "home ship" waited. An unknowable future beckoned, and I sensed that this was my last chance to change my mind. Once I went through that door, I'd be committed.

I gaped at it like a drooling moron.

What was the big deal? I'd traveled most of the way to the Moon in about an hour aboard an alien spacecraft. This was just another, larger, spacecraft. Capable of interstellar travel. Again, I didn't know much about spaceflight at the time, other than being able to cover those kinds of distances was in fact a very big deal. To them it was part of the background, like packing up the family car for a trip to the beach.

I drew a breath to collect my thoughts. "What do I do now?"

Bjorn made a sweeping gesture toward the door. "Step through that portal, and take off your clothes."

"Excuse me?"

His brow furrowed, the first indication I'd seen of anything approaching uncertainty or even humility. Not that they came off as arrogant, mind you, it was more like they were quite comfortable being masters of the universe compared to a puny human like myself.

"Please do not be alarmed." I'd been hearing that a lot lately. "It is a precaution that must be followed whenever we bring new life-forms aboard. With your background, you certainly appreciate the need to avoid unknown contaminants."

"That part I get. What I don't get is the need to strip naked in front of you two."

"Oh." He relaxed. "The portal will close behind you once you step inside. You will have complete privacy." His tone suggested their society valued that as much as ours, which eased my anxiety enough to replace it with the anxiety of being closed up alone on an alien spaceship. "It will also scan your measurements for appropriate clothing."

I looked down at the duffle bag slung over my shoulder. "I wondered if my clothes were inappropriate."

"It is a safety feature, not a stylistic concern," Bjorn said. "The garment complements the ship's inertial dampening field. In time you will find it to be barely noticeable. In fact, it will enhance your comfort."

"Okay . . ." I stepped into the anteroom and the portal winked shut behind me. I shrugged off my duffel bag and slipped out of my utilities. As I rolled them up to stuff them into the bag, the finality of it was jarring. I'd been wearing that uniform for years. Standing buck naked inside of their ship, my heart pounded. This was really happening.

As I took a calming breath, the oval room filled with violet light. Was it that simple? There had to be more to their decon protocols than a UV bath. They hadn't given me eye protection, so there had to be something more subtle at work than being in a giant alien tanning bed.

The violet light disappeared, and the room returned to its original pale yellow glow. I wondered if that was normal lighting for them, like our sun.

"Very good," one of them said, sounding as if he was in the room with me. "Now, please remain still with your arms outstretched."

I did as he said, and a bright beam appeared above my head, a layer of pure white light that began to descend over me. This must be the dress sizing.

It didn't just take my size, it deposited a thin film over me from the neck down. I didn't dare move while it was at work; I had a feeling that would screw everything up. The film was a type of fabric, that much I could tell, but I didn't have a clue as to what the material might be. It felt oddly metallic, but there was no friction or roughness to it. And it breathed; I could still feel the faintest movement of air around me.

Air. Hadn't thought about that until now. They apparently breathed the same oxygen/nitrogen mixture we did, or at least close enough to where I couldn't tell the difference. Those little gray creatures I'd encountered must have as well. They hadn't been wearing any kind of respirators or spacesuits.

My mind started racing as the white light did its work. How similar were they to humans, exactly? I'd encountered only two of what were supposed to be at least a dozen species, and we'd all breathed the same air. I didn't want to jump to conclusions, but it implied a lot, mainly that their bodies needed to exchange oxygen in similar concentrations to ours.

Thinking about the diversity of life on Earth, with millions of species springing from the same evolutionary tree, it wasn't shocking that oxygen-dependent life might develop on other worlds. Bodies had to metabolize to function, which meant their cells needed oxygen. Maybe the necessary ingredients for life on Earth hadn't been that much different from the rest of the universe? If our planet's life was carbon-based, how many others were? Was that a fundamental building block?

The questions swirled through my mind, multiple unresolved trains of thoughts heading in all different directions. I was going to have to take good notes. Did I remember to pack a notebook and pen?

As I stood there in my freshly spun metallized underwear, contemplating alien metabolism, I realized I was thirsty. If they breathed oxygen, chances were they also needed water to stay hydrated.

"Can I get something to drink?"

I hadn't noticed the portal was open again. Bjorn and Sven were standing beside me, as if they'd appeared out of nowhere. Once again they were simply *there*, like space ninjas.

"Of course," Bjorn said with a gesture inviting me to move ahead. "We can supply anything you need." He studied my new threads. "Does the inertia garment suit you?"

I pulled at the metallic fabric. "Just fine." Though I was a little self-conscious of it being so formfitting. "Is this all I get?"

"You can create more later, if you wish. For now you are welcome to put on whatever you feel like over that."

Create? That sounded interesting. For now, I needed something other than alien underwear to be comfortable, and grabbed a sweater and jeans from my bag. I could study galactic fashion trends later.

As Bjorn and Sven led me through a tour of their ship, I was struck by how minimalist everything was. Clean and functional, almost Spartan. There were no hints of personalization, but then so many features were hidden until one of them would touch a panel or wave a hand across an embedded light, that it could've been filled with personal touches that didn't appear until they wanted them. For all I knew, the walls could've been plastered with posters for alien rock bands. I wondered if music was part of their culture; yet another loose thread to clutter my mind.

It was sheer force of will that allowed me to tamp down the amazement factor and focus on what they were showing me. I had to treat this like my first day of school, where everything was new and the sheer volume of knowledge was overwhelming.

We'd begun in the back of the cigar hull. This section was dedicated to logistics and what they said were "engineering spaces," which was where they'd go if something needed fixing. It didn't look like much to my eyes, but I did recognize the same kind of pedestal-mounted sphere that powered their shuttle. This one was much larger, easily a few feet taller than me, and I felt that same odd attraction to it. Not aesthetic, it was physical in that I could feel the sphere pulling at me. I supposed that made sense if it was able to shape gravity.

We moved down an oval corridor—the shape seemed to be a recurring design characteristic—into an open area with counters built into the walls and more of the same types of contoured couches I'd seen in their shuttle.

"This is what your kind would call a 'living area,'" Bjorn explained. "It has nutritional synthesizers and hydration ports."

"Meaning food and water?" I was still thirsty.

"Yes." He waved his hand across a blank panel, which promptly lit up with characters in the same undecipherable script I'd seen earlier on their slates. That was going to be a problem.

"This menu will allow you to choose whatever appeals to you." He pressed against an adjacent panel, which opened up to reveal something I immediately recognized: plates and cups. It was a relief to find something so mundane among all of this technology that was otherwise beyond my understanding.

He must have noticed my reaction. "We are not so far beyond your experience as you might think. Everyone needs to eat."

I finally mustered up the courage to ask the question that had been burning in my mind. "Are you human?" They certainly looked the part.

"We are not, though we share much in common. Our race came from an environment very similar to yours. That drove our evolution in a certain direction."

"I wondered about that, since we're breathing the same air. I figured it wasn't only for my benefit."

"It is not. You'll find most of the life-forms within the Union are carbon-based, which means they require oxygenation for metabolism. This of course also means they require food and water." With that, he tapped a brief series of commands into the panel and slipped a metallic cup into an opening beneath. Water didn't pour out of a hidden spout so much as it just appeared.

Bjorn looked amused as he handed it to me. "One of your notable authors proposed that any sufficiently advanced technology is indistinguishable from magic."

Once again, my reaction had given me away. I was going to have to get that under control. They seemed to have a pretty good bead on our culture, which led to another question that had been bugging me. But first, I drained the glass. "How long have you been watching us?"

"We have been aware of your civilization for over three thousand years, measured in your time. Watching from a distance, as you would say. We have been observing with greater interest for the past eighty of your years."

I did the mental math. "Since World War II." The last "good" war, if there can be such a thing. "It was kind of the defining event of modern history."

"We consider your first world war to be even more so. That set events in motion which ultimately led to the second war and affects your global politics to this day, though not enough of your kind seem to have learned the lessons from it."

"Yeah, we're not particularly good at that. At least, the people in charge aren't. Seems like the rest of us see things clearly and wonder what the hell they're doing."

I handed my empty glass back to him, trying to remember the history of that time. They'd been watching us like primatologists studying apes in the jungle. A global war between competing clans would surely draw closer scrutiny, especially when it threatened to bring down civilization. "It was the nukes, wasn't it? That's what got your attention?"

"It was. The first atomic weapons test alerted us that your race had crossed a critical threshold. It was not surprising that they would be used in the war, although it's quite encouraging that they have not been employed since. Your postwar period had us 'holding our breath,' as you might say."

"It had a lot of our people holding their breath." I wasn't nearly old enough to have experienced it, but my parents and grandparents had plenty of stories of backyard bomb shelters and duck-and-cover drills. It had all sounded ridiculous, but what else could they have done?

"Every technologically advanced society eventually reaches a series of critical thresholds. The ability to harness nuclear power is the first. More will follow. What lies beyond each is up to your people."

That wasn't encouraging, as I didn't hold a lot of faith in the collective wisdom of "my people." "You said nukes are the first. What other traps are waiting for us?"

"There are many," he said, with a touch of sad resignation. "Nuclear weapons are simply more obvious. There are others which are equally dangerous, and more subtle. Gene editing is one example. It can lead to medical innovations which you would find remarkable. If employed carelessly, it can also create biological weapons which could be as destructive as a nuclear war."

"How about climate change?" I wasn't all aboard the global warming doom train, but there was no denying we tended to be messy.

"It is a threat, though not as immediate as many of your kind imagine. Every advanced society needs reliable energy to thrive, and the sources evolve with the technology. Yours began with burning wood and coal, until you found petroleum to be more efficient. The most efficient resource you currently possess is the same one which holds the most immediate potential to destroy you."

That drove the point home as to why they considered nukes to be such a big threshold. It felt completely normal to be having a philosophical discussion in what amounted to their kitchen. I took a seat on one of the couches. "You're talking about nuclear again?"

"I am, but there are even greater sources of energy." Bjorn followed my lead and took the seat facing mine. "I mentioned the ability to control gravity being the key to interstellar travel. That is not possible without a sufficiently powerful energy source."

I was having a hard time imagining what that could be. "What's more powerful than nuclear? What can we do beyond splitting atoms?"

"Fusing them is the next step," he said, laying open the gaps in my own knowledge. "Fusion is the basis for many of your nuclear weapons, though your kind have not been able to control it enough to use as an energy source."

Once again, we were better at blowing shit up than we were at actually using it. "Suppose we do. What happens next?" I looked around the ship. "Is fusion where your energy comes from?"

"We have progressed beyond that, though 'what happens next' will come surprisingly fast once your kind has mastered nuclear fusion."

I wanted him to get to the point. "So what is it, then? What's your miraculous clean-energy source?"

He raised an eyebrow, which were so lightly colored it was easy to think he didn't have any. "Antimatter."

Another sci-fi trope. I had no idea it was real. "You're serious."

He seemed perplexed. "It is by far a more efficient energy source, though it must be rigorously controlled and contained. That is the dichotomy which all advanced civilizations eventually face: the more effective their energy sources become, the more destructive potential they hold. If a single gram of antimatter was intermixed with 'normal' matter, it would create an explosion powerful enough to annihilate one of your largest cities."

"Then where do you find the stuff? It can't just be lying around."

"You are correct, it must be synthesized. Human researchers have been able to do so for some time with particle accelerators, but in exceedingly small quantities. The antiparticles they've created exist barely long enough to be detected before being annihilated. Synthesizing and storing them at scale is a daunting technological hurdle. Successfully moving beyond that threshold is one of the key characteristics of a society with long-term viability."

"In other words, we don't use it to blow ourselves up." Hopefully our track record with nukes was a good sign, though I had a feeling these guys were waiting to see how that played out.

"In so many words, yes. The mechanics of antimatter are what you might call a 'chicken and egg' problem. It promises vast amounts of energy, but requires vast amounts of energy to create and store. Once the manufacturing process is begun, it becomes self-sustaining."

I looked over my shoulder, toward the tail end of their ship, with more than a little unease. "That's what powering us? Antimatter?" Enough to level a good-sized city, if I understood him.

"Also correct." He sensed my worry. "There is no cause for concern. This is a well-understood technology. Our fuel core is secured within a magnetic containment field with three layers of redundancy. Each layer's integrity is under constant surveillance, and if the containment field falls below a certain reliability level, the core is ejected for our safety."

Somehow that didn't make me feel any better. I didn't ask what would happen to us if they tossed their energy source out into space. I hoped they kept plenty of batteries on hand.

I decided to shelve the discussion of nuclear physics as my brain couldn't absorb much more. It was time to move on to more mundane topics. I pointed at the darkened panel behind him. "What about that food generator, or whatever you called it? How can I use it if I don't know the language?"

"For now, we will bring you whatever you need. Once we arrive at our processing station, you will be implanted with a translation wafer. After a time, it will permit you to read and converse effortlessly."

I'd forgotten about the wafers. There was so much to absorb, it was like drinking from a fire hose. "How much time?" No matter how accommodating Bjorn and Sven appeared, I couldn't rely on them forever.

"That will depend on you. The more you read and converse, the better the translator will learn the intricacies of your language. It responds to your input, and is most effective if you try to limit your exposure to a single language at a time."

"Will I have that option? Or am I going to be thrown into some kind of mass immigration center?"

He smiled. "Not at all. To ease your acclimation, your initial exposure will be limited to our race and the Reticulans. The ones you encountered at the accident site."

Maybe it was better to ease me into this Union with a species that was barely distinguishable from our own, but I was eager to meet the others. It was my whole purpose for being here, and I was anxious to get on with it. "Will I be able to spend much time with them?"

"Quite a bit, once you have the ability to converse. But I must warn you, it could be something of a culture shock. The Reticulans are nothing like what you might expect."

"I figured as much." The gray skin and giant heads had kind of given it away.

"It will require more than adapting to their language. You will have to become comfortable with telepathic communication, which has proven to be difficult for the humans we have previously interacted with."

It was another hint that I might not be the only Earthling in the Union, though it was completely lost on me given the context Bjorn was laying out. "Telepathic," I said. "They're going to be able to read my mind?"

"Only to the extent which you allow. Compartmentalizing one's thoughts seems to present the most difficulty. It is an acquired skill. The Reticulans' minds function on many different levels, and separating their private thoughts from those they choose to express is what you might call 'second nature' to them. It has made them quite effective survey drones."

"Drones" was a term I'd only associated with aircraft and ants. For thinking beings, it held some unpleasant overtones. Slavery, for starters. "You make it sound like they're programmed. Like they have no autonomy."

He shook his head. "Reticulans are not programmed, but they are exceptionally organized and self-disciplined. They have a shared sense of purpose, along with an innate curiosity. Surveilling other intelligent races outside of the Union is a delicate and demanding task, at which they excel." He gave me a disarming grin. "Why do you think they are the most frequently identified beings in your culture's 'UFO' encounters?"

"They're doing all the grunt work." It made sense, and it also implied there was an awful lot of that activity going on. "I presume they try to avoid being seen."

"Yes, but they are not always successful. Despite the many precautions we take, sometimes accidental encounters are impossible to avoid. Sanctioned encounters are strictly controlled, and the study subjects are left with no memory of the event."

"Yeah, that doesn't always seem to work out. As you said, there are plenty of stories." Most came from nutcases in the pages of supermarket tabloids, but I left out that tidbit.

"Unfortunately true. The human mind is quite unpredictable, yet surprisingly resilient. Most of the encounters you refer to occurred some time ago. The bulk of our surveillance is accomplished through autonomous survey craft now."

Actual drones, then. "But you're still coming in person, otherwise I'd have never found that crashed ship."

"We are, though the work is presently limited to data collection and vehicle maintenance. Yours is our first direct interaction with humans in some time."

"You mentioned 'sanctioned' encounters. What about unsanctioned?" I made a sweeping gesture at their ship. "If everybody in your Union has access to this kind of technology, it must be hard to control individuals setting out on their own expeditions."

"It can be a challenge," he admitted. "The penalties for unsanctioned contact with unincorporated civilizations are among the severest in the Union, beginning with lifetime excommunication."

I wondered how that would work. Did they have some kind of prison planet? We could get into intergalactic jurisprudence later, though it occurred to me it'd be a good idea to learn enough to keep from unintentionally breaking the law.

As I wondered what kinds of 'unsanctioned' contacts may have already happened on Earth, I heard a chime and the cabin lighting turned salmon pink.

Bjorn looked up. "That is a movement warning. We are about to get underway." He got up and waved for me to follow, with a hint of anticipation. "I think you will want to experience this from the navigation bridge."

Now we were talking. If I was going to be on a starship, I wanted to see where the action was.

⚕ 9 ⚕

The bridge was not what I expected, not that I had any idea what to expect. As with everything else, my assumptions were based on old movie tropes. The real thing was both overwhelming and surprisingly empty; no captain's chair, no workstations manned by busy people doing busy things in front of monitors filled with indecipherable technical gibberish.

What it did have was Sven sitting in another one of those contoured acceleration couches, in front of a semicircular panel that constantly changed presentations in response to his hand movements. Behind him was a row of similar couches, which Bjorn pointed me toward.

The 'overwhelming' part was the holographic display in front of us. It was a three-dimensional map of space that filled the forward half of the control room, so clear and detailed that it seemed like the ship had been laid open to the void. Text in their language scrolled down one side of the floating display, which I presumed was important information about whatever we would be doing. A lime green ribbon arced through the space ahead, pointing toward a bright bluish-white star.

Sven gestured toward the ribbon. "This the path we'll follow to our first destination. Your astronomers call it Beta Orionis, popularly known as Rigel." He tapped at the panel and the display zoomed in on our destination.

I gulped, forcing down my astonishment. It felt like if I took a step forward, I'd tumble off into space. "Rigel. It's . . . big."

"It is a blue giant, approximately twenty times larger in diameter than your sun. There is a Union transit station in orbit at the edge of the system. That is where you'll go through initial processing."

"How far away is it?"

"Eight hundred sixty light-years. Our travel time will be slightly more than two days, by your reckoning."

I grasped enough to know that was a lot of distance to cover in two days. "Pretty sure we touched on this before, but I don't think you answered me. Isn't it impossible to travel faster than light?"

"It is. Again, your Einstein was correct in that it would require an infinite amount of energy. It would also violate causality." He must have recognized my deer-in-the-headlights look. "Put simply, cause and effect would have to be reversed. That cannot happen."

It wasn't clear to me that he meant reversing causality was impossible, or that it was just a horrendously bad idea. "How does this work, then? Warping space, like we did to get here?"

"That is the preferred method. We are in essence reducing the relative distance between ourselves and Rigel down to something we can easily traverse. There is another method, best described as trans-dimensional jumping. It is technically feasible, but is not yet sanctioned by the Union transport ministry."

That sounded interesting, whatever "trans-dimensional jumping" entailed. That it wasn't officially sanctioned made it sound a little reckless and therefore probably quite effective, enough to make the big shots uncomfortable. As my mind wandered to whatever unsavory elements in the Union might take advantage of this, Sven's console began flashing and he turned to give it his attention. "Excellent," he said. "We have received our route clearance to Rigel." He gestured for me to sit in the acceleration couch behind him. "Please settle into the gel cushion. We will be underway shortly."

It wasn't a long wait. That same barely perceptible vibration I had felt in their shuttle began to course through the ship, jiggling my insides like driving over a rumble strip on the highway. Another wave of nausea and confusion began to wash over me like before. Whatever that funky gravity ball was doing, its effects were much more pronounced now.

The stars ahead appeared to move toward us, though not all at once. This wasn't like jumping to hyperspace in the *Millennium*

Falcon, it was more like riding waves on a surfboard. Space itself seemed to swell and fold up ahead of us, distorting the foreground like ripples on a pond. If the universe was an ocean, it was as if they'd dropped a giant rock into the middle of it and we were following it down through the concentric waves spreading in our wake.

"Are we actually moving stars out of our way? Wouldn't that be a problem for whatever might be there?"

Sven was focused on driving, so Bjorn explained. "Not at all," he said with some amusement. "You are correct, moving stars would be very bad indeed. Those are gravity waves, moving ahead of us like the bow waves a ship would create on the ocean." He pointed at the virtual windshield. "The effect is concentrated enough to bend the light we see from the stars ahead."

I was relieved that we weren't moving stars out of our way, but now I was concerned with my own corner of the celestial neighborhood. "What about nearby planets? Wouldn't this move them around somehow?"

"It would perturb their orbits if we were to pass close enough. Our wake field eventually negates the bow wave, but we do have to plan our routes carefully."

As he spoke, I tried to imagine a ship on the ocean. It kind of, sort of made sense that way, but thinking of space as having structure threatened to break my brain. I had never considered that "vacuum" was not the same thing as "empty."

Bjorn kept talking. "Our local gravity field contracts the space ahead of us and expands it behind, until it reaches equilibrium in our wake. Our trajectory had to be cleared with Union transit control before we could depart, specifically to protect any celestial bodies near our path."

"Galactic traffic cops," I said. Every answer led to yet another question. If they had to request clearance, that meant the transmission would've traveled immense distances. I knew enough to understand that radio signals or whatever they used couldn't be instantaneous, and it seemed doubtful there was a Union control tower hidden somewhere nearby. "How do you communicate across that kind of distance? Wouldn't it take years to get an answer?"

"Do you recall what I said about your species' understanding of 'quantum' physics? We utilize a property your scientists call 'entanglement' to communicate beyond light-wave range. Entangled particles can be manipulated, so that inducing change in one creates the opposite action in its 'companion' particle, regardless of their separation. This makes it possible to communicate across interstellar distances, though it is limited to discrete messages using predetermined phrases."

I understood his use of 'particles' had to mean stuff at the atomic, maybe even subatomic, level. Entangled atoms—probably the wrong way to picture it, but it was all I had—could be separated by immense distance, and tweaking one had a mirror effect on the other. How did they know which ones were 'entangled' in the first place?

Yet it kind of made sense. A Navy veteran I'd known in college had once told me how submarines could receive messages deep underwater from an ultra-low-frequency transmitter, but everything had to be reduced to three-letter codes. Then I thought of something else. "It's like Morse code."

I'd said it more for myself, but Bjorn had heard me and looked puzzled. After a moment's thought, there was a delighted glint in his lustrous eyes. His dimwitted student had stumbled onto a revelation. "That is, in fact, a quite appropriate comparison."

Maybe I shouldn't have been surprised. If they'd been watching us since before World War II, they'd have been exposed to our antiquated methods. I was just happy to have made the connection. This "babe in the woods" feeling was not something I was used to, nor comfortable with. It was a relief to think I might actually be up to the task ahead.

I nodded to myself, satisfied with my tenuous grasp of what we were doing. It didn't mean I was out of questions; far from it. When so much information comes at you that fast, sometimes you have to take a breather and file some things away for later. I settled into my gel cushion to absorb what I'd learned, demonstrated in real time as space itself continually folded up ahead of us and fell away behind.

Once the Solar System was well behind us, our acceleration slowed to where it was safe to get out of the gel chairs and move about. That was a relief, as I couldn't imagine spending the whole trip confined to a couch, no matter how comfy it was. While Sven continued to monitor our progress, Bjorn showed me around the rest of the ship. The tour consisted mostly of his telling me which spaces were strictly off-limits, with a promise to show me more later. They couldn't trust me around certain equipment yet, and I was fine with that. It wouldn't do for the new girl to accidentally break something important or open a hatch into space.

My room aboard their ship was comfortably familiar, though it shouldn't have been surprising that beings so similar to humans would require a place to sit down and a bed to sleep in. It was another lesson in alien biology: every living species had its own unique metabolic cycle, which meant their bodies eventually needed rest to regenerate.

The room was small, about the size of a decent walk-in closet. A bed was recessed into one wall, and another one of the gel couches was mounted to the floor. Bjorn tapped on a nearby panel and a small table extended from the wall.

He tapped at the crystal slate that had held my contract. "There. Your crystal is now connected to our ship's network. I've loaded it with a primer on the Galactic Union, including descriptions of each member race with basic physiology and information on their home systems. There is also a summary of Union ordinances with which you will need to become familiar."

"So I don't unwittingly break the law?"

"In so many words, yes. As a newly authorized resident you will be accorded a certain latitude; however, you will be expected to fully comply if you decide to remain."

Play by the rules and you stay in the club. I got that part. I swiped my thumb across the slate. The words seemed to float within its glass. In that respect, it worked a lot like my phone. I pinched at it, trying to zoom in on the fine print to no avail. "It's awfully small type," I said to Bjorn. "Is there an easier way to read this?"

"It is responsive to your touch, perhaps not in ways you are accustomed to." He leaned across and placed his hand on the slate, then drew it up quickly as if he were pulling the words themselves out of the page. All of a sudden its text was floating in the air above the crystal, as big as a TV screen.

"Okay," I stammered. "That's, uh, much better." Once again, I was gaping like a moron.

He gave me another one of his patient smiles. "It is a simple holographic projection. Most of our interfaces work the same way. You will find it to be intuitive, much like your touch-screen devices." He gestured at the floating display. "Place your hands on opposite corners, as if you're holding it. Then move them apart."

I did as he said, and the page expanded or shrank in response to my motions, like pinching the text on a tablet. I decided on a little experiment and pulled my hands together, then swept them down. Sure enough, the page shrank to nothing and reappeared on the slate. I mimicked his motions to open it up, and once again the holographic text floated in the air in front of me. I made a swiping motion and it turned the page, like an e-reader would. "I think I've got it. Just show me how to not accidentally delete anything important."

"Not possible," he assured me. "Think of this reader as you would one of your physical books. You can't change anything, accidentally or otherwise."

I presumed they'd set it up that way to keep me from doing exactly that. I leaned back in the gel couch and swiped through more pages of Union ordinances. "There's a lot to take in. Do I have to read through all this before we get to the next stop?"

"It will facilitate your entry processing if you have a basic understanding of our civilization. We wished to give you a 'head start,' as you might say."

Bjorn was awfully accommodating, but then that was part of an Emissary's job. "Guess I've got some homework ahead of me."

He nodded. "I shall leave you to your studies, then." He motioned to another holographic panel embedded by the door, which gave off a pale orange glow. "You may use this to contact me directly if you require any assistance." With that, he bowed slightly and left me alone.

There I sat, in a room so sparsely appointed that you could be forgiven for mistaking it for a prison cell. I got up and swiped at the door to make sure it would open. Nope, not a prison. But man, was it empty.

I studied the bare walls, wondering if they worked like the ones in the shuttle. I walked up to the paneling between my bed and desk and pressed against it. Sure enough, another of their holographic projections opened up, filling the empty space with . . . empty space.

Like their shuttle, and their control room, it was as if a window had opened up to the outside. I stared into the black. Distant stars seemed to move past as if along the crest of a wave, and I remembered what they said about gravity bending light.

It was too much to absorb, and far too easy to become lost in such an incredible sight. There was work to do, and sightseeing threatened to be a crippling distraction. Maybe I could save it for bedtime, which by my watch would be coming in a few hours. I tried the same crushing motion with my hands that had compressed the other hologram, and it disappeared.

I turned back to my homework. It was going to be a long night.

⚕ 10 ⚕

I started with Union history, which originated with the Emissaries, originally known as Pleiadans.

When it became clear the lights of their dying home star were about to go out permanently, they'd begun a scramble to move their population somewhere other than the Pleiades. Of course there could never be enough ships to move a whole planet's worth of people, but the construction continued until their sun exhausted itself. They got everyone they could out, but in a tragic display of Darwinian selection, this didn't necessarily mean it was women and children first.

They were advanced, but not so much so that they could afford to take just anyone aboard. Each colony ship was a small, self-contained city with limited resources. That meant every soul aboard had to be productive. Children were a necessary burden, but they could only bring so many. The problem with that was for any society to grow and thrive, there has to be a sustainable replacement population. If not, they'll eventually die out. The Pleiadans needed to start making new babies pronto, but first they needed a habitable planet to settle.

This problem was somewhat alleviated by their long lifespans. A regular-Joe Pleiadan without gene tweaking could easily live for a hundred and twenty human years. They could last over twice that long with genetic enhancements, so there hadn't been an immediate danger of their kind dying out. But they were still in a race against time, because it's a big galaxy and it was taking them way too long to find a new home.

The first civilization they encountered was the gray guys, the Reticulans. And while the two races would develop deep bonds that laid the groundwork for the Union, that initial encounter was the first in a string of disappointments.

The Reticulans' planet was livable, and therein lay the problem. Their home was bursting at the seams with its native population, and the Grays were already in the process of scouting out new worlds for themselves. They didn't have room to take in hundreds of thousands of refugees. And to their credit, the Emissaries' forefathers didn't want to lay claim to a world that was already spoken for.

They were both on the same quest for different reasons. And where the Pleiadans' original colony ships had been immense, nuclear-powered slow boats to nowhere, the Reticulans had by then figured out how to manipulate gravity. Their much smaller flying saucers (and that's exactly what they were) could zip around like mad, bending space and time to their will. This had been a revelation to the Pleiadans, and a source of great hope.

Unfortunately, it didn't last because every other compatible planet they found was occupied. Most of the civilizations they'd met had all been understanding of the Pleiadan's dilemma, and many offered to let them stay. But this still didn't sit well.

Without a permanent place to settle, they weren't making babies at the rate they needed to carry on. Still aren't to this day, but they keep finding ways to extend their lifespan. Some of them think it's possible to live for a thousand years given the right combination of gene editing, diet, and exercise.

The Grays were finding the same problems on their scouting expeditions, and together the two races came to the same conclusion: If a planet was capable of producing life, it would. If that life was capable of achieving sentience, it would. Therefore any habitable planets they might find were presumed to harbor life, which they would not disturb to make more room for themselves.

Their restraint was remarkable, given how desperate their situations were. Despite being so physically different, the Pleiadans and Reticulans recognized their shared values and complementary traits. They took what they'd learned to map out their corner of the galaxy, and got to work. If they couldn't find unoccupied planets to settle, they'd have to get busy building a place they could call home. Maybe several of them.

Even with their combined resources, the two founding species needed help. They brought in beings from a handful of worlds they'd explored, all with different talents. Some were wizards at construction. Others knew the galactic neighborhood well enough to protect the others from races who couldn't be trusted to behave themselves. The Pleiadans' empathic abilities made them particularly good at diplomacy, which is how they became known as the Emissaries. Eventually, every race they'd contacted was invited into this mutual support alliance, the Galactic Union.

The whole story was fascinating and heartening. They could've easily gone primitive and started killing each other over territory. We'd certainly done enough of that on Earth. It gave me hope that we humans had the same potential. It also made me wonder how the more well-behaved races in the Union must have seen us: like precocious toddlers, constantly looking for creative ways to get ourselves killed.

The primer on Union law was predictably eyewatering, though it was amusing to see that other species apparently suffered from the same legalese we did on Earth. Lawyers had a way of making the simplest concepts sound like brain surgery. Boiled down to its essence, it in fact sounded like their code of law was lifted straight out of our Ten Commandments: no killing, stealing, or slander, and mind your own business. That last part was couched in the language of "respecting the customs of member civilizations," which on the surface sounded like a libertarian paradise.

The part about "thou shalt not murder" was interesting. I wasn't surprised that they didn't want their members going around killing each other; that's a basic requirement for any functional civilization. The unexpected part was that it extended to most "non sentient" beings, so alien deer hunting was apparently not a thing. Fine with me, I never much cared for it. The most we did on the farm was go after nuisance animals like groundhogs and coyotes, though it made me wonder about the Union's food sources. Were they all militant vegans, or did everyone rely on the same kind of food synthesizer Bjorn had shown me?

When I got to the section on business and commerce, it became considerably more intricate. They'd devoted an awful lot of thought to this, which I supposed was necessary. That kind of thing could get complicated in a hurry. My exposure to business dealings had been limited to our farm and Dad's veterinary practice, but that was enough to turn me off. I wasn't planning to start an extraterrestrial McDonald's franchise, so I skimmed over this part and moved on.

There was more complicated legalese on "interspecies relations," which was kind of amusing. It led to many more questions, though: apparently they were concerned about different races getting frisky with each other, and what that might result in. How many of them shared similar enough biology to make crossbreeding possible?

I closed the law primer and opened up the section I was most interested in: the Union's different member species. This was going to be the meat of my job and I was anxious to get a head start, as medic school with this bunch promised to be challenging.

The first species happened to be the one I was most curious about. I'd already encountered Reticulans at the crash which kicked off this whole improbable chain of events. I'd seen them, touched them, struggled to find their vital signs, and was keen to learn more.

The lesson started with information on their home world. Zeta Reticuli is a double-star system, both stars comparable to our Sun. It has a scattering of what we'd call "minor" planets, and a single rather small one orbiting the second star of the pair, in our language Zeta 2 Reticuli. Its orbit regularly brings it almost dead center between the two stars, so for several months the whole planet is in full daylight. Not that the Reticulans saw much of it.

Their home planet, "Reticuli Prime" as translated into English, is about two thirds the size of Earth. It's rocky like ours, but has almost no surface water except at the poles. Being regularly baked between two suns, its surface temperature is too high for life to flourish. Everything evolved underground, where there are vast subsurface oceans, and this is where their civilization took root.

Once I read this, their appearance made perfect sense. The small stature, grayish skin, and those big, black, almond-shaped eyes would've been a natural evolutionary path for a race of cave dwellers. What led them to think there was something more above the rocky ceiling they'd lived beneath in the first place?

I recalled what Bjorn had said about their role in the Union: observation. The Reticulans were unusually curious and shared something akin to a "hive mind" like ants, only much more intelligent and self-directed. It seemed like an impossible combination.

The "Grays." That's what the UFO nuts called them, and knowing that they'd been right all along didn't make it seem any less improbable. I'd touched one of these strange beings with my own hands, and now here I was reading about their culture and biology.

Average height, one and a half meters. Five fingers, five toes. Exceedingly long fingers, I should add, with a secondary distal joint. How had I missed that? It was like having a fingertip that could fold back on itself. What benefit would that provide? They'd lived beneath the surface, perhaps that had something to do with it. Scrabbling around inside caverns, they had evolved with what amounted to prehensile fingertips.

They were mostly herbivorous, with oxygen-based metabolism. Of course there had to be more than just rocks underground; they needed a food source, and for them to evolve as they had it would've been exceptionally diverse. An advanced civilization couldn't get by on moss or whatever else grew down there. Their brains needed protein.

Turns out their subsurface environment was remarkably diverse. Their light source, such as it was, came from bioluminescent plants growing from the roofs of their caverns. And their underground seas were teeming with life, much of it also bioluminescent. They had explored every nook and cranny of their subterranean world until someone had decided there had to be more, so they started looking up. What must that time have been like for them?

Our civilization had looked to the oceans and wondered what lay beyond them. The Grays had looked up at the stony roof of their world and wondered if there was something more on the other side. For a race that had been accustomed to the pale glow of luminescent plants, it must have been shocking to find shafts of sunlight blazing through the granite above. Someone had eventually gotten the nerve to climb up through it; to them it must have felt like ascending to heaven itself. How many had attempted, but not survived?

That could not have been an easy leap to make. Combined with an innate curiosity and what amounted to a type of collective consciousness, it made sense that they would be the exploration "drones" of this galactic civilization. They readily volunteered for a duty not many others were drawn to.

I wanted to understand their shared consciousness, as this was completely foreign to me. How did this work for an intelligent race—was it a way of absorbing and sharing information, or was there more to it? Could they sense each other's feelings, feel each other's pain? This seemed important if I was ever going to be called on to treat one of them again.

I flipped past the overview and dug deeper into their anatomy. Those big heads housed sizeable brains, and I wanted to know more about them.

Their brains weighed about four kilograms on average, roughly twenty-five percent more than your average human, in bodies that weighed a little more than half of ours. That implied a lot of potential. It was connected to the rest of their nervous system through a spinal column and network of neurons and ganglia that looked a lot like ours.

I touched a floating diagram, which popped out into a three-dimensional view of a typical Reticulan's brain. What immediately caught my attention was the cerebrum—this is the largest part of our brains, divided into two hemispheres of densely folded tissue called "gray matter." Theirs was not only larger, it was structured differently. There was a third hemisphere, which I suppose made it a "semisphere," nestled near the brainstem. It was like a bridge between their information-processing, "thinking" region and their sensory region. According to the text, this was the key to their collective consciousness.

The primer said damage to this region would almost invariably lead to death; even if everything else was functioning normally, being cut off from their peers eventually led to the individual's body shutting itself down. That was perhaps the strangest part of their biology, and there was plenty of strangeness to absorb.

Their digestive system held more notable differences which piqued my interest. While small compared to humans, they had a remarkably complex stomach. It was like a cow's, with multiple compartments. Most people think cows have four stomachs, but that isn't quite correct: It's better to think of it as one organ with four separate compartments. They're classified as "ruminant" animals, along with horses, goats, giraffes, and so forth. Think about what they eat all day: grasses and grains. Their bodies can't digest all of this plant matter immediately, so it happens sequentially within all of those different stomach chambers before moving on to the intestines.

Finding similar features in what I was loosely terming "humanoid" wasn't that surprising. If these beings had lived off of a diet of whatever they could find underground, their digestive systems would've adapted accordingly.

Their circulatory system was what I'd expect from beings which weren't far removed from humans: one heart, located in the center of the chest cavity, squarely behind the sternum, not offset to the left like ours. Their respiratory system included two lungs, much like ours, though they appeared even more complex. The lung tissues were folded in on each other, almost like an accordion. What aspects of their environment would've driven this kind of evolution?

I finished with the "naughty parts," their reproductive systems. This was fascinating. They were hermaphrodites, each containing both male and female organs, though individuals over time tended to develop traits belonging to one or the other. Combined with their hive-like shared consciousness, I could picture millions of short, gray humanoids going about their daily lives underground, communicating telepathically and getting frisky in whatever way seemed appropriate for the moment. How did that work when everyone essentially knew each other's business?

I set aside my prurient interests and moved on to something more familiar, the Emissaries. They shared an awful lot in common with us humans, down to having the same number of teeth, though a few oddities stood out like a sore thumb. Like the Grays, their brains were among the most obvious differences. Largely similar to ours, their frontal lobes were actually smaller, which was surprising for an advanced intelligence, but it didn't tell the whole story. I noticed the folds were smaller, tighter and more numerous, so there was more surface area crammed into the space. It suggested more efficient information processing, but it also seemed like this would make them more vulnerable to head injuries—think of it as having all of the most important stuff concentrated in a smaller area.

On the other hand, their parietal lobes were considerably larger, a good twenty percent. This is where spatial reasoning comes from, which I supposed would be important for a race of spacefaring geniuses. I once read about studies of Albert Einstein's brain, that it held some small but significant deviations that were thought to have enabled him to make associations that "normal" people couldn't. Could the Emissaries visualize the physics that enabled them to do what they did? A race of Einsteins was simultaneously awe-inspiring and a little frightening. It implied an awful lot of concentrated brain power.

This carried over into the rest of their nervous system. It was robust, to say the least. Two separate spinal cords extended from their brain stems, encased in vertebrae that were radially larger than ours for obvious reasons. If you were going to have two spinal cords, the bones protecting them had better be big enough for the job.

So was this redundancy, or did each cord have different functions? It looked to be the former. Their nerve endings were densely packed and more evenly distributed than ours, which was consistent with an enlarged parietal lobe, because that's also where our senses of pain and touch are processed. It implied their entire bodies were as sensitive as our most delicate parts, which made me wince. Every bump would feel like smacking your funny bone.

Having a couple years of veterinary school might have prepared me for this new gig more than I'd imagined. Now that I'd had a glimpse of what made them tick, it was a lot easier to understand their demeanor and anticipate their behavior. They possessed a degree of empathy and understanding that made them perfect for their "emissary" role, and their stoicism may have been cultivated as a way to cope with having such heightened sensitivity. I might have been drawing conclusions that weren't exactly right, but it fit with what I'd seen.

My stomach started rumbling and I took a quick glance at my watch. Time tended to get away from me while studying, and I'd been at this for almost six hours. I skimmed over the remaining files to get an idea of what else I was in for, and it only got weirder. A few were downright frightening: reptilians, insectoids, the "hextopods" I mentioned earlier, and a translucent blob which seemed impossible to possess any intelligence.

One was especially improbable: a race of whale-sized beings that lived in the upper atmosphere of a gas giant. They were enormous creatures but exceptionally light, essentially living hot air balloons floating among the clouds. Not spacefaring, but still intelligent enough to be offered citizenship.

What did that say about us, that whale-sized floaters were more deserving of Union membership than humans? Maybe we had a longer way to go than I'd thought.

I put away my crystal and headed for the door, trying to remember which direction their kitchen was in.

11

I found the kitchen and its "nutritional synthesizer" panel, down at the opposite end of the corridor from my room. I was going to need to come up with a less clunky name for that device, though.

Standing in front of the dispenser, I waved my hand across its blank control screen as Bjorn had showed me earlier. A menu appeared above the panel, all in undecipherable script. I cursed under my breath. I'd forgotten about the language barrier, my body clock was ticking toward midnight, and I was getting hangry.

"Excuse me, but may I be of assistance?"

The voice startled me. I wheeled about to find Sven standing behind me. He was at a respectful distance, but once again the Emissary seemed to appear out of nowhere. *Space ninjas.*

"Geez," I said, catching my breath. "Do you guys always pop out of thin air like that?"

Sven looked troubled. "I am sorry, I did not intend to frighten you. I anticipated you might need assistance."

"How did you know I was down here?" I checked the ceiling for surveillance cameras, not having the faintest idea what they might look like in this place. "Are you guys watching me?"

"Not at all. We wish to respect your privacy, though we can anticipate your needs and sense your emotional state. As we explained, it is part of our nature."

I recalled their extraordinarily sensitive nervous systems. Their empathic abilities must have been related, which I resolved to dig into more when my training started. "You could tell I'm hungry, then."

95

"More to the point, I anticipated your metabolic cycle. It has been several hours of your time since your last meal."

He was right, I'd been so consumed with my studies that I'd completely forgotten supper. But there was a more immediate problem. I jerked a thumb at the dispenser behind me. "I can't read the menu."

Sven flashed a thin smile of recognition. "Ah. We have been able to address that." He pulled one of those crystal slates from his tunic and pointed it at the blank screen. "We have translated the menu items into English for you. In the future, you will be able to do this without our assistance."

I turned back to activate the screen again. Sure enough, it was readable now.

"The translations may appear awkward at first, but it will adapt to your lexicon as you use it."

He wasn't kidding. Late as it felt, I was more in the mood for breakfast and typed in "omelet." It offered me everything from pancakes to "egg mixture, frothy."

"It will adapt more quickly if you use the voice interface."

"I can tell it what I want? Cool." I ordered a ham and cheese omelet with hash browns, as if this was an extraterrestrial Waffle House. And since I was talking to a futuristic food synthesizer, there could be only one choice of beverage: "Tea. Earl Grey. Hot."

I waited in anticipation, but nothing happened.

"You still have to place receptacles in the dispenser," Sven explained patiently.

Of course. I reached into the cabinet, set the "receptacles" into the slot, and was rewarded with a cup of steaming hot tea and a pile of scrambled eggs mixed up with something resembling ham and cheese.

"Not much of an omelet, but it'll do."

"If you describe precisely what you need, the dispenser will learn from you."

"I'll try that next time. I'm too hungry to get picky."

We sat down at a nearby table and I dug into my midnight meal. It had a taste that can only be described as artificial, and I hoped the synthesizer could learn a few things about seasoning as well. It would've been a good idea to bring a jar of hot sauce with me. The tea wasn't bad, though. "Do you ever sample our cuisine when you're on Earth?" It sounded hopelessly snooty but that was the word which came to mind. "If you're able to, I mean." Their appearance was so humanlike that it was easy to forget I hadn't learned enough about their metabolism. Chocolate might be tasty to us, but it can be fatal to dogs. Same principle.

"We have. The human race is one of the few which shares a compatible diet with ours," he said. "Personally, I quite enjoy your black coffee. Perhaps too much."

I was starting to warm up to this guy. "How about cheeseburgers? Pizza?"

"We have had both, but there is a certain loss of fidelity when the synthesizer tries to emulate your protein sources."

I considered the almost-eggs I was currently inhaling, more out of sheer hunger than enjoyment, and hoped that problem would resolve itself over time. "You don't stock up on actual food for these jaunts, then? Seems like there's enough room."

"We do not permit the cultivation of lower species for food. It is largely forbidden by the Union's code of biological ethics, with a few cultural exceptions."

Either he read the quizzical look I was wearing at that moment, or it was his empathic ability at work again. He continued. "Over time, it became clear that many animal species harbor a form of intelligence, though most have not evolved enough for it to be readily apparent. The Union determined that it was prudent to not interfere with their natural development. Though it may not be obvious to a local observer, even insects have their own native intelligence, however narrowly defined."

I could see his point. "How an ant colony functions may not seem like intelligence, but it works for them. What you're saying is a lot of what we think is a species' 'instinct' is simply their way of thinking through a problem."

"In its simplest form, you are correct. Some species take longer to progress than others, while some never do. We are resolved to 'let nature take its course,' as you would say. Too often, intelligence is assumed when a species shows the ability to modify its own surroundings to its needs. But many creatures are limited by their physical traits and do not evolve in such ways."

"Aquatic mammals," I said. "Whales, dolphins, manatees... they're all pretty clever."

"More than you may realize," Sven said. "We established contact with them around the same time we first began observing your race. They are quite intelligent."

"You're talking to them?" This was incredible. "I mean, we always thought they were communicating between themselves, but actually being able to *converse* with them..." I trailed off in thought, wondering what the implications might be. What did they think of us?

"They are quite fond of humans, for the most part. They do have concerns about the treatment of your environment, though recent trends have been encouraging."

"Yeah, we're working on that." I'd never been a tree-hugger, but I also liked clean water and air. If you can avoid polluting, then by all means do so. "So they like us humans?"

"You share much in common. They are all generally docile and patient beings. They understand your species faces challenges which theirs do not, which you are steadily overcoming."

"Kind of like you guys watching us for admission to the Union," I surmised, when something else came to mind. "There've been accounts of whales and dolphins protecting humans from predators. There's accounts of them protecting divers, for instance, because they knew hungry sharks were in the area."

"An excellent example. They welcome your desire to experience their environment, but are frequently dismayed by your obtuseness. The ocean is a dangerous place," he said. "To your point, they are not especially fond of sharks. They're considered to be thoughtless bullies."

"Reminds me of a line from an old movie: they swim, they eat, they make little sharks. Yeah, I'm not a big fan of them either." Not that I ventured into the ocean much. Spotting a dorsal fin slicing through the water once at Myrtle Beach had been enough. He was—they were—dead right about the ocean being a dangerous place. There were some enormous, toothy creatures swimming around in the murk, outside of human sight. "What does your 'biological code of ethics' have to say about predatory species?"

Sven became pensive, which suggested this was a personal struggle for him. "We have similar species within the Union, though not all are waterborne. They must be allowed to evolve just as any other creature. That does not mean we don't take precautions to protect ourselves. Avoidance is the first priority."

"Don't wander into places where you might get eaten," I said. "Makes sense, but sometimes it's unavoidable. Right?" I wondered how much of the Union remained unexplored because someone might get hurt. It didn't square with my idea of an advanced civilization.

"You will learn more about this in time. We employ many layers of protective measures, but yes, sometimes taking a life to protect another is sadly necessary." He paused a moment. "For similar reasons, you might be surprised to learn that many of your mammals generally do not mind if they are captured and placed in one of your zoological parks."

That was surprising. "I'd expect they'd think it was like being put in jail."

"Some facilities are certainly more desirable than others. But you must consider the environment they came from, what you term the 'food chain.' Survival is a continuous struggle which demands constant vigilance. Many individuals, particularly the older ones, are often relieved to have that stress removed from their lives."

"That's the dolphin retirement plan, happily swimming in a shark-free pond and having fish thrown at them all day?"

"If they are well cared for. As I said, some facilities are better than others."

A lot like retirement homes. It made me want to go back and spread the word to every zoo and aquarium in the world: Be nice to these guys, they've had a hard life. Let them enjoy what's left.

I finished my late-night meal and placed the dishes in the recycler. Sven was proving to be less of a cold fish—pun fully intended—than I'd thought. Thinking of the dolphins enjoying their respite from a hard life in the ocean, I realized how exhausted I was and made my way back to my room.

Sleep came quickly, and deeply. That was a good thing, because the next day I was in for a wild ride.

12

It's easy for an experience to beat your expectations when you have no idea what to expect, which was the case for me at Rigel Station. That's not its official name; it was Galactic Union Transit Depot 03A. That's translated into English; its name in Galactic common language is even more of a mouthful. Official bureaucratese is apparently a universal plague.

The Emissaries had called Rigel a "blue supergiant" star, and they weren't kidding. It dominated the black sky like an enormous zillion-watt lightbulb, even at the far edge of the system it was bright enough to wash out the light from background stars. From our perspective it was about the size of a basketball at arm's length; when Sven explained we were farther away from it than Pluto is from our Sun, I finally had some sense of its incredible size.

"Was it always this big?" I remembered the tale of their home planet's star burning out to become a similar giant.

Bjorn was seated beside me again in the control room. "No, but it has been in this phase since before the founding of the Union. It is near the end of its life cycle, but it is difficult to predict when its terminal phase will begin."

"Terminal phase" sounded ominous. "What happens then?"

"A star of this class will eventually exhaust its remaining fuel and collapse in on itself from its own mass. Rigel has enough mass to explode in a supernova, and eventually leave its core as a black hole."

I knew what those were, and I didn't want to be anywhere near one. "And you guys put a station near it?"

"This was one of our first transit depots; at the time this location was near the center of the Union. Our member systems have grown to the point where this is no longer the case. In time it will have to be either moved, or evacuated."

"Seems like it'd be a good idea to get on with that now."

Bjorn appeared distressed, which I hadn't seen in him before. "It is more complicated than you imagine. Remember, Rigel is eight hundred sixty light-years from your home system, so how it appears in your sky is as it was nearly a millennium earlier. This is another reason why our trajectories have to be cleared in advance using the entanglement network; it is otherwise impossible for us to know the actual condition of any destination based on our local time reference."

Once again, he was making my brain hurt. "If the Union waits too long to clear the station, Rigel could blow up tomorrow and there'd be no way to warn anyone headed this way."

"That is one of many reasons why interstellar navigation is complicated. Many residents of 3A have elected to move on their own rather than wait for the Union to act. You will find the station to be sparsely populated."

It sounded like a typical government operation. Some facts of life were constant, advanced civilization or no. "Is that why you brought me here—to ease me into this Union of yours?"

"Correct. There are transit depots closer to Earth, but they are rather crowded. We believed it best to take 'baby steps,' as you might say."

I'd have done the same in their shoes, but it didn't make me any more comfortable being this close to a star that could blow up at any time.

"There is no need to worry," Bjorn said, sensing my growing anxiety. "While we cannot precisely when a star will become a supernova, the signs of an imminent event are quite well understood. You are in no danger here."

No danger. I suppose whatever happened to me would happen to them as well, assuming they were going to remain my guides into this new world. "Are you staying with me through all this?" I didn't want to be thrown into the deep end to figure out how to swim.

"Of course. We will remain with you until you are comfortably able to make your own way."

"Good." I hadn't made my way through life on Earth by having someone else hold my hand, but in this case it was fine with me.

Rigel's brilliant glow filled the control room, like an industrial spotlight hung in the window. Sven dimmed the holographic viewscreen, stepping it down until we could see our destination.

The station lay straight ahead, steadily growing larger as we approached. It looked simple at first, a collection of long cylinders arranged in a circle around a central hub, like spokes on a bicycle wheel or teeth on a gear. As we drew closer, rings of light from individual windows appeared at irregular intervals. It was a city floating in space, with each building anchored to that common hub. We were aiming for its center, where a ship similar to ours looked to be pulling away. The spacecraft was dwarfed by the structure it was leaving.

I stood up for a closer view and pointed at the station. "How big is this place? How many live here?"

"3A is somewhat less than six kilometers' diameter. It has a maximum capacity of a quarter-million beings, depending on the species. Some require less individual space than others. The depot currently hosts fewer than a hundred thousand."

A hundred thousand didn't sound sparsely populated at all, but if it was designed to house over twice that many then I guessed living space wasn't going to be a problem. "How long will we be here?"

"Entry processing will not take long, but we won't depart for the capital until tomorrow. We have arranged for overnight quarters."

"I won't have my medic training here, then?"

"Oh no. That will be at an education center at Medical Corps headquarters. Your time here is strictly for entrance processing and acquaintance with our culture. Once you have become reasonably acclimated, we will continue on to our capital."

That sounded annoyingly bureaucratic. "Who decides if I've been 'reasonably acclimated'?"

"Ultimately that is up to you. However, it will largely depend on how well the translation implants adapt to your native language. Once you can converse, you will find it much easier to adapt. The more willing you are to engage, the faster the process."

"I'm ready to get on with it. It won't take me long."

Bjorn arched one of his silvery blond, near-translucent eyebrows.

"I would caution you to not be so certain. The culture shock for a being with no previous exposure to so many of what you call 'alien' races can be daunting, particularly for your kind. We have seen individuals become so isolated that assimilation becomes impossible. It will be best if you start with 'small bites,' as you might say."

How different were our native languages, anyway? And he'd dropped another hint that I might not be the first human in the Union. Would it help if I sought any others out? It was a question for another time, after getting whatever passed for an entry visa.

Everything had happened so fast, so unexpectedly, that I'd been living in the moment. The most time I'd had to ponder anything had been spent familiarizing myself with the different Union species, and I hadn't thought enough about what it would mean to live among them. To treat them when nobody else could.

Attitude adjustment is crucial if you're going to carry your weight in emergency medicine, whether you're an ER doc, a medic, or the poor sap who has to clean up after us. You have to separate your personal interests from the task at hand, and remember that whoever you're treating is probably having the worst day of their life. It was some comfort that I'd already seen a couple of Grays in that condition and it hadn't fazed me.

Or had it? I was in the middle of treating one, then all of a sudden I wasn't. One minute I was there, the next I was in my bed at home with vague memories of responding to a plane crash.

Of course one of the Emissaries had zapped my brain, but something about that troubled me. "Why did you wipe my memory at the crash scene? Was it to keep me from going public?" Not that I would have. The media would've painted me as one more country bumpkin yammering about little green men.

"In part," Bjorn said hesitantly. I could see he was processing my sudden realization. "While our protocols require that we remain undetected by the local population, we also must protect any individuals who might stumble upon us."

"By that, you mean protect us from ourselves," I guessed. "You were worried I might have a psychotic break."

"That is always a concern during first-contact situations. In your case, it had begun as a traumatic event and only threatened to become worse. We could sense this immediately."

"Wait . . . *you* were the one who wiped my memory?"

"Of course. The crew aboard the survey craft was in no condition to do so. We had begun our descent from orbit after the first transmission from their emergency beacon. We arrived shortly after you. If you had passed by a few minutes later, there would have been nothing for you to see."

"The 'cloaking device' thing." Another sci-fi trope, but there was no denying they all seemed to fit perfectly. And once again, an Emissary had snuck up on me. I didn't know if I could ever fully adapt to their tendency to appear out of nowhere, which only added to my defensiveness. "You also took me out of play while I was working an accident scene. What happened to the crew?"

Bjorn drew his lips tight. "Sadly, they all died of their injuries." I think he could read my simmering anger—maybe if they'd let me do my job, those guys might still be alive. "You must trust me that there was nothing you could do, even if you'd had a better grasp of their physiology. Their craft's inertial dampeners experienced an anomaly. Some races can withstand this better than others, but above a certain acceleration it is always fatal."

It wasn't the fall that killed you, it was the sudden stop at the end. I thought about the pilot I'd seen slumped over his control panel. "The Emissary was already dead, wasn't he?"

"He was. The Reticulans you encountered survived somewhat longer, but in the end their internal injuries were too severe."

"Would you have been able to do anything for them, or is your race one of those that is afraid to treat others?"

"We are not," Bjorn said, holding his hand to his chest, "though it is not our specialty."

"What did you do with them?"

"Their remains are aboard this ship, preserved in our cargo hold until they can be returned to their home worlds."

So the Union at least respected their dead in a manner similar to us. That said a lot about their culture, but I didn't like thinking about what had led to that crash. It was obvious from the name that "inertial dampeners" protected us from being squashed like bugs on a windshield. "How often does that kind of accident happen?"

"Rarely. There has only been one other incident on an Earth

survey mission, many decades earlier. It was not long after your second world war."

I furrowed my eyebrows. He'd just dropped a big hint and was waiting for me to pick it up. "You're kidding... *Roswell*?"

"Precisely. The incident resulted in significant trauma among the humans who found the crash site. There were no Emissaries assigned to the mission; an oversight which we have since corrected."

I don't know why it was so surprising; my presence here should've led me to reevaluate every crackpot flying saucer story in existence. I wish I'd paid more attention to them now, it might've left me better prepared for what followed.

13

As we drew closer to the station's central hub, I noticed a familiar object in its center. It was another one of those dark metal spheres, much larger than any I'd seen before, attached to the inner face of the hub by a framework of gossamer-thin lace glinting from the distant sun. Bjorn explained it was placed there to create a gravity field so the outer building's occupants could go about their lives normally.

I counted at least a dozen ships docked around the hub; only one of them similar to ours, cigar-shaped with rings mounted on either end. It felt odd to think of this as "ours" but that was a sign that maybe I was already getting acclimated to this strange new environment.

The other ships were of odd shapes and sizes. One was bulbous, trailing a long conical tail, which made it look like a flying horseshoe crab. Another was a simple cylinder, unadorned with any other structures I could see. The largest was ovoid and was also the brightest of the bunch, its outer skin sparkling with hundreds of brightly lit windows. The remaining few were good old-fashioned flying saucers.

Bjorn took note of my reaction. "Each of the ships you see are unique to the cultures that built them. The largest one is a colony ship; they serve to transport races that cannot otherwise tolerate relativistic travel."

That was interesting; some species' biology relegated them to the slow lane. "And the saucers—those are all Reticulans?"

"For the most part, yes. As you might imagine, they are the source of many of your culture's UFO legends."

It didn't feel like legend anymore. I was about to land dead center in a world whose existence was believed in with a near-religious fervor by the types who most "normal" people dismissed as nutjobs.

It all began to make sense. If the Union's "prime directive" was to remain undiscovered by the civilizations they were surveying, they'd want to avoid major population centers. That so many UFO encounters had been out in the boonies—including mine—was simply the result of them keeping out of sight.

The colors shifted on Sven's control panel; he responded by taking his hands away. "Our approach has been approved. The station is guiding us into our berth now." His voice gave away no emotion, but the subtle droop in his shoulders suggested otherwise.

"My companion prefers to pilot our ship himself," Bjorn explained, "but the gravity gradient and proximity to other vessels necessitates automated control." Not long after, the view outside changed as the station seemed to pivot around us, pulling us toward an open berth at the far edge of the hub.

Was this a chink in Sven's armor? He liked flying and was irked at the prospect of giving someone else control. Maybe I could actually get to know these guys, given enough time.

Before long, the station's bulk filled our view. It was hard to tell how close we were; the few visible surface features were so utterly foreign that there was no sense of scale. As we drew nearer, the reality of this new world began to weigh on me. There was no changing my mind now, and there would be no going back, not for a long time. It made me question my mental preparedness, but now there was no choice but to press on, as if the station's artificial gravity was pulling me into a new life unlike anything I was capable of imagining.

Docking with the station was so smooth as to be barely noticeable. Sven's hands danced across the control screens, methodically shutting down one system after another. Or rather, I assumed that's what he was doing, as it had the feel of shutting down a piece of heavy equipment at the end of the day.

While Sven tended to the technicalities, Bjorn led me back to my room to collect my things. It was surprisingly hard to leave even after only a couple of days; I was clinging to anything that felt the least bit familiar.

Bjorn sensed my trepidation. He swept a hand toward the corridor in a welcoming gesture. "I know you are having second thoughts. There is nothing for you to be anxious about. You will find our collective civilization to be quite accommodating."

I nodded shakily. "Oh, there's plenty to be anxious about. I've always been kind of a homebody, and this"—I paused—"is definitely not home."

"Then I hope you will eventually come to think of it as such. I understand your unease at the prospect of encountering so many new cultures at once. Rest assured, we will be by your side for as long as you require." He motioned for me to follow him. "Come now, it's time to bring you into the Union."

My entry into the Galactic Union wasn't exactly a welcome-aboard party with balloons and banners. It started with an unspectacular elevator ride through a portal in the top of their ship, ending in the first level of what they explained was the "transit hub."

As the next portal opened, we stepped into a cavernous chamber. Its size was the only indication that we'd left our ship; otherwise it looked identical to one of the spaces we'd recently left behind. The arched ceiling glowed as if it were pure light, and rows of oval doorways were recessed into the chamber's gently curving walls.

The startling difference was its occupants. Three of the Grays were waiting, each holding up one of their elongated hands in what I assumed was a greeting. I gulped. Standing face-to-face with actual, living extraterrestrials was nothing like when I stumbled onto a pair of incapacitated ones. Had Bjorn and Sven not been there, I can't say I wouldn't have wet my pants in terror.

They weren't threatening at all, but their being so far removed from normal human experience was hard to process. I didn't have a clue what to say. A tentative "hello" was all I could manage. They nodded in recognition, and I felt a tingling sensation deep inside my skull.

"It feels like they're trying to get into my head," I said anxiously.

"Translated, they are saying 'We welcome the human Melanie Mooney,'" Bjorn explained. "Remember, their primary method of communication is telepathic."

Only then did I notice the thin slits of their mouths hadn't moved. One of them extended his hand to me, revealing two small discs. I took them from him with trembling fingers. "Thank you."

The Gray answered with another nod.

"I reminded them that you cannot yet hear them, and that it is discomforting to feel their attempts to communicate," Bjorn said. He pointed to the chips in my hand. "Those are your translation wafers. Place one inside of each ear. They will embed themselves and begin assimilating your language."

I studied the tissue-thin wafers skeptically, each about the size of a fingernail. They didn't feel mechanical at all; if anything they were more like human skin than a computer chip. I inserted one into each ear as instructed, and immediately felt them going to work. "It tickles."

"That will pass. The wafers are embedding themselves in your epidermis and seeking out your auditory nerves."

It felt like thousands of microscopic tendrils were working their way into my ear canal, right beneath the skin. I shuddered against the overwhelming urge to dig them out. All I wanted was to jab a finger down there, but before long it was done. The tickling was replaced by disembodied voices in my head, which might've been even more disturbing.

Welcome, Melanie Mooney. Are you able to understand us now?

I looked up at the middle Gray. Somehow I knew it was him—or her. *Right*, I reminded myself. They're hermaphroditic. "Yes," I said nervously, not sure if they preferred for me to think it.

You may speak per your normal custom. I shall do the same for your benefit. Of course he knew what I was thinking. This was going to take a *lot* of getting used to. His slit of a mouth began to move, and his vocalization came in a torrent of unintelligible clicks and chirps. After a brief lag, the chips began turning his chattering into words I could understand. "In time, you may find it easier to communicate with us telepathically."

"I'll keep that in mind." Never much for small talk with strangers, I was ready to move on. "So, what's next?"

The lead Gray motioned toward the nearest door, which opened as he pointed to it. "Before you are allowed to enter the facility, you must undergo a medical examination."

I turned back to face the Emissaries, my imagination swirling with visions of being probed by alien abductors. "Exactly what kind of 'medical exam' is he talking about?"

Bjorn held up his hands to calm me. "There is no cause for alarm. This is a sterile processing area. Before leaving it you must be tested for any biological contaminants that could potentially infect other Union citizens. You will also be immunized against any of our illnesses which are known to be communicable to humans."

I didn't like the idea of being poked and prodded by a trio of extraterrestrials who'd just gotten access to my thoughts. Oddly enough, I was equally afraid of insulting them through sheer ignorance. "I thought the whole reason you brought me was that other races aren't comfortable with treating . . . aliens." It was the first time I'd ever thought of myself as such.

"That is true, though you may recall we explained it is a *rare* trait. These Reticulans are among the few who willingly do so."

That wasn't any less disturbing, but there was no use arguing.

They led me into an exam room. There was a padded table, a few chairs (because even vaguely human-shaped beings need a place to plant their butts), and what looked like a privacy screen in one corner. An array of unrecognizable metallic instruments sat by the exam table. I turned to Bjorn again. "I don't have to strip, do I?"

As the Grays traded looks with each other, Bjorn gave me another of his disarming smiles. "Not at all." He pointed to the privacy screen. "There are examination garments in the changing area. They will allow the necessary access without requiring you to be needlessly uncomfortable."

"Okay . . ." I said tentatively, and stepped behind the screen. A collection of cream-colored body suits were hung along the wall. I took one that was about my size, stripped out of my clothes, and slipped it on. It felt only slightly better than being buck naked, and the medic in me wondered how they'd be able to do what they needed. I poked at my arm out of interest, and the fabric opened up just enough for my finger to slip through. When I pulled away, it closed back up. Cool.

With my dignity mostly intact, I stepped back into the exam room.

"Thank you," the lead Gray said, his voice raspy through the translator. He motioned toward a bright metallic column, not much taller than me, which held two semicircular arms on either side. "Now, if you please, step in front of the scanner."

Seemed harmless enough. I stood in front of the rack and the two arms closed above me, forming a circle. White light emanated from the circle as it began descending down the length of my body, then back again. If this was some kind of alien X-ray machine, nobody seemed particularly concerned about radiation.

As it finished, the wall behind them turned black and a three-dimensional image of my innards appeared. Two of the Grays busied themselves with studying my scan, highlighting and making notes on the same type of crystal slate the Emissaries had given me. They seemed particularly interested in my glands and lymph nodes.

The head Gray placed a small disk on my neck, cold and metallic, right above the left carotid artery. I assumed this had to be a type of biomonitor. Sure enough, more information appeared on their wall screen, in a script similar to what I'd seen aboard the Emissaries' ship. I might not have been able to decipher it yet, but I recognized the traces right away: heart and respiratory rates, O_2 saturation, blood pressure, body temperature. I wondered how my vitals compared to other species.

"Your heart rate and blood pressure appear to be high compared to our baseline human database. Are you experiencing any unusual stress?"

I stifled an ironic laugh. "Two days ago I was minding my own business at home. Now I'm on the other side of the galaxy getting poked and prodded by aliens. Yeah, I'm a little stressed."

"I suppose that is understandable for a human in your situation. In time you will adjust to your new environment. You have nothing to fear."

Easy for him to say, but it was equally likely they'd spent enough time among us primitives to become jaded. Still, I was beginning to feel an odd attachment to this one. I couldn't put my finger on it, but he had a gentle manner that was about as soothing as you could find in a short, gray-skinned extraterrestrial with a giant head and black, almond-shaped eyes. "Do you have a name?" *One that I can pronounce*, I didn't add.

You may find our pronunciations are not as difficult as you expect.

Whoops. Forgot they were telepathic. I needed to learn Galactic Union etiquette, and quickly.

Translated into your tongue, my name is Xeelix. I am this station's chief physician.

"Thank you. It's easier to get comfortable with a new doctor if I at least know what to call him."

He reverted to old-fashioned vocalizing. "I am not a doctor in the sense you may think of one. My role here is less focused on patient care than it is screening new arrivals for any latent illnesses, so as not to contaminate the station."

I couldn't help but think it was like a vet checking new cattle before adding them to the herd.

Based on our understanding of your agricultural methods, that is an apt comparison.

Damn. That mind-reading thing again. I glanced back at the wall screen with my vitals, and noticed a change. Not in my heart rate or anything, but in the numbers themselves. They were slowly becoming readable. They were fragmented, not entirely complete, but I understood most of them now. I pointed at the screen. "Is that translating for me?"

"It is not. That is the implant adapting to your language. It is beginning to access your optic nerves."

Nice. So I'd eventually be able to read as well. That would take me a long way. I was just starting to relax when Xeelix lifted a small, bullet-shaped silver object from a nearby tray. "There is one final procedure, Melanie Mooney. If you please, lie face down on the examination table."

So much for getting comfortable. The shock of realization shot through me like a lightning bolt: All of the trailer park, supermarket tabloid abduction stories had in fact been true. "Wait, *what*?"

He was annoyingly detached about it. "The rectal prophylactic is standard for new arrivals. It will disperse compatible DNA imprints which will enhance your immune system's adaptation to any communicable diseases you may encounter. It is quite harmless."

My inner reactionary crank finally asserted itself. "*Nobody* is sticking an alien probe up my ass!" I snatched the silver bullet from his hand and slipped back behind the privacy curtain. If Doc Xeelix was shocked by my reaction, he didn't show it. If you want to do something right, do it yourself. Especially when it involves shoving things up your tailpipe without anesthesia.

There's not much left to say about this part, at least nothing I'm willing to talk about. I examined the gleaming alien suppository, looking for any hidden machinery that might make the experience even more unpleasant.

It will be better if we administer this for you, he said in my head.

"No thanks, I'm good," I said from behind the curtain as I assumed the position.

This is why we sedated humans for this procedure, I heard one of the Grays remind him.

Understood, I heard Xeelix think back at him. *However, she is not like most of the others. This will in fact be an excellent test of her abilities.* I could tell he was directing his next thought at me: *You may find this to be a disconcerting experience.*

More than it already was? "In what way? This thing dissolves, right?" It had damned well better, otherwise my stay here was destined to be short and unpleasant.

In a sense. It dissipates to distribute nanoprobes into your lymphatic system. Your physiology is not adapted for the types of infections we have acquired immunity to; think of this as a broad-spectrum vaccine. It is for your protection.

He'd answered a question that I'd been mulling over: Just as it was rare for animals to pass diseases to humans, how compatible was the biology of all the different Union species with our own?

It helped to think clinically as I was, well, doing the deed. And Xeelix wasn't kidding, it felt weird. I could feel the thing disintegrate, releasing millions of microscopic machines to settle inside my glands and lymph nodes. It felt as if my bloodstream had been turned into an ant farm.

I clenched my teeth and resisted the urge to claw at my skin like the junkies we too often ran across back at County EMS. My last run had only been a few days ago, but it felt like a lifetime. "How long does this take?"

Typically twenty-two seconds, by your time reference, to deposit the nanoprobes throughout your lymphatic system. It will take somewhat longer for them to acclimate to your physiology.

It was surprising how long twenty-two seconds could feel. Beyond the privacy screen, I heard some approving noises from the other Grays. *Excellent, Melanie Mooney. The nanoprobes have completed initial distribution and are establishing their monitoring network. You may come out now.*

"Wonderful," I said, collecting my self-respect to emerge from behind the curtain, shaking off the creep factor. Xeelix waited for me as the other Grays were watching the network depositing itself throughout my body. I pointed at the screen. "So you're monitoring me right now? For how long?"

"For as long as you are with us."

I didn't care for the sound of that. "Someone is going to be watching my bodily functions around the clock?"

"Not at all. It is a passive system. We are only concerned with the initial setup, as you would say. If you experience any anomalies, it will alert the nearest Medical Corps facility."

Ah, yes. The Medical Corps. My whole reason for being here. It's easy to forget when you're dealing with alien butt probes. "They send a squad whenever someone trips a circuit, or however this works?"

"By 'squad,' I presume you mean a medical transport. Not always. Maladies are categorized and prioritized before dispatching a team."

"You mean triage."

Xeelix paused, and there was a slight twitch in his eyes. His own translator must have been working overtime. "Yes, that is correct. A most useful term which we will add to our collective dictionary. You must pardon my hesitance, we have not yet encountered a human with your degree of medical knowledge. It may take some time for the translators to digest your idioms."

"I'm surprised you haven't run across any doctors or nurses. Hard to believe I'm the first."

I can't explain how, but he looked sorrowful. "Some of our kind encountered human medical professionals during an earlier survey, under traumatic circumstances. Our cohorts did not survive the experience."

I turned to the Emissaries, who were still observing me from the corner of the room. "Roswell?" I mouthed silently. Bjorn answered with a solemn nod.

"I am so sorry." It felt like I was apologizing for the entire human race, and maybe I was. "I'm sure they had no idea what they were dealing with."

"They did not. Unfortunately some of the humans preferred to observe rather than render aid, though their efforts would have been unsuccessful regardless. As you well know, some injuries are not survivable."

He wasn't kidding. I'd seen it among their own kind not long ago. Of all the unimaginable things I'd experienced in such a short time, this left me at a loss for words, maybe because it was the first thing I could personally identify with.

"We appreciate your empathy. It will serve you well during your time here." Xeelix looked to his companions by the monitor, who gave him slow, approving nods. He then turned back to me. "Your admission scans are complete. You are not carrying any diseases which are communicable to Union races, and we cannot detect any which may be of immediate concern to you."

Good to know. As I reached for my clothing, he handed me a black crystalline ring. "This ring enables an interface with the lymphatic nanobots you implanted. It also contains all of your biometric information, and will enable your access to Union facilities. Wear it at all times. Do not lose it."

He seemed deadly serious about that last part. It was strangely disappointing to be moving on; I could sense a bond growing with this little Gray man. He had a kind manner which was difficult to explain, considering his utter lack of expression or body language cues.

"Thank you, Xeelix." I offered my hand, and he seemed confused. "It's a human custom. We call it a handshake." Us girls typically were more of the hugging type, but that seemed wildly inappropriate here. He cautiously extended his own hand, those elongated fingers wrapping themselves around my own. His skin felt cool to the touch, and I'd be lying if I said it wasn't a little unnerving. Here I was, shaking hands with a no-kidding extraterrestrial. I was stumped for a moment, and decided to finish in his "native tongue." *I enjoyed talking with you. I hope we can do so again soon.*

As have I, Melanie Mooney. I am confident we will have much to learn from each other.

⚕ 14 ⚕

The Emissaries led me out of the exam area and through another oval door at the end of a long corridor, where we stepped into another small room. The door whispered shut behind us. Sven waved his hand across a panel nearby; for the first time I noticed they were both wearing rings identical to the one I'd been given. Soon after there was movement and I realized we were in a garden-variety elevator. I felt the floor rising up beneath us; we were moving quickly.

When it came to a stop my stomach felt like it wanted to float up into my chest, like going over the top of a rollercoaster. It didn't seem to fully settle. "It feels like there's less gravity here."

"There is," Sven explained. "The farther we get from the station's gravitational center, the lesser the effects. Standard gravity within the Union is approximately ninety percent of what you perceive on Earth. As we move farther out into the structure, you will feel less. At the outermost levels, it is roughly forty percent of your normal gravity."

A great way of fooling myself into thinking I'd lost weight, a too-frequent obsession with us girls. If there were bathroom scales here, I wouldn't be paying much attention to them. "I'm guessing each level is populated by different races, depending on their local gravity?"

"Exactly, though the base level targets a median gravitational force which is comfortable for all Union races." He reached with his ringed finger to open the door, then paused. Before we could exit, he cautioned me. "We are now at the receiving level. Here we will complete your entrance process. You will be exposed to many more races which you have not encountered before. You may find it to be something of a culture shock."

With no idea of what to expect, I could only think of my recent experience with the Grays. "It seemed like I got along fine with the docs downstairs. I'll try to keep an open mind." Just not so open that they could easily read it.

"That is wise," Bjorn said. "Your interaction with Xeelix was more significant than you realize. The Reticulans are generally averse to social contact. Did you sense a bond with him?"

"It's hard to explain, but yes. I'm surprised that's the case if they're your survey drones." I still didn't like using that word for intelligent beings.

"Their aversion is purely social. They are quite comfortable with contact in a clinical setting."

Ah, yes. All that probing and scanning. They were what we'd call "process oriented." My thoughts raced back to the UFO loonies and their abduction stories. No wonder the Grays suppressed their memories.

My escorts exchanged a look that seemed like agreement. Sven swept his hand across the panel and the door swished open. Before us stood a female Emissary, wearing the same iridescent tunic as my companions, though she was different in ways which weren't very subtle. She held up a hand in the same manner as the Grays. "Welcome, Melanie Mooney. I will be your entry control escort."

While she was obviously an Emissary, a few physical differences stood out. The eyes were the most striking—hers had no color; the irises were translucent, almost as white as her sclera, and her pupils were black pinpoints. It was a little unnerving. Where I'd first referred to my guys by their eye color, this one presented a challenge. "Whitey" was out for obvious reasons, so I settled on "Pearl."

Her eyebrows were more prominent, and her cheekbones were especially high and sharp. Her features were a lot further removed from a human's than either of my escorts. I was tempted to ask them for an explanation, but right now that seemed rude. *Open mind, girl.*

It occurred to me that I'd stood there staring like an idiot for far too long. They'd tried to warn me, hadn't they? I raised my hand, mirroring her gesture. "A pleasure to meet you," I finally replied, a little stiff. She answered with a crisp nod.

"Please follow me to Entry Control. We will have you on your way shortly."

Extraterrestrial Customs. It was an enormous and busy facility, like an airport terminal, large enough that the floor curved away from us in either direction. I assumed this was still part of the central ring, and a glance at a nearby overhead screen confirmed it. It was a map of the station, and our level was highlighted with directions to each of the cylindrical buildings that sprouted outward from here.

That was when I first noticed the other beings scattered around the terminal, and the shock threatened to overwhelm me. I watched a group of Grays move past nearby, and behind them stood a cluster of crablike beings with elongated necks which bobbed up and down in what looked to be an animated conversation. It was like being dumped into the middle of an alien petting zoo.

I'd unconsciously gone into this with tunnel vision, focused on the more humanlike Emissaries instead of all the different races teeming around us. It was the chaotic mix of unfamiliar sounds— and smells—that had grabbed my attention. There was a faint odor of cucumber salad; the kind of scent copperheads give off when they're startled.

I turned to my right and saw a family of reptilians heading for one of the entry control stations. Two of them stood tall above a gaggle of smaller ones, all having iridescent golden eyes with catlike slit pupils. Or snakelike. I preferred to think of them like cats because I hate snakes with a passion. Each adult had a scaly ridge protruding from above their eyes that met at the crowns of their heads at a sharp angle. It lent their brows a heavy, menacing appearance that again resembled snakes. I had to remind myself that if they were in the Union, they should be well-behaved.

At the end of lanky arms, their hands each had three fingers and what approximated an opposable thumb, which is kind of crucial if you're going to build complex structures or need to work in fine detail. The thick claws at the ends of their digits had apparently been filed down, which made them look a little less threatening.

They walked gracefully in a hunched-over, birdlike fashion, on reverse-jointed legs which reminded me of a dinosaur's. They were balanced by tails that were easily half their body length; when the female stood to her full height, she had to be at least seven feet tall. I'm assuming this was the female because it looked an awful lot like a mom corralling rambunctious kids, waving her gangly arms at them in a *get your asses over here* manner.

The little ones, three of them, acted like they were ready to bolt at every distraction. And there were a lot of distractions; I'm guessing this was their first time at a Union terminal as well. Maybe they were going to Galactic Disney World.

I stopped gaping at the reptilian family when another unexpected smell caught my attention—seawater. I turned left and saw my first hextopod scrabbling past nearby, heading in the opposite direction. It was colored with blotchy shades of gray and purple, and stood a bit taller than me. It seemed to be in a big hurry as it muscled its way toward the docks. It didn't move like an octopus on land, flattened and pulling itself along. Instead it walked upright on its six tentacles, which was remarkably nimble in its own way. I marveled at how muscular they must have been; for an invertebrate to move like that required a lot of strength.

"That one is heading for the large transport we saw earlier," Bjorn said. "The vessel contains an entire deck of seawater tanks. Their species can move about on dry land, but they are much more comfortable in aquatic environments."

Made sense to me, and it was a reminder of how much there was to learn. I'd read all of this in the study materials, but to see these beings in person going about their lives was an entirely different matter. Textbooks couldn't prepare me for the jolting sights of what amounted to intelligent dinosaurs and a walking octopus.

As the hextopod hurried for the docks, its colors began changing to placid hues of pink. "That's how they communicate," I said, remembering my brief study. I searched the terminal for more of their kind. "But there aren't any more of them around."

"It is expressing relief," Bjorn told me. "It has probably been out of water too long for its comfort. It will be safe in its normal environment soon."

I wondered how long they could hold their breath; I didn't

recall the study guides mentioning anything about them being amphibious.

My fascination with the walking octopus-like being was short-lived. A portal adjacent to the one he (or she) disappeared into opened up, and a swarm of pale white creatures emerged. My skin crawled instinctively, and my scalp tickled. It was a gut reaction which I was ashamed of; hopefully my escorts didn't pick up on it.

They were insects. Enormous, ten-legged arthropods with eye stalks, antennas, and mandibles. I mentioned they appeared pale white; on closer inspection I could see their segmented exoskeletons were almost translucent. Each creature was about three feet long, which may not count as "enormous" in the usual term, but these were *insects*. They poured out of the opening, climbing up the walls and spilling into the terminal by the hundreds. I instinctively drew closer to my escorts.

They quickly organized themselves into a procession, three abreast, and began marching toward one of the other entry gates. Another Emissary, accompanied by three more of the insect's own kind, waited for them. The floor beneath us vibrated with the patter of thousands of cuticles.

Sven placed a calming hand on my shoulder, no doubt sensing my reaction, if not expecting it. "As we cautioned you, this would be something of a culture shock. Many of our races evolved from species you may have a natural aversion toward."

"Everybody has something that gives them the creeps. For me, it's insects." Growing up on a farm, there were lots of them, especially in the barn. A parade of giant bugs was like something out of a horror movie. I shook off my initial revulsion to dispassionately study the herd as it passed, like the vet student I used to be.

These creatures were disciplined. They moved of one accord, like a company of soldiers marching past. But I failed to see how they, or the giant walking octopus thing, would be able to manipulate their environment in a precise enough manner to harness the kinds of technology necessary to make it into space. "How are beings like this . . . what's the word I'm looking for . . . spacefaring?"

"Not all Union races are natively capable of space travel, but that is only one of many qualities we screen for. Those who are found to have sufficient intelligence and suitable cultural characteristics are invited into the Union based on their civilization's collective potential. If they choose to join, they are provided with interstellar transport by those races who can do so." He nodded toward the mob skittering past us. "The Gliesans are particularly adept at what humans call 'civil engineering.'"

"Did they build this place?"

Sven shook his head. "We constructed this outpost with the Reticulans. We did not make contact with the Gliesans until much later. You'll find their designs to be more . . . organic. Rather artful, in fact." He nodded at the swarm. "This is most likely a construction team en route to their next project."

The Union gave them a lift when they needed it. Not a bad arrangement. It made me wonder again how far removed we humans were from having the kind of "collective potential" the Union looked for. It was a reminder of how much might be riding on my shoulders.

I'd delayed long enough, standing in the middle of the terminal atrium and gawking at the natives like the tourist I was. There were a few more Grays and a smattering of Emissaries, nearly all of whom had the same features as the one we were following. A quick glance back at my companions strongly suggested they'd been modified for duty on Earth, either through old-fashioned plastic surgery or genetic tweaking. My money was on the latter.

They led me to an open entry control point, which was staffed by another Emissary. This one was male, but looked an awful lot like Pearl with the same spooky eyes, prominent brow, and sharp cheekbones. They could have been twins, though I imagined there were distinctions that would be obvious to someone of their own race.

It was yet another lesson in the shortsightedness of Earthbound prejudices, so let's get this ugly aspect of human nature out of the way: We tend to look for patterns in nature, so we become accustomed to the variants of people we are most frequently surrounded by. Those we don't normally encounter fall outside of our internally defined patterns, which is why we tend to think "others" all look alike. It's an age-old human trait that isn't confined to cranky old white guys; they just get blamed for it the most. Spend enough time among population groups outside of your own and you'll soon learn to spot the subtle distinctions between individuals. I'd had something of an immersion course in that as a medic.

I tried to identify those distinctions while this new Emissary processed my entry paperwork—not really "paperwork," but that's the gist. Trying not to look like I was staring, I searched his features for any differences. They weren't easy to spot, but I could see a hardness to his features that the female didn't have: brows a bit sharper, cheeks a bit hollower, with long hair so brilliantly blond as to be almost white.

Blondie exchanged some words with Pearl as she handed him my data crystal, then looked me over like I was a bug on a microscope slide. "Melanie Elizabeth Mooney," he read dispassionately. "Terran, female, aged twenty-nine Earth years." He raised one eyebrow, prompting me to answer.

"Um, yeah. That's correct."

He swiped at the crystal's glowing text and glanced down at the duffel bag slung over my shoulder. "Those are your personal belongings?"

I was flummoxed for a second. Were they going to have a problem with my stuff? "Yes," I finally said, and began to shrug off the bag. "Do you need to inspect my things?"

"That will not be necessary," Blondie said. "It was scanned as you entered the terminal." He glanced down at the crystal again. "I see you are here for admission to the Medical Corps. Unusual." It was impossible to tell if he was perturbed, impressed, or simply trying to rattle me. He gestured toward a slot in the podium between us. "Please insert your hand with your identification ring here."

I did as he said, though it was impossible to tell that anything important was happening. Characters begin to blink on the crystal, and a polite smile crossed his face. "Excellent. Your physiological profile and biometric data are now accepted." Moments passed as I stood there like a dummy with my hand still in the slot. "You may withdraw your hand now. Welcome to the Galactic Union."

I turned to my escorts. "That's it? I'm in?" I'd had more hassles from customs in my own country.

"You are," Bjorn said pleasantly. He took the crystal back from Blondie and handed it to me. "Your personal data terminal is now connected to Union information services. Your ring will grant you access to whatever you need, within the parameters of your resident status. It must remain on your person at all times."

I guessed that meant it limited me to whatever I was authorized to do here. I also guessed that meant I'd be royally screwed without it.

⚕ 15 ⚕

After leaving Union customs, my Emissary escorts led me to another bank of elevators. This part was pretty unspectacular; it could have passed for a ritzy office complex on Earth if it hadn't been for the collection of Grays, reptilians, and insectoids all waiting along with us. The scene was much more crowded than the expansive terminal had been, and the crush of alien beings, the unfamiliar smells and sounds, all combined to make my head swim. My knees began shaking and I braced myself against a nearby wall.

Sven moved past them and waved his ring across one of the elevator doors, which slid open silently. He motioned for me to follow him in, which attracted some unwelcome attention from the crowd. Nobody protested that I could tell, but they couldn't have been happy. After all, who was this scrawny human chick to be getting special treatment?

I closed my eyes and blew out a long breath after the door closed behind us. Bjorn turned to me as our car began moving. "You are perturbed."

"Just curious. How is it we get to skip to the head of the line?"

"Our diplomatic status accords us certain privileges, though we use them sparingly."

So they didn't like to throw their weight around, another point in their favor. "Aren't all of you Emissaries diplomats of some kind?"

"Of a fashion, yes, but not all of us perform the same roles. Since Earth does not have membership in the Union, admitting you as a resident falls under our first-contact protocols. That requires us to tightly control your exposure to other races."

"Ah. So you didn't want me hanging out with the riffraff for too long."

"We could sense your anxiety," Bjorn said. "Your first exposure to other Union kind was in the expanse of the terminal. While no doubt shocking to you, we kept them at a distance for your comfort. Being pressed into a crowd of alien beings is difficult for anyone to absorb. Many fail. So far, you have not."

So far. "And you'd like to keep it that way."

He nodded. "True, for you and for us."

Bjorn noticed me raise an eyebrow at that. "We are not concerned for ourselves. It will be good for the Medical Corps to have someone like you in its ranks, and if that experience leads to the Union extending membership to humans, it will be good for everyone."

"In the meantime, we have to take it slow. I get it."

"Baby steps," he reminded me. The lift came to a stop and we stepped into another wide, curving corridor lined with more oval doors.

Sven checked his crystal and began walking. "Our transient quarters are not far at all." He stopped in front of a door and began to lift his hand, then paused. "Perhaps you should try your ring, Melanie."

"Sure, but how'd you find our room?" There were no markings and it looked easy to become hopelessly lost.

He pointed to the crystal in my pocket. "That will provide everything you need to learn your way around. You will find it to be invaluable the longer you are here." He pointed to the ring on my finger. "But first . . ."

"Yeah. Got it. Try the room key." I waved my hand in front of the door and it whispered open.

We stepped into a cozy living room furnished for Emissaries, which made it compatible with humans. A pair of tub-styled easy chairs sat across from a semicircular divan, all made from a fabric of variegated colors that dazzled against the platinum-gray walls. A small kitchen with a food synthesizer occupied one wall, similar to the setup on their ship. Next to it was a triangular dining table. Doors on opposite sides of the living room led to private bedrooms, which I was elated to see. "Transient quarters" had sounded mighty austere, and I was beginning to crave some privacy.

Before I could settle in for the night, Sven tapped a white rectangular screen on the far wall. When it lifted, the room was filled with Rigel's brilliant sapphire-blue light. "Ah. Excellent. We have a spectacular view."

I held my hand in front of my eyes. "It's awfully bright. Can you dim the screen?"

"It's not a monitor, if that's what you mean. It's a window made of transparent alloys. But yes, we can adjust the light filter." He showed me how to swipe at the window, dimming the light to a more comfortable level by simply drawing my finger across the surface.

"How long are we here for?"

Sven moved over to the food synth. "Overnight, by your time reference. Longer if necessary. For now, I believe we all need nutrients and rest. Are you hungry?"

"Starving. What's on the menu?"

"Whatever you want, assuming the synthesizer recognizes it."

That seemed like a tall order. "Cheeseburger with lettuce and tomato, chocolate shake." The machine chirped to let me know it was working on my order.

It took a minute, but damned if it didn't produce. I grabbed my tray and plopped down at the table. "Looks about right," I said, and took a bite. "Tastes about right, too. How does this thing know what humans like?"

The Emissaries shared a look. "We added some menu items based on our observations among your kind."

"Will this be the same wherever I go?"

"Wherever you go. The synthesizers are networked throughout all Union outposts."

"You've got much better IT support than anything on Earth, then. I wouldn't trust my food supply to a computer network if you put a gun to my head."

They winced at my lame joke.

"Sorry. Human expression. Maybe a little too aggressive."

After savoring my first extraterrestrial burger, I picked up my shake and said goodnight.

My room was small and sparsely furnished, but then it didn't need to be extravagant. So long as there was a place to clean up and crash, I was happy.

I opened the screen, dimmed the window to something below retina-burning level, and sat on the edge of the bed.

Rigel looked close enough to touch. With the filters on full, I could study it for the first time. I'd never seen anything like it. There was texture to the surface, like the pebbling on a basketball, but it bubbled and boiled in a froth like milk in a hot saucepan. There were a handful of black spots on its surface, and filaments danced around its edges like loose hair blowing in slow motion.

Occasionally spacecraft would move in and out of view, of all shapes and sizes. One of the big horseshoe-crab-looking transports drifted past, speckled with hundreds of lights on its way to who knew where. It reminded me of a vacation with my parents a long time ago. We'd watched the giant cruise ships moving out of Miami harbor at night, lit up like casinos as they headed for the Caribbean.

All of this, right outside my bedroom window.

What in the world was I doing here? What could I possibly offer these people that they didn't already have, or hadn't already thought of?

"Unique ability," they'd said. They'd also gone to a lot of trouble to bring me here, so maybe it was time to relax.

Of course, relaxing wasn't part of my nature. If there was a type A-plus personality, it would've applied to me. I was too amped up to sleep and it wasn't like I'd be able to do anything useful on the next leg of our trip. The best use of my time would've been to study the materials they'd given me, but something else had put a burr under my saddle.

They'd made it clear I wasn't the first human the Union had encountered, and it sounded like there might already be a few others here. In fact they'd been rather cagey about it. Instead of studying alien anatomy, I pulled out my crystal tablet and began poking around in their network to see what was there.

It took some doing. First I had to figure out their interface. So far the tablet had done everything I'd needed it to in the moment, like it knew what was coming. I suppose that's predictable when going through customs or looking for your room, but now I was freelancing. After a few minutes of swiping and poking, I was getting frustrated. If our comparatively primitive tablets had voice control, why wouldn't theirs? It was worth a try. "Main menu."

What do you know? Main menu. Now it looked a lot more like my iPad, absent the cute little icons. This was a bit more sophisticated and businesslike, with blocks of text in small print that expanded with touch. There was a lot of that.

After a time it was like trying to navigate a clunky government website. If you didn't know exactly what you were looking for, you'd never find it. Of course, stubborn old me had tried to stick with the meat interface instead of voice commands. I decided to be as specific as possible. "Record of Union interaction with human race."

A tab marked "Archives" appeared, which opened up a disturbingly long list of events. Judging by the numbers tagged to each, it looked like they were in chronological order. "Are these cataloged by date?"

The crystal answered in a voice that sounded for all the world like a live human. It even had a vaguely Midwestern accent. "Affirmative."

"Can you translate the dates into Earth . . . err, human . . . reference?" I had a sneaking suspicion that "Earth reference" would be in billions of years.

"Which cultural calendar would you prefer? Judaic, Indian, East Asian . . ."

The voice kept going. I had no idea what to tell it, and frantically searched my memory. There'd been something in Western civ, way back during freshman year . . . "Roman . . . no, Gregorian!"

"Converting to Gregorian calendar references. Please stand by."

The numbers instantly changed to something more recognizable. The first event on the list was recent, which was my encounter with that crashed spacecraft. Of course. I flipped at the list, scrolling down further. They went back a long way . . .

Holy shit. *BC.*

I stopped cold. They'd been observing us since before the friggin' Babylonian empire. I tapped on one report at random. It was pretty dry reading, describing the time, place, human activities, soil samples, air samples . . . but all the locations were referenced to a planetary grid they'd set up. I'm sure it worked fine for them, but it told me nothing. "Can you convert these locations to modern human references, too?"

"Affirmative. Please stand by."

And just like that, grid squares turned into text. I went to the first entry.

"2579 BC. Cairo, Egypt. Extended observation of construction activity by intelligent primates. Structures are pyramidal and impressively large for their current technological level. Estimate completed height will be 146.7 meters above local surface. Hominids exhibit rudimentary understanding of algebraic mathematics and engineering principles. However, their construction methods remain primitive, relying on beasts of burden and manual labor from other hominids. First Contact protocols not recommended at this time. Further cultural development is required."

Extraterrestrials hadn't helped build the pyramids like some fanatics thought, but they'd been there. The Old Testament would have a thing or two to say about the "primitive manual labor" part a few hundred years later. No signs that these guys had anything to do with the plagues or miracles, though, so my Sunday School lessons remained unmolested. That came as something of a relief.

I tapped on a subfile marked "Imagery" and about fell out of bed. There were *pictures*. No kidding, 3D holographic images of the Great Pyramid of Giza while it was still under construction over four thousand years ago. I'd gone looking for confirmation of tabloid abduction stories, instead I was getting deep insights into our own history. No matter what else happened to me here, this alone would be worth the trip.

There was too much to read through each account, so I kept scrolling and stopped on whatever looked especially interesting. The next entry was a hoot.

"AD 788. Skiringssal, Norway. Technical malfunction aboard survey ship led to inadvertent contact with a large tribe of humans. Survey party was unable to maintain concealment due to failure of transparency field. Our sudden appearance led to great confusion and alarm among the humans.

"The tribe our team encountered is one of a warrior class which dominates the region. Tribal traditions and societal structures are centered on agriculture, harvesting of local aquatic and land animals, and wanton aggression against neighboring regions. There is considerable warring between tribes as well.

"It is a primitive, quarrelsome culture. One Emissary was gravely injured by a particularly agitated human male wielding a heavy melee weapon known as a 'battle axe.' As punishment, this individual was then subjected to a gruesome ritual they call 'blood eagle,' which will not be described here.

"We attempted to dissuade them to no avail. The tribal chieftain's insistence on this dreadful punishment is symptomatic of a more unfortunate consequence of our appearance: they now worship us as deities. Further contact NOT RECOMMENDED."

This time I did fall out of bed, laughing my ass off. Thanks to a mechanical glitch, the Emissaries had unwittingly become the foundation of Norse mythology. Gods. Odin and Thor's invisibility cloak goes tits-up and what happens? They're immortalized in legends that would be carried through the ages in oral traditions, ancient Norse texts, and modern comic books.

It was literally epic. I could have great fun at my hosts' expense with that tale.

I skipped over the rest of our secret history with the Union's survey teams, moving up to more current events. How many of those wild stories were true? Now that I'd seen the Grays face-to-face, along with proof of their butt-probing proclivities, they had to be.

Short version: It's true. All of it, at least the more notorious incidents. Roswell? True. Betty and Barney Hill? True. The Pascagoula Abduction? True, but to be fair that one was an unsanctioned contact and the perps got into serious trouble with the Union science ministry. I felt sorry for the two guys caught up in that mess; they'd only wanted to go fishing after work and ended up having the living shit scared out of them by some Grays on a bender.

The Union seemed less and less intimidating as I read through each account, in fact some stories sounded all too familiar. You know who gets the scut work on a big university-funded anthropological expedition? The grad students. They're sitting around in the jungle, bored out of their skulls while watching some remote Amazon tribe from afar. One of them smuggles in some booze to stave off the boredom, and next thing you know they're screwing with the locals for shits and giggles.

Judging by this history, the same thing occasionally went on in the Union. Where do you think crop circles come from? Bored alien research assistants.

They made mistakes and it looked like they'd owned up to them, which was more than I could say for too many of my own kind. Especially the ones who think they're in charge.

I went to bed content in the knowledge that I could make it here. It was the best sleep I'd had in days.

⚕ 16 ⚕

Rigel station had been impressive, but nothing could prepare me for the spectacle of the Galactic Union's capital city. It resembled our last stop (as they seemed unusually fond of circles), but my puny human perspective was not adequate to process how absurdly *big* it was. I expected it to be larger than the transit station, and was it ever.

The city encircled an entire *planet*. The Union capital was an enormous artificial ring suspended high above a lush, green world. The inner edge of the ring sparkled like a richly jeweled necklace, with millions of lights that gave it the appearance of a rainbow. There was no telling how it appeared to other beings who perceived a broader spectrum than humans could.

More lights danced around it at random; hundreds of enormous ships moving about the perimeter. The city was a physical demonstration of how expansive the Union truly was. Huge numbers like the distances between stars become meaningless because we have to reduce them to manageable scales: A light-year is easier to work with than six trillion miles. It's when you see an individual piece of that puzzle laid out before you, itself more massive than any structure a normal human could conceive of, that it becomes real.

The crushing sense of scale and distance could've ended with the capital city, but it didn't. Beyond it, in the deep background, hung a radiant cloud of gas which the Emissaries said we puny Earthlings had named the Crab Nebula. Still dozens of light-years distant, it dominated the sky, a smear of bluish haze interlaced with tendrils of red and orange. They told me it was the remains of a supernova, a star that had collapsed on itself and exploded like Rigel was expected to do in the future.

It's a cliché to say I had to pinch myself, but it's also the truth. This glittering gem of their capital had to be tens of thousands of miles across but was only part of a much larger civilization, which itself covered only a small slice of our galaxy. My head couldn't absorb what might lie beyond.

The surprises didn't stop coming as we drew close enough to make out more detail. The entire inner surface of the ring was studded with transparent domes, which made it look all the more like a jeweled necklace floating in space. Beneath them were smaller structures surrounded by forests and fields. Each dome was like a small town to itself, hundreds of them set across the face of the capital.

"Those are environment structures, tailored to mimic the conditions of individual planets from all of our member races." Bjorn, as usual, was right behind me playing tour guide.

Thousands of smaller cities, with giant parks and playgrounds, studding the inside of the capital ring. "Are they where everyone lives?"

"Most do, depending on their cultural preferences. Some live in the structures beneath the domes; all work either within the structure or along its outer rim."

Spectacular as it was, I'd expected to see something even more dramatic, like a giant capitol building. I pointed out clusters of buildings spaced at even intervals between the domes, miles apart. "What about those?"

"Each complex serves a different purpose within the capital." One slipped by as we passed, a jumble of brilliantly lit cylindrical buildings like the ones at the entry station. "That's the administrative complex. The next one you see will be the judiciary."

Space court. I resolved to stay clear of that one. "Does the Medical Corps have its own complex, then?"

"Oh yes. We're currently passing the governmental quadrant. The Medical Corps is part of the services quadrant, which we'll be coming upon shortly."

Sven flew us in a lazy circle around a cluster of jagged white buildings, each one successively taller, ending with an elegant spiral in the center which towered over the rest. It was the Emerald City of Oz in real life, and I was feeling more like Dorothy with each passing minute.

"That's the Medical Corps complex. The surrounding buildings are treatment facilities and trauma centers. The center spiral is administration."

Of course it was. The suits always had the best offices. I noticed a flurry of white teardrop-shaped craft with green stripes moving around the complex, some zipping away with flashing beacons. I watched one slowly maneuver itself into a massive open bay. "Are those what I think they are?"

"Patient transports," he said. "Ambulances."

Cool. No more bouncing around on rough country roads, though I was still a little uneasy at the idea of being a flight medic.

After one final pass around the complex, we continued on above the inner face of the ring. More of the domes passed by beneath us, each containing a different biosphere. One looked like desert, all pale yellows and burnt ocher. The next dome held a verdant forest that could've been transplanted from back home.

Our ship settled into a landing bay between the two, and came to a gentle stop. Soon after, a band of pulsing white light appeared around our door. "That indicates outside pressure has equalized. It is safe to leave the ship," Bjorn explained. "Always wait for that, unless you are wearing a vacuum suit."

Right. Don't stumble out into open space. Good to know.

We left our ship and made for a nearby bank of elevators, as if we'd never left Rigel Station. The ride seemed interminably long, another indicator of how big the capital city was. We eventually came to a stop, and the elevator opened up into a massive atrium. From where we stood, it appeared sparsely populated. In the distance I could make out rows of what looked like fruit trees. A light breeze carried hints of lemon and sage with it, and it was making me hungry.

"Is that the bio dome we saw outside?"

"It is," Sven said. "This is our sector, cultivated to resemble the environment of our home world. Or rather, how it once was." There was a tinge of sorrow in his voice, as if he craved more. "This biodome is the one most similar to Earth in the capital. You may even find some of the vegetation to be familiar." He took a deep breath. "It is refreshing to spend time here. I highly encourage it."

"I don't see many people about. Is this all Emissary territory?"

"We share this sector with the Gliesans, the insectoids you saw at Rigel Station. They have a similar home world."

I wasn't sure how to feel about sharing space with a colony of meter-long bugs, but if they were part of the Union I'd have to get used to it.

"It is also after hours. Most residents have retired to their homes for the evening. That is where we are headed next." They waved me along. "Come, we will escort you to your quarters."

Another long, circling hallway with more nondescript oval doors, though this looked more well-appointed than the temporary quarters we'd had on Rigel. The walls were adorned with sconces alive with drooping vines, while the gently curved ceiling glowed with indirect lighting that made it feel like late sunset.

Sven took note. "The lighting adjusts automatically with time of day, to simulate a normal solar cycle. Our day is twenty-eight of your Earth hours. The Union standard is closer to thirty."

I checked my watch out of habit. "That's going to take some getting used to."

"It will," he admitted. "Rely on your crystal for time reference."

We stopped in front of a nearby door. "This is your suite," Bjorn said, and a number appeared in floating digits above the arch: 1302C. Before I'd been afraid of getting hopelessly lost; now I at least knew my own address. With a quick pass of my ID ring across the panel, the door slid open.

My suite was, well . . . sweet. And private, no adjoining bedrooms this time, though I hoped my guides would be close by. "Where do you guys live?"

Sven tipped his head toward the hallway. "We are at the end of the corridor, suites G and H."

Reassured that I wasn't being completely cut loose on my own, I dropped my bag on the floor to check out my new home. It was nice in a resort hotel kind of way, well-appointed but not ostentatious. A couple of pieces of artwork hung on the wall, generic depictions of what I imagined the Emissary's home world had once looked like. They could have graced a suite at a Hilton on Earth. A large picture window filled the far wall, with a first-class view of the biodome below. The furniture was designed for Emissaries, so it was also compatible with humans. The suite featured a larger kitchen and food synth, which I hoped meant it also had a wider-ranging menu.

I peeked into the bedroom and found a closet already half-filled with green and white coveralls, along with random bits of other clothing hung opposite them. On the floor beneath them sat two pairs of sleek black boots and two more pairs of slip-on casual shoes. "What are these?"

They exchanged an amused look. "Your uniforms, of course. They were tailored using dimensions from your body scan at Rigel. The others are items we thought you might find appealing, and more in line with current fashions."

It was a sideways hint that my frumpy Earth clothing might not be up to snuff here. What can I say? I like my sweats. I held up one of the uniforms in front of me. The girly stuff could wait.

Sven tried to be encouraging. "Feel free to try them on."

I raised an eyebrow.

"After we leave, of course," he said.

"Of course." I hung the coveralls back in the closet, not ready to put on a fashion show for two men who were still largely strangers to me. "Anything else I should know?"

"You should find the nutritional synthesizer's menu has expanded, based on information uploaded from previous surveys." Sven stepped into the bathroom. "You may also find this feature to be more to your liking." He tapped a control behind a shower enclosure, and actual hot water streamed from a port in the ceiling.

Hallelujah. Now I could actually feel settled in.

"If there's anything else you require, you can contact one of us through your crystal. There are comm panels by the doors of each room as well."

I placed my hands on my hips and surveyed my new home. "I think I'm good, guys. Now if you don't mind, I need to rest up and get ready for tomorrow."

"Understood," Sven said. "I will be here after breakfast to escort you to the training center."

I followed them out, trying to not-too-obviously hurry them along, but that hot shower was calling my name.

☤ 17 ☤

The next morning I stepped outside in my spiffy new Med Corps uniform to find Bjorn waiting for me. He led me out of our building and into a subway-like transport tube that shot away with alarming speed for the training center outside the hospital complex. With no idea of what to expect going in, I was relieved to find the classroom was surprisingly familiar. I might not yet know anything about how the Med Corps went about their business, but this room's purpose was obvious to anyone with a medical background.

The dead giveaway was the arrangement of training dummies in the back of the room. They weren't the plastic and silicon mannequins we practiced on in EMS school; these were amazingly realistic simulations of each race in the Union, enough to make me first think they were especially well-preserved cadavers. There were Grays, Emissaries, reptilians, insectoids, even a human back in one corner. I wondered if they'd put that one here for my benefit; and exactly how much interaction did the Union have with my species?

Along the adjacent wall sat an array of what looked to be the types of equipment we'd be using in the field. I recognized a smaller version of the scanner they'd first run me through, which already seemed like a lifetime ago. The rest I'd learn as the course went on.

To my dismay I was the last student to file into class, though there weren't many of us to begin with. Besides myself, there were only a couple of Grays and a reptilian who looked especially uncomfortable behind a desk that was way too small for him. I was mesmerized by his sea-green skin, iridescent under the glow panels in the ceiling. He seemed overly conscious of keeping his tail from spilling out into the aisle between us. Over a tunic that barely covered his torso, he wore a small chest pack with tubes which wrapped around his abdomen and limbs. It was for regulating body temperature, which a cold-blooded being would definitely need in here.

He was intimidating, and there's no better way to get past fear than by confronting it head on. I took an empty seat next to the towering reptilian, who introduced himself with an imperious nod as T'Ch'on-ukk-R'Baal. His voice came as a hiss that made the translator stutter at first. "From star system called Th'u'ban."

Even through the translator chip in my head, his name was a mouthful and they seemed awfully fond of their apostrophes. "I hope you don't take offense, but in my language that's what we'd call a tongue twister. Mind if I call you Chonk?"

He paused, his tri-forked tongue sliding across his scaly lips as he considered whether I'd just insulted him. Maybe I used too many words? "Yes. Is acceptable abbreviation. Your name?"

"Melanie Mooney."

More thoughtful flicking of that trident tongue. "Is likewise difficult. Much"—he paused—"alliteration. I address you as Mel?"

I could feel the smile spread across my face, and I hoped he understood what that conveyed. "That's perfect, in fact. That was my nickname back on Earth." I intentionally left out the "Tiny" part. He was almost twice my size already.

Chonk answered with an approving nod. "Excellent. I look forward learning"—he paused again—"together, Mel."

"Thank you. As do I."

Bjorn leaned in close. "Very good, Melanie. I am pleased to see how well you are adapting to your new environment."

"Learn or burn," I replied. "You're staying in class with me?"

A thin smile from Bjorn. "Of course. I am a student as well."

My eyes widened. "Seriously? You don't have to do this on my account."

"It is part of my assignment as your cultural escort. It is also something I wish to learn for my own purposes. It is why I requested assignment to your case."

My *case*? How far ahead had they thought this through? Had that accident in the woods even been, well, an accident? Had I actually been recruited on purpose?

If so, that was an awful lot to put on my shoulders. Like so much else recently, I compartmentalized it. That info would be tucked away in a little mental box for later.

The class grew quiet with the entrance of another being. The door whispered shut behind him/her/it.

It was another Gray, who exuded an air of age and wisdom I'd seen before.

He stepped behind a podium at the head of the classroom and began speaking. Not thinking at us, actually vocalizing. It took a moment for my translator to catch up with his rasping voice.

"Greetings, students. My name is Xeelix. I am a physician assigned to the Medical Corps station at Union Transit Facility 03A. I will be your primary instructor for this course."

Xeelix! I had no idea what kind of teacher he'd be, but it was good to have a familiar face, such as it was.

He continued. "As you are already aware, the Medical Corps is in constant need of individuals with an ability to overcome their parochial nature and provide aid to beings of other races. You were selected to be here because you have each demonstrated that ability."

I couldn't be sure, but he seemed to single me out with an approving nod. The two other Grays in the class turned slightly to look me over. No pressure there.

"Some of you have formal medical training specific to your race. Regardless of your background, you will find the material to be uniquely challenging." He pointed one of those long, bony fingers at our desks. "Please activate your instructional materials."

I watched as the others placed their data crystals on their desktops and waved their ringed fingers across them. I followed suit, and a holographic screen appeared in the air above my desk.

"The materials are organized by topic with competence exercises at the end of each section," Xeelix explained. So it would at least follow a format I was familiar with. "The course will begin with an explanation of the Medical Corps' organization. Then we will immediately proceed into a study of each race's anatomy and physiology. You will likely find this to be the most challenging."

We'd see about that. If vet and medic school had taught me anything, it was how to drink from the proverbial fire hose.

Being the first day of school, I instinctively reached into my bag. While the data crystals could be enormously useful, I'm a pen-and-paper girl at heart. The others stared in curiosity when I pulled out an old-fashioned spiral notebook and pen I'd brought from Earth.

"You are likely to find that is not necessary," Bjorn said in a low voice. "It may even be counterproductive. I am told this class moves quickly."

I was feeling a little defiant. "I'll try and keep up." Popular as tablets and e-readers had become on Earth, it was still well established that your average human retained information much better by writing it down. I'd even packed extra pens, which made me feel clever.

The holograph projection blinked to life and quickly translated itself into English. The first text to appear was "Stabilize patients and alleviate their suffering to the maximum extent of your abilities."

Xeelix waited a moment for us to take that in. "This will be your ultimate responsibility as emergency medical specialists," he explained. It felt a little like the Hippocratic oath: "First, Do No Harm." But their phrasing carried some subtle differences. What did "alleviate patient suffering" actually mean? You could alleviate an animal's suffering by putting it down, but that would absolutely be considered "doing harm" to a human. Did this mean we were expected to euthanize patients if they were too far gone?

He must have sensed my concern—I mean, of course he did—and elaborated: "You may find this to be a vague admonition, though it must be considered in the context of the individual you are treating." He looked at each of us in turn. "Each race recognized by the Galactic Union possesses its own moral code, which you will have to consider when rendering aid. It is as important as understanding your patient's anatomy."

He swept an elongated hand toward the other two Grays sitting up front. "For example, our civilization condones euthanasia at the patient's request. This presents certain complications if the patient is not conscious."

I'll bet it did. This was going to lead to some interesting discussions.

"Other cultures do not permit medical personnel to provide such assistance." He focused on me now. "I understand this is a contentious issue within the human race."

My eyes darted left and right. I was being expected to contribute already? "It is. Some nations permit it, others don't. My own country doesn't, but not everyone agrees with that." I didn't mention that I thought the practice was ghoulish, no matter how well intended.

Chonk turned to me and hissed; again my translator needed a moment to catch up. "What is 'nation' and 'country'?" The Grays looked interested, too.

Not being familiar with Chonk's culture, I needed to think about that. Did all of the Union worlds have unified governments? "Think of them as smaller civilizations that make up the whole. Each one has their own culture, their own laws, unique traditions."

"World not unified," he said flatly. "Is what keeps you from Union."

I couldn't very well argue his point, not that this was the place for it. Much as I loved my own country, it made sense that the Union might not want member planets who were still bogged down with what amounted to tribal factions. Maybe technology drove civilizations to either unify or self-destruct, given enough time? No wonder they were still keeping an eye on us; to them we must have looked like tribes of quarrelsome monkeys. Monkeys with nuclear weapons.

Bjorn leaned over again. "Do not take it personally. Thubans are known for being rather direct, and the translators often have trouble with their language."

"No worries," I said under my breath.

Xeelix used our interruption to illustrate his point. "A perfect example of the thorny issues this mandate may present, and why your cultural studies will become as important as your physiological studies. When called upon, you will not have the luxury of time to consider competing philosophies. You will have to rest on the knowledge you already possess."

Now he was speaking my language. When you're elbow-deep in a mangled patient, there's no time to think so you'd better have your wits about you. And two is better than one—you learn to treasure the kind of partner who's on the same wavelength, the kind who brings their own experience to the table without second-guessing. I wondered how that was going to work as the only human in this group.

Xeelix moved on. "Now that we have established the central precept of your service, we will begin with the background and organization of the Medical Corps."

A three-dimensional map of the galaxy appeared above each of our desks, with text translated into our individual languages. "The Medical Corps was established with the Union's founding agreement in annum 9331." "Annum" was a year in their time reference, and I had a feeling my notion of calendars was about to become hopelessly outdated, pun intended.

Amber points of light appeared on the map, which were clustered around a single region of the Milky Way labeled "Perseus Arm" with a few scattered in the "Sagittarius Arm" closer to the center. Apparently this arm was the Union's boondocks; Xeelix explained that the closer one gets to the galactic center, the less habitable it becomes. I made another note to check which races emerged from those worlds, because they had to be tough as nails.

A single yellow dot appeared in a region between the two, named "Orion Spur." The dot was labeled "Sol"—our star. Apparently our entire region was something of a no-man's-land between the Union's two biggest neighborhoods. It was interesting to see how the Union was concentrated in one section of the galaxy. Had the rest not been explored, or was it something else?

"The Medical Corps has treatment centers in each member star system to supplement their home civilization's medical facilities. They are located within the system transit stations." The map disappeared, replaced by a diagram of one of those wheeled stations like the one I'd recently visited. One of its outer bicycle-spoke buildings began flashing for our attention.

"Treatment centers are equipped for short-term and emergency care, which is of course where you will be placed upon successful completion of your training. Each center's purpose is to care for patients until they are well enough to travel to their home worlds if longer-term treatment is necessary. Each center maintains a fleet of Class III transports equipped with the tools you will need to treat and stabilize patients until they can be brought to an appropriate facility."

That sounded a lot like how we did things back home. The fundamentals didn't change, whether for a dog, a human, or a dozen different species of space aliens. The Med Corps was a network of urgent care centers.

I didn't have much time to ponder as Xeelix kept moving. A diagram labeled "Class III Transport" appeared above my desk. It looked like the one the Emissaries had parked in my front yard, another flattened teardrop-shaped vehicle, with the addition of a pair of stubby pods along either side. A neon-green slash ran diagonally around the little ship's midsection, signifying it was an emergency vehicle. I wasn't sure that mattered in deep space, but they must have figured it was important. I leaned over to Bjorn and whispered, "Class III?"

"Intra-system transport," Xeelix explained for him. "For traveling between planets in a single star system. They have limited interstellar range."

The holographic flying ambulance split in two lengthwise, each half of the ship rotating outward to show a cutaway view. "The transports are furnished with generalized equipment which can be used for any Union race, in addition to vacuum and exposure suits tailored for its crew."

It was sparse compared to what I was used to, but still familiar. Lockers for loose gear were embedded into one side, with assessment equipment mounted along shelves beneath them. The other side was filled with patient monitors. Sleek-looking spacesuits were hung next to them, near the back of the bay. A complicated-looking gurney hovered between the two; it had complex origami extensions folded up beneath it which could be used to accommodate whatever being was strapped to it. Ahead of the bay was the pilot's station, which I wasn't about to try and comprehend. I wouldn't be driving one of these things for a long time, if ever.

Each piece of gear glowed as Xeelix explained them. It all looked impossibly simple, kind of like the data crystals I'd become familiar with. "Interior equipment is limited to that which can be adapted to any Union race." He ran through each, front to back along each side of the bay. The first piece of hardware looked familiar. It was a rectangular bag made of material I could only guess at, in the same neon green as the stripe across the ship's side. "The aid kit contains analgesics and tranquilizers formulated for use on any race. Syringes with blood-clotting foams are carried in the side pouches with race-specific instructions. Audiovisual transducers are located in the main compartment, which will synchronize with your translation implants."

That sounded interesting. Was that their version of a stethoscope? I raised my hand, which caught the others off guard. Maybe it was some kind of insult in their cultures, but Xeelix looked like he knew what I was doing.

"Yes, Melanie Mooney."

"Is that for listening to the patient's heart and lungs?" I was oversimplifying, given the diversity between species, but it was the only thing that came to mind in the moment.

"Correct. When placed over a patient's vital organs, it will transmit sounds of the circulatory and respiratory functions directly to your auditory implants." He walked over to an equipment table along one wall and handed me a metallic disc about the size of a hockey puck. "Place this on your chest."

I eagerly did as he said. To call it a stethoscope was not doing it justice; it would've been like comparing high definition TV to a 1950's black-and-white set. As soon as I placed it over my heart, my ears were filled with a cacophony of bodily functions, as if a microphone had been inserted into my chest cavity. Details I could never pick out before were suddenly loud and clear, changing as I moved the disc around my body. The air moving through my lungs sounded like a whirlwind as it left the trachea for the bronchi, becoming like a breeze across tall grass as it filled the alveoli. I couldn't just hear the thump of my heartbeat and the blood moving through chambers, I could hear the muscles contracting. Out of curiosity, I placed it on my arm and could hear blood rushing through my capillaries like a running stream. I have no idea what dividing cells sound like, but I swear they made noise too. Moving the disc further down to my hand, each fingertip sounded like rustling leaves. It was the sound of my fingernails growing.

"That's amazing," I stammered. "I've never heard such resolution, not even with the most expensive stethoscope." What wonders did the other gear hold?

Chonk seemed amused at my human lost-in-the-woods naïveté.

Xeelix studied him. "You may be unfamiliar with this device as well. Would you care to try?"

The big lizard guy sat stiffly. "Unnecessary. Have seen before."

Xeelix was unmoved. "Have you *used* one?" Not that I'd had a wealth of experience with Grays yet, but it was surprising to hear him become even a little forceful.

"Have not on myself," Chonk said. He held out a clawed hand. "Will try."

I handed over the disc. The slits of his eyes widened as he moved it around his body. "Can hear everything," he said as he settled the disc over his long neck. "Everything."

It was my turn to be amused. "I know, right? Isn't it awesome?"

Chonk paused as he processed my language. "Yes. Awesome is good word." He moved the disc to his tail. "That strange. Hear"—the translator hissed as it tried to process his words into my language—"crackle. Breaking."

"How much time has passed since your last molting?" Xeelix asked.

"Over one annum," Chonk said.

"Ah." Xeelix nodded. "Then what you hear is the sound of your scales preparing to shed."

Chonk handed the disc back to our teacher. He seemed embarrassed, his regal posture slightly diminished. It was as though acknowledging an inherent vulnerability grated against his nature.

From the corner of my eye, I saw Bjorn tapping away on a holographic keypad projected onto his desktop. He made a swiping motion toward me and a message appeared on my desktop: *Thubans are a warrior culture. They are reluctant to display weakness.*

I answered Bjorn with a slight nod: Message received and understood. But it seemed strange that they'd be ashamed of fundamental biology. The teenage years must be rough on them; I'm sure the rapidly growing critters were shedding every couple of months.

It also seemed strange that the Union had seen fit to admit a warrior culture into the fold. Was there some external threat they hadn't told me about? Maybe they'd only recently learned to behave themselves. Either way, it put the lie to the notion that any advanced civilization would have to be peaceful, otherwise they'd have destroyed themselves. I remember hearing that in some science documentary back in high school and thought it was hopelessly optimistic even then. There was a pretty good argument to be made that ensuring peace required having a kick-ass military, especially if your country had stuff that other countries envied.

Contemplating galactic politics would have to wait. Xeelix was still talking about the little disc we'd been playing with.

"You will find the transducer to be particularly useful. In addition to its auditory input, it is the primary tool for assessing your patient's vital signs. I will demonstrate."

He stepped over to a rectangular device on one of the equipment shelves. It was about the size of a paperback book, a little thicker than a standard data crystal, and was otherwise unremarkable. This changed when he pressed the disc against his arm. The crystal embedded in its face flashed to life with a bright display of characters I faintly recognized as the Reticulans' language. My desktop screen changed to mirror it. Sure enough, everything was there: trace lines for heart and respiration rates, blood pressure, oxygen saturation, and temperature, all helpfully translated into English. It even had what looked like an EKG trace, once my head got around the three-dimensional presentation.

It didn't end there. He pressed a thumb—which wasn't exactly a thumb but that's the closest analogy—against the disc, and the display changed. Now we were seeing three-dimensional views of his blood vessels. As he pressed the disc more firmly against his skin, it probed deeper to show his thin bones sheathed beneath wiry muscle tissue, all of it clearer than the best MRIs.

If the other students were impressed, they didn't show it. This must have been as familiar to them as a stethoscope and BP cuff was to me. I, on the other hand, was properly amazed. "How deep will that thing go?" I wondered. "Will it show internal organs?"

It was hard to tell but I think Doc Xeelix was amused. "Of course." He pressed the transducer against his upper abdomen, and soon we had a 3D picture of his insides. As he moved the disc around we could see his lungs, intestinal tract, and beating heart. His bones looked stick-thin, and I wondered what they were made of, if not calcium. Anatomy class promised to be fascinating.

"You will recall the scanner we used for your processing

examination, Melanie Mooney. This is a portable version of that device. It of course cannot provide a full picture of the patient's inner workings, but it is sufficient for localized assessments."

Pulse oximeter, BP cuff, stethoscope, EKG, MRI, all in one tidy package. What else could we possibly need?

As the day went on, I learned there was a *lot* more. The ambulance's outboard pods held species-specific gear, and we endured a long presentation on what was located where. The hextopods can't be too far from water for long, so half of one pod was essentially a big aquarium. It even had breathing equipment for the medics, though I noticed that none of it appeared compatible with humans. I wondered how long I could hold my breath if it ever came to that.

There were supplies to close wounds for every race in the Union stocked aboard our ambulances. The reptilians—excuse me, *Thubans*—had what amounted to a silicon-patch compound for repairing large areas of damaged scales. That seemed more like carpentry than medicine, but it wasn't the Thubans' fault that they couldn't be patched up with a synthetic epidermis spray like everybody else.

The rest of our inventory featured equipment with direct links to whatever Med Corps facility the space ambulances were assigned to. In the most extreme cases, I learned we wouldn't be working alone. One particularly intimidating-looking device with five multiple-jointed arms was there for emergency surgery—if a patient was in enough trouble, we'd be expected to use that sucker to repair them in the field. With a doc's advice, of course, but if we were more than a couple hundred thousand kilometers away, the signal return lag was too long for them to do much in real time. They were limited by the speed of light, like everything else in the universe.

It was a long day, and not just because we had to absorb a lot of information. Bjorn and his partner had been accommodating my twenty-four-hour cycles until now. I'd forgotten their standard day is more on the order of thirty hours, based on the average cycle for all of the Union's planets. It was a tiring reminder of exactly how much of an outsider I was. Suffice to say that sleep came easy that night.

☤ 18 ☤

It seemed like thirty-hour days would give me plenty of time to rest up and study between classes, but as with everything else I had a lot to learn. Being a night-shifter for so long helped, since I was used to living on the wrong side of the clock, but only a little. Recalibrating my body took a while; recalibrating my brain took longer.

Part of the problem was that their hours were more like an hour and twelve in human time. If classroom time on Earth feels like it's running backward, try adding another twelve minutes to it. According to the wristwatch I stubbornly wore, our class sessions were easily eleven hours.

That made sense as it was a little over a third of a standard day, so not that much different from the way we did things. It left me with close to a whole human day in between classes, and I didn't want to spend all of it in my suite.

It was certainly nice enough. It has been appointed with human-compatible furniture, which no doubt came from the Emissaries since they were of almost identical builds. The artwork on the walls could best be described as "space alien impressionist" with lots of pastels and fuzzy outlines depicting scenes from what I gathered were planets throughout the Union. As a barely initiated human, to me they were almost surreal, but looking out my window into the atrium below I could tell there was more to them.

I wandered over to my kitchen, which wasn't much more than a food synthesizer with a recycling port for dirty dishes, and considered its menu. Bjorn had assured me the synth would offer more selections as it got to know me, but for the first time in my life I was tired of burgers and yakisoba noodles. I glanced at the window again and decided it was time to get out and explore. I had about eighteen hours to kill and maybe there was a food truck down there.

Stepping into the atrium for the first time was a full-frontal sensory assault. Imagine the lushest conservatory on Earth, but easily covering ten acres under a dome that had to be a few hundred feet tall, enough for clouds to form along its ceiling.

The scents from so many varieties of alien vegetation were unlike anything I'd experienced before. The best way to describe it is a blend of citrus, herbs, and pines, but even that doesn't do it justice. Some reminded me of lemon and rosemary, but with enough difference to know that couldn't be what they were.

The map on my data crystal showed the interior was laid out with representative plants from the Emissaries and insectoids, which seemed like an odd combination, but their climates must have been similar. The reptilian Thubans no doubt had a dome somewhere that would've felt a lot like a desert on Earth.

It was easy to tell which sections were tailored for which race, as each seemed to concentrate in specific areas. Small insectoids were clambering around dense trees which looked like massive palms, with elegantly curving fronds and multicolored fruit that resembled pomegranates. The fronds were a deep indigo, and I wondered what gave them such a color—it couldn't be chlorophyl, could it? Beneath the palms sat larger insectoids, which I assumed were parents watching after their swarms of kids. It made them feel a little less creepy, and I wondered if this was where they took their meals.

My stomach growled, another reminder that it was well past suppertime. It didn't help that the fragrant plants were whetting my appetite.

The gardens were separated by a wide, carefully groomed stone walkway like something you might find in a conservatory on Earth. Where the insectoid side was dense and naturally chaotic, like a jungle, the Emissary's section was orderly and meticulously cultivated, like an orchard or Japanese garden. Deciduous trees bloomed with intricate flowers in regal shades of violet and gold, as if they'd been bred for royalty. Their brilliant jade-green leaves highlighted the richly colored blooms. It felt like I should be wandering the garden, gently caressing its flowers as I contemplated the meaning of life.

Right now I could only contemplate my growing hunger. More oddly shaped fruit dangled from the trees, some resembling curlicue-twist bananas. Others looked like garden-variety pears. The temptation to pick one of each and dig in was hard to resist, but I had no idea which ones would be compatible with human metabolism. The Emissaries had told me we were "mostly" compatible, but that meant some things weren't. I didn't want my first week in class to be interrupted by a case of food poisoning, so I reluctantly trudged back up to my suite. Maybe I could tweak the synth to create a steak with asparagus.

The synth created a decent sirloin, which was not surprising since it could already duplicate a good cheeseburger. The veggies proved to be trickier. What it thought was asparagus came out as a jumble of olive-colored sticks with the consistency of beef jerky, and no amount of extra cooking would soften them up. I needed the vegetables so I choked them down. The synth added all the necessary nutrients to whatever it prepared, but presentation is everything and that part was going to take some work.

It was enough to fill me up, which made sleep come easier. I got in a solid eight hours in GU time, which was closer to ten in human time. Going by the clock on my data crystal, I had over a full GU hour before it was time for class to start. I'd planned to get there early today and needed to hustle.

I jumped into the shower, a closet-sized compartment that felt like a car wash. It sprayed me with a cleansing mist and caressed me with sonic waves before rinsing me down with a stream of nice hot water, then finished with a blast of warm air. I was standing in a giant blow dryer. It was efficient but left me unsatisfied—I'd never wanted a hot bath and a plain dry towel so much. Maybe I could get to know a few hextopods and take a dip in their pool sometime.

My plan was to play around with that transducer disc before

class; I wanted to test it against the comparatively primitive gear I'd brought from home. How much more accurate—or not—was it compared to an old-fashioned BP cuff and pulse oximeter?

It felt a little like burglary, but the classroom door slid open as I passed my bio ring across it, so it must have been okay. I expected to enter a darkened room, but to my surprise it was as bright as day. And uncomfortably warm. At first I assumed they kept the A/C off when it wasn't in use, but then I saw why.

Chonk was hunched over his desk, his temperature regulator placed atop his neatly folded tunic beneath his seat. He turned as I walked in, apparently not the least ashamed to be buck naked. For a giant lizard, it seemed appropriate.

He hissed. "Excuse appearance," said the translator in my head.

I waved it away, then realized he might not grasp my gesture. "It's not a problem," I said, and studied the room. A lot of the equipment was out of place. "Have you been here all night?"

"What 'night'?"

How to describe that, especially being in deep space? It was always night out there. "Solar cycles," I began, and caught myself. "Sol" wouldn't mean much to him. "When your home star is in the sky, it's 'day.' When your planet rotates away from the star, it gets dark. Where I'm from, we call that 'night.'"

"Ah. Understand now. Our home world tidally locked to star. Always presents same face. One half planet always in light. Other side always dark. We live in between."

I hadn't heard of 'tidally locked' and had to think on it. It sounded like our moon, where the same side always faced Earth. "Oh, okay. I understand now. You live in the space between, then?" I tried to imagine a strip of arable land bordered by full sun and eternal darkness. It couldn't have been very big.

He thought for a minute. "Yes. Between. Is very warm."

I unconsciously tugged at my coveralls. It had to be close to a hundred degrees in here. "This is more comfortable for you, then."

"Much more comfortable."

"I don't understand. Could you not get your own quarters warm enough?"

"Could warm. Needed stay here. Learn more."

I thought about how I'd spent the last eighteen hours and felt like a slacker. He was driven and disciplined, appropriate for someone from a warrior culture. "Did you sleep here, too?"

"Sleep . . ." He trailed off in thought. "Ah. Rest. Yes. Not for long."

I'd worked with a few veterans over the years and they'd all said the same thing: a soldier learned to sleep anywhere, anytime, because they never knew how long they'd have to go without. It applied to medics and firefighters, too. "I came in early myself to play with the equipment."

"Play?" He paused again. "Not play. Serious."

I smiled. "It's an expression we use. Humans can be indirect like that."

He thought that over and seemed satisfied. "You come work? Learn?"

"Yes. Learn." I reached into my bag and pulled out a pressure cuff, pulse oximeter, and stethoscope. He regarded them in the way we might consider a collection of eighteenth-century dental tools. I didn't yet know how to read the body language of a giant lizard, but his widened eyes hinted he was appalled.

"Use on Earth? Primitive."

I jerked a thumb over my shoulder at the high-tech gear arranged along the back wall. "Compared to that stuff? Yeah, I suppose. This is standard equipment on Earth, and they work very well." I placed the pulse ox on my index finger, and after a moment its tiny screen flashed with numbers. "See? This device tells me heart rate and blood oxygen levels. Simple."

"Yes. Simple."

Of course, "simple" could have meant "easy" or "stupid." I placed the stethoscope into my ears, slipped on the BP cuff, and began pumping. "The others are a little more complicated. This will tell me blood pressure, but I have to take those readings myself with this gauge." He seemed interested in the old-fashioned dial. I held the stethoscope's bell to my chest. "This lets me listen to heart and lung function, abdominal sounds, that sort of thing."

"Like transducer," he said. "Is that not easier?"

"Much easier. I wanted to know how it compares to what I'm used to." I handed him the stethoscope, which barely fit against his ear openings. He moved the bell around his chest. "Ah. See now. Useful."

I smiled again. "Very useful." It made me wonder, though . . . "Does your race not use this kind of equipment?"

"No." He tapped the side of his head. "Ears sensitive. Can hear much direct." He removed the stethoscope and held one arm against the side of his head to demonstrate. "Good as stetho . . . thing."

Now *that* seemed primitive, not that I was going to say so to a seven-foot-tall warrior lizard. It must have worked for them, otherwise he wouldn't be here. It made me even more curious. "So how did you end up with the Med Corps?"

He sat up straight. "Was legion medico. Like physician. Treat many other races on expeditions." He seemed to be searching for the right word. "Improvised. Union impressed." The translator didn't do an especially good job of conveying tone, but he seemed proud to be selected. It was an intimidating reminder of how unique my situation was.

"You said 'physician.' In my language that means a doctor. Are you a doctor?"

"Not doctor. Much training. But not doctor."

That was a relief. I'd started to worry that I was the only medic in a room full of alien MDs. Maybe he'd been more like a physician's assistant, which on Earth was still pretty far up in the pecking order. His remark about "expeditions" piqued my interest, though. Did he mean scouting other systems, or something more aggressive? Call me naive, but the Union didn't strike me as being interested in conquest.

War stories would have to come later. There wasn't much time left to do what I'd come early for in the first place. I snatched the transducer kit from the equipment shelf and began running it over my body, comparing it to the numbers on my pulse ox and BP cuff. That was a bit of a trick, keeping the disc in place while I pumped the cuff. My numbers were all over the place, no doubt from the awkward effort of holding the disc with one hand and pumping with the other, while twisting my head to one side to see the gauge. You're supposed to be relaxed for a stable BP reading, and my contortion act was the opposite of relaxed.

To my chagrin, it reminded me of my own self-imposed limitations. For the same reason I clung to my old-fashioned paper notebooks, I'd kept a comparatively outdated manual BP cuff long after our squads had been equipped with the automated digital gear. The newer equipment was accurate, but I preferred the personal touch, relying on my own skill to pinpoint systolic and diastolic pressures. Plus the old ones didn't need electricity to work.

One nice thing about the Med Corps' device was the error bars, assuming they were correct. A healthy human's pressure should stay close to 120/80, but this can vary, and there are definite danger zones at the upper and lower ends. The "typical human" range looked awfully generous, with an upper limit that would have me worried about stroking out. Pulse and O_2 ranges were more reasonable, with the lower ends matching what I'd expected to see.

Again, I must have been telegraphing my uncertainty because Chonk seemed to notice. "Have problem, Mel?"

"Maybe. The acceptable BP ranges seem optimistic."

"Optimistic . . ." He pondered that a moment as his translator must have been scrambling to keep up. "Optimistic. Hopeful. Mean unrealistic?"

I nodded, and made a mental note to be more precise. "Yes, that's it. Unrealistic." I held up the transducer disk. "The range of acceptable human blood pressure this device thinks is healthy is not accurate."

"Ah. Will fix in time." He pointed at the crystal propped up on my desk. "Need data. Make"—my translator stuttered—"baseline." It was another indication that I was something of a guinea pig here. Chonk unfolded himself from his seat, towering over me at his full, intimidating height. He began collecting the displaced equipment and held out an opened claw. "Come. Class soon. Must organize."

It was another day of equipment familiarization, which Xeelix assured us we would have plenty of opportunities to practice with. Some of the gear was familiar enough that I understood the machines as soon as he explained their function. Some purely mechanical devices like suction units and infusion pumps were remarkably familiar once I got over the near-magical technology upgrades, because in the end they had to function by the same principles. Nearly every device could adapt itself for individual races, while some had to be crafted for a specific race—spine boards, cervical collars, and so on.

I was especially fascinated with the laryngoscope. Another purely mechanical tool, it's the flashlight-looking device we use to insert breathing tubes down a patient's trachea. Intubating is dicey work, an acquired skill that relies heavily on sense of touch. Like everything else in emergency medicine, as a patient you really don't want to find yourself in a condition where that thing becomes necessary.

This one was both smaller and way more capable than any I'd ever seen, made of something called "meta materials." Not only did it come with a case full of tracheal blades that could change shape for each race, its grips could adapt to whichever being might be using it. The settings for a Gray were a lot different than a Thuban's, for instance. Fortunately the Emissary-sized grips fit my own hands pretty well.

The neatest trick was 3D projection. We learned the displays Xeelix had used to show us what the "assessment disc" could do were for classroom illustration. In actual practice we'd be wearing transparent wraparound goggles that overlaid holographic images from whatever device we were using. With the laryngoscope, we could see exactly what it was seeing in three dimensions, projected in our visors. We tried it out on some of the training dummies and it was like looking straight into the patient's body. It made intubating almost idiot-proof. Same for the little miracle disc—with the goggles on, it was like having Superman's X-ray vision wherever you pressed it. I was dying to take this thing back home to show off to my buddies at the station.

I was less excited over Xeelix's next presentation. He pulled out a container with the green Med Corps slash and opened it to reveal a cluster of gleaming metallic cigar-shaped objects of varying sizes. I immediately recognized them and groaned inwardly.

"While you all appear suitably impressed with the variety of assessment tools at your disposal, these devices will provide you with a more complete view of your patient's vital functions." He went on to explain how each was designed for specific GU species, and the proper methods for insertion. A helpful depiction of each species' rectums and the appropriate probes appeared above our desktops.

Understand that I'm not repulsed by other people's butts. We're all meat sacks of one form or another, and it's all gross, some parts more so than others. You learn to deal with it, or you find another line of work.

This felt different. After laughing off all the tabloid stories of alien abductors probing the more tender parts of human anatomy, here I was smack in the middle of it, learning how to use said probes.

What the hell was it with these guys and anal probes, anyway? On Earth, we poked around our patient's nether regions for two things: One, it's the most accurate way to read body temperature. Two, it's a quick way to find internal bleeding in a gunshot victim. The first was hardly ever needed in the field, and the second was case-specific for obvious reasons. There's a third reason I won't get into, as it involves certain sexual misadventures which are best left unsaid. These guys, on the other hand, seemed to have a probe for everything.

Xeelix held up one of the devices, a particularly large (for me) and shiny butt cigar. "If conditions permit use, you will find these probes to be quite useful." He seemed to focus on me, sensing my uncertainty. "In combination with the other tools we've demonstrated, you will be able to rapidly assess your patient's condition to the fullest extent possible, even generating preliminary diagnoses."

That was a big leap. As medics, we *never* diagnosed. That was an MD's job. "Excuse me," I said. "I feel like we need to understand scope of practice here. Where I came from, medics and nurses can't diagnose patients. Only doctors like yourself can do that."

Xeelix nodded in acknowledgment. "I understand the differences may seem profound, and I assure you that we will explain your limitations under Union Code in more detail." He took a seat beside his podium, indicating that we were in for a bit of a philosophy lesson. "This is an excellent opportunity to discuss the legal boundaries of your position." While he was addressing the class, I had the distinct feeling this was mostly for my benefit.

"Your role is to treat and stabilize patients for transport. Melanie Mooney, this is similar to what you are familiar with on your home world. However, the distances and time scales involved are significantly greater."

"I understand the time lag for light-wave signals." I inclined my head toward Bjorn. "They also explained the 'entanglement' device you use for long-range communication."

"Signal lag and the limitations of entanglement are certainly factors. However, I don't believe you have been adequately prepared for the true impact of relative time."

Now I turned to Bjorn. Relative time? It seemed like everyone else in the Union had an innate understanding of mind-bending physics. It was a reminder that here, *I* was the alien.

Xeelix continued. "Are you familiar with the effect of velocity on perceived time?"

"Barely," I admitted. "It slows down the faster you go, right?"

"For the individual traveling, it passes at the same perceived rate. But relative to an outside observer, the traveler's time slows down. It is a difficult concept for one who has no need to understand it."

"But your ships can't travel at light speed. That's still impossible."

"Strictly speaking, yes, though many travel at a considerable fraction of light speed. This creates time-dilation effects. What you may not yet grasp is that gravity has the same effect. Our use of gravity-manipulation drives to cross interstellar distances results in the same phenomenon, as if we were traveling faster than light. You will not know if the medical team you left behind on station is the same that will be there when you arrive. Or for that matter, what diagnostic tools they may have available. In extreme situations the facility may no longer be operable; however, this is quite rare."

Once again, my brain hurt, but now was accompanied by a sick feeling in my gut. I'd been here not quite two weeks, but how much time had passed on Earth? And how isolated would we be on long runs? The idea of leaving one of the Med Corps' orbiting hospitals and coming back to a completely different place—or no place at all—was a lot to digest.

It was one more thing to compartmentalize for later. I had to focus on the immediate questions. "That's why these ambulances"—and I could tell that word tripped a few of my classmate's translators—"are more like self-contained ERs." That also made their translators skip. "Emergency Rooms," I explained.

Xeelix nodded appreciatively. "That is precisely correct, Melanie." It was the first time he'd dropped my surname, which felt like progress. Maybe he'd needed time to catch up with human cultural norms. The Grays could be scrupulously formal. "Recall that I said the probes and transducers can generate a diagnosis. It is all automated and ready for access by a physician. Your personal observations are vital, but they are not the 'final word,' as you might say."

That made me feel better about the GU's standard of care. But now there was a bigger question to ponder: How much time had I already lost back on Earth, and how much more would I lose in the future?

I would find out soon enough.

☤ 19 ☤

Everyone in our class was paired with an experienced medic for training runs, each with one from his or her own species. While that wasn't going to be the case as working medics, for training it made things simpler to go on runs with someone who spoke the same language and came from the same culture. That presented certain difficulties in my case, so Xeelix took it upon himself to work with me personally. It was probably the obvious choice, but I couldn't get past the feeling that they'd singled me out for special attention.

First runs as a trainee are a roller coaster of emotions, a constant flow of new sensations clamoring for attention. You have to quickly figure out how to keep your head under pressure, and most of all learn from the more experienced medics. Just a few weeks ago training runs had been a distant memory, but here I was in the middle of it once more.

We met in a cavernous hangar in the bottom level of our sector's medical center—I wished they'd just call it a hospital—where we were paired up with our training preceptors. Like everything else in the Union, it was impossibly neat and tidy. Glow panels in the high ceiling shone like natural daylight, making the already airy space feel like we were outdoors. The back wall was filled with supply and specialized equipment lockers.

Enormous openings were evenly spaced along the opposite side of the hangar, as if the entire deck was open to space. Xeelix explained that they were force fields taking the place of mechanical doors. Apparently they were more reliable, but it left me with the willies. What happened if the power went out? A low-frequency hum permeated the hangar, the sound of those electromagnetic fields keeping the vacuum at bay.

The Class III transports, our flying ambulances, had looked interesting as holograms; in person they were pretty impressive. Larger than the shuttle I'd left Earth in, each was about the size of a city bus and emblazoned with the Corp's green slash, beginning at the tips of the outrigger pods and coming to a point midway atop each ship. Each slash bore alien script which my visor translated as numbers. Ours was 5.

I mentioned they were teardrop-shaped, the equipment pods flaring outward as the fuselage tapered to a sharp point. They bore evidence of wear and tear, with subtle scuff marks and dings around the access panels along the top of each pod. It made the vehicles feel more lived-in, more real.

Each transport was lined up in front of a force-field opening, between rails on either side. "Those are additional field generators," Xeelix explained. "When a transport is dispatched, it is surrounded by a local field before its bay is opened to vacuum." They must have had a lot of confidence in those devices.

As if to illustrate his point, a high-pitched klaxon sounded overhead, like the squawking of irritated birds, and I heard a message through my translator. "Alert bay twelve, alert bay twelve. Prepare for immediate departure."

Xeelix pointed toward the far end of the hangar, where a translucent yellow wall had appeared. Behind its shimmering electromagnetic curtain, a transport began powering up. "The field is in a visible spectrum to warn away others," he said, and pointed to the rail nearest us, which was also cast in high-visibility yellow. "It is important to avoid these areas." Good to know, as I wouldn't want to stumble into one of those things when they threw the switch. Same reason we painted safety lanes around our ambulance bays in high-viz colors, though nobody in the firehouse was in danger of being cut in half by a force field.

I was mesmerized by the whole ballet. An amber beacon began flashing on the transport's belly, a warning that its gravity drive was being spun up. The field bowed outward as the ambulance began to hover, which was more than a little unnerving. "Is that a gravity wave?"

"Highly localized, but yes. Just enough to move the ship out of its launch corridor."

There was a flash of white light around the rim of the portal as the outer force field opened, letting the ambulance slip through along a current of escaping air. The field quickly returned to its normal invisible state and the sparkling yellow curtain disappeared. There was a tickle of moving air and my ears popped as the hangar's pressure equalized. "Bay twelve is clear," I heard. "Bay twelve is clear."

Xeelix seemed satisfied. "Quite a good introduction, I think." He motioned me onward. "Now, let us become familiar with our own transport."

He led me through an exterior inspection, allowing me to open the outrigger compartments to check the gear inside. For this, we used the same goggles he'd showed us for patient assessments. As I opened each panel, an inventory list appeared in front of me. Species-specific immobilizers, breathing masks, atmosphere tanks, oddly shaped cervical collars, and the ever-present array of brightly polished butt probes were precisely arranged in each compartment.

At his direction, I waved my bio ring across one side of the ambulance and a large opening appeared. I stepped inside and found it to be exactly as depicted in our training holograms. An automated, moldable gurney sat in the center with scanning and assessment gear mounted atop shelves along one sidewall. Outlines of monitoring screens were embedded in the opposite wall. I pointed them out to Xeelix. "I have a question," I said, tapping my visor. "If we can see everything through these, then what are the monitors for?"

"They have a number of uses," he explained. "They can function as 'repeaters' so others can see what you see. They can also display physiological information which would otherwise crowd your field of view. Often they are simply used as windows to the outside. This is an important psychological benefit to both patients and technicians."

That was more than good enough for me. I liked being able to see where we were. We'd been exposed to every piece of gear in class except one, and that had been bugging me. In the back of the compartment hung three vacuum suits in transparent lockers, one of which was clearly tailored for a human of my size. "What about those? We were never trained on how to use them."

"An oversight, I admit," Xeelix said. "They are used commonly enough among our spacefaring races as to be an afterthought. It would be like teaching you to put on a coat when it is cold outside."

I stared at the simplistic-looking spacesuit. "This seems a little beyond dressing for the weather."

"I suppose so." He led me back to where the suits were hung. "Come, let us have you try yours on. As with your uniforms, it was tailored based on your initial entry scan."

I swiped my ring across the door and lifted the immaculate white jumpsuit from its hanger. It was light, no more cumbersome than my medic coveralls. A small backpack was mounted below the helmet rim, and the helmet itself was a clear ovoid bubble. "This isn't glass, right? More of that transparent metal?"

"Correct." He pointed to the backpack. "This is the biopack, your 'life support.' It contains power cells, communications, temperature controls, and air circulators. It is controlled by a panel embedded in the left sleeve."

Sure enough, there was a small rectangular crystal above the wrist, seamlessly woven into whatever this fabric was. I turned it over to check the backpack. "Seems awfully small. And it's all so light."

Xeelix lifted the suit from my hands to show me its features. "The biopack is what you would call a 'rebreather.' It contains a small supply of breathable air in a mixture tailored to your species. Its circulation pumps include catalysts to remove carbon dioxide before reintroducing it to your helmet."

"Doesn't seem like that would be enough to keep everything under pressure." My skepticism was asserting itself again. Of course, all I knew about spacesuits had come from watching old films of astronauts on TV. They were supposed to be bulky and stiff, necessary to keep the human inside at a survivable air pressure.

"The air is confined to your helmet." He pointed to its rim. "Notice the material beneath the neck; it will seal off the rest of your body. The suit works through mechanical counterpressure. The fabric is woven with flexible alloys that are constantly adjusting to your movements." He pulled at the skin on his arm, then gently poked at mine. "Our epidermis is already a sufficient containment vessel for most environments. In vacuum, we only need a way to keep air molecules from escaping."

The inner layer would be skintight, which made me thankful for the loose outer covering. "What is this layer for?" I couldn't imagine it was for looks.

"Radiation shielding. It requires something more 'low tech,' as your kind might say. It consists of simple physical barriers, many of which are similar to the materials your own space travelers use. A force field would offer full-spectrum protection, but those require considerable amounts of power. Equipping the biopacks with antimatter reactors seemed...impractical."

I laughed. "Was that a joke?"

"That was my intention. I understand humor is important to humans, particularly in unfamiliar environments."

"It certainly makes some things easier."

"Excellent." He opened the adjacent locker and pulled out his own suit. "I wished for you to be fully at ease before exposing you to vacuum."

I took a step back. *Exposing* and *vacuum* were not words I wanted to hear strung together.

Xeelix stripped out of his coveralls. "Do not be anxious. I will be with you."

Contemplating the naked gray alien before me took my mind off the "exposure to vacuum" part, if only for a moment. If he was this comfortable around me, I'd have to be likewise around him, but it was going to take some getting used to. "No, uh...underwear, then?"

He was halfway through sealing up his suit and looked at me, cocking his head to one side. "What is...ah. I understand now. Underclothing is not recommended. It can become quite uncomfortable."

I frowned, still unconvinced. My "underclothing" was already light enough that I didn't see how it could make a difference, so I shed my coveralls and left everything else in place.

The suit went on easily enough, with a barely noticeable closure running the full length in front. It wasn't a zipper, but it did the same thing, following my finger up and down to connect seamlessly. Cool air caressed my face as I set the helmet into place. It was comfortable so far, the inner layer in fact feeling like a second skin. It pressed against my underwear a bit, but nothing to complain about. Maybe I could retain some of my dignity after all.

Xeelix showed me his wrist controls and pointed to a pulsing white light, which apparently meant "A-OK" in the GU. His voice sounded in my ears. "This is an integrated diagnostic for suit function and integrity."

I followed his lead and lifted my left wrist. As promised, the same pulsing white light indicated I was good to go. "What about warnings?"

"It will glow steadily if you are in vacuum. If it turns off, there is a problem with your suit. The wrist panel will inform you of the precise malfunction."

Lovely. That seemed backward. No news was not good news, apparently.

Xeelix closed the side door and began tapping at a nearby embedded panel. "I am venting cabin atmosphere into our recycler tanks. We will be in vacuum shortly."

It didn't take long. The hiss of moving air grew steadily quieter until the cabin was utterly silent. The counterpressure material began to squeeze in response. The white light on my wrist panel pulsed more rapidly, and began glowing steadily as Xeelix announced "vacuum."

And now I fully understood what he meant about underwear. It was as if the counterpressure fabric was trying to meld itself with my body, forcing every stitch and elastic strip to dig into my skin. It only got worse when I shrugged my shoulders and rotated my arms, trying to get a feel for the suit. All I'll say about that is thank God I didn't need underwire bras.

"You should try it through the full range of motion."

I remained as still as a stone, afraid to move any more. "I don't think that's a good idea."

"Perhaps not." This was a definite teaching moment. "Let us turn our attention to your helmet. Do you feel at all claustrophobic?"

If that was going to be a problem, it was overshadowed by the sensation of my undies cutting into my skin. I closed my eyes and took a deep breath, the hiss of circulation fans matching my rhythm.

Turning my head was the one physical movement that didn't hurt, and the helmet was big enough that it didn't feel restrictive. "No, I'm good. Feels natural."

"Excellent. This has been a satisfactory exercise." He tapped another command into the panel and I heard air returning to our little mobile ER. The pressure garment began to release its vise grip on me and I let out a sigh of relief.

"I believe you see what I meant now."

I hurriedly drew my finger across my chest to unzip the suit and began tenderly poking beneath the elastic of my underwear. My skin was an angry red stripe beneath, chafed in some places and bruised in others. It was sure to be even worse under my bra. On the other hand, the pain had kept me from obsessing over being separated from horrific instant death by a few millimeters of metallized alien fabric. "Yes. I see what you mean."

The rest of my orientation was uneventful, mostly reiterating what Xeelix had showed us in class. The only question I had left was who would be driving the bus. Where I'd come from, we were crewed in pairs and partners would swap driving duties. LifeFlight helicopters were, of course always flown by a qualified pilot with a pair of medics in back, one of them usually a registered nurse. I'd never been interested in that kind of work; I'm too scared of heights.

I'd figured our ride was going to be more like a helo's, which proved right. Not long after Xeelix finished my orientation, another Gray climbed aboard, this one already in a vacuum suit, carrying the helmet under one arm. Androgynous or not, this one tended toward female by the graceful way she carried herself, with a slight sway of her hips. It was subtle, just enough for another chick to spot, alien or otherwise. She paused to study me; maybe I was the first human she'd encountered.

"Greetings, Melanie Mooney. I am Needa, your pilot." She turned to Xeelix and they apparently had a private, telepathic exchange which my translators didn't pick up. Needa finished with a respectful nod and settled in at the pilot's station. A flick of her hand brought the ship's control panel to life.

"She was asking if your orientation was complete. It is a necessary condition to check in with central dispatch. I hope you took no offense; you are her first encounter with a human."

Aha! I'd been right on both counts: female, and first contact. Cool. "Your race is hermaphroditic. How often do individuals settle on a specific gender?"

"It is situational. Often it is driven by the name given at birth. Translated into your English, male names traditionally end in consonants. Female names traditionally end in vowels."

That wasn't much different from our traditions, which was interesting. I was starting to develop a real affinity for these little gray guys, and wondered how much else we had in common. "So it comes down to the parent's preference?"

"It is left over from ancient practices, before we evolved into a form that was more . . . adaptable."

That held some interesting implications, and made me wonder what humans might be like in another ten or twenty millennia.

"I have informed central dispatch that we are on active status," Needa said. "We are currently number one for ready alert."

"Excellent," Xeelix said. "We will be on the next run, as you would say."

I was beyond ready to get moving, and began to feel edgy from anticipation. "Awesome."

It was an exercise in hurry-up-and-wait, a fact of EMS life that was apparently fundamental across the galaxy. We spent the next couple of hours hanging out in the bus with Xeelix reviewing procedures and quizzing me on the various GU physiologies. Despite having that information implanted in my head, recalling everything on the fly was a real challenge. That wasn't the same as having knowledge ingrained in my memory, it was more like files I could access if I concentrated enough. It was teaching my brain to work like a user interface.

"Do not worry," he reassured me. "It is my pleasure to assist you."

I sighed. "It's a lot to digest."

Perplexed, Xeelix rubbed his chin. "I do not understand how that relates to your gastrointestinal function."

"Sorry. I meant *comprehend*."

"Ah. I see now. I did not believe you had eaten the files."

I laughed. "Feels like it sometimes. When I was studying to be a veterinarian, we spent a lot of time on different species' anatomies. I wished they could've just downloaded it all into my head back then. I'm not so certain now."

"We have observed that humans retain complex information more readily if they spend considerable time in study. I was curious how our methods would work for you."

"I'll get used to it. It has reminded me of vet school a little."

Xeelix shifted in his seat. "I am curious about that as well. If my understanding is accurate, you were close to completing your course of study. May I ask what caused you to change your plans?"

He wanted to know why I'd quit for something presumably less challenging. Fair enough, considering all they'd done to bring me this far. It wasn't something I enjoyed talking about, even after all this time. The guys back in the firehouse had known not to bring it up, but I couldn't blame Xeelix for asking.

I absentmindedly smoothed out my coveralls—a pointless gesture, as they stayed remarkably wrinkle-free. "I came from farm country. Agricultural region. We had more than enough vets around; my father was one of them. What we didn't have enough of were emergency medics." I was ready to leave it at that, fortunately the dispatch center ended the conversation for me.

"Alert bay five. Alert bay five. Prepare for departure."

Rolling out felt familiar. The sudden burst of activity, the rush of adrenaline as we shot out for the unknown. Xeelix and I pulled out our data crystals and read through the dispatch notice:

ALERT 149883-46 / ASSIGN MED 5
SINGLE VEHICLE ACCIDENT / SKIMMER CLASS
    TRANS-ATMOSPHERIC FLYER
THREE OCCUPANTS ABOARD, TYPE CHALAWANI
LOCATION: SECTOR 00, SUBSECTOR GAMMA 338,
    REPORTED BY EMERGENCY BEACON
HAZARD RATING: 3 / NO G.U. PRESENCE REPORTED

"Chalawans," Xeelix said as the capital ring receded behind us. "You recall their anatomy and physiology?"

"Working on it," I said, forcing my brain to call up their file. "Partial exoskeleton. Four lower limbs for mobility, four upper limbs for manipulation. Quadrilateral symmetry," meaning all eight limbs were evenly spaced around their centers. "Elongated neck, four eyes arranged vertically in pairs."

"And their most vulnerable regions?" Xeelix pressed.

"The neck and underbelly." Imagine a crablike shell with a giraffe-like neck.

Xeelix pointed to my crystal. "This information is rather thin. We have no reports of injury types. As you surely practiced on Earth, we must be mentally prepared without jumping to conclusions."

"We're going into this blind. How'd they get the report in the first place?"

"According to the alert message, it came from their flight plan and emergency beacon. Traffic control is aware of a skimmer accident, the number and race of occupants, but no more."

"What's a skimmer?"

"As the dispatch notice says, it's a trans-atmospheric flyer. Perhaps the closest match to one of your rocket-powered vessels. They rely on similar methods of reactive propulsion, thus the hazard rating."

I did recall that 3 was higher up the scale than I'd like. We'd have to be careful. I had no idea what they used for gas, but rocket fuel on Earth could be very nasty stuff. "I'm surprised anyone in the Union still uses them."

"Some citizens still prefer them for short trips. Many use them for recreational purposes."

Interstellar hotrodders, then. "Is that a popular pastime?"

"For some more than others. Chalawans tend to be fond of antiquated technologies. It is an avocation which often lands them in trouble."

I looked up toward the pilot's station in a vain attempt to figure out where we were going. "It's not on the capital ring. Where are we heading?" I was wondering how much time we were about to skip, but asking that seemed brash for a rookie.

He pointed at my crystal again. "Not far. Sector zero-zero is the Union center, the planet the capital ring orbits. We are approaching from its night side, which is why it is not yet visible."

In orientation they'd said the planet was uninhabited, at least by sapient creatures. It was something of a galactic nature preserve. "That's interesting. I'm surprised the Union would allow a vehicle like that."

The corners of his mouth turned down ever so slightly. "They are not generally permitted," he said grimly. "But that is not for us to determine, of course. Constables are en route. For now, it appears we will be the first on site."

That was completely opposite from the way we did things back home. The cops were almost always the first to respond. "What do we know about those skimmers? What kinds of hazmat do we need to be worried about?"

"Haz . . . mat?" His translator was having trouble with that one.

"Sorry. It stands for 'hazardous material.' Dangerous chemicals."

"Ah. Yes. Skimmers tend to be highly customized, though most use a propellant compound based on the elements you call boron and lithium. It is energetically reactive with oxygen and toxic to most races if ingested."

I didn't plan on swallowing the stuff, but that didn't mean there weren't other ways to ingest it. "Fumes?"

Xeelix nodded. "Fumes will be a concern." He pulled at his jumpsuit. "Our uniforms will be adequate against exposure, but I anticipate we will need to wear protective hoods."

I glanced over at an equipment locker that was marked with a black slash. It held our protective gear. This first run was going to be complicated.

Despite the inertial dampening, our little ship shuddered as we plummeted through the planet's upper atmosphere. I flicked on one of the outside viewscreens and could see only a sheath of incandescent plasma streaking past us, like we were flying through a neon tube.

"Atmospheric entries for emergency response calls are more exciting than usual," Xeelix explained. "Time is of the essence."

I nodded, as if I knew enough to understand the difference. After a few minutes we'd left the light show behind. High-altitude clouds zipped past as we flew in an ever-tightening spiral on our way down. Needa had targeted our entry to put us right on top of the emergency beacon. She looked busy up front, and I had the distinct sense that she was enjoying herself.

Soon the clouds gave way to reveal a dense forest below. Verdant trees with multicolored blooms turned beneath us in a kaleidoscope of alien vegetation as Needa continued her spiral, too fast for me to identify anything.

A clearing opened up ahead and we began to aggressively decelerate. I could tell this by looking outside; with the dampener field we couldn't feel anything.

We settled into a large clearing surrounded by curling, funnel-shaped trees. I only call them "trees" because they were enormous; otherwise they looked like ornamental flowers. It messed with my sense of scale. A stream ran along the far side of the clearing, leading into more dense forest. Light reflected off exposed metal scattered across its banks. That was our crash site.

Xeelix opened the hazmat locker and pulled out a pair of transparent breathing hoods. They were a lot like the helmets on our vacuum suits, with a respirator pack mounted behind the neck closure. He handed me one along with a pair of disposable gloves. In this, they were much more "low tech" and comparable to the vinyl exam gloves I was used to. Honestly, they're not even worth mentioning except that it was comforting to have something so familiar.

I opened the main door and was assaulted by a potpourri of new smells. Even through the respirator pack, the competing scents were as overwhelming as if I'd stumbled into the perfume section of a department store.

Xeelix noticed right away, of course. "GU Prime is what your people call a nature preserve." He looked across the clearing at the tangled mess of metal, appearing to be thinking about something else. "Access points are tightly controlled. Recreational flyers like skimmers are not often found here."

I grunted acknowledgment as I popped open one of the outboards to retrieve the Chalawani gear. I figured we'd need breathing masks, exoskeleton patch kits, and elongated cervical collars. There were only two of the latter; hopefully all three didn't have spinal injuries.

Xeelix watched approvingly. "Excellent. I had assumed the same."

He slung a field bag across his thin shoulders and headed to the scene. For being no taller than I was, he had a surprisingly long, loping gait. I snatched my own bag and ran to keep up.

The site was nothing like the crash I'd come across back home, where the vehicle was mostly intact. This thing was a mess; debris was scattered across a hundred-meter fan pattern. They'd hit hard and their vehicle had disintegrated; more of what I was used to finding in a high-speed crash. It was hard to see how anyone could have survived it. "Do these things have inertial dampeners?"

"They typically do not. Skimmer enthusiasts are attracted to the unbridled sense of acceleration."

My hotrodder analogy had turned out to be pretty close to the mark. Some of the larger pieces were brightly colored with iridescent shades of crimson and violet.

Xeelix pulled a thin wand out of his field bag and held it in the air. "Residual traces of boron and lithium. We must keep our respirators on."

"I expected a lot more fuel spillage."

"If their tank ruptured, the fuel would have reacted with the native oxygen. It would have been quite energetic."

I paused in my search for victims and studied the nearby vegetation. Sure enough, the tops of the closest funnel plants were badly singed, all curled up and crispy. The skimmer had gone up in a big fireball. "We might not have any survivors."

"A distinct possibility."

We spread out, searching opposite sides of the debris field. It wasn't long before I came across our first victim. Or rather, pieces of him. A mottled yellow shard of exoskeleton, about the size of a dinner plate, lay on the ground. Its color signified the victim was male. Nearby was one of his lower extremities, snapped off at the mid joint. I followed a smear of purplish blood across the cornstalk-thick grass and found the rest of him.

It was my first encounter with a Chalawan. His shattered carapace lay in pieces atop its thorax and abdomen, still attached but so fragmented as to offer no protection. Two pereiopods—his walking legs—were missing. His neck was bent at an odd angle—granted everything was "odd" to me at this point, but trust me when I say it was obvious. "Found one!" I shouted to Xeelix. "Chalawan male. Missing two lower extremities. Neck appears broken." I pulled out the transducer disk from my trauma bag and pressed it against the base of his neck. "No vitals. I think this one's a goner."

Xeelix was by my side within seconds. He knelt and motioned for me to move the transducer down to the victim's abdomen. He shook his head sadly. "You are correct, Melanie." He tapped a note into his data crystal, transferring everything we'd read from the transducer. He closed his eyes, and I heard him call to Needa telepathically. *Needa, report to central dispatch. We have located one victim, deceased. We are continuing our search.*

Understood, Needa replied. *Constables report they are on approach.*

"Very good," Xeelix said, and straightened up. "Come, there is nothing we can do here. Let us keep moving."

I stowed my gear and stood, giving the broken Chalawan one last look before moving on. At least we wouldn't be running short on cervical collars. That sounds grim, but in truth when you're responding to an accident with multiple victims, you're hoping there's enough gear to go around.

We found the next one a little farther ahead; this one I located by smell, like roasted oysters. That's in essence what we found. The poor guy was burnt to a crisp, no doubt closest to the fuel tank when it went up. Legs and arms were curled up beneath him. His carapace may have offered momentary protection, but his head and neck were gone.

"Vaporized in the blast," Xeelix said. "Sadly, I have seen this before." He called in his report to Needa.

This didn't make sense. "Why wasn't the other one burned?"

"Impossible to know without a constable investigation. I suspect this one survived the initial impact and went back to try and isolate the fuel cell."

Damn. Poor guy tried to do the right thing and it literally blew up in his face.

Xeelix quickly moved on ahead. I was still running to catch up when he came to a stop and kneeled over another mottled yellow exoskeleton. "Melanie! Come quickly!"

I ran over to his side and dropped down to my knees, hurriedly opening up my bag. This one was still alive. His lower extremities appeared to be in place, but two of his uppers were bent at odd angles between the joints. He moved groggily, with all four eyes fluttering at random. Probably a head injury. We worked together to put the cervical collar in place around his meter-long neck.

I tried talking to our patient as Xeelix placed a full-face breathing mask over him. "Can you hear me?"

He answered with clicking sounds my translator couldn't yet decipher. Xeelix repeated the question in Chalawan. More clicks. "He can hear us."

"Great. Can you tell me your name?" I asked without thinking. They apparently didn't have names in the way we thought of them, but I was going by habit now.

After a couple more clicks, my translator started to keep up. "Lusanii brood, four of twenty."

"Thanks, Four. You can call me Melanie." I held up my hand with two fingers extended. "How many fingers am I holding up?"

Again, I was relying on old habits. It apparently confused him even more.

"Rely on your assessment tools," Xeelix said patiently. "Remember, you are almost certainly the first human he has ever encountered. He is afraid."

Oh. Hadn't thought of that. It was easy to forget that I was the alien here. Again. I pulled out the disc and began moving it slowly across his thorax and abdomen. "Irregular heart rate. O_2 sats low, respiratory rate also irregular," I said. I pressed the center of the disc and began looking for internal injuries. The transducer functioned as it had in class, projecting images of the patient's anatomy in my visor.

Xeelix kneeled beside me and began directing my movements. A jumble of internal organs appeared, the Chalawan's long eight-chambered heart beating randomly beneath his carapace. Breathing was harder to assess because Chalawans exchange gas through "book lungs" like spiders. Their chambers look like a folded book and don't expand and contract like ours; they function more like gills, letting air pass over them. He was lying belly-down, which would've impeded airflow, so Xeelix held the cervical collar in place and while we gingerly moved our patient onto its side. No matter what kind of creature you're dealing with, you don't want to move them when there's a possible neck injury. But if they can't breathe, none of that will matter.

Xeelix made a tsking sound. "It is as I feared." He pointed at the Chalawan's thorax, which appeared scorched from the blast. I placed the disc next to his respiratory opening. "There are burns around his atrial cavity."

As I pressed the disc more firmly, we could see the seared folds of his lungs, like scorched pages of a book. "I'm surprised he's still alive."

"Chalawans are partially amphibious," Xeelix reminded me. "They can survive for extended periods without being in open air." He leaned in close, focusing his thoughts on me so our patient wouldn't hear. His voice sounded like a whisper in my head. *But this one does not have long. We must act quickly.* He laid the patient back on its belly. "Tell me, what would you do?"

This seemed too urgent to use for a teaching moment, but one glance at the wounded Chalawan told me what to do—he needed a tracheotomy, fast. "We have to crack his carapace. Drill through his front dorsal quadrant, between the second and third abdominal segments, and insert a breathing tube inside the atrial cavity above the lung folds. We can use the respiratory pump to start airflow once we've secured him aboard."

Xeelix stepped back and rubbed his chin. "Excellent." He placed a hand on my arm, fixing me with those black almond eyes. "We must work quickly, Melanie. Prepare the breathing tube and field instruments. I will calibrate the drill."

Xeelix set the transducer dead center on the Chalawan's front quadrant, gauging the exact depth. The drill was a handheld plasma cutter, and we needed to match its beam to the shell's thickness. Going any deeper risked more damage to internal organs. I was still pulling out the field surgery tools when Xeelix announced he was ready.

I spread sterile mats across the carapace, leaving an opening for our drill, while Xeelix administered a sedative. It wouldn't do to have our patient jerking around while we fished a breathing tube down around his vital organs. I laid out forceps, retractors, and a long section of tubing. "Ready."

Xeelix had replaced his sterile gloves with a heat-resistant pair. "Very good. Keep your hands clear until I say so."

I knelt back and kept my hands on my knees while he put the drill in place. It worked almost instantaneously. There was a flare of pure white light and a wisp of smoke curled away, carrying the sickly smell of burning calcium with it. Xeelix set the drill aside, stripped off his insulated gloves, and slipped on a fresh pair of sterile ones. There'd be more to cut, apparently. "The site is safe for us now. Retractor."

I handed him the retractor. Fortunately our hands were of similar size, so we didn't need separate sets of tools. He reached into the opening and began pulling folds of epidermal tissue aside. Now we could directly see the Chalawan's innards. Xeelix studied the opening as I ran the transducer disk around the patient's side to get a clearer picture. "No visible obstructions." He gestured for me to move the disc directly over the hole he'd drilled. Our visors showed a clear path down to the atrial chamber.

"Excellent," he said. "Our next task is more delicate." He lifted a long metallic tool from his field bag. It was an impossibly thin, articulated probe with an ablation blade at its end, similar to the arthroscopic instruments surgeons used on Earth. "We must make a small incision in the atrial sac to expose the lung folds." He motioned for me to move the transducer disc. "Fix this over the left forward quadrant so we can see exactly where we are going. When I am finished, you will follow with the breathing tube. Are you ready?"

I set the disc in place with an adhesive patch. "Ready."

Xeelix nodded and carefully inserted the ablation device down through the opening we'd created. I followed his progress through my visor, mentally mapping out the path I'd have to follow. He stopped right above the atrial chamber, gently placing the blade against the tissue. With a quick press from Xeelix, it sliced through to expose the book lungs. The ablation blade instantly cauterized the tissue, creating a nice, neat opening about the size of my index finger.

He deftly pulled the device out in a precise reversal of his movements. He turned to me. "Now."

Without a word, I tore the tube free from its sterile wrap and began fishing it down into the Chalawan's thorax, mimicking Xeelix's motions. I wasn't even thinking at this point, I was just *doing*. It felt no different than intubating a human patient; in fact I had a much better picture of where I was going with the tube.

It helped that Union gear was more advanced than the simple

silicon tubes we used on Earth. These little beauties could be made as rigid or as flexible as we needed simply by twisting our fingers around them. In short, they reacted to our movements. On the one hand it required more precise control, but with enough practice you could make them do whatever you needed. I'd played with them enough in class to have a decent feel for it, but there's nothing like doing it for real out in the field.

Fortunately, my first real-world use didn't require much complex maneuvering. I fished it down past a major artery, around the upper digestive tract, then straight through Xeelix's incision into the atrial cavity. "I'm in." My eyes darted over to the vital signs floating at the edge of my field of view. "O_2 sats are low, but stabilizing." We still needed to seal off that opening around the tube. I kept it in place while Xeelix pulled out another long, thin instrument with a handle shaped for his hands. He knelt beside me and slid it down alongside the breathing tube until it rested against the opening. "Keep it in place," he said, and gave the handle a quick squeeze. Bio-adhesive paste extruded from the opposite end, securing the breathing tube in place and sealing up the incision around it. As he removed the tool, he set another blob of paste in place around the opening we'd made in the shell.

"Something's wrong," I said. "O_2 sats are still too low."

"Agreed," Xeelix said. "Passive airflow is not enough. We must connect him to a respirator."

I searched the scene. Needa had landed us at a safe distance from the crash, mindful to keep us clear of any toxic fumes, but that meant we had a hike ahead of us. "Wait. I have an idea."

I yanked a hose free from my rebreather pack and shoved my thumb into its open end to seal it off.

"Melanie! What are you doing?"

"Getting air moving," I said, and held up my hose-tipped thumb. I turned my back to him. "Here—shove his tube into my open port and seal it."

Xeelix didn't argue but I could tell he was upset. "This is most unorthodox," he said disapprovingly as he fed the breathing tube into my pack and injected a plug of adhesive around it. "You are putting yourself at considerable risk."

"I'll hold my breath. Let's go." I was going to be rebreathing my own CO_2 until we got this guy aboard, so it was time for me to shut up and move. Xeelix lifted the Chalawan to one side as I slid the gurney under him, and we pushed and pulled against his carapace until he was centered. We each unfolded a pair of wings from beneath the gurney to accommodate his width, which was a good bit more than your typical humanoid.

Fortunately that was the hard work, as the gurney was self-propelled. Once we had our patient strapped in place, Xeelix activated the gurney's lift coils and the whole contraption began floating in air, waist-high. We ran back to our waiting ship. Or rather, Xeelix did his usual loping gait while I ran to keep up.

Needa was waiting for us by the main doors with a pair of semicircular wands in each hand. "For decontamination," she reminded me. She moved the wands around each of us in turn until she was satisfied we were safe to board. "Hazardous residue has been neutralized," she said as the door closed behind us. "You may remove your breathing hoods."

I stripped mine off with a sigh of relief. It had fogged up to the point where I couldn't see where we were going; I'd just been following Xeelix's lead. He turned on the respirator pump as I pried the breathing hose loose from my pack. After cleaning off the adhesive paste, I inserted the tube into the respirator and waited for the Chalawan's lungs to respond. Behind us, I could feel the odd push/pull of the gravity drive spinning up, our ambulance swaying as it lifted off.

"We must still be careful," Xeelix said as he adjusted the pressure. "Their aerobic exchange is based on the free flow of air, not active respiration like ours." It was striking to hear him compare us so easily.

I had taken off my goggles and was now watching one of the repeater displays on the wall behind him. "Sats are coming up," I noted. "Looks like they're staying above ninety percent."

"They are," he agreed, but I could sense he was perturbed. "Tell me, Melanie. What compelled you to take such drastic action? You put yourself in considerable danger."

"It was a calculated risk. He needed airflow at that moment much more than I did. Where I'm from we call it 'buddy breathing.' I figured we could make it back here before I was in danger."

"And if you figured wrong?"

"I assessed the scene. There appeared to be no further danger. We'd already determined the area was largely clear of contaminants."

He removed his visor to study the more complete picture on the sidewall repeaters behind him. "In this case, I believe your actions may have saved this one's life. He was on the verge of complete respiratory failure. In the future, please ensure that you don't place yourself in similar danger."

"I promise you if we weren't ready to transport, I wouldn't have done it. An unspoken rule among paramedics is to not add yourself to the body count." I didn't offer that my old boss had reminded me of that a few times.

"That is of some comfort," he said. "Your kind is known for improvising."

"Is that considered a good thing, or a bad thing?"

"I suppose we shall see."

☤ **20** ☤

Needa had us back at our sector's hospital in minutes; she must have put the pedal to the metal, or whatever one does with a gravity drive. She pulled us up alongside a docking bay, flashing yellow and white to announce our arrival. I barely felt us make contact and it wasn't long before the main door opened up into the GU's version of an emergency room.

There was no guessing where to take our patient. As soon as the lift doors opened, a luminous red line appeared in the white floor ahead. An unseen force actually pulled the floating gurney along for us, tracing the line; all we had to do was follow. Along the way, I got a good look at their ER.

Like so much else in the Union Med Corps, it seemed immaculately sterile. But there was a difference that stood out, which made me smile inside: The place was chaos. Magnificently controlled chaos, like a trauma center ought to be. Despite the wildly advanced technology, there were more than enough similarities to make the place comfortably familiar. Beings of every GU race were here in various states of activity. Some ran between bays, others huddled in consultation, a few were slumped dead-tired in chairs tailored for their body types. If anyone who works in trauma says they don't get a charge out of it, they're either lying or they need to find another job before they hurt somebody.

If anyone noticed the new human running past in Med Corps green, they did a superb job of hiding it.

Our trail ended at an open receiving bay, where two Grays and a

Chalawan waited for us in sterile bodysuits. As soon as the gurney stopped, they removed our monitors and began placing more of the little black discs at strategic points around his body. Xeelix motioned for me to brief them, which seemed to catch them off guard. I hoped my translator was fully calibrated by now.

"Patient is male, age estimated one hundred and nine annums based on shell layers. Left quadrant lower extremities are broken below both stifle joints. Second-degree burn injuries to his lower lung folds; airway was opened with a ten-millimeter breathing tube, inserted through the forward quadrant." I pointed to our homebrew tracheotomy. "Oxygen saturation was at sixty-four percent, restored to ninety-two percent after we connected the respirator."

The Grays looked back and forth between me and Xeelix. The Chalawan clicked at him as the others attended to the patient. It sounded rapid, urgent. My translator picked up a little of it: "This... assist... you?"

I heard Xeelix's reply through my translator. "Correct. This is Melanie, the human female recruited for our emergency response teams. Did you not see the notification?"

Didn't you get the memo? Awesome. The speed of bureaucracy was a universal constant, like the speed of light.

"Did see." The Chalawani doc studied me with his four crimson eyes, then turned to our makeshift tracheotomy. "This... unusual. Severe."

Xeelix tilted his ovoid head in my direction. "It was her idea. I approved of her actions. The patient would not have survived otherwise."

The doc gave me another look, this time with an appreciative nod. He turned back to his patient, which was our cue to leave. Our part was finished, so we headed back to the lift.

Xeelix was silent until the doors closed. He clasped his hands behind his back. "You comported yourself well, Melanie. That was rather intense for a first run. You maintained composure under pressure, and took appropriate courses of action. However, I am curious regarding your understanding of their cultural norms. You recall our classroom discussions?"

When you're a trainee, any praise is always followed by, "You did great, *but*..." He'd suggested I missed something important, and was giving me time to think about it. I was still pondering Chalawani culture when we arrived back at our ambulance bay.

"The exoskeleton," I finally said. "They're proud of them."

He nodded. "Our patient was a fully mature Chalawan, so he will carry that scar for the rest of his life. They avoid intentional modifications in all but the most severe cases."

"By 'modifications,' you mean repairs."

"Correct. However, I fully agree that your solution was the proper course of action. The Chalawani physician needed to hear that from me."

"One doctor to another," I said. "It's the same way on Earth."

It's hard to describe, but there was a kind look of understanding in his black eyes. He placed one of his elegant hands on my shoulder. "As you're seeing, the practice of medicine varies greatly with species and technology. However, many truths remain constant." He looked ahead toward our transport and motioned me to follow. "One of those is cleaning the vehicle at the end of a shift. Come."

I'd been thinking about cultural differences a lot as we prepped our ship for the next crew. *Alleviate suffering to the maximum extent possible.* That was the motto, but the "maximum extent" part promised to be a moving target.

Would remembering the Chalawani obsession with their shells have influenced my decision? The way I'd seen things, he would've been a goner if we hadn't cut through it. The alternative would've been removing the damaged lung tissue to expose the inner folds, which to me had seemed much more radical. Xeelix had clearly decided the same: We'd have been doing surgery at a crash site with potential toxic fumes in the air. Our patient may not like the permanent scar it would leave, but it was better than being dead.

I put that out of my head for the moment, busying myself with restocking supplies and making sure all the equipment was in working order. While I did that, Needa inspected our rig from nose to tail in a routine that was indistinguishable from the way I'd seen air ambulance pilots preflight their choppers.

Cleaning an ambulance at the end of the day could be a real chore, wiping every surface down with disinfectant and hosing out the back if it's messy enough. Here it was much simpler. Once we'd finished our inventory and tested every piece of gear, Xeelix motioned me over to a locker embedded in the floor of our ambulance bay. He removed a large transparent tube, mounted to a pedestal that unfolded beneath it. "This is a sterilizer boom," he explained. "It will remove any foreign particles and contaminants."

Together, we fed it through the main door and centered it inside the ship. We stepped back outside to what Xeelix explained was a safe distance, and he pressed his ring against a small control screen on the pedestal. The tube flooded our rig with a luminous, pulsating blue light that hurt my eyes. This went on for several minutes until it turned itself off.

I looked inside as we removed the sterilizer. The back of our ambulance was spotless, as shiny as it must have looked coming out of the factory. The purple Chalawani bloodstains were gone, as were our handprints on the cabinets and footprints on the floor. It smelled pristine, and I couldn't see so much as a mote of dust. "Did this vaporize all that crud?"

"Atomized it, to be precise."

I looked around our squeaky-clean rig with amazement. "The guys on Earth would love this."

"Your race is closer to this technology than you may realize. You are already using ultraviolet light as a sterilizing agent for certain applications, correct? This is a more energetic version. And quite precise."

Energetic. As in, don't get too close. I stepped back out into the bay as the next crew made their way toward us. Another Gray pilot conversed with Needa, while a pair of insectoids clambered up into our rig. "Is that it, then? We're done?" By now I'd normally be sweaty and up to my elbows in antiseptic wipes.

"Our shift is complete," Xeelix said. "You did well today. As we already discussed, I would suggest you spend some time studying cultural differences. Be here at the same time tomorrow."

That's the way I liked shift debriefs. Short and sweet. I spotted my classmate Chonk striding away from his rig, and started thinking about cultural studies again. No better way to learn than by being in person. I waved him down. "Wait up!"

✠ ✠ ✠

The other universal constant is trainees commiserating about their first live runs. We parked ourselves on a bench along the back wall of the ambulance bay, watching the activity and trading stories. As we talked, our translators seemed quicker to catch up. There were fewer awkward silences as they worked to turn Thuban hissing and human babbling into recognizable words. Judging by Chonk's reaction, I'd had a more exciting day.

"Chalawan skimmer crash?" He seemed jealous. "Exceptional. Our runs . . . dull. Sickly Reticulan infant. Much coughing. Administered steroid vapor. Parents worry much. Then called to Th'u'ban suffering *lo'to'oh*. More steroids."

My translator skipped on that. "What's 'loto-oh'?"

Chonk tugged at his abdominal plating. "Skin condition common to molting Th'u'bans. Can develop if old skin shed too soon." He nodded at a row of succulents sprouting from pots along the wall. "Used to treat with *te'mau* leaf. Better medicine now."

"She called a squad for a skin rash?"

His vertically slit eyes rolled upward, showing his exasperation. "Preceptor say this one call often. Little complaints." He reconsidered his words, calibrating to my language. "Small stuff."

I laughed. "Where I'm from, we call those 'frequent flyers.'"

Chonk's trident tongue darted in and out, which I think signaled that he was amused. "Good word. Will remember." He paused. "How . . . familiar . . . this? Like Earth?"

I folded my arms and studied the bay. Other than the technology and the various skittering, chittering aliens, it was a lot like the firehouse back home. Just bigger. With spaceships. "More familiar than I expected. Once we were on a run, the old reflexes took over." I pointed toward the lifts nearby. "And I'd have recognized the ER for what it was, even without our training."

"ER?"

"Emergency Room. Trauma center."

"Ah. Understand. Your . . . slang . . . sometimes difficult."

"Sorry. We tend to use a lot of acronyms. Initials. Makes some things easier."

"Easier if knew language. Knew culture."

"Yeah, I'm learning that the hard way. The Chalawani doc upstairs seemed a little put out with us drilling into that guy's shell."

Chonk shrugged, his emerald scales rippling with his massive shoulders. One clawed hand traced a line across his thigh, where his scales had once been broken and patched. There must have been a good story behind that. "You did right thing. Better to have scar than dead."

"Exactly!" I said, a little too loudly. "Sounds like not everyone sees it that way."

"Do not," he agreed. "Benefit of not having war. Narrows choices."

"I have a lot to learn about cultural differences."

"Same." He patted his chest. "Am Union citizen whole life. Still feel . . . outside."

I stole a glance at the scar on his thigh. "Because you're from a warrior culture. The others can't understand, can they?"

Chonk nodded with a faraway look. "Cannot. Believe violence not necessary." He turned to me and thumped his chest. "Our kind know better."

This was taking a somber turn, and it felt like both of us needed to let off some steam. "Tell you what. Maybe we can help each other out with 'cultural studies.' It's been a long day and I need a drink. Food, too. Where's a good place around here?"

"Now talking!" He slapped my knee with one of those massive, clawed hands. I tried not to wince, but *damn*. "Come! Know good place."

Chonk led me to a transport tube, essentially a subway that traveled the full length of the capital ring. We were surrounded by representatives of most every race in the Union. It was noisy, crowded, and filled with the scents of individuals going about their daily lives. So a lot like a human subway. It wasn't filthy like New York subways are said to be, but it definitely wasn't up to Med Corps standards of cleanliness.

Grays huddled together silently. Insectoids clung to the walls, which was apparently more comfortable for them. Chonk nodded at a pair of Thubans who gave him a questioning look as he moved past with me at his side. In the corner, an Emissary sat reading his data crystal, oblivious to his surroundings.

I tugged at Chonk's tunic. "Where are we going?"

"Place called Wa'xi'ya'de, in Th'u'ban sector. Believe you call it 'bar.'"

An actual bar, in Thuban territory. This was going to be interesting, maybe a little dangerous. But if I wanted more cultural acclimation, it was hard to think of a better way to get started.

I tried to repeat his pronunciation and stumbled over my own tongue. "Wayside," I finally said, contracting it into something I could remember. Sounded enough like a bar, too. "They have food?"

He patted his stomach. "Much good food. Very satisfying. Excellent drink."

I was all about an excellent drink at this point. It wasn't long before our tube came to a stop. The pair of Thubans made their way out, and we followed. A wave of arid heat washed over us and I could tell Chonk was loosening up already. He let out a deep, satisfied hiss. "Like home," he said, and stripped off his temperature-regulating pack. He was about to place it in a pouch on his waist, but something stopped him. He turned and offered it to me. "You want use? Climate not comfortable for many others."

I rolled up my sleeves and unzipped my coverall as far as prudence would allow. "I'll be all right. We have some pretty hot places on Earth, too." Without a word he stuffed the regulator into his pouch, looking glad to be free of it.

We walked up a broad, short flight of stairs into the Thuban sector. Like the one where I lived, it was a massive transparent dome, but instead of being filled with extraterrestrial vegetation, this one looked more Earthlike. It reminded me of Arizona, all hues of burnt ochre with sprinkles of sage where extremely hardy plants grew. Bulbous cacti and squat paddle-leafed palms surrounded fields of pointed succulents that resembled aloe and agave.

"This is what your home world looks like? We have deserts on Earth that are almost identical."

"So have been told," he said. "You like?"

"I do. It's hot, but I'll manage. I need to stay hydrated."

"Hi-drayt? Ah. Water. Yes, much water at Wa'xi'ya'de. Come."

I followed him to a low-slung building of sculpted stone. Its outside walls were decorated with gracefully cut swirls; its windows were circles of multicolored glass that changed with perspective. Lilting melodies from wind instruments emanated from its open doorways. It was beautiful and inviting, almost making me forget that it had been built by highly evolved dinosaurs.

The music might have been calming to me, but to the Thubans it must have been like death metal. The inside was as intricately decorated as outside, but the activity within reminded me more of a roadside bar. The whole place was one big exercise in contradictions.

Thubans huddled around tables, either quietly nursing drinks or raucously playing a game that looked like a cross between backgammon and chess. I didn't try to get my head around that one.

It was a pair of Thubans along the back wall that captivated my attention. They stood about fifteen feet apart, each in front of a target circle, throwing knives at each other. Imagine axe-throwing with the stakes being a bit more personal. Apparently whoever got closest without hitting his opponent earned the most points. *Warrior race*, I reminded myself.

I must have been staring at the dueling pair for a while, because Chonk felt the need to lean over and explain. "They play *ta'au'ae'he'lee*. Game of skill."

My implant translated that simply as "knife fight." I was about to turn away when one of them caught one square in the chest, the blade stuck in one of his scales. I was about to run over to render aid when Chonk stopped me. He seemed amused. "Wait. Watch."

The injured Thuban held out his arms and roared, and I thought for sure we were about to get caught up in an alien bar fight. I was hopelessly vulnerable. Here I was, barely five feet tall, surrounded by warrior lizards that stood a good two feet taller.

It turned out the roar was laughter. The other Thuban hung his head in dismay.

"Th'u'ban who caught knife just won. Body hit automatic victory."

I watched in amazement as the "victim" pulled the blade free and handed it back to his opponent. They each sheathed their knives and returned to their table, where their companions raised their drinks and roared in unison.

"This is normal?" I wondered.

"Believe you call 'letting off steam.'" Chonk pointed to the knife-throwing pair. "Soldiers on leave from border patrol. Hard work. Hard play."

Out of the corner of my eye, I studied the plated scales on my companion's chest. They did appear pretty thick, and those knives looked to be surgical-quality sharp.

Chonk found us an open table and held up two clawed digits. Soon a female Thuban barkeep came over with a pair of small clear glasses filled with golden liquid. "You enjoy this."

I was a bit more circumspect, having no way of knowing if this stuff would kill me. My eyes fluttered as I mentally searched the files on Thuban physiology; for all I knew they could drink radiator fluid and be just fine. After a moment I was satisfied that methanol was as deadly to them as it was to humans. I took a sniff, and it smelled strangely familiar. "What is this stuff?"

"Is called *ka'vaa'ma'loi*. Made from ka'vaa nectar." He pointed to one of the same type of succulents I'd seen outside, the ones that looked an awful lot like agave.

No way. Throwing caution to the wind, I took a sip. Light, a tad fruity...

"Holy shit! It's tequila!"

"You familiar?"

More than I should be. I was grinning like an idiot. "We have this on Earth! Very popular."

Chonk held up his glass in a satisfied salute. "Ah! To good day."

"To a good day," I said, and we downed our drinks. It went down smooth, but the warm sensation welling up inside me was a warning to be careful. Thuban tequila promised to be potent.

Chonk smacked his glass on the table and waved for the barkeep, who brought over a whole carafe of the stuff. "Will be good night too."

It was indeed a good night. For being a race of hard-ass warriors, the other Thubans were decidedly less aggressive when it came to checking out the human chick carousing with one of their own. One or two made their way over to say hello to Chonk, eyeing me cautiously. Their back-and-forth hissing was too much for my translator to keep up with, until I heard Chonk introduce me and explain that we were in training together. That's when the dam broke.

More of them surrounded our table, pulling up stools and peppering me with questions. They'd heard of Earth, but had never been anywhere near our vicinity as it was one of the quieter parts of the galaxy. That was good to know; whatever threats these guys protected the Union against apparently didn't have their eyes on my home planet. It made me wonder what else was out there, beyond the Union's borders.

"Earth like this?" one asked.

"Some places are exactly like this," I said, and explained deserts. "Others are jungles, very humid. Lots of vegetation, filled with other creatures. Much of Earth is like the Emissaries' old world, or at least that's what I'm told."

They paused to consider that. "Is mostly cold, then?"

"Cold" was relative. Room temperature to a human would put a Thuban in torpor without a regulator pack. "Parts of it would be to a Thuban, I guess. Some regions are very cold, but many humans still thrive there."

"Humans strong, then. Much good." They celebrated human tenacity with another toast of *ka'vaa'ma'loi*. I took a small sip, afraid to drain my glass. Judging by their size alone, these guys would put me under the table if I wasn't careful. They seemed amused by my moderation.

My stomach growled, a reminder that if I was going to keep this up I'd need to get some food in me soon. The smells wafting from behind the bar suggested they were actually cooking back there and not simply giving commands to a food synth. I began scrolling through the menu on a data crystal embedded in our tabletop. It helped that each description was accompanied by a picture, like a Chinese restaurant, because it wasn't translating well into English. I pointed to one that looked promising. It resembled a burrito bowl. "What's this—*la'mo'a'pini*?"

"Tasty. Much popular," Chonk said. "Much spicy."

That sounded like a warning, which I of course ignored. A quick press on the menu made the item glow, then disappear. That apparently meant I'd ordered it. A few of the Thubans lifted their heavy eye ridges, either surprised or impressed. "*Fa'ka'apa!*" they shouted in unison as they lifted their drinks in another toast. "To humans!"

"To humans!" I repeated. This time I downed the whole thing.

✠ ✠ ✠

Chonk and his buddies all ordered the same dish as mine, which was their custom for welcoming new friends.

And it did feel friendly. There were a lot of "last things" to expect when I was inserted into this world, and partying with a bunch of giant warrior lizards was absolutely near the top of the list. Pleasant as Xeelix and Bjorn had been, this was the first time anyone had made me feel like part of their group. I hoped for more opportunities like this with others in the future, but right then it was a joy to feel like part of their tribe.

It wasn't long before one of the barkeeps arrived at our table, deftly balancing three hot bowls of *la'mo'a'pini* on each of her scaly arms. The dish was pungent in a good way, reminding me of peppers and cumin. Alien Tex-Mex. We each took one, and the Thubans waited on me before digging in themselves.

The *la'mo'a'pini* came in an enormous (for me) dish, definitely not sized for a human. Maybe next time I should look to see if there was a children's menu, but then I've always been one of those fortunate few who can down a double-patty chili cheeseburger with a basket of fries and burn off the excess calories by just existing.

It was a mishmash of what looked like sweet peppers, little glistening orange balls in a reddish-brown sauce over a bed of something akin to long-grained rice. It was topped with chunks of segmented meat similar to lobster.

I poked at it with a broad-handled ceramic scoop that approximated a spoon, again meant for Thuban hands. To me, it was about the size of a serving ladle. "What's this?" I asked, picking up a piece of the mystery meat.

"Pa'lop'a'le m'aka," Chonk explained. It translated as *stone bug*. "Most popular delicacy. Hearty. Easy to harvest."

Bugs? That was a mite revolting, but I was careful this time to not let my expression give me away. Plenty of human cultures used the bigger ones for meat; thankfully mine hadn't been one of them. Closest I'd ever come to eating bugs was dishing on crawdads in New Orleans once, but they're in the same family as lobsters so they don't really count.

Not wanting to be rude, I finally dug into my bug burrito bowl with a comically small bite at the end of that absurdly large spoon. My Thuban companions watched with great interest. Judging by their expectant looks, I waited for it to feel like a volcano erupting in my mouth.

It was good. *Very* good. It's a cliché that any unusual meat—possum, rattlesnake, you name it—tastes like chicken, but this did taste exactly like blackened chicken. The peppers, meat, and grains swirled together in a mix of smoky sweetness and spice, almost like curry. There was a bit of heat to it, but nothing like my new friends had warned me about.

With my taste buds and stomach ringing their approval, I dug in with gusto for another, larger bite. Around the table, my companion's golden eyes widened in surprise.

Chonk leaned back on his stool. "You like?"

"I like. Very good," I said around a mouthful of stone bug and peppers.

"Not hot?"

I wiggled my hand in a so-so gesture. "A little. I've had worse." No doubt our taste buds were attuned quite differently. What must have tasted like liquid fire to them was sweet as honey to me. If anything, I'd have liked it to be a little hotter.

They chattered amongst themselves, their quiet hissing once again confusing my translator. In the end, they acted surprised and impressed. They lifted another round of drinks in salute before digging into their own dishes. "To humans!" they shouted. "Much strong!"

It was a long night of raising toasts and telling stories. They were fascinated with my tales of Earthbound medic runs and humans in general, while I was eager to learn more about their culture. As I fished for stories of their exploits along the Union frontier, I began to pay more attention to them as individuals. Each bore scars that spoke to a dangerous life of keeping nastiness at bay, and wore crimson sashes decorated with badges which were equivalent to our military insignia. They were the apex badasses of an already badass race, the Special Forces of the Union, yet they were more interested in hearing my stories than sharing their own.

They were not unlike the soldiers I'd met back home. The ones who'd seen the worst were circumspect about it; it was the ones on the fringes who usually wouldn't shut up, like they were trying to cover for their own shortcomings. "In the rear with the gear" was how one former combat medic had explained it.

The largest Thuban, their leader, leaned against our table while nursing his drink. "You were"—the translator scrambled to interpret—"animal doctor?"

"We call them veterinarians." I waited for their translators to catch up. "My father was, and I was in school to become one." I left it there, not wanting to dig too deeply into my own story. In that, I shared some commonality with soldiers. Some things are too unpleasant to relive, no matter how much *ka'vaa'ma'loi* they put in front of me.

"Why animal school?" another asked. They seemed fascinated with the concept; veterinary medicine was not a common practice in the Union.

"Animals are important to our culture." I lifted a piece of stone bug meat from my almost empty bowl. "You raise them for food, right? Keep some as pets? Our culture thinks it's important to care for creatures who can't care for themselves."

They exchanged looks, trying to comprehend what I'd said. After a bit, I could tell the thought was revolting. "No. Animals not food. Not slaves." He pointed at my nearly empty bowl. "Harvest only non-sapient beings."

Sapient? Slaves? I recalled what Bjorn had told me about the different types of intelligence that weren't obvious to us, particularly some of Earth's sea mammals. "So you also believe that all animals harbor some form of intelligence?"

Chonk interjected, shaking his head. He put a clawed hand on my arm, and I wondered if that was a native gesture to their culture or if he was mimicking ours. "Not all. Some. Others potential. Not interfere with evolution."

I took a sip of my drink, slightly chastened. I'd loved every animal on our farm, from dogs to dairy cows. That the Union considered keeping them to be slavery was an unsettling reminder of how far we had to go before they considered Earth worthy of membership. We might never get past that particular hurdle. "I had no idea," I mumbled over the brim of my glass. "It's not like we don't take good care of them."

The lead Thuban also placed a claw on my arm, so apparently this was a native gesture to them. "Not worry. You are excellent human." He thumped his chest. "Strong heart. Take care of others. That why you . . . leave animal school? Go to human school?"

And here we were, back to that thing I didn't want to talk about. I certainly didn't feel it was due to any altruism on my part. It was more like shame. I took a slug of *ka'vaa'ma'loi.* "I left for . . . many reasons." I prevaricated, as I had with Xeelix. "Where I'm from, we had more than enough veterinarians. What we didn't have enough of were emergency medics." Which wasn't entirely true, we just hadn't had any close enough to do any good. My friends thought ditching a university veterinary program for community college paramedic school was nuts, but there are times in life when you can't live with the alternative.

Chonk gave my arm a squeeze. I tried not to wince. "This why Union recruited you. Also have not enough medics. Union growing . . . busy. Much activity. Expanding." He seemed to be looking for the right phrase. "Spread thin."

That explained things a bit. It also put Thuban activity along the Union's borders in context. Probably getting too tipsy for my own good, I pointed my drink at Chonk's buddies, happy to redirect the conversation. "Is it the same for you guys? Spread too thin?"

The subordinate Thubans looked to their leader. He set down his drink. "Union not hostile. Is how it . . . sees itself. Does not mean others not hostile."

I'd heard enough hints of problems along their frontier. "What's causing you trouble?"

He ran his tri-forked tongue across the ridges of his mouth, which I gathered meant he was considering how much to tell. "Much . . . nuisance. Raiders." The translator skipped a beat. "They not big problem. We handle."

I imagine they did, but that didn't feel like the whole story. "What else is out there, beyond the borders?" Images of marauding aliens filled my head.

"Not beyond. Within. Through. Underneath."

Underneath? I tried to picture what he was talking about. "Does the Union have trouble with . . . insurgents? Rebels inside its own borders?"

"Not only union. Whole galaxy." He spread his arms in an expansive gesture. "Universe."

Chonk's translator had spent a lot more time with me, so he tried to explain further after giving the leader an inquisitive look. The leader nodded his approval. I could see my friend was choosing his words carefully. "Are more . . . manifolds. Dimensions most races not perceive." He pointed to his snout. "We perceive. Use heat. Cannot see with eyes. See with nose."

Now I was confused. "You're at war with a race of invisible bad guys?"

"Not war. Defend. Is different."

If it involved shooting, knives, and claws, it was hard to see how that was any different. I didn't know much about military campaigns, but it seemed like one man's defense was another's offense.

He continued. "Also not invisible. Underneath."

"I'm sorry, I don't know what you mean by 'underneath.' Underneath what?"

"Underneath space. Underneath universe." He seemed frustrated, like he'd reached a point in our language barrier the translator chips couldn't overcome. "Best speak with Emissary. Can explain better."

It was a long night, but thanks to the insanely long Union standard day, there was still time to get in a few hours of sleep before the next shift. As Chonk escorted me back to my quarters like a true gentleman Thuban, I mulled over their talk of invisible troublemakers. What could be "underneath" space?

Safely back in my suite, I took several drinks of cold water to flush out the haze of Thuban tequila and collapsed into my bed. Any lingering worries I might have had evaporated as I drifted off to sleep.

⚕ **21** ⚕

"Dad? What's wrong?"

His breathing was forced. "Don't know, punkin." He steadied himself against one of the cattle pens before falling to his knees, clutching his chest.

"Lie down, Dad."

He did, in a filthy pile of straw on the barn floor. Stubborn as ever, he began fumbling for the cell phone in the pocket of his worn jeans. "Call…"

I snatched the phone from his hand. "I've got it, Dad. Just hang on." I stabbed at the keypad. It was an eternity before someone finally answered.

"911, what is your emergency?"

I frantically explained what I thought was happening. The dispatcher on the other end was infuriatingly calm, asking for name, age, et cetera. Didn't she know how critical this was? When she asked for the address, I drew a blank. What? I'd lived my whole life here! Couldn't they see my location? The words eventually fell out of my mouth.

"Do you know CPR?" the voice asked me.

"I…I do." Why the hell hadn't I thought of that myself?

I laid the phone on the ground beside him and began compressions to the beat of "Staying Alive" in my head.

I woke up screaming. Happens every time.

I came to hate that song, no matter how many times I'd use it for the exact same thing in the future, maybe because of how often I'd have to use it.

I'd worked summers as a lifeguard and they'd taught us to use that ditty in our first aid class. Had it again in EMS school. No matter how hard I tried to unlearn it and find another song with the same beat, it was still there, the memories stabbing at me like an ice pick every time I had to do chest compressions on a patient. No matter how hard I tried to suppress those memories, they always found a way back. Assholes.

The data crystal on my nightstand was blinking and chirping, growing brighter and louder with each pulse. It was time to get up. I pushed the covers aside and sat on the edge of the bed, rubbing my eyes with my palms. My head pounded, smothering the lingering memories with a killer hangover. Despite doing my best to pace myself last night, Thuban tequila packed a wallop. On the bright side, I'd made a bunch of new friends and that was worth the headache. Being small even by human standards, it felt like victory to be accepted by a group of reptilian warriors almost twice my size.

After going through my morning bathroom routine—and yes, they'd provided human-compatible plumbing fixtures—I pulled on a fresh set of coveralls and turned on the food synth. "Coffee, black. Toast, plain. Electrolyte juice." When the little door slid open, I had a fresh cup of hot coffee, perfectly done toast, and a glass of something that looked like liquified algae.

I picked up the glass and studied it with a healthy dose of skepticism. "Is this stuff compatible with humans?" I asked the machine. It was the first time I'd tried talking to it.

A pleasant voice answered. "Affirmative. It is formulated for your individual physiology, augmented with known human athletic beverages."

"Can you at least change the coloring? Because this looks gross."

"Affirmative. Please replace your glass and select your preference."

I did as the machine said. "Orange juice, please." The little door slid shut and reopened to reveal what looked and tasted like a fresh-squeezed glass of OJ. I gulped it down, and by the time it was finished I was already feeling better. If there was a way to reproduce this extraterrestrial miracle hangover cure on Earth, it'd be worth a fortune. It also made the coffee much more enjoyable. With electrolytes in balance and a clear head, I left for work.

⌗ ⌗ ⌗

The hangar swarmed with activity, more so than usual for a shift change. I was assigned to bay five again with Xeelix, and the warning beacons were already flashing. Our ship sat atop maintenance lifts as a team of Grays and insectoids scurried underneath, mounting a long cylinder to the hull as Needa watched. She seemed particularly interested in the attachment points. Elastic webbing hung from one of the outrigger pods.

Xeelix came over to meet me with Bjorn in tow. "You are early. Excellent. We have been assigned to what could be a challenging run."

I hiked my bag up my shoulder. "I'm always up for a challenge." That's always easy to say when you have no idea what you're about to get into. I looked up at Bjorn. "You're coming with us?"

"This will be a "big job," as you might say. Dr. Xeelix wanted an extra medic aboard."

That got my attention. Bring it on. "Cool. Where are we going?"

They eyed each other. "A planet called Aegir, in the Ran system," Bjorn explained. "Your astronomers named it Epsilon Eridani."

"Okay . . ." I said warily, not sure why this was such a big deal. "What makes it so challenging?"

Being our instructor, Xeelix stepped in. "Recall your studies of Union civilizations. Aegir is a gas giant, the only planet in the system. The upper strata of its atmosphere is compatible with organic life. Its lower regions become exponentially denser, with a high concentration of sulfuric acid. The Aegirans will be unlike any species, sapient or animal, that you have encountered. They are quite large, and quite light."

Aegirans were "floaters," massive gas bags that lived in the upper reaches of their planet's atmosphere. They looked like jellyfish the size of hot air balloons and moved about on essentially the same principles, living off of microorganisms in the upper atmosphere. Like whales back home, Aegirans were one of those intelligent species which were physically incapable of manipulating their environment, and so were entirely dependent on Union technology for anything beyond scooping up food in the air. "I remember. They're new to the Union, right?"

"Quite so," Bjorn said. "A pair of Emissaries made first contact with them only twelve annums ago, and they have been Union members for less than two. Construction of an outpost at their world is still underway. Currently there are no medical services available."

I remembered that from class too. The Aegirans were so massive that we couldn't keep species-specific gear in the outriggers; they had to be attached externally. We turned at the sound of a pneumatic hiss as our ambulance was lowered back to the deck, loaded up with the custom gear we'd need.

Needa signaled to Xeelix, who motioned us to get aboard. "I will brief you on the patient's situation once we are underway. Come, we must hurry."

As I stowed my gear, Bjorn hung an extra set of exposure suits in the aft lockers. He closed them up and sat in the seat beside mine. "There is one more thing which you must know." He met my eyes apologetically, and I wondered where he was going with this. "We are the closest treatment facility, though Aegir is still quite distant." He looked ahead at Needa's pilot station. "It will require us to hasten our travel."

"So?"

Bjorn seemed chastened, as if he realized he'd been hiding something. "I do not believe we have adequately prepared you for the effects of time dilation."

The low-frequency hum of the gravity drive began to spool up around us, and I felt our ship begin to lift off. Outside, warning beacons pulsed as our bay emptied itself to the vacuum, jetting us out into space. The drive's hum increased to an intensity I hadn't experienced before. My innards could feel it moving us along.

Ahead, the star field had once again warped into concentric rings of blurry starlight. It was different this time; everything outside had taken on a distinct bluish hue. Remember my rock-in-a-pond analogy from that first time leaving Earth? This looked more like a boulder had been thrown ahead of us.

I was passingly familiar with the concept of relative time, if only through the dumbed-down explanations from Discovery Channel programs. It was the kind of thing I'd watch at three in the morning to decompress after a late shift. "I don't understand. I thought we couldn't go faster than light?"

"We cannot, though the effect becomes more pronounced as

relative velocity increases." He looked to Xeelix. "Our vessel will be traveling at its maximum rated dilation factor, correct?"

Xeelix nodded silently, and Bjorn continued. "Our relative velocity will be fifty percent of light speed, which equates to a time dilation factor of roughly fifteen percent. For each hour that passes in our time reference, close to an hour and ten minutes will pass back at the station."

He'd helpfully put it in human time reference, but I got the point. Add in the Union's longer hour, and it would feel even more pronounced. I'm ashamed to admit this impressed me in purely selfish terms—every hour we spent in transit would be an extra ten minutes back at the barn, which meant our shifts would be over sooner. Cool. Maybe another trip to Wayside with Chonk after work? My stomach was growling already, needing something more substantial than a hangover breakfast.

Xeelix had been listening patiently until now, and snapped me out of my contemplations of relativity and stone bug curry. "If you are comfortable with Byyruumn's explanation of relative time, I will brief you on our dispatch order." He tapped on a nearby panel and files appeared on the sidewall screens. "Our patient is an adolescent Aegiran, approximately twenty annums old. Her parents report that she is having difficulty breathing and cannot maintain directional control. The symptoms began after she strayed too deeply into their lower atmosphere." He prompted me for an initial assessment.

"Poor gas exchange and impaired directional tendrils . . . sulfur poisoning?"

He seemed satisfied. "I suspect so as well. Please continue."

I didn't want to mess this up, and so pulled up the files on Aegiran physiology on my crystal. Living in an environment just above the clouds of sulfuric acid that dominated its lower atmosphere, mature Aegirans were supposed to be resistant to its effects. Her rhopalium, the sensory organs that dangled from the lip of her outer hood, could have been damaged as well. That would also explain the loss of directional control. "They say anything about chemical burns?"

"Unknown, but I suspect we will find some damage to her hood and subumbrella at the very least. Twenty annums is a young adolescent. She likely has not had enough exposure to trace amounts of acid for her epidermis to develop the protective callus of an adult."

"If she's having trouble exchanging gas, it sounds like she ingested a lot of it."

"Agreed. What would you consider to be a proper course of treatment?"

"She'll need a broad-spectrum counteragent." I thought back to my own training from poison control back home. The mantra they'd taught us was *the key to pollution is dilution*. "They're oxygen-breathers. We'll need to administer O_2." I tried to imagine what that would look like with an airborne jellyfish that could be bigger than our ship. "We don't pack that kind of gear."

"We do not," Xeelix confirmed. "Recall your training. We have other methods which you may find unconventional."

I thought of the big metallic cylinder mounted beneath our ship. I pointed at the deck. "That's another anal probe down there, isn't it?" The Grays sure did like their shiny suppositories.

"For an Aegiran, the distinction is moot. Recall their central orifices perform both intake and elimination functions."

I suppose it helped that Aegirans didn't have taste buds, but... *yuck*. "The probe's full of nanobots, right? They'll disperse and distribute the counteragent."

"Correct. In this case, the probe also contains catalysts to dissociate its component compounds. The patient's initial reaction will be unpleasant. We must keep her immobilized in the restraining net Needa rigged between our outboard pods while the reaction proceeds. It will become messy, as you say."

"She'll end up expelling the hydrogen and sulfur." Thank goodness for those exposure suits. It was going to get smelly. Explosively so, if we weren't careful. "Those compounds could ignite, too."

Xeelix fixed me with his black almond eyes. He was prodding me to think through it more, but it was especially unnerving coming from a nonhuman.

"This is going to be traumatic for her," I continued. "We'll need to monitor for signs of shock."

"All correct." Xeelix pointed a long, delicate finger at the dispatch briefing on our sidewall screen. "The entanglement receiver only transmitted the patient's condition and location. We must deduce the rest from what we know of them. Are there other factors we should consider?"

He was talking about cultural differences now, which I'd overlooked on yesterday's run. "Aegirans are herd creatures. The scene could be crowded. Her parents will be on us like stink on a stick."

Xeelix looked momentarily caught short. His translator must have skipped at that last one. "The parents will indeed be watching closely and will no doubt be upset by their child's reaction to the catalyst treatment. Considering their size, that could present an additional hazard. Is there anything else?"

I searched my memory for what we'd learned of the Aegirans. "We won't be able to communicate with the patient. They don't take translator implants until adulthood."

He seemed satisfied now. "Very good. Melanie, this will be an excellent opportunity for you to apply your veterinary training." He looked to Bjorn. "I would prefer you to be our interlocutor with the parents while we perform the procedure. Will this be acceptable to you?"

Bjorn nodded. "Of course, Doctor."

We entered orbit around a massive planet completely shrouded in clouds which stretched around its circumference in bright bands of yellow and white. I reminded myself that it was almost all clouds. Hovering high above one side of the planet was a semicircular smear curving across space.

I must have been gaping. Bjorn leaned in close and pointed at the half-ring. "That used to be one of Aegir's moons. It was torn apart by tidal forces several hundred annums ago. In time it will become a ring system, like your planet Saturn's."

It might be spectacular in the future but right now it looked threatening, like a crescent poised to slice the planet in two.

Up front at the pilot's station, Needa tapped at her console and a swooping curve of light illuminated our path. "I have located the herd and plotted an entry path to their position," she announced. "Please remain in your acceleration couches."

I watched Bjorn tuck his arms and legs into their rests and

followed his lead. "The upper level winds reach several hundred kilometers per hour," he said. "Wind shear will be considerable." Apparently there was a limit to what the inertial dampeners could absorb. I didn't have to know much about meteorology to understand that rivers of near-supersonic air changing direction as we passed through them could make the ride down hair-raising.

To be honest it wasn't much worse than airliners back home. There were a few jolts and sudden dips, which must have been more unsettling to my companions being used to the dampeners shielding them from such unpleasantness. I chuckled to myself that maybe all this technology had made them soft.

Pillars of sulfur-yellow clouds swept past as Needa piloted us deeper into the atmosphere. Ahead we could see a swarm of white specks moving in a gentle circle. She began to slow down. "I have the herd in sight," she said.

Xeelix stood to lean over her. "Have you identified the family?"

She swept at her holographic display and isolated a trio of the white specks at the center of the swarm. We'd slowed down to the point where we were now hovering at a distance. "There. It appears the herd has moved to protect them."

Xeelix made an almost-human *tsk* sound. He was perturbed. "That is . . . not optimal. Can you maneuver clear of them?"

"It will be difficult."

Damn. I'd seen this before back home. Crowds of hysterical concerned onlookers getting in the way of the cops and rescue squads; happened way too often. Especially if there were kids involved. One more trait that seemed universal. "Xeelix, can you communicate with them at this distance—telepathically, I mean?"

His eyes were closed, and he held up a hand to quiet me. "I am attempting that now. Please wait."

Chastened, I turned to Bjorn and jerked my head at the exposure suits. "While he's doing that, we'd best get prepped."

We pulled on skintight temperature-regulating garments before slipping on the environment suits. Other than the hood and respirator pack, this gear wasn't like our sleek vacuum suits; these were meant for keeping nastiness out, not for holding air in. Loose-fitting and in an attention-grabbing shade of orange, they were still better than the "bunny suits" I'd worn for hazmat accidents back on Earth. Once the coveralls were on and the helmets pressurized, Bjorn and I checked each other for tight seals. He gave me a quick thumbs-up which almost made me feel like I was on a run back on Earth.

Almost.

Xeelix must have been able to warn the floating rubberneckers away, because he was hurrying back to join us and get into his own suit as Needa cautiously brought us down through the top of the circling herd. Outside it looked like a hot-air balloon festival, that is if the balloons were giant jellyfish.

Once Xeelix was suited up, he led us to the main doors and watched as we each secured ourselves to restraints in the ceiling. There was a warning tone and the side doors opened to a howling wind that buffeted the inside of our ship.

I held to my safety tether and peeked over the sill, spotting our patient for the first time. We were maybe a hundred meters above her now, and she was almost as big as our ship. Her parents hovered nearby. Even more massive, their undulating opalescent hoods streaked with pink. They were taking turns nudging her up higher to keep her from falling deeper into the atmosphere. I'd never seen Aegirans before, but I'd sure seen my share of exhausted parents. Mom and Dad were running out of steam, and their girl was running out of time. Her color was badly off, a sickly gray pallor. The younger Aegirans were supposed to be a healthy pinkish white; my book learning was backed up by the young ones I saw circulating amongst the herd, now at a safe distance. Out of curiosity I looked beyond our patient, down to the planet's surface.

Yeah, that was a mistake. There was no surface, just pillars of clouds that stretched down into a depthless dark. Lightning flashed miles below, like flashbulbs buried beneath cotton. Farther down, somewhere there was a "surface" of solidified gases, but first you'd have to get through the clouds of sulfuric acid.

I froze. My hold on the tether had turned into a death grip, to the point I could feel it digging into my hand through my gloves.

Xeelix reached out to slap his hand against the side of our ship and a pair of railings folded out from its skin. Oblivious to the danger my own nervous system was screaming about, he grabbed hold and swung himself onto the outrigger pod.

I tried to follow his lead, fighting the urge to look down. The wind buffeted me as I hooked an arm through the railing, desperate to stay attached to our ship. Xeelix showed no such concern, holding on with one hand as he watched Needa maneuver us closer to the ailing Aegiran. He fully trusted his harness, and I wished I could've been so confident. Did I mention I'm terrified of heights?

I heard Needa's voice in my helmet. "Stand by. Deploying collection net." I stole a look down—ignore the depths, watch the gear—and the elastic mesh ballooned out beneath our ship. "Are you ready?"

There was an edge to Xeelix's voice as he looked at me. "Ready."

Needa moved us in slowly. The poor kid was clearly struggling, her skin quivering erratically compared to her parent's graceful, measured pulsations through the air. As we moved over top of her, the poor kid collapsed onto the net and settled into its mesh. Resting on her side, our patient expelled a torrent of yellow fumes. Her body was trying to reject the toxins, but it wasn't working fast enough.

Xeelix lowered himself into the restraining net. I followed cautiously, fighting to keep my handhold and footing against the howling wind. I had to close my eyes and let go. It was only a short drop, not even a second in time, but my stomach heaved as if I'd jumped off a building.

The mesh held and I heaved a sigh of relief. Our footing was surprisingly firm, where I'd expected to feel like we were trying to work on a trampoline.

I took a deep breath to collect myself. We were here, we weren't falling into an acidic abyss, and we had a patient who needed us to be on our game right freaking now. EMS work meant that sometimes you had to wade into some scary shit to get to your patients. This was no different, even if it was next-level terrifying. Time to get to work.

I began setting the transducer discs in place. Soon a full picture of her inner workings appeared in my visor. The graph of vitals looked dangerously low—not that I had Aegiran vitals memorized, but the traces had a helpful reference baseline hovering above them. The wheezing and low O_2 saturation confirmed what we could tell by her gray pallor and fluttering hood.

Xeelix moved around to her rear, tenderly probing and prodding. He lifted a flap of tissue-thin skin to look beneath her outer hood. "It is as suspected. Her vital signs and gas exchange are consistent with respiratory acidosis." He moved to her opposite side and began unlocking the probe. "Come. We must work quickly."

Bjorn's voice cut in. "The parents wish to know what you intend to do."

Xeelix answered for us. "Please tell them we are administering the nanobot counteragent. It will work quickly."

I left the transducers in place and followed Xeelix's movements, snapping open the probe's remaining restraints. The silvery, meter-long probe fell into our hands, light as a feather. Together we carried it around behind the wheezing Aegiran. This was the touchy part, as inserting rectal probes tends to be. Her single orifice winked open and shut with each labored breath.

Xeelix eyed her rhythm and patted the air with one hand, cautioning me. "We don't want to force this. Stay in time with her." We waited through at least half a dozen cycles before he tightened his grip around the probe. "Next inhalation. Ready . . . *now*."

Her orifice opened, expelling air, and we swiftly guided the probe in as she inhaled. She convulsed reflexively, fighting to expel it. Xeelix didn't flinch, coaxing it along while I held it steady. "Hold it in place. Good. Good."

In my visor, the probe's business end was already getting to work. I could see it dissolve inside her, billions of nanobots dispersing themselves throughout her body and getting to work separating the ingested sulfur and hydrogen. As she gasped for air, we shoved it the rest of the way in.

Her body was wracked with spasms, her hood rippling with convulsions as the probe did its work. Xeelix motioned me to move away as he did the same. "She will feel like she is drowning at first. The probe is momentarily blocking her airway while it disintegrates."

I watched as the car-sized gasbag between us shuddered. "Pulling all that hydrogen and sulfur out of her system isn't going to feel any better."

"It will not. But once the catalyzing reaction is complete, she will expel the toxins quickly."

Kids had a way of finding creative new ways to try and kill themselves, and this was no different. I don't know how many times I'd had to administer ipecac or help pump some poor kid's stomach after getting into something they shouldn't have. Sometimes the parents didn't have any business raising kids, but more often than not the little rugrats had found a way around Mom and Dad's best efforts. I turned to see this one's parents hovering on either side of us, their blimp-sized bodies casting a shadow over us. They were the ultimate "helicopter parents."

My visor lit up with activating nanobots, like a swarm of fireflies had infested the Aegiran's body. "Get ready," Xeelix said. In a single wrenching, convulsive burst, our patient soon expelled a stream of lemon yellow gas in the loudest, longest fart I'd ever heard in my life. The hassle of wearing an environment suit felt like a pretty good tradeoff because I could only imagine what all that sulfur smelled like.

Her paper-thin skin began to regain its color within minutes, the gray pallor fading into a healthy pinkish white. This was mirrored by her vitals creeping back into normal range. I sighed with relief. "I think she's going to be okay."

"Her gas exchange is greatly improved," Xeelix said. "But the tendrils of her rhopalium did sustain chemical burns, as I feared."

On instinct, I gently stroked our still-quivering patient to try and calm her. "Anything we can do for that?"

"Not here. If the Union outpost was complete, we could call for a medium-lift transport and place her in rehabilitative care." He looked across at me. "But do you believe that to be necessary for this patient?"

I wasn't used to having to make that sort of call as a medic. It was another sign that GU work would be a lot different, closer to being a vet in the field. If we were out on a long run like this, far removed from Med Corps facilities, triage would be part of the package. Here I was, standing in a net suspended miles above a churning stew of toxic clouds, and my mentor was asking me to decide if our patient needed neurological rehab.

This time I had to consult the implant files. The answer came surprisingly quickly. "It shouldn't be necessary, in fact. Adolescent rhopalia can regenerate, but she needs to stay away from clouds of toxic vapor." Which seemed easy enough, but I was learning it was a universal constant that kids were wildly unpredictable.

Bjorn interjected. "Would you like me to communicate this to the parents?"

"Please do," Xeelix said. "Tell them the catalyst treatment has expunged the toxins. Her visual and tactile senses will be impaired for a time due to chemical burns, but they will return to normal as her tendrils regenerate. Also, please have them tell her we are waiting for her system to expel the nanobots. When that process is complete, we will free her from the restraining net."

I spent our remaining time at Aegir watching the swirl of straw-colored clouds that surrounded us, spiraling into a bottomless well of condensates hundreds of miles below. The herd had gathered closer, circling us and the parents in a protective swarm. I rested my head against the netting and drew my knees up, studying how they moved.

They floated about us in silence, hundreds of them gliding past in wide circles above, around and below. Their hoods would contract and expand, inhaling and expelling the microbe-rich gas in an act of both feeding and breathing. Bjorn had explained that at this altitude, oxygen became a lifting gas like hydrogen or helium was on Earth. And while the Aegirans were enormous creatures, their low mass density kept them afloat exactly like the hot-air balloons they resembled when expelling gas.

It was hard to see them as intelligent beings at first but as we waited with our patient, my translator implant began to interpret more of their language. After a time I could begin to hear multiple conversations, most of them marveling at our ship and the odd-looking beings tending to one of their wayward youth. Apparently diving into the depths of Aegir's atmosphere was a constant game the younger ones played. The parents didn't exactly encourage it, but I learned from listening to them that it was also something of a rite of passage. As the herd circled us, I realized their natural buoyancy meant that it would take some effort to dive down into the denser layers.

I suppose it paid to understand your environment, but this seemed like playing with fire.

A chime sounded in my helmet, drawing me out of my reverie. "The last of the nanobots are expelled," I said, and stood up to make one last check of our patient. "Vital signs are stable. Cardiac and respiratory rhythms are holding in normal range. I think she's ready to go."

"Agreed," Xeelix said. He began stepping around to join me, pulling his safety tether behind him. "Patient is stable and ready to release," he reported.

"Understood," Bjorn answered from above. "Advising the parents now."

It was hard to hear, but I could pick out a series of low snorts and puffs. The young Aegiran responded with a jolt, ready to get out of here. "Steady, girl," I said, placing a calming hand on her. "You'll be on your way soon." I knew she didn't have an implant, but it felt like the thing to do. I was rewarded by a thin tentacle wriggling out from beneath her hood to tickle my leg. I won't lie, it was a little freaky, but it felt like she was saying "thanks."

Xeelix climbed back onto the outrigger and waved for me to follow. I patted her tentacle before hopping back onto our ship. "Now go, and behave yourself."

We grabbed the handholds and watched as Needa released the net. It gave way and retracted into the opposite outrigger, and the young Aegiran quickly righted herself. Her hood expanded to its full diameter, easily as big as our ship. She sank, then with one smooth contraction, she expelled air and shot away to join her parents who closed ranks around her before they all jetted off to join the herd. Without being told, the mass of floaters dispersed so we could make our way clear.

Xeelix gestured for me to climb back aboard, then followed me in. He pressed the handrails and they retracted into the hull. "Safe aboard. Restraints secure." I felt the caress of the gravity drive spinning up, and we were soon rising above the cloud tops.

⚕ 22 ⚕

Safely back in the hangar, as we hopped out of our ship I noticed the force fields were still activated around us. "We were working in a toxic environment," Xeelix said as a decontaminant boom was lowered into place above us, a larger version of the ones we used to sterilize our ambulance's innards. "The Aegirans have evolved with a natural resistance to the caustic compounds in their upper atmosphere. We, of course, have not."

The bay was soon awash with brilliant light. We stood with our legs spread and arms outstretched as beams of sterilizing energy reached into every nook and cranny. When the boom was finished with us, we took the extra step of shucking off our environment suits and stuffing them into a disposal bin to be incinerated. We were left standing in our coveralls when the force fields shut off.

Our crystals chirped in unison and Xeelix pulled his out of a hip pocket. "We are off duty for the next two hours. I believe the human term is a 'lunch break.'"

I slapped my hands together, a little too enthusiastically, but it'd been at least six hours since my breakfast of dry toast and coffee. "That sounds awesome. Where do we go?"

"I intend to remain here with Needa. Our needs are minimal. But you are free to find sustenance wherever you wish, as long as you can return here on time."

When he put it like that, it sounded like foraging. But I was also in the mood for a little foraging. "The last actual meal I had was over in Thuban territory. It was good, but they really like their *ka'vaa'ma'loi.*"

Xeelix looked at Bjorn, who arched an eyebrow. "You were with Thubans? In their sector?"

"Chonk took me to a neat little place in their corner of the dome. Can't remember the full pronunciation, so I just call it Wayside. We hooked up with some of his buddies who were back from border patrol. It was fun."

A flash of recognition crossed Bjorn's face. He must have known the place. "I'm impressed. Thubans are a stern people. They aren't known for welcoming outsiders. You no doubt made a good impression."

"That's all thanks to Chonk being a good host. If I'd wandered in there by myself it probably would've been a different story." My Thuban friend was different from the rest, which was the whole reason he was training with us. I looked down and guiltily dug my toe into the decking. "I may have had a little too much fun for my own good."

Bjorn laughed. "Of that, there is also no doubt." He placed a hand on my shoulder. "I will take you somewhere less lively. Xeelix, I promise to have us back in plenty of time."

We took a lift back up to the biodome and stepped out into a fragrant orchard. I recognized it right away as the Emissaries' sector, though we appeared to be in a different corner than the one I'd briefly explored weeks ago. In the distance I recognized my own apartment block.

Paths of smooth stone wound their way among the orderly rows of meticulously pruned fruit trees. This end of the orchard was bounded by towering conifers, like something you'd find in northern California or Oregon. It was gorgeous, but at this point I was starving for real food. "I hate to sound ungrateful, but are we here just to pick fruit?"

Bjorn smiled knowingly, as if he'd been keeping a secret. "Not at all, though you are welcome to. It could make for a nice appetizer." He pointed to a nearby tree, heavily laden with purplish peach-sized globes. I pulled one off its stem and turned it in my hands. It was firm and waxy, like a fresh plum. "What is this called?"

"In your English, the best translation is 'sallawine.' Which I know doesn't mean anything, but it sounds appealing."

Right now a withered pear would be appealing, so I took a bite.

The flavor started out tart, like a lemon, then turned sweet. It was like a blend of plums and peaches finished off with a dash of cinnamon, all in one bite. My eyes popped. "Bjorn," I said between munches, "this is *fantastic*. I've been dying for fresh fruit, and this is like every single one I love rolled into one."

"I am pleased to hear that. These began as surviving species from our home world, and have been cultivated over many generations to produce the variety you see here."

I looked up and down the lengths of the orchard. "Is everything here okay to pick?"

"As long as you only take what you can consume in one sitting, you are welcome to try any varieties we grow. As they are bred for our race, they are also compatible with human metabolism. You'll find numerous varieties of fruits and nuts, perhaps comparable to what is grown in your California."

I laughed. "California has plenty of fruits and nuts, all right. Just not the kind you're thinking of."

The joke almost went over his head. "That region can be rather . . . eccentric. Though it is quite scenic." He paused. "Much like our home world."

"Sorry. Didn't mean to be a downer."

"There's no need to apologize. You will learn that over cosmic timescales, such events are inevitable. We were fortunate to have formed alliances with the Reticulans. It is their ingenuity which made all of this possible." He looked up to the dome curving far above us, then ahead, deeper into the orchard. "Come, we have a place I believe you will enjoy."

In the center of the Emissary's grove was a round building that sparkled like polished chrome, encircled by large picture windows. It reminded me of a space-age diner. It was telling that all of the quaint little footpaths through their gardens seemed to end up here.

Inside, tables jutted out from the walls with chairs arranged neatly around them. And it smelled exactly like a good diner. Like the Thubans' Wayside dive, they were doing actual cooking here. We took a seat at the nearest open table. There were plenty of those; apparently we were well past rush hour here. A single pair of Emissaries sat at the opposite end of the circular restaurant and waved at Bjorn.

"This looks great. Like something from back home. How come no one ever showed me this place before?"

"Your induction schedule was rather compressed and we didn't want to overwhelm you. It was also feared that introducing you to anything too familiar would hamper your assimilation into our wider culture." He studied me as I opened up the menu crystal embedded in the table. "However, I now see that may have been a mistake."

I thought about my earlier wanderings and that night out with Chonk. "Maybe not. It did a lot of good to broaden my horizons. If I'd known about this place right away, I might've never made it out." Admittedly, I could see spending a lot more time here after hours.

The menu looked even more human-friendly than I expected, but the translation was still kind of wonky. I pointed to one that looked tasty, though the description was disgusting. "'Flesh and spawn'? What the hell is that?"

"It's steak and eggs."

That was more like it. "They have steak and eggs? Where do they come from?" I tapped in my selection, too excited to wait for an answer.

Bjorn ordered the same, then gestured toward a distant corner of the grove. "The eggs are collected from a hatchery in the eastern quadrant of our sector, from a species similar to your quail. We do not raise fowl for production; they are what you'd call 'free range' animals."

"Even better," I said. You could always taste the difference. I was never a fan of grocery store eggs, but the ones we used to collect on the farm were delicious. "What about the meat? You guys don't raise cattle for slaughter."

The corners of his mouth turned down at the thought. "We do not. The meat is replicated from bovine DNA and grown in vats."

"You guys took samples from cows..." I wondered how they might have differed from ours when the realization hit me. "You stole them from us!"

Bjorn sounded embarrassed. "It was a very limited quantity, I assure you. Strictly for tissue sampling and DNA extraction. Early efforts were a bit messy, I'm afraid."

"So all those wild stories of cattle mutilations..."

"All true, unfortunately. The tales you are familiar with were the result of misaligned collection fields. Those incidents occurred early in the project, by insufficiently vetted harvesters. The remaining cattle were returned safely."

So the hyper-advanced Galactic Union occasionally made mistakes, too. It was one more bit of trivia that made them seem a little less Utopian and a little more accessible. It also made me even more wary of force fields.

It wasn't long before our food arrived, which I enthusiastically wolfed down. It might've been unladylike, but it was also the most authentic taste of home I'd had since leaving Earth. However screwed up their little cattle-wrangling project had been, the results were yummy. I felt human again.

We had four and a half hours left on our shift when we stepped off the lift. One look told me the Med Corps was having a busy day, as nearly half of the ambulance bays were empty. Xeelix was waiting for us, sitting at a cluster of tables along the back wall of the hangar and sipping from a bottled nutrient drink. I plopped down across from him with a full tummy and happy heart.

"Better now?" he asked.

"Absolutely. A good meal can work wonders when you're running low."

He seemed a little displeased, once again fixing me with his black eyes. "Quite so, particularly for humanoid metabolism."

I gave him a sideways look, and noticed Bjorn had turned away uncomfortably. "Is something wrong?"

He sat upright and pushed his bottle aside. "Your performance on our last run was ... hesitant. I believe you were hampered by your escapades with the Thubans last night, though I am also willing to allow certain accommodations for the extreme environment."

I sank in my chair, chastened. He was right on both counts. I hadn't set out to get hammered, but that's how it goes sometimes. I'd rationalized that the GU's lengthy standard day would give me plenty of time to recover. It hadn't helped that I was also terrified of heights, and hovering among the cloud tops of a massive planet that was nothing *but* clouds had nearly paralyzed me. "You're right. No more drinking on work nights."

Thankfully, Xeelix nodded in a gesture that signaled he was ready to move on. "That is wise. You would also be wise to remember that you are one of very few humans in the Union. You will not be able to metabolize most of the nutrients our component races thrive on, and I do not wish to see you harmed. In this case, you were lucky. Thuban diets are largely compatible with humans."

There it was again—other humans. He'd come right out and said I *wasn't* alone out here. Now that we'd addressed last night's binge, I wasn't going to let this go. I crossed my arms and leaned across the table. "Back up a second. You mentioned 'very few' humans." I wagged a finger between him and Bjorn. "That's not the first time you guys have hinted there might be others besides me. How many, and where are they?"

The two exchanged a glance, and Xeelix gestured for Bjorn to explain. My Nordic friend shifted uncomfortably. "As you know, we have been covertly observing your world for a very long time."

"Not covertly enough," I interjected, a little too tartly.

"The human mind, particularly its capacity for storing memories, is quite resilient. More so than many Union races, in fact." Bjorn pursed his lips. "Memory suppression has been challenging."

"I'd say so, judging by all the stories. Some of them go back decades."

"Centuries, in fact. The last century in particular has been quite eventful, which of course means our survey craft are more likely to be detected. As time progresses, such events will be carefully 'stage managed,' as you might say."

"Let me guess—a slow drip to prepare us for the Big Reveal when you think we're ready?"

"Exactly. There have been some individual humans, however, who expressed interest in becoming Union residents after their encounters with us." He paused, looking away as if he were embarrassed. "This was quite some time ago. We were not as discerning as we should have been. Some seemed grateful to be free of 'Earthly' concerns and happily lived out their days in the Union. A few found they could not cope and had to be confined to Med Corps sanitariums for their own well-being until we could safely return them. One in particular has thrived."

"Who?"

"He goes by 'Gideon,' though I do not know his full name. He has managed to amass a great fortune and chooses to remain private." Bjorn's words were clipped, as if he could taste their bitterness.

I rolled my eyes. "Ah. One of *those* guys. I'm surprised you let him stay."

My friend's lips drew thin. "Gideon found a way to make himself essential, inserting himself into most aspects of commerce and administration. Apparently he was quite good at this on Earth."

"And so found an opportunity to expand his sphere of influence," I finished for him.

Xeelix interjected. "At first, Gideon proved himself to be quite valuable. He was particularly gifted at logistics—he could anticipate problems and visualize solutions in ways that eluded us. He also displayed an acute interest in developing mass-produced, modular energy sources; I suspect in order to eventually introduce to Earth."

I could sense how this had played out. "Introduction" could turn to "exploitation" in short order. Vision and ingenuity can bring great wealth, which often translates to great power. Too many humans had shown themselves to be incapable of handling both without turning into complete assholes.

Don't get me wrong, I'm no commie. I'd rather live in a world that allows Scrooge McDuck levels of wealth instead of one that pretends they can control it without dragging everyone else down. No doubt some people accumulate too much for their own good, and most of the time they're just gaudy. It's when the super-rich leverage their wealth to keep others out of the game that I start having a problem. Judging by my companion's reactions, the GU felt the same way.

I was about to ask where in the galaxy this Gideon person had set up shop, when the klaxon blared overhead: "Alert bay five, alert bay five. Prepare for immediate departure."

⚕ 23 ⚕

Almost as if the Universe had intended to offer a counterpoint to our contemplations of wealth and privilege, this run offered a glimpse of the Union's decidedly less wealthy and privileged. I was about to be thrust into this alien utopia's seedy underbelly, the kind of place that might spawn either hard-boiled detective novels or tedious "message" fiction.

We'd been called to a colony ship, an ancient one by Bjorn's reckoning. It had been in transit for centuries, built long before gravity drives and almost-light-speed travel. Technology had leaped ahead generations by the time the travelers were even halfway to their destination, yet they'd elected to stick with the bucket of bolts they'd first set out in.

Imagine this: The Mayflower sets sail for the New World, but instead of a two-month trip, it takes a couple of centuries. Entire generations are born, grow old, and die aboard ship, all the while being isolated by thousands of miles of ocean in all directions. Meanwhile, the Native Americans in New England and the Viking descendants in Newfoundland grow into industrial societies and become friendly. They eventually set out across the ocean in steamships and come across the decrepit Mayflower somewhere in the North Atlantic. They offer to bring its passengers and crew aboard their steamers for a quick, comfortable trip to America, but the hardheaded Pilgrims decline. We'd like to stick to the plan, thank you very much, but we're happy to partake of some of that wonderful food and medicine you offer.

Imagine being aware the rest of the world has leapfrogged ahead of you, from sailing ships to steam power to internal combustion to nuclear power, and you elect to not participate. It sounded like bad reality-TV fodder: Space Puritans. Amish Aliens. But maybe it is such a cultural shock that it'd be natural to decline that first-class upgrade out of simple fear of the unknown.

It seemed so unlikely in this present case, yet there they were. They'd been at the nuclear stage when they'd left their home star, Tau Ceti, centuries earlier on a quest to settle the galaxy. They'd had the ability back then to identify stars with promising worlds and build ships big and powerful enough to move hundreds of people, along with the ability to grow food. Technology shouldn't have been a stumbling block for a species capable of building something this big.

And it was indeed a *big* ship. It was made of six spheres, each one nearly a half-mile in diameter and strung end-to-end, like beads on a necklace. At one end was an enormous device that resembled a mechanical tulip; Bjorn told me it was a fusion rocket engine. Way more advanced than anything humans had ever built, it was still antiquated tech to the Union.

We were close now. Every viewscreen was filled with the Cetan colony ship. I still didn't know a lot about spaceships, but I knew old and worn-out when I saw it and this one had been put through the wringer. The skin of its six spherical hulls had been battered by slamming into cosmic dust at high speed and were bleached white by centuries of solar radiation. I was afraid we'd break it if Needa took us in too close.

I hovered behind her at the pilot's station. "I can see that tub wasn't built with us in mind. How do we get aboard?"

Needa pulled up a diagram of the colony ship. "This is not the first time the Medical Corps has been called to this vessel. They have a landing bay which is large enough to accommodate us, in the central sphere." She pointed to a series of rectangular openings along the sphere's equator. "Their terminal guidance is antiquated. But it works."

I had no doubt that "antiquated" to Needa would be wildly advanced for a human pilot. Outside, the stack of battered white spheres rotated as she pivoted us to align with an open landing bay. Yellow light shone from within, and we were soon inside.

The bay was more like a big garage or airplane hangar on Earth: a little messy, with instructions painted on walls and safety lanes painted on the floor. Equipment cabinets and massive bottles of compressed gasses lined its walls. Wheeled carts trailing power cables and air hoses were scattered around the bay. It all smelled faintly of lubricating oil.

If that all sounds very human, the Cetans themselves resembled us closely enough to give me the willies. They had elongated limbs and torsos, with exaggeratedly large frontal and parietal bones—in essence, big heads for big brains. The Cetans were no dummies, so I had to accept they had their reasons for declining the Union's superior technology.

The call was for what, in humans, superficially sounded like a nuisance condition that didn't need an ambulance run: fungal infection. Xeelix informed me that this was not going to be a simple case of crotch rot or athlete's foot. They called it *phoetima*, which roughly translates into "zombie fungus."

It worked similarly to the cordyceps fungus that could infect certain insects, taking over the host's bodily functions as it hollowed them out from inside. Eventually it would kill off the host and use its body's decomposition to disperse more spores. It was dreadful to see, even in a spider. And I hated spiders.

We all wore environment suits again; there'd never been any such infection in Xeelix's species, but he wasn't taking any chances with me or Bjorn.

We'd been led from the landing bay to a lift that ran through the center of the sphere, leading to decks that grew smaller as we neared the top of the sphere. The rest of the Cetan colony ship didn't look much better than the hangar. It was dank and cluttered, the result of generations of use, repair, and reuse. Dents and scrapes, multiple layers of paint, corrosion and mold around the air recyclers gave it the "lived in" feel befitting a ship which in fact had been lived in for centuries.

Our Cetan escorts communicated telepathically like Reticulans, so Xeelix took the information on our patient's condition and translated for us. I could hear the Cetan's "voice" in my head, but at this point my translator still couldn't make heads or tails of it, just random words that didn't make sense without context. I could tell he was gravely concerned, though. He wore all white with a sunburst crest on his collar, I guessed that signified he was some sort of physician. But that didn't make sense—if they had their own docs, what did they need us for?

The answer came when he led us to what I gathered was a quarantine room, with two doors to get in and out, basically an airlock. The Cetan opened the outer door and led us into an antechamber, then closed it behind us. He remained conspicuously outside.

"He seems a little jittery. Is he a doctor?"

"Roughly equivalent," Xeelix said. "And yes, he is 'jittery' with good reason. I am familiar with variants of *phoetima* in other Union races. It is fast-acting, and invariably fatal to Cetans."

"I don't understand. Why are we here, if they have their own doctors?"

"This was until recently a novel infection for the Cetans. They did not bring it with them inadvertently, nor did it evolve naturally among them."

"Where did it come from, then?"

"The Thubans, quite by accident. They were the first Union race to encounter the Cetans. *Phoetima* is a minor irritant to Thuban scales, but it mutated into something radically different among Cetans. The original outbreak was contained early, before it could infect their entire population. This is the first case they have seen in a generation."

Xeelix slid the inner door open to what looked amazingly like a hospital room on Earth: a little more advanced, but still wholly recognizable. In the center of the room was a bed surrounded by plastic curtains hung from the ceiling. There was a humanlike silhouette within, a little rough around the edges.

Xeelix stood with a hand on the curtain and studied me with those big almond eyes. "I must warn you, Melanie. This could be unpleasant. You must promise that you will keep your composure and do whatever is necessary."

How bad was this going to be? I swallowed. "Promise."

Cordyceps is pretty disgusting just to observe among insects on a nature show. To see something like it in a being approximating a human was nothing short of horrifying.

When Xeelix pulled the curtain aside, we stood before a naked Cetan male strapped into the bed. His skin was discolored in mottled shades of violet, as if his entire body had been bruised from within. Toenails and fingernails had turned into spongy gray masses. And the less said about his genitals, the better. Looked like a mushroom garden, and I'll leave it at that.

Xeelix pointed at his hands and feet. "The parasite spores first take root in the nail beds, then spread across the body through touch."

Once he explained that, the pattern of spread was obvious: rubbing his eyes, picking his nose, scratching his junk. The effects on his face were shocking. His eyes had been completely covered (replaced?) by strands of gray fungus. More of the stuff grew out of his ears to encircle the back of his head. Speaking of which, his already large parietal bulge was easily twice its normal size, judging by my embed files and the Cetans we'd passed on our way here. That strongly suggested the fungus was growing inside his brain. He was in the final stages of infection.

I clenched my fists, hard. I was *not* going to lose my cool. "You said this is their first case in a generation. How did they contain it before?"

"Physical isolation," Xeelix said. I could sense his remorse. "The outbreak was isolated to the ship's aft sphere, their engineering section. It thrived in the damp conditions around their air and water recyclers. They were forced to shut off the entire structure until the infection burned itself out."

"Closing off their engineering section seems drastic. We call it cutting off your nose to spite your face."

Bjorn considered that. "An apt analogy, but in this case it was their only recourse. The fungus could have killed off their entire ship's complement, had they not moved so quickly. They would not have lasted for long on secondary and tertiary systems."

I stared at our patient in grim astonishment, imagining hundreds more like him all confined to one of these spheres. "They left an entire section of their ship to die." It was that, or expose the whole population. Still . . . "Then what are we here for? I assume it's because they don't have a treatment regime."

"There is no treatment regime once the infection reaches this stage," Xeelix said. "We were called to make a final assessment and deliver a fungicide. Do you understand the effect this will have on the patient?"

I looked at the infected Cetan, bruised and bulging from the invaders multiplying in his body, waiting to burst out. I didn't have to consult the embed files; I knew what this would mean. "The fungal infection's reached his nervous system. It's probably already taken over, otherwise they wouldn't need the restraints. If we administer a fungicide at this stage, it'll kill the host." I was revolted by my own rationalization—calling our patient a *host* made it easier to think about.

Xeelix reached into his bag and pulled out a jet-injection syringe. "Do you recall our protocols for administering euthanizing agents?"

I'd hated that class. I detested the whole concept of mercy-killing patients in the field. Yes, we'd learned it in vet school but that had been different—we weren't putting down sentient creatures. At least we hadn't thought so; one other accepted truth that was blowing up in my face here among Union civilizations. "Yes," I finally answered. "Senior medic on scene administers, junior medic monitors."

"Correct." Xeelix was an actual doctor by GU standards, so he'd be the one to do the deed. I'd set up the transducers and watch vital signs.

Knowing what the outcome would be, the process of setting up was less rushed and more somber than treating a patient in the field might normally be. Xeelix carefully loaded the vial of fungicide, calibrating its dosage based on the volume we estimated to be eating its way through our patient.

I placed scanning transducers on either side of his head and torso, like setting up an EKG on a human. As they started talking to each other and feeding data to our visors, my translator started chattering at me in a muffled, confused mess of almost-syllables. Xeelix seemed unaffected. I angrily smacked one ear with the palm of my hand—because if you don't know how to reboot something, just beat on it, I guess—and shot a glance at Bjorn. "I think my implant's gone screwy."

Bjorn looked as troubled as I felt. "Your translator is working properly." He was subdued, his tone detached as if he could somehow keep the awful truth at bay. "The invading fungi has taken root in his nervous system, as Dr. Xeelix suspected."

That sounded awfully certain coming from someone at the same level of Med Corps training as me. "You've seen this before, haven't you?"

"I have." He lowered his eyes, focusing on the data crystal recording our patient's vital signs instead of the patient himself. "After contracting this malady from the Thubans, the Cetans became especially uncomfortable around non-humanoid races. I accompanied the medical response team as their translator. It was a most unpleasant experience, for a number of reasons." He met my eyes. "I was exposed."

I considered our patient, a grotesque humanoid caricature of molds, tendrils, and folds of organic matter that belonged on a forest floor—anywhere but in his ears and eye sockets. I turned back to Bjorn, unable to hide my revulsion. "You caught *this*?"

"I was fortunate that it came after our cohorts had identified the pathogenic mechanism and before it could spread to my nervous system. As I said, it was most unpleasant."

"Melanie." Xeelix interrupted our little campfire horror story. "Have you established contact with the patient?"

I turned back to what I should've been doing in the first place. "Not certain. It sounds as if he's trying to get through to us, but I'm having trouble identifying anything." It didn't help that our patient was telepathic in a language my implants hadn't translated into English before.

"That is another sign of late-stage infection, I'm afraid. The spores are competing for dominance over his neurological system."

"They're *talking*?"

"Mimicking, to be precise. Even as a collective organism, they are incapable of independent thought. They are simply imitating characteristics of the host." Xeelix paused sadly. "The disjointed voice you are hearing is the patient trying to speak."

Now that was horrifying, an infestation right out of a zombie movie. I screwed my eyes shut, listening anew for anything intelligible from my translator implants.

A disembodied voice formed in my ears: *Me . . . help. Late.*

My eyes widened. I shot a look at Xeelix. "You heard that too, right?" He answered with a grim nod of his head.

I heard the voice again, weak and muffled, like speaking through a filter as our patient fought to assert control over his own nervous system. "He keeps repeating 'late' and 'help.'"

Xeelix acted as if he'd fully expected it. "Yes, I heard that as well."

Then there was a single, chilling word: *Kill.*

I heard it again, in that sickly muffled timbre, like he was trying to speak through a mound of dead leaves. *Kill.*

I fought to keep my eyes from tearing up as I searched our patient for any remaining shred of his essence beneath the invading growth. I focused my thoughts on him: *We understand. This will end soon. Please try to relax.* It sounded so pointless—what do you say to someone whose body has been hijacked, and the only way out is death?

Still, he understood. *Will try. Must do. Help. Save others.*

I gulped. Xeelix seemed to be watching my reaction as closely as he was our patient. "He knows what we have to do. He said to 'save others.'"

Xeelix locked the vial in place, activated the injector, and pressed it into the fungal mass growing out of our patient's left ear. "That is precisely what we are doing."

I watched as the fungicide went to work. Right away, the mass began to change color. Its edges turned gray before disintegrating into black dust. Without being told, Bjorn pulled a handheld vacuum out of his bag and began sucking up the dead spores with what amounted to an alien dustbuster. "We will follow up with a portable sterilizing boom. It is vital that all traces of contaminant be removed." Again, he didn't need instruction. It was obvious he'd done this before, perhaps many times. That he'd been here for the first outbreak a couple of generations earlier made me wonder exactly how old Bjorn was.

As the fungicide progressed through our patient's body, his vitals responded in kind. There was a brief, encouraging jump, but I knew it was a false hope. His heart and lungs had responded happily to their newfound freedom, only to be stopped in their tracks by a nervous system that had been so thoroughly corrupted by parasitic spores that it could not survive their removal. Minutes later, he flatlined.

Xeelix dutifully recorded the time of death, but we weren't finished. We had to wait for the fungicide bots to root out every trace of infestation.

I rested my hands on my hips and studied the Cetan's isolation ward. "Do I understand this right—we have to decon the room, too? They don't have the tools to do that?"

"They are unprepared and unwilling. They are afraid," Bjorn said. "Understand, an isolated population such as this responds differently than their larger civilization might. The Cetan colonists tend to be risk averse."

That made me furrow my brow in frustration. Thousands of them had committed themselves—and their offspring, which introduced a whole other moral question—to being isolated aboard a multigenerational ship going who-knows-where. Seemed like they'd be a little more risk tolerant. "So they treat this like humans treated the Plague in our Dark Ages." I poked my head outside of the isolation curtains and studied the room in more detail. It was musty and damp, with flaked paint and traces of corrosion around the joints and seams of the environment filters embedded in its ceiling. It was especially appalling for what was supposed to be a medical ward. "Seems like they can do a lot better, given their technology level. Are these conditions typical?"

Bjorn nodded. "I'm afraid so. A single vessel can only endure for so long before it requires major overhauls."

I'm pretty sure he intentionally left out *or gets scrapped.* "How long until they reach their destination?"

Bjorn's eyes darted about as he did the math. "If memory serves, another three decades by your time reference." He looked to be as skeptical of their chances as I was. A whole other generation would pass before then.

"Then they've got bigger problems. Maybe we can do something to help." I wasn't about to try talking the Cetans into taking the Union's offer to get them there faster. If an Emissary couldn't do it, what hope did I have? But still . . .

Bjorn's cautious demeanor didn't change; I'd only given him something new to be skeptical about. "What are you thinking?"

I tapped my foot on the floor, trying to put a plan together. "They're committed to going the distance in this ship?"

Xeelix answered this time, just as frustrated by Cetan obstinance. "Very much so."

I turned to Bjorn. "But they accepted Union help during the first outbreak. They're not above taking charity."

"If you're thinking of supplying them with antifungals, they are reluctant to accept our standard preventative treatment." He finished with a glance at Xeelix.

This was only getting more confusing. Were the Cetans closer to being Space Amish than I'd thought? I looked around the empty medical bay and considered the rest of this massive ship and the absolute faith they'd have had to put in it. "Why is that? People this comfortable with technology shouldn't be averse to basic medical care."

Xeelix answered. "You are correct. They are comfortable with more traditional standards of care, such as the invasive surgeries and chemical-based treatments you are familiar with." He reached into his bag and pulled out yet another silvery, cigar-shaped implement.

I rolled my eyes. "Can't blame them. What is it with you guys and the anal probes, anyway?"

Xeelix's big eyes narrowed. "Their distrust is not about the delivery mechanism. It is about the nanobots."

"I still don't get why they couldn't be persuaded. It weirded me out a little at first, too, but I dealt with it." Despite my ribbing, releasing millions of microscopic machines to root out infections and repair tissue was a lot more effective than cutting someone open or administering a barely understood vaccine. Bad outcomes from either were rare, but they did happen. Nanobot treatments had driven the GU's "adverse event" rate down to almost zero, but the Union was oblivious to exactly how much of a running joke their delivery system had become among UFO-skeptical humans. If either side ever knew the truth . . .

"Despite their utter dependence on technology for survival, the Cetans are what your race might call 'Luddites.'" Xeelix swept his arms in an expansive gesture. "Being confined to this vessel, however large, has confined their development to whatever materials are aboard. There is very little margin for experimentation or growth. Without realizing it, over the generations their culture became insular. Parochial. Almost cultlike."

Bjorn interjected. "If the Cetans didn't bring it with them, or have the ability to replicate it themselves, they don't trust it."

"Not invented here." I grunted my disapproval. "Cultural isolation will do that to you."

"Quite so. It made for an interesting anthropological exercise . . . after the initial outbreak had passed, of course." Bjorn studied me. "You know, their technological level is not much more advanced than your own. Perhaps a hundred years."

"Only a hundred years?" I scoffed. "An awful lot can happen in that time."

Xeelix inserted himself back into the conversation. "Technologically, yes. A hundred years can mark the difference between coal power and nuclear fusion. Any changes that may impart to cultural norms is largely superficial. Changing a society's fundamentals takes much longer, unless it is compressed by extreme enough conditions."

It made me think about the people back on Earth who were obsessed with colonizing Mars: Would they end up in a similar cultural straitjacket? This place was living proof that just because you *could* do something didn't mean you *should*.

A chime sounded from our crystals; the nanobots had finished their work. A quick scan around the room showed no active spores; the nanobots had gone about their business like microscopic ninjas.

It was time to finish what we'd started. As Xeelix and Bjorn lifted the deceased Cetan off the bed, I pulled a tightly rolled bag out of my kit and unrolled it beneath him. We zipped him up inside and ran decon wands above and below. The whole process was silent and solemn, as familiar as if we'd been doing the same thing on Earth.

As we cleaned up the scene, stuffing bedspreads and clothing into hazmat bags, I considered everything they'd told me about this strange cult of expatriate Cetans. No one aboard had any personal memory of what home had been like. This aging colossus they lived in was their home, and would be for the foreseeable future. The end was theoretically in sight, a star still so far away that it was no more real than the light at the end of a long tunnel. They were a culture on a perpetual journey. What would it do to them when they finally made landfall? Would they embrace their new home, or cling to this artificial world in fear? If Cetan nature were anything like humans', too many of them would opt for the latter.

Maybe this ship wouldn't give them a choice. Maybe it'd be too far gone by that point. In the meantime we had a more immediate problem, and it was laying in the body bag before us. "If they're as insular as you say, how quickly do you think word of this will get around?"

"Their medical service will no doubt attempt to suppress it," Xeelix said. "And they will no doubt fail. An infection which terrifies their populace like *phoetima* is bound to lead at least one person to slip. Perhaps even intentionally."

Especially intentionally, if they were anything like humans. "Word's gonna get out. I think we all know it. And it'll probably lead to a full-scale panic, in a confined space."

"Yet they will not accept our prophylaxis regime," Xeelix said. "What would you suggest?"

I rested my hands on my hips and gave the ward a final once-over. "This place needs a glow-up."

⚕ 24 ⚕

I have to admit at this point we were acting more like Doctors Without Borders than on-scene medics. When we emerged from the isolation ward with the deceased on a gurney, the Cetan doctor seemed awfully eager to get him the hell off of their ship.

My translator was getting better at keeping up, and the bits of telepathic conversation I heard between him and Xeelix left no doubt that he was terrified of another fungus outbreak: "You must leave. Now."

"He will be secured aboard our vessel for transport and interred per your established customs," Xeelix assured him. He turned to the gurney. "We have activated a containment field around the deceased, and sterilized your ward. Rest assured we did not detect any residual live spores. But I must ask: Do you know who else this patient may have been in contact with? Has he left your ship for any reason, or have there been any other Union races aboard?"

"We initiated contact tracing as soon as he presented symptoms and identified fourteen potential exposures. They have all been quarantined in a separate ward. We confirmed through transport logs that there were no excursions from our vessel, and no outside visitors."

"Excellent. May I presume the isolation ward's air circulation is segregated from the general population?"

The Cetan doc was growing impatient. "Of course." His thin, lanky body and oversized head exaggerated his body language. He was anxious for us to get moving, but Xeelix was stubborn.

"There is more you must do to prevent another outbreak. We can arrange for a decontamination team with the necessary equipment to cleanse the entire vessel."

The Cetan stiffened as he realized we weren't going anywhere yet. "That would be complicated. I will have to relay your proposal to our ship's master. I suspect he will be reluctant."

Unbelievable. I closed my eyes tight, trying to join the conversation by projecting my thoughts into the translator. It worked. "You can't be serious. You won't accept our preventatives, and your ship's captain might not even let us remove any spores? Are you suicidal or just ignorant?"

Xeelix turned to me in surprise, which is saying something as Reticulans don't show much emotion. The translator had worked a little too well, turning my immediate thoughts into unfiltered telepath-speak. I liked to think my spoken words would've been a bit more diplomatic. The Cetan's eyes narrowed as he regarded me.

Xeelix tried to defuse the situation. "You must excuse my colleague. She is the first of her race to join our Medical Corps, and her kind tends to be rather outspoken."

"That is actually refreshing," the Cetan replied, loosening up. He placed a six-fingered hand on his chest. I hadn't noticed that physical trait before. "Our own kind was known to be that way, long ago. Before our journey. Many generations have passed since. Our behavior has become subdued over time. Compliant."

Xeelix used that opening to drop the hammer, which shocked me probably as much as it did the Cetan. "Since we are on the subject of compliance, I am compelled to mention Union statutes on nonmember species crossing our space. We have laws against permitting the transit of any vessels which are unable to contain biological contaminants. Failure to comply could result in your ship being rerouted out of Union space."

The Cetan was taken aback. "That would add generations to our travel time." He looked up and down the corridor, eyeing its worn surfaces and gunky recycling vents. "It is not likely we would be able to reach our destination. Our ship is already nearing the end of its design life."

Xeelix was undeterred. "Then I would advise you make that case to your ship's master, and soon. We will have to file a report with

Med Corps operations, which will no doubt be prioritized for the attention of the Union immigration ministry. They are likely to act swiftly."

Doc Cetan appeared resigned to the inevitability of a Union cleaning crew swarming through their ship. "I will inform our master. Thank you for your assistance. Now, if you please . . ."

We took the hint and began fast-walking down to the lift, propelling the deceased ahead of us on the anti-grav gurney with the Cetan following at a safe distance.

Once we were secure aboard our ambulance, I collapsed into one of the gel chairs as Needa piloted us away from the colony ship. "That was a slick move back there, Xeelix. Were you serious?"

"I am always serious. You ask about what in particular?"

"The transit laws. Immigration. Would you really kick them out of Union space?"

"It is not up to me. Our report will be routed to the immigration ministry, with my recommendations. I cannot know for certain how they will respond, though they rarely overlook a Medical Corps assessment."

"That was all true, then."

"I would not mislead about something so serious." His slit of a mouth curled up ever so slightly. "Though I have been known to exaggerate."

Bjorn stifled a laugh. This might have been the most emotion I'd seen out of either of them.

We arrived back at the barn almost an hour after the end of our shift, illustrating the downside of relativity: Go on a run too late in the day, and you end up working even later than you thought. The clocks on our data crystals reset themselves to Union standard time as we emerged from the ambulance with our dead Cetan, safely zipped up in a body bag behind a containment field.

As we silently went through the motions of decontaminating ourselves and our ship, there was a tingling sensation on my wrist, behind the biosuit gloves. I looked down to find a tear, maybe an inch long, right along the seam.

"Oh shit."

Bjorn wheeled about, his eyes widening when I showed him the tear in my suit. "Xeelix..."

Whether from being a doctor, or by being from a generally stoic race, our Reticulan leader was far more collected than I felt at the moment. He gently grasped my wrist and examined the tear. "Yes, this is concerning," he said, in the understatement of the year.

Nightmare visions of turning into a human mushroom raced through my head. "You're damn right it's concerning! Am I in danger of contracting that crud?"

As Bjorn hurriedly pulled a patch kit from his bag and began taping me up, Xeelix quietly consulted his data crystal. His answer wasn't encouraging. "It is impossible to know for certain without case history, but your race does share some genetic markers which suggests vulnerability."

Oh no. *No no no...*

He placed a calming hand on my shoulder. For being so thoroughly alien, the Reticulans could be remarkably soothing once you got past the freaky black eyes. "You recall we have a preventative treatment? I trust you will be more agreeable to its use than the Cetans."

I let out a wry chuckle. "Yeah. The shiny little probe." I looked around the open bay. "I'm gonna need to find some privacy."

He left his hand on my shoulder. "I apologize, Melanie. You are quite capable, but our protocols require this procedure to be performed by a qualified physician."

Ugh. I can't say why the thought bothered me so much. Probably my own cultural aversion, though at least it wasn't Cetan-level obstinance. That running joke had just run head-on into me for its punchline.

"There is more," he continued. "For your protection, the treatment must be followed by an extended observation period."

"You mean an isolation ward. For how long?"

Xeelix thought about that. "I am uncertain. Considering your common DNA markers against Cetan physiology, my recommendation is at least one standard week."

That worked out to a little over eight days by my reckoning. I hung my head. This was going to seriously disrupt my training schedule.

Xeelix must have sensed my mounting anxiety. He took out his crystal and began adjusting his schedule. "I am assigning myself as your attending physician." He paused. "That is, if you consent."

It made a lot of sense. No one else would be a better fit out here, but it drove home how exposed I was. And there was this nagging, creeping feeling in my fingertips, the way your skin crawls at the sight of a teeming mass of insects. I told myself it was psychological, but the tingling sensation beneath my nails wouldn't go away no matter how much I wished for it.

Before I could answer him, a pair of Reticulan orderlies approached to collect the deceased Cetan. I watched as the two Grays carted him off to who knows where, knowing there'd be an incinerator at the end of the line. I sure as hell didn't want to end up in the same place. I clenched my teeth and turned to Xeelix. "I trust you. Just do it."

I won't get into the treatment for obvious reasons, mostly out of embarrassment. Xeelix is a good doc, and the procedure was painless. That doesn't mean it wasn't uncomfortable, because having a few million nanobots skittering around beneath your skin will do that.

Xeelix seemed satisfied as he watched my progress on a monitor above the exam table. "The nanobots are fully dispersed and over ninety-nine percent functional. You are not showing any signs of rejecting the treatment." He laid a hand on my arm. "This is very good, Melanie. I believe you will fully heal."

That was reassuring, but at this point all I wanted was to get some sleep. A wave of fatigue had begun washing over me almost as soon as the probe had dissolved. It had already been a long day, but this felt different, nothing like the immune system booster they'd given me at the transit station. "Why am I so tired?"

"It is your body responding to the nanobots, working with them to root out any contaminants." He glanced up at the monitor. "You are running a slight fever."

I turned to see for myself: 100.5. "That explains a lot. It's like my immune system went into overdrive."

"That is precisely the case. The booster bots we gave you during your initial exam are dormant until they recognize an infection, but *phoetima* is not one they are programmed for. The antifungal treatment is active, and works with your lymphocytes to destroy invasive spores."

I scratched at my arm. "That's why I can still feel them at work."

"Ordinarily I would say that is psychological, but this treatment regime has not been applied to humans yet. You are the first."

"I'm a guinea pig." Xeelix looked at me quizzically. "Lab rat. Human slang for test subjects."

He blinked in recognition. "Ah. I see. Forgive me, but it has been quite some time since we used animals for testing."

That made me wonder what they did use, but this wasn't the time to get into the philosophy behind their research standards. Whatever they did, it seemed to work. I mumbled an unintelligible reply. I was so tired . . .

Xeelix turned down the lights. "I was prepared to offer you a sedative, but that does not appear necessary. It is time for you to rest. You have earned it."

I awoke to sunlight filtering through the window. I instinctively reached for my phone on the nightstand, eyes shut against the light and hanging on to the gauzy remnants of a deep sleep. After a minute or so of groggy fumbling around, I noticed the texture wasn't right. It felt cold and impossibly smooth, not at all like the poplar furniture I'd had in my room since childhood. And that sunlight—something inside reminded me it wasn't natural.

Oh. Right.

I laid back against the pillow and pulled the sheets over my head. This wasn't home; it was a Med Corps isolation ward. The light came from artificial glow panels embedded in the biodome outside, creating day/night cycles for the millions of alien residents in the Union capital.

I sat back up and rubbed the sleep from my eyes. I opened them to find a seven-foot lizard sitting across from me.

"Chonk?"

"You awake now. Very good. Doctor wanted to know." His claws tapped an entry into his data crystal.

"Where is Xeelix, by the way?"

"With other students. Asked me stay with you. Monitor your condition."

I reflexively scratched at my arms and legs, knowing those microscopic insectoid bots were still somewhere beneath my skin. I was concerned for his safety at first, then remembered: "You can't catch this, can you?"

"Am immune. Exposed long time ago. Th'u'ban children most risk. Adults, not big deal."

I looked down at my hands. There were black specks beneath my fingernails which hadn't been there before. A chill shot down my spine. *Oh God.* "Chonk, I ... it's ..."

My Thuban friend crossed the distance between us in one loping step, and took my hands in his claws. His golden eyes narrowed as he studied me. For being such an imposing creature, Chonk had a gentle manner. "You okay." He pointed to my nail beds. "See? Black. Means spores are dead. Body expelling them. You recover full."

Now that he was close, I noticed a white film had grown around the edges of his scales. I took my hand from his and ran them across the ridges. The film peeled away beneath my fingers. "You're molting, aren't you?"

He seemed embarrassed. "Am. Xeelix thought good to stay with you." He gestured between us with a claw. "Good for both." The ridges of his mouth, a reptilian approximation of lips, turned up in a tight smile that would've suggested I was next on the dinner menu if I hadn't gotten to know him already. "Also get credit for hospital rotation."

I laughed. "Glad I could help."

"We help each other. Molt embarrassing. Cannot do much for self." He lifted a pair of pumice stones from the pouch on his waist. "These good for removing scales."

"You can't reach everything by yourself, can you?"

He shook his head. "Cannot. Perhaps you can."

I giggled, relieved to have something besides my own plight to think about. "Of course. I've done this before, you know."

He cocked his head. "How before? Not enough time here."

"It wasn't here. I used to have a pet lizard, named Homer. Sometimes I'd rub his back with this same kind of stone when he'd shed."

He considered the idea of my keeping one of his distant relatives, and didn't seem very fond of it. "Strange concept, 'pets.' Better off living free."

"I assure you he was well cared for. He seemed to welcome my help, for what it's worth."

"Understand. Th'u'bans once kept pets, many generations ago. Small primates. Suppose not much different."

So the giant lizard race had once kept distant relatives of humans as well? "I suppose not." I reached for his shoulder, where the old scales appeared close to sloughing off. "Just let me know when you're ready."

"Will be soon. Watch you in meantime."

I arched an eyebrow. "Watch for what?"

He returned to my fingernails, brushing away a clump of black dust. "Expelling spores take time. Can be messy. Need much cleaning."

As in bathing, in front of a man. Didn't matter that he was of a completely different race, the fact that he was sentient drastically changed my perspective. This wasn't going to be like changing clothes with a pet in the room. Every time I thought the cultural shocks were behind me, up came another one. Still, I felt an innate trust in him. Thubans were a justifiably proud race, living by a strict code of honor that we humans could learn a thing or two from.

I rested my hand on his and gave it a squeeze. "Thanks. You're a good medic, Chonk."

He lifted his head, his eyes meeting mine. "You think so?"

"Of course I do. You've got heart. You stepped out of your comfort zone to come work with the Med Corps." I made a sweeping gesture around the room. "All of this is new to me. Every day holds a different surprise, because I came into it as a blank slate. But you've lived here for decades, grew up in a race that's been part of the Union for centuries. In some ways I think that'd make it harder."

Chonk looked away, his trident tongue brushing across the ridges of his lips. "Has been difficult. Did not volunteer. Following orders."

"You were sent here?"

"Union request medic from admiralty staff. Select me. Not say why."

"I don't understand. Wouldn't that be obvious? It's because they thought you were the best candidate."

He shook his head slowly. "Military not always work so. Sometimes get rid of problems. Troublemakers."

"You? Causing trouble? I find that hard to believe."

Chonk leaned back, the end of his tail flicking back and forth. I gathered it was a nervous habit. "Hard to find word. Not trouble. Questions. Asked many questions."

I crossed my arms behind my head and settled back against the bed. "Now you're going to have to tell me everything. You know that, right?"

He let out an irritated hiss and began pacing the room. "Was medic for Th'u'ban expeditionary brigade. Respond to border raid. Trading outpost. Many injured. Not all soldiers. What you call . . . civilians? Yes." He thumped his chest. "Me only medic on scene. Lost many civilians. Not understand physiology. Not have correct medicine."

"They attacked civilians?" I didn't like the sound of that one bit. "Who? Was it those invisible beings you told me about?"

He shook his head. "No. Three dimensional, like us. Nomads. Mongrels. Not join Union, not keep to home worlds. Better to steal. Pillage."

Space barbarians. Great. "And they raided a trading center. Do they often go after civilians?"

"Not direct. Civilians get in way when they come take."

Random Union civvies had been caught in the wrong place at the wrong time. That sounded depressingly like Earth. "You said you didn't have the right medicines for them. How did you deal with that?"

"Best as could. Bandage wounds, set bones. Only had medicines for Th'u'ban anatomy."

"Like clotting compounds? Blood plasma?"

"Yes. Needed much. Not have. Complained to admiralty staff in report."

Now we were getting somewhere. "You raised a ruckus, and the people in charge didn't like it." That sounded all too familiar.

Chonk nodded. "Very much. Said expeditionary brigades need prepare for all species. More training, more medicine."

"Sounds like that would've been a big project."

"Is so," he agreed. "Admiralty not like." He thumped his chest angrily. "Say *I* need better training. Not up to job."

"Wow. That there's some bullshit, Chonk."

He looked confused. When his translator caught up, he roared with laughter. "Yes! Good word! Will remember."

"I find it useful sometimes." Too often, in fact. "But on the good side, they sent you here."

"Staff upset, and Union ask for Th'u'ban student. Timing good. Union knew human would be in class. See how well we work together. Test."

And with that, my new friend had just confirmed my lingering suspicions. They hadn't brought me here by accident, at least not entirely.

"Don't you worry about us working together. If we're going to be stuck in this ward, that'll take care of itself." But now I had even more questions.

Chonk hadn't been kidding about the mess. As the days passed, my skin excreted more of the nasty black dust and I couldn't bathe often enough. The stuff seemed to come out of every pore, interspersed with convulsive fits of sneezing that produced even more crud. I was terrified that the fungus had settled in my lungs, but Xeelix assured me that wasn't how *phoetima* propagated.

"The contaminating spores remained confined to your epidermis," he said during one of his regular morning visits. "Dead spores are collecting in your nasal passages, which you are expelling naturally." He placed transducer discs on my back and chest, and a three-dimensional image of my respiratory system appeared on the monitor beside us. "As you can see, your airways are free of contamination." He slowly moved the discs down toward my feet, scanning my entire body in the process. "In fact, you have expelled most of the contaminants. We should be able to release you from isolation soon."

That was a relief. I tugged at the waist of my skintight "observation garment," ready to get out of this and into some real clothes. The Med Corps' version of a hospital gown was the same kind of lightweight bodysuit I'd worn for my entry physical, a bit less degrading than what we used on Earth. It wasn't exactly flattering, but at least my ass wasn't hanging out in the breeze.

Watching from across the room, Chonk seemed relieved as well. His old scales had largely been shed, with a few remnants stubbornly hanging on amidst the more pronounced ridges and folds. A long session in the sonic-wave shower would take care of those in short order. His new skin was a regal emerald green, flecked with gold highlights that matched his eyes. Freed from the constrictions of his older skin, he seemed to stand even taller than before.

We were beyond ready to get out of the ward and back to work. I finally broached the question to Xeelix: "How much longer?"

Xeelix took one last look at the holographic scans above us. "I will visit you again tomorrow, and I expect you will be cleared for release then." He pulled out his crystal. "In fact, I have taken the liberty of placing you back on the training rotation the following day." His tone became apologetic. "You both need to make up for your time in isolation. I'm afraid this will require an aggressive schedule for the remainder of your rotations."

He handed the crystal to me. "No days off, for the next ten. I've done worse." And with a lot less opportunity to sleep in between.

Xeelix eyed me. "We shall see."

🜚 25 🜚

The compressed schedule meant that I was going to be paired up with another trainee, and for my first day back on the job it was a relief to see a familiar face waiting for me in the hangar.

"Bjorn!" I dropped my gear to the deck and instinctively gave him a hug, which he awkwardly accepted.

"Hello, Melanie." He studied me at arm's length. "It is good to see you again."

"I kind of missed you in isolation. Were you busy filling my slot in the schedule?"

He seemed evasive. "Not quite. I wished to visit you, but could not risk exposure."

"Oh." I backed away. Stupid me hadn't realized why he was so awkward. "Oh crap. You're susceptible, too."

Bjorn smoothed down his jumpsuit. "I am." He placed a hand on his chest. "Like you, we have similar evolutionary pathways to those of the Cetans, with similar vulnerabilities." He turned apologetic. "Doctor Xeelix kept me under observation after your exposure. It was forbidden to visit you during isolation."

"That's okay, it wasn't your fault. If anything, it was mine. I should've been more careful."

"You were doing your job. My task is to act as your chaperone during your transition to an independent Union resident. I should never be far from your side."

I laughed and shouldered my bag. "No offense, but the most fun I've had here has been entirely on my own. I'm a big girl."

Bjorn followed me as I headed for our waiting ship. "You are acclimating quite well, I must admit. More than any of us expected, in fact."

I hopped aboard and began stowing my gear. I glanced up toward the pilot's station, and Needa greeted me with a curt nod. "You guys didn't notice that I tend to jump into things headfirst? That should've been obvious from the beginning."

"Perhaps you are correct. If anything, I now have a better understanding of your attraction to this service. Sometimes our preconceptions can blind us to reality."

"Then we have more in common than either of us thought," I said. "Must be in our DNA."

The day started off slow, which came as a relief after being out of the game for over a week. Of course, that's when you know something big is sure to drop. I was settling down to catch up on my studies of Med Corps regulations (it's easy to procrastinate on that topic) when Xeelix popped his head out of the ambulance door and waved for us.

"Come, collect your gear from the ship. We have a call."

We hopped up and climbed aboard. Xeelix had already shouldered his own bag and was headed back out. We both looked at him in confusion. "Where are you going?" I asked, then noticed the lack of alarms and warning beacons. "You said we had a run."

He held up his crystal. "We have. It is local, here on station. Meet me at the equipment locker behind bay four."

My mind raced to remember which specialized gear was stowed in which lockers. My eyes widened when it came to me. "That's for confined-space rescue."

"Correct." Xeelix waved for us to hurry. "I believe you have some expertise in that discipline?"

I grinned and snatched up my go bag. "You bet your pale gray ass I do."

The confined-space gear wasn't all that different from the stuff we used on Earth. It was mostly recognizable, if considerably more advanced. There was a folding tripod with motorized winch, which housed a carbon-filament cable that looked impossibly thin.

Retrieval lanyards, body harnesses, air pumps, and helmets were all light as a feather. We piled everything into a repulsor-lift cart and headed for the nearest elevator.

Xeelix briefed us on our way up. "Part of a tunnel collapsed beneath the biodome, in the Gliesan sector. Most were able to climb out through a ventilation shaft, but several were left behind with injuries which are preventing their escape. Two remained to stay with the injured."

I gulped. "Gliesans?" We were about to climb down into a tunnel full of insectoids. Yay. I tamped down the creep factor by focusing on the job ahead. "What can you tell us about the tunnel?"

Xeelix swiped at his crystal and a topographical map appeared to float above it. "The Gliesans live beneath the surface in their sector of the biodome, where they've carved out a rather elaborate system of tunnels and chambers. I've never been, but understand it to be quite impressive. I can only presume they were in the process of constructing another chamber."

I rotated the hologram with my hands. It looked like a whole underground city. "That explains why I never saw any of them inside our building. Did see a few scurrying around in the dome, though."

"Quite so. It is a close approximation of their natural environment on Gliese II."

"Not close enough." A more troubling thought occurred to me. "How much can they dig down there without putting the whole dome at risk of collapse?"

"The Gliesans constructed the dome, including the grounds and foundations. They understand its limitations better than most."

"Their underground structures are continually evolving," Bjorn interjected. "However, all plans are supposed to be cleared by the infrastructure ministry."

"Plans are just that. Reality eventually has a say."

Xeelix's mouth slit turned down. "Quite."

We emerged from the lift in the Gliesan sector, and it wasn't hard to find the accident scene. A swarm of them were gathered around in a circle, skittering back and forth and crawling over each other in a writhing mass of agitated insectoids. A few on the edge of the mob spotted us and scurried over, excitedly scraping their forelegs together. They communicated through a complicated system of tapping and clicking, much the same way crickets chirped. This being my first up-close exposure to them, my translator lagged a beat as they chittered away.

"...quickly. Many of us are hurt. Please hurry."

Another focused on me, his eye stalks reaching up to my level. He seemed to be sizing me up. "You assist the doctor?"

I hoped his translator was working as well as mine. I held my hand to my chest. "Yes. I'm here to help."

"Good. Come with us. Hurry." He nudged me with his mandibles, and believe me when I say it took every ounce of self-discipline to not bolt. I defy anyone to not run away screaming when confronted by a giant bug with jaws that could snap you like a dried twig.

These two must have been some kind of leaders in their collective hierarchy, because the teeming mass of insectoids drew themselves apart for us like Moses parting the Red Sea. Their noise was like a forest full of cicadas in high summer. I couldn't hear a thing over the cacophony of chirping and chittering.

The two leaders reared up on their back legs, waving their forelegs at the crowd to give us room as we arrived at the mouth of the air shaft. It looked perfectly natural, as if it belonged there, and I made a mental note to watch my step in Gliesan territory. There could be hundreds of these holes all over their grounds.

As we began unloading our gear, I took a look at our access point. It wasn't big, maybe two feet across. "Going to be a tight fit."

Xeelix had slipped on his safety harness and craned his elongated neck past me for a look. "Quite."

While Bjorn set up our tripod winch above the opening, I climbed into my own harness. Other than being made of gossamer-thin material, it wasn't much different than something we'd have used on Earth. The straps automatically tightened themselves to the point of being uncomfortable, which satisfied me they were secure enough.

I pulled a helmet from the gear box and slipped it on. With a quick press on either side, its liner gel molded itself to my head. I clipped my bag to a ring on the bottom of my harness, then let Bjorn hook me up to the cable.

I tugged hard at the wire, as it wasn't much thicker than

monofilament fishing line. None of our gear seemed stout enough to do the job compared to what I was used to. "This is going to be enough to hold me up?"

"More than enough," he assured me. "It's graphene, a material your own people have been trying to mass produce for some time. It could hold up our transport if need be."

I peered down the hole. "I'll take your word for it." I was ready to rock. I'd done this before back home, on a run to a cave system in southern Indiana where a bunch of amateur spelunkers had gotten themselves into real trouble. I kept telling myself this was exactly the same thing.

Without realizing it, my instincts had kicked in and I'd kind of turned myself into the on-scene commander. I was issuing orders, laying out our plan without even realizing that I was probably stepping on Xeelix's toes, but he seemed content to let me run the show.

"First things first: nobody goes near this shaft without a full body harness secured to a winch." There wasn't much danger of Bjorn falling in, but we also couldn't be too sure about the integrity of that shaft.

I looked to Xeelix as I shrugged on a rebreather pack. "We mask up before we go down the hole. Bjorn, we'll signal you when we're ready for you to feed the ventilation hose down to us. Air's got to be getting close down there."

"Correct. The Gliesans exchange air beneath the thin walls of their carapaces," Xeelix reminded me. "Trachea are distributed along the inner surface. They are dependent on air movement. We will need to begin ventilation as soon as possible."

The two insectoids with us were in a hurry. "Come. We will lead you." With that, they scurried down the hole. They hadn't gone very far when the shaft began to glow with a pale light.

Right. Bioluminescent. That'll help. I sat on the lip of the shaft, slipped on the rebreather mask, then tugged on the graphene wire to reassure myself it wasn't going to snap as soon as I put weight on it. I gave Bjorn a thumbs-up. "I'm ready."

Bjorn stood by the winch. "Ready."

I pushed off and steadied myself with my arms. "Let's go."

✠ ✠ ✠

Bjorn was appropriately cautious with the winch, which meant it felt like an eternity to get down there. The two Gliesans had scurried well ahead, and the only light came from the glow pad on my helmet. The shaft walls were perfectly smooth, not the roughed-out passage I'd expected to be carved by giant insects.

After a time the shaft filled with dim light from beneath. I had to be getting close now. "Almost there," I called over the helmet comm. I felt my feet dangling free, and soon after I was through the shaft and hanging above the chamber.

My eyes still had to adjust to the bioluminescent glow, but I could tell the chamber was huge. It had to be at least fifty yards across, a dome of rock beneath the surface. As my eyes adjusted, I could begin to discern patterns in the walls curving away from me. Intricate serpentine arches, spirals, and curlicues belied an artful attention to detail which, once again, I didn't expect. At the very least it was more comforting than being lowered into a dank cave with a mass of giant alien bugs.

Not much farther to go. The floor beneath me was smooth, with a clear area for me to drop in amongst them. The two healthy Gliesans scurried around their injured comrades, who were lined up against one side of the chamber in a faintly glowing mass. Their luminosity dimmed with injuries, as if their body chemistry recognized there were more important matters at hand. Their shells were like built-in vital-sign monitors.

I felt the ground beneath my feet and took a moment to steady myself. First things first: assess the scene.

The ground was firm, but the far end of the chamber was a pile of rubble. The elegant arches and bas-relief sculptures were broken and crumbled into a heap on the floor, blocking their exit. I hoped none of their group had been trapped beneath it.

Under the light of my helmet, I scanned the rest of the dome for any signs of cracking. Everything looked to be in place, but it was best to stay as far away from the wrecked side as possible. If there were any more impending structural failures, that's where they'd be likely to start.

Next, check my oxygen flow. The rebreather controls on my wrist showed it was working. With solid ground, clean airflow, and a mostly stable ceiling, I unclipped the tether and called up to Bjorn and Xeelix on my helmet comm. "I'm down and okay. Scene is secure, but we're going to need some structural braces brought down here. I'm beginning triage."

"Very good," Xeelix answered. "I am on my way. Bjorn will begin lowering the braces after me."

I looked back up the shaft at the glow from his lamp high above as Xeelix began his way down. He wasn't wasting time. Good. I grabbed my bag and headed for the two healthy Gliesans, who were scurrying back and forth among their injured companions like mother hens. If I felt out of place, they didn't seem to care that this strange-looking human would be tending to them.

The first one they led me to looked to be in bad shape indeed. His forelegs were canted outward at odd angles, with chartreuse-yellow goo leaking from the cracked exoskeletons. That would be hemolymph, the insectoids' approximation of blood. They didn't have blood vessels like humanoids; instead, this fluid circulated throughout their bodies in direct contact with tissue.

This guy had at least two compound fractures, but his eye stalks were what concerned me the most. One of them was completely gone, sheared off in the collapse. His companions had packed the opening with what looked like mud to stop the bleeding. The transducer showed me his vitals were thready, and the lack of air movement wasn't helping matters. I tapped my helmet comm. "Bjorn, we're going to need that ventilation hose down here stat."

Xeelix answered. "I have it right behind me. We'll start air flow as soon as I reach ground."

Even better. My first impulse was to begin rendering aid to this poor guy right now, but triage doesn't work that way. You have to assess each patient before deciding who's going to be first in line. There could be others who were even worse off but it might not be immediately obvious. The mud pack was crude but it worked. He wasn't gushing hemolymph, and while his vitals weren't great, he wasn't in imminent danger of crashing quite yet. Unless one of the others was even worse off, this guy would be first.

The next one was more straightforward. All but three of his ten limbs had been broken like the first patient's, and one of his mandibles was hanging loosely from his mouth. Vitals were steady, but he had to be hurting. A quick swipe of the transducer didn't show any internal injuries, so after giving him a dose of painkillers it was on to the next one.

It was obvious the third Gliesan was going to be on the short list for immediate treatment, and a good example of why we do triage. He was lying in a puddle of hemolymph after his shell had been crushed in multiple locations, with more of the vital fluid still oozing out through the cracks. My first thought was that he looked like a bug on a windshield, which felt wildly inappropriate and "species-ist" in context. One more example of instincts I'd have to unlearn.

His vital signs were in line with what to expect from massive blood loss. Without veins and arteries to carry the fluid along, there's no measure of systolic/diastolic pressure like we'd see in a typical BP cuff. It was supposed to remain in a constant range of acceptable levels, and his was on the verge of bottoming out. I called up to Xeelix.

"We've got one who'll need a hemolymph infusion, or we'll lose him. Carapace is crushed in multiple locations, with signs of internal injuries. Right now he's our priority." I might have been jumping the gun, but I reasoned that if anyone had even worse injuries then they'd already be dead.

Xeelix emerged from the shaft, ventilation hose in tow, as I was finishing up with the last few victims. They were in good shape, considering the circumstances. Lots of broken legs, injured eyestalks, and cracked carapaces, but nothing immediately life-threatening. I had already moved to our crush victim, and was pulling compression bandages and hemo-packs from my bag when Xeelix dropped down at my side.

He seemed particularly interested in the patient's eye stalks and shined a light on them. "Sluggish. Typically they are quick to respond to sudden changes in illumination. You are correct, this one must have priority."

I pointed to the first victim nearby. "He's not far behind. Compound fractures like everyone else, but his left eye stalk is sheared off above the ocular tendon. Looks like they packed it with mud or something."

Xeelix nodded. "A common practice among their kind. It is a sufficient first aid response, but you are again correct in your assessment. Hemolymph flow is considerably higher in that region."

Made sense, as that's where their brains were. I laid out the compression wraps and began calibrating the infusion pump. Normally this would call for an IV but there were no veins to inject into. We'd do a direct infusion of hemolymph, but it had to be carefully managed. Too much in one place could create as many problems as it solved; it needed time to evenly distribute through the patient's body and at this point it wasn't clear we'd have enough time. None of this would matter if it kept leaking out of his crushed carapace, and his injuries were too extensive. We had to get Humpty Dumpty's shell back together first.

Once the pump was ready, I placed the wrap alongside our patient and tried to talk to him. It. Whatever. "Hey there. I'm Melanie. What's your name?"

"They don't have names," Xeelix said. "Not in the sense we are accustomed to. They have a collective consciousness. They only identify by clan."

"Got it. No names." That kind of small talk was normally for the patient's benefit, to calm them down. In this case, it was as much for me as it was him—remember, giant insect with yellow slime oozing out of every crevice.

He clicked his mandibles weakly and scratched at the floor with one foreleg. The translation was equally shaky. "We are Chitherii clan." He turned an eye stalk toward me and scratched out more words. "You are different."

On top of being creeped out, now I was self-conscious about it. "I'm new. Not from around here. My home is called Earth."

He grew agitated, his ten limbs twitching along with his eye stalks as if he wanted to get away. "Earth? We know of Earth. You are Gideon clan."

There was that name again. Whoever this Gideon was, he didn't seem especially popular around the Union. That explained why they were acting as wary of me as I was of them. "I don't know anyone . . . any clan . . . called Gideon. My clan is called Mooney."

"Moo-ney," he pronounced awkwardly. "A happy name."

Used to be, I thought to myself. Or at least I'd been, a long time ago. It was nice to know it sounded happy to somebody from a completely different evolutionary tree.

He clicked his mandibles. "Hurts."

"I know, and I'm sorry but we can't give you anything for the pain yet. You've lost too much blood. Do you understand?"

"Blood . . . hemo. Yes."

"Good." I held up the compression wrap for him to see. "I'm going to coat this with a gel that will fill in the broken parts of your exoskeleton, okay? We'll wrap it around you good and tight. When the gel hardens, we're going to start replacing your lost hemo."

"Then you can give . . . pain . . . killer?"

I smiled, not knowing if the gesture meant anything to him, but that's how we humans roll. "We'll see, okay? Once the gel wrap sets, you may not need it."

Xeelix handed me the first wrap and gently lifted the injured Gliesan on his side. "We cannot use the repulsor lifts for this one," he said. "The localized gravity field might do even more damage."

I nodded silently and went to work, being careful to not put too much pressure on the shattered parts of his exoskeleton as I smoothed the bandages in place. It was like trying to fix a cracked eggshell with masking tape, and the delicacy of the task took my mind off of any lingering revulsion. Because, once again, giant insect.

We had to work quickly, not only because we needed to replace his hemo fluids quickly, but because the wraps themselves threatened to do more damage. Hairline cracks began to emerge from beneath the bandages as the underlying gel hardened. It was vital to get him wrapped up from head to tail before the fragmented shell could spill its way out from under the compress. Xeelix gently rocked him from side to side, giving me space to work.

Soon we had a freshly wrapped Gliesan. I ran a hand across him, testing where I knew the worst damage had occurred. "Feels like the gel is setting."

Xeelix did the same, but with a transducer. "It is. Pressure is still low, but consistent. Stable. He is no longer losing hemo volume."

I grabbed the infusion pump. "That's good. What about internal organs?"

"Bruises to his alimentary canal and . . . Malpighian tubules." The translator stuttered over that last one, as it was a purely human term. Malpighian tubules were an insect's excretory system, named for the scientist who discovered them. Whatever they called it, it meant our patient was going to be on a liquid diet for a while.

It could've been much worse. Even better, it meant there was nothing to keep us from starting the infusion. I placed the infuser by our patient. "The gel has hardened enough for us to get started. This pump will replace your lost hemo. You should start feeling better soon." I held up two clear tubes, each with needles on their ends. "We'll insert these lines beneath your shell and start the infusion. It'll pinch a bit."

Xeelix took one of the lines and moved opposite me. "We must do this together. Trust me."

In unison we plunged the needles into his skin, just beneath the lip of his shell and beneath his eye stalks. His mandibles snapped reflexively, and it was all I could do not to pull away in terror. He still had enough strength to snap one of my arms clean off.

Xeelix placed a firm hand on the Gliesan's back. "Good. Keep moving," he coaxed me. Together we watched the leads on our visors as we pushed them along. As they approached the joint between the prothorax and mesothorax, Xeelix relaxed his grip and motioned for me to do the same. "Hold here. You can begin the infusion."

I tapped the control screen and the pump began whirring quietly. "We've got flow...no backpressure." Our visors showed the hemolymph fluid begin to distribute itself beneath the bandaged shell. "Looks like his exoskeleton is holding together."

Xeelix rocked back on his knees with relief and made one last check of vital signs. "Patient is stabilized. Excellent." He tapped on the floor to get one of the healthy Gliesans' attention, and motioned him over to our freshly swaddled patient. "We require your assistance." He pointed to the infusion pump's monitor and the two graphs tracing their way across its face. "This trend line is ambient fluid pressure, the one beneath it is backpressure." There was a solid line between the two. "This is baseline pressure. It does not change. If either one of these values approaches baseline, let us know right away. Do you understand?"

The Gliesan bobbed his eye stalks. I assumed that meant yes.

I stood and moved to the next victim on our triage list. We had been so busy with patching up our first patient that I hadn't noticed Bjorn had already lowered a pair of structural braces. "I will get these into position and secure the first patient for lift," Xeelix said. "You tend to the next one."

"Aye, captain." I snapped off a half-assed salute and got back to work.

26

As the last patient was pulled up the air shaft, I collapsed into a heap between the stanchions Xeelix had muscled into place. For being so scrawny, he was remarkably strong.

"Tired?"

I pulled off my breathing mask to wipe the sweat away. My hands shook from the adrenaline letdown. "Exhausted."

He handed me a bottle of electrolyte juice. "This will help."

I downed it in one long pull. Whatever alien magic they brewed into that stuff, it was better than anything on Earth. The taste was nothing to write home about, but I could feel the goodies percolating through my body with each gulp.

He held out a hand and helped me to my feet. "Excellent work, Melanie. Once again, you comported yourself well under difficult circumstances." He studied me with his almond eyes. "I believe this is indeed a calling for you."

I slipped my helmet back in place and reached for the cable dangling out of the air shaft. "This line of work? It has to be. It's all-consuming. You either live for the rush, or you eventually find something less demanding. On Earth, there's plenty of jobs that will pay better."

"Ah. Commerce, yes. Perhaps that is something else we could explore when time allows."

I was reminded of my conversation with Chonk in the isolation ward. "Come to think of it, I—"

A handful of loose stones landed on our heads and around our feet. Our eyes met. "That's not good."

"It is not." He hurried to get us both hooked up to the cable. "You must go first. I will be right behind you."

As we got into position there was a dull rumble from overhead, followed by a sickening, earthy crack. The ceiling above began to crumble around the rim of the air shaft.

We unhooked and ran for the relative safety of the stanchions. Whatever was happening to the shaft, we weren't going to get caught beneath it. In our scramble to get clear, I hooked my foot on a rock and fell flat on my face. Xeelix grabbed me beneath my armpits and dragged me the rest of the way. I was dimly aware of a shooting pain in my ankle.

Bjorn's voice sounded in my headset, but it was drowned out by a thunderous cascade of falling rock as the shaft caved in on itself.

It was over in seconds, but to me the collapse seemed to happen in slow motion. A few bits of gravel bounced off the floor, followed by bigger stones, ending with a crash that filled the chamber with choking dust. I scrambled to get my rebreather back in place and blew the mask clear.

Our only illumination came from our helmet lamps, creating a small cocoon of light that shifted as we moved. I turned to stare at the dimly lit debris pile in disbelief. The air shaft above had closed up completely. A trickle of loose dirt from the ceiling was the only hint that something other than solid ground had once been there.

Bjorn's voice sounded in our headsets, through the hundred or so feet of compressed dirt between us. I'd never heard him sound rattled before. "Xeelix! Melanie! Are you okay?"

Xeelix looked at me. I answered with a shaky thumbs-up, with way more confidence than I felt. "We are intact," he said, "but we appear to be trapped. The braces likely prevented a complete collapse, and that is where we are situated now. What is your status?"

"The other response teams are transporting the patients to our trauma center. The air shaft began to collapse from below, creating a sinkhole up here. I am well, but need to extricate myself."

"Do so with utmost urgency," Xeelix cautioned him. "If the surface is unstable, conditions could become worse."

Bjorn's reply was terse. "Understood." As in, *you don't have to tell me once.* Welcome to EMS, buddy.

"What about the other Gliesans up there with you?"

"They dispersed almost immediately, converging on a nearby cave entrance. They appeared to be in a considerable hurry."

Xeelix sagged against a stanchion and closed his eyes. Was that relief I saw? He checked his wrist monitor, then motioned for me to show him mine. "We each have two-point-four hours of breathable air. Let us hope that is sufficient."

"Understand two-point-four," Bjorn said. "I will communicate that to the Gliesans."

"Thank you. Please keep us apprised of your progress." Xeelix stood and stretched his elongated limbs. "We will be here for some time. It is critical that we conserve our breathing supply." With one finger, he made a circling motion on his wrist monitor. "I am reducing mine to the minimum level. I suggest you do the same."

I tapped at the "O_2 Saturation" icon on my monitor and dialed it down until it flashed a warning. "I'm at eighty-eight percent. That's as low as I dare go." It was far from ideal, but as long as I wasn't exerting myself it would be survivable. I slumped against the opposite stanchion and pulled off one of my boots with a wince. "I wrenched my ankle."

Xeelix scooted over beside me to examine it under his headlamp. An ugly purple bruise was already starting to spread as he moved a transducer around my ankle. "You certainly did." He fished in his bag for a splint and went to work setting it in place. "That will require some time to heal," he said as he finished. "We have accelerants to knit broken bones together, but muscle and tendon damage cannot be repaired as quickly." He was apologetic. "I'm afraid you will have to be on light duty for a time."

That was the least of my worries. I'd deal with it when—if—we made it out of here. "What happens now?"

"We wait." He splayed his hands out on the floor and closed his eyes, as if searching for something.

The ground was cold, a harbinger of the tomb I was afraid it might become. I didn't know what Xeelix was expecting, but judging by his stoic demeanor it couldn't be anything like what was rushing through my head: hundreds of light-years from home and left to a dark, choking subterranean death.

What in hell was I even doing here?

I felt Xeelix's hand take mine. He exuded a contagious optimism, and thank goodness for that. Whatever he might have been feeling, it wasn't resignation to a horrible fate.

"They are coming for us," he said with a reassuring squeeze.

"How do you know that?"

He placed my hand on the rock floor. "I can sense them. You cannot?"

"I'm not telepathic."

His slit mouth turned up in that almost-smile he sometimes used for my benefit. "You do not have to be. Quiet your mind. Listen with your fingertips."

Sure. Use the force, Mel. But he had a point. It was deathly quiet, but for the metronomic hiss of our rebreathers. I turned mine off to listen. Xeelix did the same, again for my benefit. The chamber became utterly silent.

I closed my eyes and concentrated on the feel of the rock beneath my fingers. There was an ever so slight, steady vibration, like something big was coming. I pulled off my helmet and pressed my ear to the ground. Now I could hear it: a churning, chattering symphony, like thousands of tiny shovels working in unison.

I sat up sharply, switched my rebreather back on, and sucked in my breath. "That's them!" I twisted to face the chamber entrance behind us. "They're digging us out!"

"They are. I do not know how much distance lies between us, but the fact that we can both hear them is encouraging."

A troubling thought occurred to me. "Why didn't they do that to begin with?" Not that it would've stopped us from coming down here in the first place.

Xeelix shrugged. "I am a physician, not an engineer. But it is reasonable to assume they feared doing so would risk further collapse."

I leaned my head back against the stanchion. If it hadn't been for those trusses, we'd have been crushed under a few hundred tons of dirt. "Good point." I began impatiently tapping my good foot. "I presume they're not as concerned now."

"The Gliesans are quite industrious, and equally loyal. We aided their clan; they no doubt feel the need to respond in kind."

"They freaked me out at first. I'm not fond of insects."

"A surprising trait, considering how diminutive their relatives are on your world. It is interesting how evolutionary pathways can work. Their native environment favored insects over, say, mammals or reptiles."

I looked up, casting my helmet light on what was left of the ceiling. "They weren't anything like I expected. That's impressive work up there. They did all of this themselves?"

Xeelix followed my gaze. "They did. Notice the carvings? Each tells a story."

I strained my eyes; he was no doubt able to see much more in the dark than I could. The elegant curves flowed in a spiraling pattern, each one leading to the next. Glyphs were etched inside of them, all in different configurations. It was obvious now that this was their writing, but it was too far removed from anything remotely human for my visor to translate. "I can tell those are characters, but they're all coming up as gibberish."

"Quite so," Xeelix agreed. "Their written language is rather opaque. My translator has never been able to adequately interpret it, despite our kind having a long history with theirs. Telepathy has likewise been difficult. It is easier to communicate with them face-to-face."

"My translator eventually figured out their chirps and clicks. Maybe they prefer to keep some things to themselves?"

"An interesting observation. I have thought that myself."

I took a deep breath. We were going to be here a while, so it was a good time to press him for some answers to my lingering questions. "There is something that's been bothering me. When they learned where I'm from, I could tell they weren't happy. Have they been to Earth before?" I wouldn't come out and say it, but it was easy to see how a ship full of Gliesans could seriously freak out unsuspecting humans. It wouldn't have ended well.

Xeelix looked away. "They have not. Though their clans have had interactions with a particular human."

"Gideon."

He turned back to me but said nothing for a moment. "Yes, Gideon. Their history with him is unfortunate. Tragic. He held to some rather primitive human notions of labor, which I'm afraid he used to exploit the Gliesans once he understood their potential."

"He saw them as useful drones, didn't he? Giant carpenter ants he could control."

"An apt analogy. Recall that Gliesans are not capable of space travel on their own. They rely on others for transportation, which renders them helpless if they are removed from contact."

It sounded like the bad old days of mining towns and owing everything to the company store. "That made it impossible to quit. To leave for something better."

"Precisely. A Gliesan clan had contracted for one of his early construction projects, and they soon realized he considered them little more than indentured servants. Their legend tells that conditions were dreadful. Many of their clan perished."

"Legend? How long has this Gideon character been here?" And how old was he? I wondered.

"Several decades, by our reckoning. Well over half a century by yours, though his tale seems to be laden with as much rumor as fact." He subtly moved the subject back to the Gliesans. "You must understand 'legend' carries a different meaning for them. Recall that they have a collective consciousness. When the Union brought that particular clan back from isolation, their recent history became one with the rest of their race as they reintegrated. Their memories became part of a collective folklore." He pointed to the ceiling and its intricate carvings. "The artwork you see depicts a continuous record of Gliesan history. They are constantly building new chambers as their legend grows."

"It's a library," I realized, one where the books were part of the walls themselves. It was a sign of advanced intellect I'd never expected. "They may not be able to bind books or build semiconductors, but that doesn't mean they aren't thinking. They're expressing it in a different way." I waved a finger at the carvings. "Is this what got them into the Union?"

"Correct, and quite perceptive." He studied me for a moment, which was a little uncomfortable. "Your veterinary training has benefited you, as I expected it might. Now, if I may ask: What led you to abandon your schooling? My understanding of human hierarchies would suggest a paramedic is considered a 'lesser' profession compared to physicians."

I laughed. "Compared to MDs? Yeah, they'd tell you it is. Vets are a whole other career path. We don't intermingle species."

"You seem to be avoiding the question."

I absentmindedly scratched at the ground. "I'm surprised you don't already know. Haven't you been reading my mind?"

"Not recently, out of respect for your privacy. Forgive me, but that trait is innate to our kind. It is like suppressing a reflex, which I have learned to do among certain beings. You are perhaps the most challenging."

"Why is that?"

"I can sense that you harbor lingering emotional turmoil. Your outward self-control is admirable, considering the conflicting thoughts and desires which burden you."

I snorted. "Maybe you should add 'psychiatrist' to your resume."

"I am aware of that discipline in your culture. It seems unscientific. Subjective."

"A lot of humans would agree with you." I didn't happen to be one of them; medicine wasn't nearly as straightforward as people imagined it to be. I rubbed my eyes with the palms of my hands. "Later. We have to conserve our oxygen."

"Now you are most definitely avoiding the question."

"You really want to know, don't you?"

"It is purely from personal curiosity. It will not affect your standing in the Medical Corps."

"It's not something I like talking about," I sighed. "But I think about it all the time. Barely a day goes by without it popping into my head."

"Would you be agreeable to 'thinking about it' with me?"

I stared at Xeelix for a long time, considering his offer. Here I was, trapped underground with this strange extraterrestrial. Only a few months ago this would've left me paralyzed with fear, but his gentle manner and deep wisdom had become so endearing it was hard to resist. I trusted him unquestioningly. And Bjorn. And Chonk. Hell, even the giant bugs who were right now working their asses off to get us out of here.

Why not? "You win. Just tell me what I have to do."

He took my hand. "Not a thing. Relax and think of whatever you wish for me to know."

"911, what is your emergency?"

"It's my father, I think he's having a heart attack!"

"*Can you describe his symptoms?*"

My hands were shaking uncontrollably. It was all I could do to hold the phone steady, and they wanted my assessment? "He lost his balance, couldn't stay on his feet. Fell to the ground, clutching his chest. Said he couldn't catch his breath." *I touched his face; it was cool and sweaty.* "He's clammy, turning pale!"

"*Okay, we're sending a squad right now. Do you know CPR?*"

Did I know? Yes, yes I did! Lifeguard training, back in high school. Had it again in college; I was one of those nerdy dorm RAs and first aid was part of the job. "Yes," *I stammered, and tossed the phone to the ground. I knelt beside him and began compressions, counting out the beat to that stupid disco song while the dispatcher stayed on the line.*

The worst part wasn't that my Dad might die, it was that I could feel his ribs cracking under my hands, like I was making things worse. Our ribcages are there to protect our heart and lungs and don't give way without a fight. Most people don't realize how violent you have to be for CPR to do any good.

I shouted at the phone. "Where's that ambulance?"

"*It's on the way. The Carthage unit is on another run. The next closest station is in Greenfield, fifteen miles from your location.*"

Fifteen miles of winding country roads. It was hard to do the math in my head while counting out compressions. An ambulance would be hauling ass, but they could only go so fast. We'd be lucky to have them here inside of twenty minutes, and I was already getting tired.

My mind raced with all of the things I still wanted to say to him, all of the things we had left to do. Dad had been one of the top large animal vets in the state; even in retirement he couldn't stay far away from the work he loved. We had more animals on our small farm now than ever before. Who was going to take care of them?

Of course I had planned on being here to help. He'd already taught me a lot during summer breaks, tending to our livestock and accompanying him on calls for the county ag extension. After graduation next year, he was finally going to fully retire and hand me the keys to the family business.

When the squad finally arrived, I collapsed against the stall next to him while the medics did their thing. My arms were numb and I was out of breath. I could only sit there and watch, barely comprehending what was happening in my exhaustion.

They slapped an oxygen mask on him, followed by a shot of epinephrine. One medic gave the injection while the other kept up the chest compressions. When Dad didn't respond, they pulled out the defibrillator.

Charge. Clear. Shock.

More compressions.

Charge. Clear. Shock.

I have no idea how long it went on like that. One slipped a stretcher beneath him while the other kept pumping his chest. At that point they probably knew he was gone, but they weren't giving up. I watched them load my Dad's limp body into the back of their ambulance. They tore off down our drive in a cloud of dust.

The turnout for Dad's funeral was massive. Every vet, farmer, rancher, and ag agent across three counties showed up. A parade of dual-wheel pickups and SUVs wound its way from our church to our home. Burying Dad in the backyard had been more complicated than expected, and it didn't matter that Mom was already there. Zoning codes had apparently changed since we lost her several years before, and it took some special attention from an outraged state agriculture director to convince the local bureaucrats to look the other way.

There wasn't much family at the service, which isn't to say nobody cared. There just wasn't much family left. My parents had been in their early forties when I came along as their only child. After years of not being able to have kids, you can imagine my arrival was something of a surprise. So no siblings, very few cousins, and even fewer aunts and uncles.

Of course, they were all helpful. Dad's younger brother and his son stayed with me for several days, helping to get affairs in order. The house and land were paid for, and the livestock would be worth a lot at auction.

Still, there was no way I could take care of this place from school. And for that matter, I'd already missed two weeks of class. Catching up in time to finish the semester was going to be brutal, if it was even possible.

Of course I tried anyway, and fell flat on my ass. I'd missed too much, and despite my professor's best efforts, my mind wasn't ready

to absorb the material. After bombing the midterms, I dropped out
and told myself I'd start over after winter break.
  That was my last day of veterinary school.

"You never went back. You chose a completely different path."

I tore off my mask, angrily wiped at my eyes, and blew my nose on my sleeve. Pathetic. "What can I say? Lost my taste for veterinary work after that. When Dad needed me most, I was next to useless. They told me it was a 'widow-maker' heart attack, the kind that comes without warning. They're hard to detect unless you're actively screening for signs of arterial blockage." Of course Dad had a family history of heart disease, but one of the realities of life in farm country is the quality of vets frequently outclasses the quality of small-town docs.

"Why not become a . . . what did you call it . . . MD? You seem to have the academic background."

"Entirely different schooling. I'd have had to start over. Thing is, I didn't want to. Waiting twenty minutes for an ambulance while my Dad slipped away? It was *infuriating*. We needed more good doctors, but we needed even more first responders. They're the ones who make the difference when everything is going to shit in the middle of nowhere. After what happened, I couldn't think of anything else."

"Do you feel like you have made a difference?"

Dropping my postgrad work for a community college EMS course had given me purpose, but it hadn't been enough. Doing my part to beef up the firehouse roster was chump change, so I sold off a few acres—arable farmland can bring a *lot* of money—and made an anonymous donation to our county EMS. It was enough to buy three brand-new ambulances stocked to the brim with first-rate equipment. None of the medics I worked with suspected they were driving around in rigs that I'd paid for.

"Yeah. I did my part."

"Then that is all any of us can do."

Sitting with him in the dark, I pondered that. Too often, we never know what we're capable of until we're pushed. Tested.

"Am I a test case?"

"I beg your pardon?"

"A test case. Trial run. Guinea pig. Is the Union using me as a proxy for the rest of the human race?"

Xeelix tilted his head. "Why do you ask?"

"Some things I've been piecing together ever since the Emissaries came for me. It sounded like the Union had been making advances toward us, then pulled back. From the first day of class, it was obvious to me that my skills aren't as unique as they'd have me believe. Then Chonk filled in the rest while we were in isolation."

He closed his eyes for a moment. "Yes. I thought he might. Unfortunate, but also unavoidable given your circumstances."

"So I *am* a proxy. That accident I came on wasn't an accident, was it?"

"That was in fact an accident you happened upon, though it did lead us to you. There are many things the Union looks for when assessing new worlds, and the needs of the Medical Corps are only one small part. It is something of a crucible: If individuals from a prospective race can demonstrate their ability to take on such a demanding role without fear or prejudice, it provides us with valuable insight into their kind's overall potential."

It was an epiphany. They'd seen the worst of us, but weren't convinced we were a lost cause either. "This Gideon person left the Union with a bad taste. I'm here to prove we're redeemable."

"In a sense, yes. It does not all fall upon you, though it will inform how we proceed." He paused, as if deciding how much to tell me. "There is great potential with your kind, and we are always cautious about establishing formal contact. It takes centuries of observation, of understanding the culture. Yours is complicated by the fact there are so many diverse cultures to contend with. If we initiate contact too soon, it can be devastating. But there are times when it becomes necessary to accelerate the process."

I understood his point. It had happened time and again on Earth. "Why the hurry now? The Emissaries mentioned 'threshold events.' Are we about to kill ourselves off or something?"

"That is a risk, though there are other factors." Xeelix took a deep breath. "Earth may be in danger."

"What kind?"

"There is reason to suspect the beings our Thuban citizens have been defending against have become aware of your planet. This is partly our fault. As the Union expands its reach into other parts of the galaxy, it tends to attract the attention of bordering civilizations."

"And the Union is trying to make it right."

"Correct. Your civilization is close to being eligible for first contact, likely within this century. But we fear that may have to be accelerated. Without your knowing it, Earth is currently under Union protection. If we are to increase our presence, formal arrangements will need to be made."

"I'm here so they can decide if we're worth the risk."

"In so many words, yes. I am sorry, Melanie. We felt it best if you were protected from that knowledge, as it could affect your performance."

"I'm a woman who worked in a male-dominated profession. I'm used to having to prove myself. And being here was my choice." Maybe it was a bit too cavalier considering the stakes, but what else could I say? I massaged my tender ankle. "Besides, this is going to limit me more than anything else. I'm going to lose a lot of training time."

Xeelix leaned back against the support beam. "I believe you have satisfied your training regimen. And now, the best use of our time is to rest. We have talked enough. We must conserve our oxygen while the Gliesans do their part."

Xeelix had been right, of course. Jabbering away in the dark was the single worst thing we could have been doing, so I laid back against the floor and promptly fell asleep. Between the letdown after a complicated rescue and reliving the single worst day of my life, it was easy to let the exhaustion overtake me.

I awoke with a start at the rumble of another rockfall. I shot upright. The rest of the chamber was caving in . . .

No. There was light, way more than our headlamps could produce. The chamber was filled again with bioluminescent glow. The Gliesans had broken through!

Xeelix was talking to me, but I couldn't make it out. It sounded like "hurry." Yes. Hurry. Get the hell out of here.

I was scrambling for my go bag when I felt a sharp pressure around my calves, and looked down to see two Gliesans with their mandibles locked onto my legs. My dormant, fearful monkey brain took over for a split second: *This is how it ends. Eaten by giant bugs.* I might have peed myself.

I clawed at the ground, but they were too strong. They were pulling me out of the chamber on my back, into a tunnel filled with a glowing, teeming mass of insectoids, piled one atop the other all the way to the ceiling.

I heard Xeelix's voice in my head. *Remain calm, Melanie. Do not be afraid.*

Calm? I was being dragged through a tunnel full of creatures out of a nightmare. "What are they doing?"

Pulling us clear. Trust them.

Right. Trust. I took a deep breath. It was hard to read intent from a disquieting mass of insects, but it looked like the ones surrounding us were working. Straining. "They're holding the tunnel up for us!"

Yes. They can get us through much faster than we can ourselves.

He wasn't kidding. The two dragging me were moving with purpose, their ten legs scrabbling against the stone beneath us. Xeelix was a few feet ahead, being pulled the same way. His arms were crossed on his chest as if it were the most natural thing in the world.

I heaved out a sigh and followed his lead. The Gliesans' grip was firm, a little uncomfortable, but I could sense they weren't taking any chances. Now I was more afraid the passageway they'd carved out might not hold. How strong were a few thousand of them against tons of dirt?

We emerged into another, larger chamber. As soon as we were free, the lead Gliesans began frantically clicking their mandibles. That must have been the signal for the others, because soon after the tunnel entrance exploded with more Gliesans, scrambling to get out of there. It took less than a minute for them to empty the tunnel, finding safe space wherever they could. That included climbing the walls of their subterranean dome, which was a little freaky.

There was a deep rumble behind us as the makeshift tunnel began to collapse on itself. Soon, all that was left of it was a pile of rubble and a cloud of dust.

One of the Gliesans approached, mandibles clicking and forelegs dancing on the floor. "You are well? Uninjured?"

He was checking up on me. I did a double-take and patted myself down, wiping away the dirt. "I'm good. I mean, yes. A little shaken. Thank you."

He silently held up a foreleg. Was he trying to shake my hand?

Xeelix inclined his head at me. *Yes, that is precisely what he is doing. Remember, you are not the first human they have encountered.*

I bent down and took the offered cuticle. "Thank you."

The Gliesan knelt forward and dipped his eyestalks in what approximated a bow. "We likewise thank you. You placed your life at risk for our kind. That is rare. We are in your debt."

"Please, that's not necessary. It's quite all right. I was only doing my job."

"You have a good job, then. We need more humans like you."

I turned to Xeelix in wonder. He answered me with a curt nod. *I believe you made the right choice, Melanie.*

⚕ 27 ⚕

Graduation was a low-key affair. Our class gathered in a small auditorium in one corner of the training center, dressed in fresh Med Corps uniforms. A few Reticulans showed up for the two graduating from our class. The largest—and rowdiest—crowd was Chonk's. The group I'd met before was there, plus a bunch more. It looked like the Wayside bar had been emptied out, and they beat their chests in salute when Chonk's name was called. I caught his eye and gave him a wink as he proudly took the Med Corps EMS crest: a neon green, eight-pointed star against a white background. He fixed it to his tunic to a chorus of stomping Thuban feet and celebratory hissing.

I didn't expect the same when my name was called. When I hobbled up to the podium, favoring my bad ankle, Chonk and his warrior buddies stomped in unison, as if I was one of them. I flushed in embarrassment. Xeelix stared at me intently, sharing his private thoughts. *Your father would be proud, Melanie. I believe you have found the ideal avenue for your skills. It is my hope this will become a long and fruitful relationship.*

"Thank you," I whispered back, self-consciously wiping at a tear. I proudly affixed the Med Corps crest to my uniform and stood to face my peers. The room erupted with the stomping feet and beating chests of my unlikely friends.

The throwdown that evening at Wayside was epic. It was a sight to see Thubans, Reticulans, and Emissaries happily mingling

271

together, though the crowd dispersed a bit when Chonk and his crew started one of their knife-throwing contests. Xeelix observed from a corner, probably wondering when he'd have to step in and reattach somebody's severed limb. I watched from a table by myself, with my bum leg propped on a chair.

The *ka'vaa'ma'loi* flowed freely, though this time I was smart enough to alternate it with plain old water. I was digging into a stone bug burrito bowl when Bjorn took a seat beside me.

He studied me with a lopsided grin. "You appear to have assimilated rather well."

I wiped spicy red sauce from my mouth. "We call it 'going native.' And yeah, I think you're right." At the back of the room, Chonk hooted in triumph when his opponent's knife landed squarely in his chest. They of course grasped claws and toasted his victory.

"I must admit, your affinity for the Thubans was most surprising." He watched another knife go sailing through the air from the corner of his eye. "They are a rough crowd."

"You haven't met any soldiers on Earth," I said around a mouthful of peppers. "Or firefighters. They can get rowdy."

"I have not. We purposely avoid military encounters for obvious reasons." He watched the ongoing contest with bemusement. "They perform a demanding and dangerous job. Seeking out more danger for fun seems like the last thing they would want."

I pushed my bowl away. Once again, Thuban portions were way too much for me. "They're just blowing off steam. I think it helps them keep their edge when they're off duty."

"Perhaps. Though I doubt that human soldiers shoot at each other for sport." He pointed at my leg, changing the subject. "This is something of a setback for you."

I waved away his concern. "It'll heal. But it will keep me off rotation for a while."

"What will they have you do in the meantime?"

"I've been assigned to the dispatch center."

He must have read the disappointment in my voice. "You may actually find that to be invigorating. Have you not been there before?"

"The orientation we had in class, that's all. Honestly I didn't pay close enough attention. I was eager to get down to the ambulance bays."

"It won't be long," Bjorn reassured me. "Until then, I'm sure you'll make good use of your time. I can't think of a better way to get a sense of the extent of the Union."

"The scale has been intimidating," I admitted. "There's a lot of nothing out there, until there's a lot of something."

He considered that. "I believe I see what you mean. Galactic-scale distances can be intimidating."

"And the Union doesn't even cover the whole galaxy. How far have you guys gone, anyway?"

"There have been scouting expeditions, but we found habitable planets to be sparsely distributed. Most are concentrated nearby, in this sector."

"Nearby" was relative, of course. It was another indication of the immense distances involved, and how precious life was in the universe. If people this advanced still hadn't managed to cover the whole galaxy, or decided it wasn't worth settling, then no wonder they'd decided to band together. It was too much for my puny brain to absorb, so I dulled it with another order of Thuban tequila. "This round's on me. Here's to our little corner of the galaxy. Cheers!"

Still harboring some disappointment over starting my EMS career as a desk jockey, I made myself remember what Bjorn had said. Everything is a learning experience, and I was determined to take what I could from this.

There was a lot to take in. The Med Corps dispatch center was enormous, a bowl-shaped room easily the size of a football field. Its black curved walls merged into one massive holographic screen that displayed the entire extent of the Union, like being dropped into the middle of space. Multicolored icons highlighted its member planets, colonies, and outpost stations. Swooping arcs in varying shades of yellow and white displayed ships in transit. Eight-pointed stars representing the EMS shield flashed amber to designate ambulances in transit. Others shone a steady green, pinpointing the location of each Med Corps facility across the Union.

At the base of this bowl were the rows of dispatch consoles, arranged in concentric circles. At the center was a cluster of different consoles, all staffed by Reticulans who looked busy. This was route clearance. Every EMS ship on a run anywhere beyond their local planetary space had to go through these guys first. It had to be a big job, making sure all those short-notice departures didn't inadvertently fly through a gamma ray burst or carelessly alter some unsuspecting planet's orbit by zipping by too closely.

Each dispatch console handled a different sector of Union space. Mine covered a quarter of the ring city, which I suspected was their way of easing me into it. No route clearances, no time shifts to calculate, just send the nearest available team. It featured a big semicircular holoscreen which gave me status of each crew and an ever-changing roster of incoming requests. The desktop was suspiciously bare, but when I placed my hands on it a virtual keyboard appeared beneath my fingers. They'd already calibrated the desk for human input.

Glancing at the stations nearby, I saw at least one representative from every race in the Union, each handling calls from their own kind. Each was tapping away at their desktops with hands, claws, cuticles and tentacles. A few glanced in my direction, either intrigued or suspicious of the weird-looking new girl. Their screens looked a lot more interesting, with 3D projections of each region of space they covered that mirrored the massive holographic map that encircled the room.

The odd thing was there was almost no conversation. I'd expected a cacophony of competing voices from dispatchers taking calls, talking to responders, or shooting the shit in between bursts of activity. That's how it had been back home, but that's not how they did things here. Most everything was transmitted through the data crystals, though I got the feeling the Reticulans were doing it telepathically. The Gliesans were of course a step beyond that—each individual knew what was happening to everyone else in their clan. A couple of times I could tell the Gliesan dispatcher was alerted to something before the call even came, proactively contacting the clan to find out what was wrong.

Those of us on the capital consoles were more jacks-of-all-trades. We took calls from everyone regardless of species. If it happened in your sector, you dealt with it. I was working with a Reticulan, another Thuban, and one I hadn't encountered before. We'd studied Orionids in anatomy and physiology, but seeing one in person was, well, gross.

It was a translucent blob, about four feet across. When the light hit it right, I could make out its internal organs and circulatory system. A dull gray, amorphous patch of light receptors approximated eyes. White tendrils extended from its underside, dancing across the desktop like a bundle of animated spaghetti noodles. They ate by directly absorbing food through their outer membrane, which to be honest is like straight out of a horror movie.

Orionids were also considered to be the most sharply intelligent beings in the Union, and of course they were. They looked like giant disembodied brains, after all. They were supposed to be extremely sensitive to light and touch, being in essence a bundle of exposed nerves. They also didn't hear in the way we did, instead picking up vibrations through their outer membrane.

This acute sensitivity limited where they could go and what they could do. The quiet darkness of the dispatch center apparently made for a good fit. I stood up for another look at the route clearance group, and this time noticed another Orionid at the center of the action. If they were smart enough to boss a bunch of Grays around, then that was all I needed to know.

Once the floor manager, a particularly uptight Gray named Jarra, was satisfied that I knew my way around my console, it was time to log in. I plugged in an earpiece, swiped my access ring over the desktop as instructed, and that was that. I was on duty, not quite flying solo. Jarra kept a respectful distance but I could sense her watching over my shoulder.

It wasn't long before the call screen began to light up, most of it mundane stuff. A lot of calls for children, either getting into things they shouldn't have or waiting until bedtime to become explosively ill. Parents, know that your travails are not isolated to humans: It's a galactic-scale problem. If the house is unusually quiet, somebody's about to get hurt in an inventive way. If you've had a long day, Junior will start puking his guts out as you're getting around for bed. If you're having a special night out with hubby, that's about the time your little punkin is going to take a header off the neighbor's porch.

As you can probably imagine, it can be incredibly frustrating to go from being a first responder to calling plays from the sidelines. Every run I sent someone else on felt like it should've been mine. I started tapping my heels impatiently, and the bolt of pain that shot up my leg was a reminder that they'd put me here for a good reason. The accelerants Xeelix had given would speed up the healing process, but only by so much. Muscles and tendons ultimately had to take their natural course, because monkeying around too much with tissue growth could lead to some unpleasant side effects. Like cancer.

Resigned to my circumstances, I sighed and propped my bad leg on a nearby stool. Bjorn had encouraged me to use this time to get a broader perspective, but being stuck with one section of the ring city was like having blinders on. I could sense Jarra watching from behind, and kept at it. Do a good job here, and maybe she'd move me to a more interesting desk.

My first chance came with an actual call. My console chirped, followed by a raspy hiss in my earpiece. My translator recognized it as female Thuban vocalizations right away.

"Med Corps EMS, what is your emergency?"

"Already said emergency. You not hear? Youngling has *lo'to'oh*. Very bad. Is bleeding."

I remembered Chonk telling me about the skin rash their children could get if they molted too soon. He'd made it sound like a minor problem, but the bleeding got my attention. "You said he was bleeding. Can you estimate how much?"

"All over. Bled through tunic."

That didn't sound good, and when the video came up it didn't look any better. The poor kid was miserable, with spongy eruptions between his new scales.

Their location came up on my screen at the same time. They were at the far western end of the Thuban sector, which was sparsely populated. According to this, Papa Thuban was away from home on border patrol. Mom was home alone, maybe isolated, with a sick kid. The nearest response team was already heading out on a different call, and the next closest team was in an entirely different sector. We could only pull from adjacent sectors for high-priority calls, so Mom was going to be on her own for a bit. "Okay, ma'am. I'm sending help but they can't get to you right away." I pulled up my files on Thuban physiology. What could I do to help her in the meantime? I thought back to the pet lizard I'd had back in middle school, and remembered the big succulents that grew in the arid Thuban sector. I pulled up a file on Thuban vegetation as I tried to remember something Chonk had told me. "Do you have any *te'mau* plants growing nearby?" It was close enough to aloe that it might alleviate the irritation.

She sounded confused for a moment. "*Te'mau*—ah. Understand. Very old remedy."

"Good. Do you have access to cold water?"

"Cold..." She trailed off.

I cursed under my breath, momentarily forgetting how they regulated body temperature. Cold could be bad, but it would also slow down any blood loss. "Yes, cold. For the time being, you can use cold compresses to control the worst bleeding. Then cut some *te'mau* leaves close to the stem, and apply their juice directly to the irritated areas. That will give him some relief until our medics arrive."

Her head tilted quizzically as the translator did its work. I could imagine how it would feel if our roles were reversed—you have a sick kid, call 911, and a talking lizard picks up the line. "Will try," she finally said, as if I'd told her something she already knew. Probably did, if it was an old remedy. Stress can make anyone forget. "How much time now?"

I checked the roster. The closest team reported they were wrapping up, so I promptly sent the alert to them. "Should be another...ten minutes." Not bad. "Would you like me to stay on the line until they arrive?"

"Not necessary. Must go now."

When the call ended, Jarra appeared at my side. "That was inventive."

"Something I learned from a friend," I said with a shrug. "We have similar plants on Earth. They used to be popular home remedies for burns and skin irritation. Many of our kind forgot about them as medicine improved." Same as the Thubans.

"I meant lowering his body temperature. Are you not concerned about that?"

"Not as concerned as I am about blood loss. Besides, 'cold' to a Thuban is lukewarm to us."

Jarra nodded. "That is a salient point." She made a note on her crystal, no doubt grading my performance. "Carry on."

⚕ 28 ⚕

The next several days proceeded about like the first, and the job was starting to become a drag. With every incoming call I'd feel that twitch of anticipation, only to have to tamp it down because someone besides me would be going on that run. A few of them were pretty juicy, too. The biggest deal by far had been a nasty accident on a transport inbound to the ring; apparently its inertial dampeners glitched as it was decelerating out of warp space. It was crewed by Orionids and a few Reticulans. The Orionids took some lumps, which with their gelatinous bodies must have been hard to tell. The Grays fared much worse. One fatality, the others were now upstairs in the ICU.

The first units on scene weren't even Med Corps, it was a pair of transit tugs that raced to keep it from crashing into the ring. Once they had the ship stabilized, we'd sent a heavy rescue unit and three additional ambulances. One of them had Bjorn and Chonk aboard, and I was jealous. They'd been the first on scene and were still there, having been called back to the scene by their shift commander. The transport ministry had sent an investigative team, who had lots of questions. I hoped they weren't in trouble.

Meanwhile, I held down the fort in dispatch. Yay me.

I worked with a rotating cast of Union folks, with barely a familiar face among them from one shift to the next. Jarra was the only constant, walking the circle amongst our consoles, occasionally giving advice, and taking notes. Always taking notes.

To be fair, the others weren't unwelcoming. Everyone was heads-down in their work and there wasn't much time for socializing. The job attracted a certain personality type for sure, but I also suspect a lot of it had to do with not being exposed to humans yet. Or if they had been, it may not have been entirely positive, like the Gliesans.

When my shift ended, I checked in on Bjorn and Chonk. They were still at the accident scene. With eighteen hours to kill before my next rotation, I headed down to the hangar deck.

I was sitting at a table along the back wall of the hangar, finishing off a bowl of noodles from the food synth when the alert beacons lit up for bay twelve. My friends were finally coming home after a long day, and I hoped they weren't too tired to tell some stories.

Their ship settled into its bay with a low hum as its gravity drive spun down. Soon they climbed down from the main door and went about replacing used stock while the next crew helped get the ship ready for duty. There was a lot to do; it looked like a couple of outrigger compartments had been completely emptied. I waited for them to finish with the sterilizing boom before making my way over.

"Hey fellas. Rough one today?"

Chonk eyed me silently. I could sense his tension. "Hello, Mel," he finally said. "Perhaps later." Without another word, he picked up his gear and headed for the nearest lift.

I watched him leave with my hands on my hips, a little put out. "That was awkward."

Bjorn seemed stiffer than usual as well. "Do not take it personally. It was a difficult day."

"As in the run, or the questioning?"

"Both." He arched an eyebrow. "You are familiar with the accident, then?"

"I'm in the middle of everything now, remember? You're the one who told me it'd be good to see the big picture."

"It is bigger than you suspect." He glanced left and right, then back at me. "But we should not discuss this here. In fact we should not discuss it at all."

My eyes widened. "What the hell happened out there?"

I could see he was considering his options, then reached a decision. He forced a smile. "You're correct, it has been a long day. Would you care to join me for dinner in my quarters?"

I was a bit taken aback. That sounded like an invitation to a date, which he couldn't have meant. "Lead the way."

Bjorn's suite was unexpectedly lavish, filled with trinkets that looked as if they'd come from Earth. Reproductions (I assumed) of human artwork hung from the walls, with a few busts of classical musicians arranged along a credenza beneath the window. The furniture was elegant, with graceful lines and lively colors. He tapped at a panel and relaxing piano music began to emanate from the walls.

"Where did you get all this? Please tell me you didn't steal it."

He looked taken aback. "No, of course not. The furniture is your French Reproduction style, created from patterns we observed on Earth. It appeals to me."

I supposed that fit the type: alien Renaissance man. He lit an old-fashioned incense candle in the small kitchen and ordered two cups of tea from the food synth.

"I thought you were hungry."

"A diversion," Bjorn said as he handed me a cup and saucer. "A good excuse to leave. I will eat later." He took a seat opposite me and sipped from his tea, beginning to relax. "I suppose you have many questions."

"I do. But with you acting so cagey, now I have even more."

"As did the transport ministry team. To be honest, I am somewhat exhausted from answering questions. For you, I am happy to make an exception."

"I saw the reports from the scene. Plenty of broken bones and internal injuries. Sounds like it was real mess."

"That it was." He set his tea down on a side table. "We had to hold until the transit control team could make the ship stable. After docking we found the occupants right away; they were all either in the control deck or the passenger cabin. Those in the cabin fared best, though the Reticulans in the control deck were badly injured. One was deceased. You no doubt know the medical aspects from the patient reports. You do not know the rest."

"They called you back to meet with the investigation team. Why would they be so urgent to have you back on scene?"

"We were the first to arrive, and they wanted as accurate a reconstruction of events as possible. Being an Emissary, they also wanted my assessment of the situation. There was some history of the ship's master having unsanctioned encounters with races outside of the Union."

"Like mine?"

He shook his head. "Not at all. In fact, there are none in the Union like these beings. Their existence is more rumor than fact. That is what makes this so troubling."

This was taking a turn for the spooky. "What kind of 'beings' are we talking about?"

"We don't have enough information to make a judgment. Their existence can only be inferred by the evidence they leave behind."

"And what would that be?"

Bjorn shifted in his chair and gave the window a sidelong glance. "One advantage of being an Emissary is what your kind calls 'diplomatic immunity.' I can rest assured that any conversations here are not monitored. And if they are, they are held in strict confidence."

"Wait a minute—has somebody been listening in on me?"

"Only for reasonable concerns, which in your case are not justified." He seemed dismissive, which didn't make me feel any better. "Any contact with this cryptid race is by definition unsanctioned, which would warrant surveillance."

"I think you're avoiding my first question. What kind of evidence?"

He tugged at his uniform. "Biomarkers, like fingerprints. Injuries inflicted on others. Unexplained equipment damage. In this case, there was evidence of both."

I tensed up. "What kind of injuries?"

Bjorn drummed his fingers along the arm of his chair. "Deep tissue damage which appeared inconsistent with the environment and the nature of their other injuries. It didn't escape our notice, but we also weren't overly concerned with them at the time."

"Sure. You're treating the patient, not worrying about how they got hurt." I paused. "Unless whatever caused it presents a danger to you, too."

"The Reticulan casualty appeared to have been deceased for some time. Rigor mortis was beginning to set in. The investigators found this particularly intriguing."

"Wait a minute. Do they think she was *murdered*?"

"No, though it is unlikely that her death occurred as a result of the accident." He stroked his chin. "In my opinion, it may have in fact been a contributing factor."

"Now I'm confused. Was she monkeying around with the gravity drive?" All I knew was that you didn't want to stray too close to one of those things when under power. It might never let you go.

Bjorn was silent for a moment. "This must remain strictly confidential, Melanie. If word gets out that you know, it could affect your residency status."

This felt like a test. I held up my hand. "Scout's honor."

He sucked in his breath. "Very well. This particular ship's master already had a checkered history with the Union. Unsanctioned contacts, questionable cross-border excursions, and so forth. But now he may have been experimenting with a propulsion system that would be revolutionary. It could also be quite dangerous."

"Hard to imagine something more dangerous than an artificial gravity ball powered by antimatter."

Bjorn nodded in agreement. "It is. Yet the possibility remains."

"I can't imagine you know all that just from today. If Union detectives are anything like ours, they're not going to tell you their working theories while they're asking questions."

"Also correct. No, my knowledge of the research comes from other Emissaries in the science ministry."

"Maybe we should talk about the positive aspect, then. What is it about this new technology that makes it so promising?"

"The popular term is 'trans-dimensional jump.' You may remember I mentioned the concept to you some time ago. It could enable near-instantaneous travel across immense distances without relativistic effects. A ship would simply disappear from one point in space and reappear in another."

"How can anything go that fast without affecting time?"

"That is where the trans-dimensional part comes into play." He stared at the window, stroking his chin as he considered how to describe it. "You know of the three physical dimensions we exist in—height, width, depth? Time is the fourth, but let's concentrate on the physical for now. We know there are more which we can't perceive, because we're limited to the three we can."

"I think I follow you. But I can't imagine what the others might be."

"Exactly. The Orionids can perceive at least two more dimensions, which makes them extremely valuable for any research into this problem." He pointed to my hip pocket. "May I see the notebook you brought from home?"

"Sure." I handed it over, uncertain of where he was going.

He took out a single piece of paper. "Imagine you're a two-dimensional being. Your universe would be like this sheet of paper, and everything you experience is only defined by width and depth. You wouldn't be able to perceive anything that existed with that third dimension of height. If something three-dimensional passed through your frame of reference, you would only see its width and its depth. Never its height. It would seem to appear from nowhere, and disappear as easily."

This place never seemed to run out of things that made my brain hurt. "Where's the danger?"

"The energy source. Our best theories indicate a jump drive would need a near-infinite power source, and the next step after antimatter reactions is called zero-point energy. This is something human scientists have hypothesized, so it's perhaps not as exotic as you might believe. Your physicist Feynman calculated the potential zero-point energy contained within a single lightbulb would be enough to boil your planet's oceans. All of them."

"Never saw a lightbulb blow like that."

"That's because its bonds didn't break down at the subatomic level. Zero-point energy exists in the fields between subatomic particles. It is not easily released, much less controlled."

"And this is what has the transport ministry so freaked out."

"I can assure you, it does not end with them. They are merely the frontline investigators. From their questions, we were able to gather that this ship had been powered by an experimental zero-point reactor. Their inertial dampening field was deactivated, possibly because it wouldn't have been necessary for a jump drive. It might even be counterproductive."

"They started out worried that the ship would collide with the ring. Sounds like they knew there was more to be concerned about, like blowing up the whole city."

"Quite. I understand the ship's gravity wave signature drew considerable attention when it appeared." He paused. "Because there wasn't one."

I might not be able to grasp the physics, but that sounded exactly like what he'd been talking about. "It popped into our space, out of nowhere."

"That appears to be the case. It also appears that a functioning inertial field is still necessary."

"Doesn't answer the question of what happened to our dead Reticulan, though." I tried putting the pieces together. "That's what had Chonk so upset."

"He became agitated as our interviews progressed. His cohorts have observed some disquieting activity along our frontiers in the past. I believe this struck a nerve, as you would say."

I drained my tea and set it on the table. "I need to find Chonk. Want to come with?"

We stopped by his quarters first, though neither one of us expected him to be there. Considering the mood he'd been in, there was only one place he could be.

The atmosphere in the Wayside bar was subdued, missing the normal undercurrent of pent-up energy and general rowdiness. We found Chonk at a table by himself, nursing a drink in a ceramic mug. Wisps of steam curled around its brim.

Bjorn and I each pulled up a chair on either side of him. "No *ka'vaa'ma'loi* for you tonight?"

Chonk slowly pushed his mug away. "No alcohol. Clouds mind. Need think."

A glance around the room made it clear his friends shared his mood. Maybe they'd already been talking to him, or maybe the warrior rumor mill had accomplished that for him. "Bjorn told me what you found on that ship. Told me about the kinds of questions you were being asked."

"Could not offer much help. Not want to speculate." He tilted his head at a sullen group of Thubans gathered around a nearby table. "But we know. Have seen before."

"On the frontier?"

He nodded. "Difficult adversary. Unable to determine intentions. May not be intentionally hostile, but still threat. Not compatible with Union."

Bjorn interjected. "As far as we know, no one has ever encountered these cryptids in person. As I mentioned before, we have only seen the aftereffects. Indirect traces of their existence."

I turned back to Chonk. "What kind of traces is he talking about?"

"Ships damaged, abandoned. Derelicts. Colonies abandoned. All this along frontier. Never seen inside Union space. Never this close to capital ring. Dangerous."

"Do we know where that ship came from?"

"No route clearance on file," Chonk said. "Think vessel came from outside Union space."

No wonder these guys were so grim. From what I'd learned of Union history, they'd never been confronted with a serious outside threat. The Thubans had always maintained the peace. Now they might have to go to a war footing, and I recalled what Xeelix had told me in the tunnel collapse. I prayed these beings weren't the threat he'd warned me about.

Chonk pointed to my leg. "How long?"

I was happy to let him change the subject. "Not much longer. I should be back on full duty in a week or so."

"Am glad. You are good medic." Chonk leaned back, relieved to have something else to think about. He waved at the barkeep. "Round of drinks now. On me."

"Now you're talking."

⚕ 29 ⚕

The dull ache in the back of my head was a reminder that no matter how acclimated I might be, *ka'vaa'ma'loi* still packed a wallop. I was near the end of my shift and had been pounding down the water and electrolyte juice all day. I looked forward to heading back to my suite for something that went down nice and easy. A simple peanut butter sandwich sounded awesome right now, and I wondered if the food synth could pull it off.

I'd been moved to one of the larger consoles with the big wraparound holoscreen, covering a sector of Union space that had been mostly quiet. There was a single outpost in my sector, with a few ships moving to and from. It was far enough away for light-wave transmissions to be impossible, so I was dependent on the entanglement comms. The outpost had its own EMS station, so there was little to do but wait for calls from ships in the sector that might need help. We were kind of a third wheel, keeping track of what the local Med Corps teams were doing. We could send units if they got shorthanded, but it would be a long haul for any reinforcements to get on scene.

The quantum entanglement comm might be based on exotic science, but it was easy to use. I'd started my shift with a routine check-in, sending a five-character coded signal that in essence said, "I'm here." After a few seconds the outpost sent back another signal that essentially said, "Yeah, we know."

That's pretty much how my day started. Occasional updates from the outpost, notices of ships transiting my sector, all in five-character messages I'd decode using a list of predetermined phrases that hovered in one corner of the screen. It felt like being an old-fashioned telephone operator.

KSJHI: Ship transiting sector. No assistance required.

LCHZS: EMS team dispatched.

BHSIG: EMS team returned. Patient admitted.

And so on. Not exactly the most fascinating job I'd ever had.

Occasionally rollover calls would appear from other sectors, which was mildly interesting. Considering how sparsely populated each sector was, it was rare that one would get overtaxed to the point where the call would be pushed to somewhere else. Jarra had told me it typically happened along the boundaries between sectors.

It became a lot more interesting when nearly every sector in our quadrant started lighting up. Codes began appearing from nowhere, on everybody's screens. What took things from interesting to alarming was that they were all generic distress codes. No details, no personal identification, it was like calling 911 and leaving the line open. They were appearing on comm screens all over our quadrant, by the hundreds.

"I don't understand. Is this some kind of glitch?"

Jarra moved about between consoles, looking over everyone's shoulders and trying to understand the problem. "A system error would seem reasonable. It also seems unlikely." She pointed at the newest burst of codes on my screen. "These are discrete, from individuals. Thousands of them, all in a short time."

"I don't understand. There's no location identifiers. Where do we even send response teams?" And how many, for that matter.

Jarra closed her eyes and stood motionless, as if something was drawing her attention away. "I believe I may know. Excuse me." She edged in next to me and called up a visual feed from an outpost near Zeta Reticuli. It was a starfield, taken from an observation station. At its far edge was a grayish-brown smudge. "This is Tanaan, a minor planet at the edge of our home system. It has long been used as a research facility. It is also where we maintain particle accelerators for synthesizing element 115."

"You think that's where these calls are originating from?"

"It appears so." She studied me for a moment. "Tell me, do you sense anything strange?"

I'd been too focused on where all these calls might be coming from to notice anything. "Do you mean telepathically? I don't have that ability."

"You have had such bonds in the past with your mentor Xeelix, correct? Once those bonds have been established, they may be suppressed. But they do not wane."

I closed my eyes to clear my head, and felt a tickle at the edge of my mind. Fear. Pain. "There's too much. It's all a jumble, like I'm trying to pick out voices from the edge of a crowd."

"Then you sense much more than you know."

I stared at the growing roster of incoming codes. "What do you think is going on?"

She pointed at my holoscreen. "I suspect we may find out shortly. That planet is two light-hours from the nearest system outpost. They would have recorded the same distress calls over the entanglement net, but will be unable to directly observe anything yet. In the meantime, we must prepare."

I understood. "Mass casualty event."

"I believe you are correct. If it is as I suspect, we are about to need considerably more resources." She tapped out a series of commands into her crystal. "For the time being, we will send our heavy rescue unit to assist. I am also alerting neighboring sector outposts, and advising the Zeta Reticuli outpost to prepare for a surge."

"How far is that from here?"

"Thirteen point four light-years." She looked away from the screen, her black eyes narrowing as she studied my leg. "Xeelix speaks highly of you. What is your physical condition?"

I sat up straight. "I'm ambulatory. That's good enough."

"You are hereby released from dispatch duty. If my suspicions are correct, we will require as many resources as can be spared. Get to the hangar and help any way you can."

I ran out of the dispatch center, ignoring my ankle, and grabbed the first lift up to my suite. My heart pounded as I impatiently counted off the seconds waiting for the door to open. I ran into my room to snatch up my go bag, then hauled ass back to the lift. As it took me down to the hangar, I slipped on my boots and cinched up the one around my bad ankle as tight as I could stand. I was determined to get aboard that heavy unit before it took off.

When I got to the hangar deck, every bay was buzzing with activity. Medics and pilots of every race scurried back and forth between their transports and the gear lockers in anticipation. Those who weren't had clustered in groups, no doubt trying to get a handle on what was happening out at Zeta Reticuli. I sensed the collective adrenaline rush among them.

I could also tell the rumor mill was already getting out of control from snippets of conversation as I ran past:

"...planet exploded..."

"...space-time rift..."

"...gravity lance weapon..."

When I made it to the heavy bay, it was a punch in the gut. The alert beacons were already flashing and the force fields were up. The ship was easily three times the size of our little Class III's, a fat silver cylinder with outriggers bigger than our ambulances. And it was leaving without me.

The floor vibrated as the bay opened, jetting the big transport into space.

My ride was gone.

I coped with my dejection by helping the other crews load up their rigs with as many supplies as each could hold. Every squad had a full complement, with no room for extras. We were playing catch-up with transports that couldn't possibly make it all the way to Reticuli without something much bigger to ferry them. Maybe I could hitch a ride on that. A hospital ship was supposed to be on its way, but that meant we'd be the cleanup crew, relieving the others who were first on scene.

Technically I was off duty, but when an event like this comes along no one willingly stays behind. I'd seen it before with industrial accidents back home, where medics and firefighters rolled up in their personal vehicles if they had to. It made me long for my own ship, but that would've been no more realistic than trying to pilot a LifeFlight chopper on my own.

Then again...

I pulled out my crystal to see who was off duty, and left the hangar at a dead run.

✠ ✠ ✠

Bjorn answered his door, half asleep. "Melanie?"

I shoved past him into his suite. "Good. You're awake."

"I am now." He rubbed at his eyes. "You're rather animated. Is something wrong?"

"Something's happened in the Reticuli system, a place called Tanaan. Something bad. We started getting individual distress calls by the thousands over the entanglement net, but no details. The observation post was a few light-hours away and couldn't see what was happening at the time." By now, they surely could.

As I explained Jarra's suspicions to him, Bjorn pulled out his data crystal to search for any updates. "There's nothing on the newsfeed. I know of Tanaan, though."

"We sent the heavy rescue unit. The other squads are on standby for a ferry, but—"

"It will take them too long to get there to be of any use."

"Exactly. They'll be the cleanup crew. You still have access to your ship?"

"I do. It's still docked. What are you thinking?"

"Isn't it obvious? We need to get our asses out there, pronto. I've already called Chonk, he's on his way to the hangar. Can you contact Sven?"

Bjorn looked perplexed, then understood where I was leading. "Yes, I will contact him. And that is good thinking. This will be a very long run indeed. I could fly the ship, but it sounds as if my services will be required on scene."

"You got it. Come on, time's wasting."

Chonk was waiting for us in the hangar with a pallet full of supplies. It was basic stuff, but enough to set up the Emissary ship as a makeshift ambulance. He'd thrown in a quartet of environment suits for good measure. We tossed our bags on the pallet and waited.

Soon the heavy bay's warning lights pulsed and its shimmering curtain of force fields lit up. When the bay opened to space, a familiar sight pulled in. It was the Emissary's ship, that big, beautiful cigar with the drive rings on either end. I'd never been so happy to see a fast mover.

The ship settled into place and the fields dropped. We ran alongside as Sven emerged from an open hatch, waving us aboard.

"Come, come. I had to assure your dispatch center that we wouldn't linger."

He'd get no argument from me. We loaded our pallet of gear and jumped in.

"I have route clearance to the Tanaan outpost. Access has been restricted to Medical Corps and constabulary vehicles. They made an exception in our case."

"Diplomatic privilege?"

"Let us say that I bent a few rules. There are already a number of vessels on scene. The distance involved is significant," he cautioned me. "We will be traveling at our vessel's maximum relativistic factor. You've been made aware of the time-dilation effects?"

"Not worried about that now. I'll reset my watch later."

☤ 30 ☤

We did our best to get up to speed while en route, but facts were in scarce supply and it didn't help that comms are almost useless when the gravity drive is going full tilt. Bjorn did his best with the information they had aboard, which was considerable. Such were the perks of being an Emissary. For myself, I was fighting the nausea and mental fog that hit me every time they fired up the drive.

He had a map of the system up on one of their holoscreens, with an image of the planet on the other. "This is the most recent imagery of Tanaan from the Reticuli Prime outpost, downloaded right before our departure." The picture was fuzzy, but it was enough to see the dull brown world was crisscrossed with jagged cherry-red gashes. "Those features are not normal. The planet is geologically inactive, which makes it favorable for synthesizing stable isotopes of element 115. Tanaan is one of our primary refinement facilities."

"Jarra said they do research there too. What kind?"

"Materials science and propulsion technologies. The Reticulans are constantly searching for greater efficiencies."

"So we're probably looking at an industrial accident."

"That would be my thought as well, though it would be nice to have some reports from on scene."

We'd had specialized training for mass casualty events and industrial accidents, but nothing on this scale. It felt like we were winging it. "What kind of special considerations are there? Hazards we should be aware of?"

"Ionizing radiation is certain to be a danger. Recall that unrefined 115 is an exceptionally unstable heavy element. I suspect we will find a number of burn victims and cases of radiation poisoning. Anyone working outside of the ship will have to wear protective garments at all times. We should also perform dosimeter checks on each other at regular intervals."

The decon routine after this run promised to be unpleasant, but I was still concerned with getting my head around the situation. "If the complex is that big, I don't understand why we didn't get any distress codes from them. Everything we saw came from individuals. It's like no one had any time to react."

"That may well have been the case. If there was, say, a reactor containment failure, the cascade would have occurred so quickly that destruction was instantaneous. The facility may not exist."

By "facility" he meant the entire planet.

"Very bad," Chonk said. He looked around the inside of our makeshift ambulance. "May need more help."

Bjorn studied the image. "We shall see."

The wavelike ripples in space began to subside, taking my queasiness with them, and soon we emerged in a distant orbit around Tanaan. The grainy image we'd studied on our way didn't come close to conveying the extent of destruction.

The planet was tearing itself apart. The reddish zigzag we'd seen earlier turned out to be a widening crevasse that stretched most of the way between poles, branching off crazily around its equator. Mountain-sized shards of rock had separated from the surface, flung free by the planet's rotation once they were no longer rooted in place. They moved lazily about in their new orbits, slowly disintegrating as tidal forces sheared them apart.

Fountains of molten lava erupted from the cracks, spewing radioactive globules that arced high above the surface before raining back down. It was a horrific sight, and I wondered how many Grays down there could have survived such a disaster. It was hard to see how this could be an industrial accident. "That can't be from a malfunctioning machine."

"Can be if machine covers planet," Chonk said from beside me.

"Recall what I told you about 115," Bjorn said grimly.

I still couldn't comprehend the kind of destructive power that had been unleashed here. It was like something from an end-times fever dream, as if Hell had decided it'd had enough of being confined underground.

A cluster of ships orbited at a safe distance, staying clear of the slowly disintegrating world. They weren't only EMS, a flotilla of every vessel imaginable had come. "Those can't all be Med Corps."

"Are not," Chonk said. Intermixed with the local ambulances were freighters, tankers, and brightly lit passenger transports. Their shapes and configurations varied by race: spheres, cylinders, and diamonds in addition to the cigars, teardrops and saucers I'd become familiar with. "Ships in transit nearby must answer general distress signals. Were many such calls."

One ship stood out which I'd never seen before. It was enormous, all sharp edges and angles, covered in mottled shades of gray and black. Like camouflage. "Is that a warship?"

"Is," Chonk said proudly. "Th'u'ban *Ta'loa*-class heavy cruiser. Much room."

"What kind of medical resources do they have aboard?"

"Sick bay. Surgery center. But keeps supplies mostly for our kind, not many others."

Right. The very thing he'd gotten into trouble for kicking up a fuss about. We'd have to improvise the supply situation, but right now we needed to get everyone off the surface and into a safe place. "What kind of bed space?"

"Not enough," Chonk said. "But much hangar space."

The bulky Thuban cruiser began to move itself in between the makeshift rescue fleet and the planet. The space ahead of it began to shimmer, extending into an oblong shield to protect the others from the decaying world below. It sparkled in random spots, wherever tumbling shards impacted it. An occasional random sliver would make it past the edge of their shield, only to be vaporized by a blast from the ship's energy weapons.

They were protecting the civilians, but all those fireworks were going to make it harder to do anything. We didn't dare get between that cruiser and any stray chunks of planet.

Now that we were in light-wave range, Bjorn pulled up a comm screen on an open monitor. It exploded with text as soon as he did. "Distress signals, from multiple locations. Some are from above the planet."

Those were survivors, stranded in place on continent-sized fragments of Tanaan. They had to be in environment suits or pressurized structures. "Can we tag their locations? Track them?"

"As long as their calls remain open, we will know where they are. Everyone will."

That raised the question of who was in charge up here. We couldn't have every ship running off willy-nilly, that could leave some groups stranded while others might have too many vessels converging on them. And that many ships zipping about at random would create collision risks. I watched the unending stream of distress signals scroll past. "How are those calls being prioritized?"

"I cannot tell. Some are being answered, most are not."

I pointed to the mass of ships outside. "Which one of those is the command post? We need to get patched in to the on-scene commander."

Bjorn scanned the registry of ships, focusing on the Med Corps vessels. His face was a mask of confusion. "I don't see one. All of our EMS ships are awaiting further instructions."

I spat in frustration. This was rapidly devolving into a shit show, and the Med Corps couldn't expect to run everything from the capital with nothing but entanglement comms. "What about our mass casualty procedures?" I'd been digging through them, and the Union apparently had nothing to say about a planet-wide emergency that didn't get bogged down in cultural differences between species. In class, the exercises had been confined to things like transport accidents.

"There is no protocol to address a calamity of this scale," Bjorn said. "It is as if everyone is afraid to make a decision."

Right there were the limitations of an overly polite and well-behaved society, laid bare. Everything worked just fine until the defecation hit the oscillation. I turned to Chonk. His tribe undoubtedly knew a thing or two about managing chaos. "Can we contact your people out there?"

"Yes. Common emergency channel."

"Great. You do the talking." I pointed at the Thuban warship. "That's going to be our command post. Let them know we're coming, and for God's sake *don't shoot*."

✠ ✠ ✠

Sven followed the Thuban instructions precisely, navigating us into a cavernous hangar. This one wasn't protected by anything as exotic as force fields; instead, a pair of massive doors slid open to admit us. I suppose a warship had to keep things simple, and considering the situation outside I was glad for it. There was a rush of air as the doors closed up behind us and the bay repressurized.

We climbed down into their hangar. Their technology might have been wildly beyond ours, but the hangar itself appeared not all that different from what I imagined an aircraft carrier on Earth might look like. I was drawn to a row of wedge-shaped vehicles with stubby wings, neatly lined up along the far end of the hangar.

"What are those?" I asked Chonk.

"Drop ships. For planetary entry."

"I take it they're sturdy?"

He nodded. "Combat vehicles. Armored. Very tough."

Good. They might come in handy.

An imposing Thuban approached us, flanked by what had to be either aides or guards. Maybe both.

He wore a blood red tunic with golden piping. A black sash filled with incomprehensible badges and geegaws was draped across his torso. Chonk placed a fist on his chest in what I gathered was a salute, then turned and introduced us to the ship's commander. His name was the typical barely pronounceable string of consonants, which I shortened to "Grunk." Fortunately their rank structures translated more easily, so I could address him as Commodore without potentially insulting him.

The commodore eyed me guardedly; it was obvious I was his first human, and a scrawny one at that. "You ... scene commander?"

Hadn't thought of myself that way, but somebody had to get things under control or we were going to lose a lot more people down there. "Yes sir, I suppose I am. Thank you for having us aboard."

He studied Chonk with suspicion. They exchanged some rapid-fire hisses, of which my translator only caught about half. It amounted to *the lady knows her stuff, and I trust her.*

Commodore Grunk clasped his claws behind his back. "Very well. Agree must have organization. Many hurt. Many more dead. What needed?"

I crossed my arms and studied the hangar. "Bed space, for starters. Whatever you have that can be cleared to accommodate stretchers, and any gel cushions or mattresses you can spare."

"Not here. This flight hangar. If Med Corps vessels come, need room for ship movement. Will use maintenance hangar. Can put worst injured in sick bay."

Good thinking. It would've been my next question if he hadn't thought of it himself. I pointed to the row of drop ships. "What about those? Can we use them to evacuate victims from the surface?"

He followed my gaze. "Yes. Will alert pilots. Also have medics."

"We'll want to keep some of them here, in your sick bay. They'll know your equipment better than anyone. How are they with treating Reticulans?"

"Some familiar," he said, glancing at Chonk. "Would prefer use other Reticulans."

I really wished Xeelix were here right now. "We'll have to see who's available from the other ships. We might get lucky." That brought up the next question. "We'll need to set up a communications center. I assume you already have something suitable?"

The commodore's golden eyes blinked, as if he was mildly insulted. This was a warship, after all. "Yes! Very good one." He spun about and began walking away briskly. Chonk gave me a gentle nudge to follow.

The commodore led us through a maze of corridors, all at zigzag angles and regularly interrupted by heavy pressure doors. Chonk explained that the ship was designed this way so if a compartment was exposed to space, it could be sealed off in a hurry. Exposed pipes ran the length of each corridor, their purpose a mystery to me. Lockers with vacuum suits and damage-control gear were all over the place. Everything was spartan and functional, with none of the graceful aesthetics of the Union stations. It marked the difference between mundane civilian life and the no-nonsense warrior class who protected it.

The ship's climate control was optimized for Thubans, which made it uncomfortably hot for me and Bjorn. I pulled my hair back and unzipped my coveralls, stripping them down and tying the sleeves around my waist. Bjorn quirked an eyebrow, but if the

Thubans had any interest in checking out a human female in a sports bra, they didn't show it.

We ended up in a large octagonal chamber filled with holoscreens depicting everything happening in space around us. More Thubans worked at consoles while one stalked the room, looking over their shoulders and occasionally giving directions. Chonk told me this was the watch officer in charge of running the ship in the commodore's absence.

The watch officer snapped to attention when we entered, and was waved down by the commodore. They proceeded to converse in private. The watch officer initially seemed as perplexed as his commander had been at seeing me, occasionally looking over his boss's shoulder to size me up.

The commodore returned to our small group. "Will provide all you need here. Tactical action center at your disposal."

"Thank you, sir." I rubbed my hands together while getting a feel for the room. Every display was of course in Thuban, so I slipped on my visor and let the translation routine get to work. The indecipherable characters soon began to resolve into something approximating English.

The watch officer kept eyeballing me, so I decided to break the ice. "My name is Melanie. I'm a human, part of the Medical Corps emergency service. Thank you for your help."

"T'Ch'uum-yu-K'Gaar. Tactical officer. You . . . welcome?"

Close enough. "Full names are difficult for me. May I call you Chummy?"

"That is acceptable."

It'd have to be. I made a sweeping motion at the holoscreens which encircled the room. "Can you explain to me what we're looking at here, Chummy?"

"Planet disintegrating. Reason unknown. Civilian fleet holding in stationary orbit, waiting direction. You provide?"

Somebody had to. "Yes, for now. How many beds does your ship hold?"

"Have five hundred twelve crew. Thirty beds in sick bay. Can use crew bunks."

"Keep the hospital beds in sick bay, we'll need them. Bring whatever bedding you can spare to the maintenance hangar. And let the other ships know we're setting up the command post here." I paced the room, trying to collect my thoughts. How could a civilization this far-reaching not have a planetwide disaster plan in place? Was it truly that inconceivable?

The local Union outpost had sent everything they could. Half a dozen Class III's and a single heavy rescue ship waited behind the Thuban cruiser and its protective field. More Med Corps ships were arriving as we spoke, including our own heavy rig, and joined the crowd waiting in orbit. They were simply following protocol: No one goes on scene until it's secure.

Watching the catastrophe unfold on Tanaan, it was impossible to see how it could ever be secure enough. Fountains of lava continued to erupt from its surface, and with each explosion more distress signals disappeared. We were losing lives down there at an alarming rate. I waved at a nearby screen, where each vehicle in orbit was marked with a discrete code. "Are you in contact with all of these ships?"

"Affirmative. All standing by for instructions."

Just like everybody else. I could understand the civilians, though. It was encouraging to see so many out there, but they had to be scared half to death. "This is where I'll need a lot of help, because I'm not familiar enough with them." I pointed to the biggest transport, one of those massive horseshoe-crab ships. "That's a passenger liner, isn't it?"

"Correct."

"Great. Please tell them to start preparing space. Same thing you're doing here: Every available bed needs to be opened up, preferably in a common area. Tell them to be ready to receive our response teams."

Chummy gestured to a pair of Thubans at a nearby console and hissed instructions at them. "Is being done."

"Great. Thank you." I pointed at a nearby trio of Med Corps Class III's. "Next, contact those ambulance ships, tell them to dock with the biggest transport. Have the crews unload all of their gear and stand by to receive patients."

That'd be six medics, nine at the outside, with their only equipment being whatever they had aboard. I was counting on a passenger liner having some kind of medical provisions; if they carried a ship's doctor then he/she/it ought to have been well ahead of me.

We still had the immediate problem of transporting victims off the surface. Overshadowing that was the fact that we didn't yet know what had caused this, which is the first thing to determine in a mass casualty event. Without that knowledge, we couldn't anticipate what else might be about to literally blow up in our faces. It would put first responders in even worse danger, and we needed everyone we could find.

I crossed my arms and tapped my feet impatiently, studying the situation unfolding below. The surface fault lines appeared worst toward the equator, where the planet's rotation was shearing it apart. Tanaan was tearing itself to pieces, as if the glue holding it together had evaporated.

What was the glue that held planets together? Gravity. I might be able to manage the logistics from up here, but understanding *that* was way out of my depth.

I turned to Bjorn. "What the hell happened down there?"

31

"I am struggling to understand this as well," Bjorn said. He'd been hovering over one of the Thubans, pulling up every file they could find on the Tanaan operation. "There are immense quantities of energy involved, both in production and storage. The stable 115 isotopes are created by a pair of particle accelerators which encircle the planet along its equator. The isotopes are collected and transported to containment facilities at the mid-latitudes. Production is managed from operations centers at the poles. Isotope distribution is strictly controlled due to the substance's gravitational potential."

"They're activated by applying power, right? I assume that means antimatter."

"The reactors are beneath the surface at each pole, adjacent to the production control complexes. Based on what we can see, I do not believe they are the proximal cause. A reactor accident would be devastating, but localized. The effects would be blindingly obvious." He pointed to an interactive map of the planet, or what was left of it. "You can see their containment fields are still intact. This was caused by something else."

"Sure. Of course." I nodded blankly, having no idea of what I was looking at. "Could it be as simple as a natural disaster, like a volcanic eruption?"

Bjorn looked at me as if I had grown a third eyeball.

"Hear me out. Geologists on Earth have figured out that a good-sized piece of the continent I come from is sitting on top of a dormant 'super volcano.' If it ever blows, they think it would turn most of North America into ash. Could that be what's happening here?"

He shook his head. "Tanaan is geologically lifeless. No tectonic activity, no subduction zones, no volcanism. That is why it was chosen for 115 production."

"Their current predicament would suggest otherwise," I said tartly.

He stared at the cauldron roiling Tanaan's surface. "Quite." Bjorn tapped at his chin, obviously troubled. "There had to be a catastrophic subsurface energy release. Something self-sustaining. Something that would propagate."

"Something with enough juice to melt the interior, turn all that inert rock into magma."

"That is what troubles me. For this to have happened so rapidly suggests tremendous energy, enough to cause the planet's interior matter to rapidly change states."

"You mean from solid to liquid?"

"Or to gas. This cannot simply be an artificially created volcanic event, though it is also that. It implies a sudden loss of mass density, enough to alter the planet's gravitational potential. That would also account for the shearing effects along the equator. Tanaan no longer has enough gravity to hold its remaining mass together."

"Am I right that it would've had to occur deep beneath the surface, like near the core?"

"That would be my estimation, otherwise I believe the effects would be more localized." He paused. "Do you recall our discussion of other, more exotic, energy sources?"

My eyes widened. "Zero point. Feynman's lightbulb." Enough untapped quantum whatever-it-was to boil oceans. Or rock.

Bjorn clenched his jaw, possibly the most emotion I'd ever seen from him. "That would explain a great deal." He turned to Chummy. "Have you received any communications from the surface facilities?"

The Thuban nodded. "Production control. Both stable enough to evacuate."

"Do they require our assistance, or do they have enough vehicles to evacuate themselves?"

"South complex evacuating. North need help."

"What of the mid-latitude processing stations?"

Chummy shook his head. "Most gone. Distress signals all individuals."

Watching Tanaan's rapidly deteriorating condition on screen, I could imagine the chaos on the surface. The ground was collapsing beneath them, swallowing up entire complexes. Those who escaped had gathered on whatever high ground they could find, judging by where all the calls were coming from. "We need to get the survivors off the planet. The commodore said we could send the drop ships we saw down in the hangar. Is that still viable?"

Chummy studied the shattered planet on screen. It was filled with clusters of pulsing amber icons near the processing stations. Each represented an individual call for help. There were hundreds of them. Conditions down there would be dangerous as hell, but if those drop ships were made for combat...

"Affirmative," he finally answered. "Can hold thirty Th'u'bans each. Most signals Reticulan, drop ship hold perhaps twice as many."

That would be a good start, but any Thubans we sent to the surface were going to have their hands full. "Have your medics triage on scene. Critical injuries are the first to go, if they think the patient can survive long enough to get them up here. Any minor injuries have to stay until the next ship lands."

"Agree," Chummy said. "What will Med Corps vehicles do?"

I'd been thinking of a plan for them, but needed Bjorn's expertise. I pointed at the massive fragments of Tanaan that had separated from the surface, finding their own orbits as the planet crumbled beneath them. "There's still a lot of active signals coming from those shards. Can a Class III ship land on something like that?"

"It would be difficult, but not impossible."

"Then we have a plan." I clapped my hands and raised my voice for everyone to hear. A dozen Thuban heads snapped up in surprise as their translators scrambled to keep up. "We're sending the drop ships to the surface clusters. Med Corps transports will go to the orbiting fragments. The most critical cases get brought here, the rest go to the civilians. Keep any fast-movers on standby for transporting victims to Med Corps hospitals. We start with the largest concentrations of distress signals, and move on from there."

⌘ ⌘ ⌘

Now that we had a plan, things came together quickly. Chonk helped his fellow Thubans prioritize where to send their drop ships, while Bjorn and I started dispatching Med Corps rigs. We had over thirty individual craft on the move, with more on the way, and it was a sight to behold. Thuban traffic controllers were all asses and elbows as they kept everyone from running into each other on their way to the surface.

I watched as the drop ships left the hangar one by one, each a few seconds apart before zipping away for different parts of the planet. Getting our ambulances moving was a little more delicate, and something of a crash course in orbital mechanics for me. Nothing traveled in a straight line, and so our dispatch priorities went to those ships in the best position to intercept the orbiting clusters of distress signals. It was a complex ballet that could have easily fallen into chaos, but the Thuban controllers had a lot of practice in keeping mass formations from flying into each other. Within half an hour the hangar deck was empty and every Med Corps rig was on its way to a rock which had once been part of Tanaan.

Now would come the hard part. We'd be receiving patients soon and could get overwhelmed in short order.

Bjorn would manage the logistics. Each arriving ship would need to turn around quickly for its next run, and he was in a far better position to handle that. I grabbed Chonk and had him lead me down to the maintenance hangar and our makeshift emergency ward.

The hangar was cleaner than expected, which was a welcome surprise. I'd expected it to look like an auto repair shop, but its brightly polished floor sparkled from the overhead glow panels. Whatever equipment they normally used here had been put away in storage racks along the back wall. Three hundred beds had been brought in, filling the hangar in neat rows. The only other sign this place was meant for maintenance was a Thuban drop ship tucked away in a far corner, missing some panels.

Two spaces on the floor had been left open, each a massive rectangular section marked with orange borders. Chonk explained those were lift elevators. They'd bring the arriving craft directly up here from the flight deck with our patients.

A team of medics waited for us, mostly Thubans from the ship's complement. A half-dozen Med Corps types were with them, a mix of Reticulans and Gliesans, which I hadn't expected. "We came from the Union outpost," the lead Gliesan explained. "Many of our clan work on Tanaan."

"Your kind is working there? Maybe you can help us understand what happened, keep more from being hurt. Do you know what they were doing?"

The Gliesan's mandibles clicked. "Excavation for a hardened test site, deep underground. Construction was largely complete. We do not know its exact purpose."

I turned to the senior Reticulan medic. "Do you know anything about what they were building?"

"I do not," he said, rather stiffly. If he was going to have a problem taking orders from the new girl, he'd have to get over that real quick.

"Come on," I said. "Given what they do here, even I can hazard a few guesses."

The Gray was unmoved. "My knowledge is limited to medical matters."

I ignored him and addressed the group. "First off, you can call me Mel. I'm the on-scene commander until somebody who knows better tells me otherwise. We're not going to bother with other names because I'll forget them." They weren't a particularly emotional group and I wasn't concerned about hurting feelings.

"Our first transport from the surface should be arriving soon; expect fifty to sixty patients on each run. Medics on the drop ships are doing a hasty triage on scene, and we'll respond based on how they're tagged when they arrive. We do not have time to second-guess the guys on scene. Anyone down there who is ambulatory and not in obvious distress is going to the civilian transports outside, so we'll be receiving the most critical patients." I focused on the Thubans. "Those who are at imminent risk of death will go upstairs to your ship's surgeon."

I surveyed the group. "Most of our victims will be Reticulan or Gliesan. From the distress calls we've received and the conditions on the surface, expect a lot of crush injuries and burn victims. If there's anything peculiar to your kind that doesn't get covered in training, now is a good time to inform the rest of us."

One of the Reticulans spoke up. "Given the nature of production and research activities on Tanaan, we should be prepared for radiation poisoning as well. If the accelerator coils have been breached, there would be a considerable release of ionizing radiation. Reticulans generally respond well to iodide-based prophylactics." He waved to a trio of containers and opened one. "We have brought as many as could be spared from the outpost clinic."

The crates were filled with shiny new rectal probes. Of course. I grabbed a handful and tossed them into my trauma bag, and had the others do the same.

A Thuban spoke up. "Sick bay has blood plasma. Broad spectrum. Can tailor platelets for race."

I glanced over at Chonk, who looked pleasantly surprised. Somebody had listened to him after all.

The Gliesan started clicking his mandibles again. I couldn't make it out at first, then the translator caught up: "Hyperbaric."

"You mean positive-pressure oxygen?"

More clicks. "Yes. Our exoskeletons protect against heat and radiation damage."

If it didn't cook their innards first. If they survived the initial burns, their shells would still be severely weakened. "Where I'm from, we used silver nylon dressing for wrapping burns. Do you have something like that?"

Both Thuban and Gliesan translators seemed to have trouble at first. The lead Reticulan spoke up. "Yes. You mean element 47. We have a polycarbonate wrap plated with 47. It is quite effective for protecting against skin toxicity from radiation."

Now the others understood what I'd been asking for. "Have that," the Thuban said. "Much in sick bay."

That made sense. Burn supplies were something a combat ship probably needed plenty of. "Okay, platelet-rich plasma and '47' wraps. Whatever they can spare, get it down here." Two of the Thubans took off running for a nearby lift.

"In the meantime, what about this hyperbaric oxygen therapy? We're on a spaceship, I imagine there's a way to rig that."

"Is so," Chonk said. He pointed to a row of heavy doors along the hangar wall. "All compartments adjacent to hangar spaces pressurized. Can control individually."

"Awesome. Let's get those set up. Any Gliesan burn victims go straight to those rooms. In the meantime, everybody get into their exposure suits."

It was starting to feel like we might actually be able to get this under control. A warning siren began to wail as one of the big lift elevators began to recede into the floor. Our first transport had arrived.

⚕ 32 ⚕

Clamshell doors opened in back of the drop ship before the lift had time to settle. The unmistakable stench of burnt flesh wafted out along with high-pitched wails from voices inside. I pulled down the visor of my environment suit and tightened the seal. *Here we go.*

A pair of Thuban medics hopped out with the first stretcher, an old-fashioned hand-carried job without the high-tech repulsor lifts and vital-sign monitors we had in the Med Corps. It was simple, functional, and sturdy, exactly what a military medevac team would need.

We converged on the ship and began bringing out patients in pairs. This batch was all Reticulan, easily carried by the hulking Thubans. I let the big guys do the heavy lifting and immediately got to work on our patients, hurrying down the line of beds to check their triage tags. Instead of color-coding, since we couldn't know which beings could perceive which spectra, they'd ranked everything by number. "3" needed minimal treatment and would go to the civvies, "2" would be for non-life-threatening injuries, while anybody tagged "1" needed immediate treatment. "0" was dead or close to it. All of our victims were tagged 1 with more than a few rapidly on the way to 0.

As expected, there were a lot of burns and radiation poisoning. Three of the Thuban medics walked through the rows of beds, waving their version of Geiger counters above our patients and recording the levels from each. The meters' chirping sounded like a chorus of crickets echoing through the hangar.

We had a lot of crush injuries as well. Broken limbs, internal injuries, and more than a few missing appendages.

The remaining medics each took a row of beds and began making their rounds, first hooking up IV fluids and pushing pain meds to whoever could tolerate it. There weren't many who couldn't, other than a few in respiratory distress. Those were taken straight upstairs to the ship's sick bay.

I weaved between rows, checking on the Grays who looked to be in particular trouble. One had third-degree burns over almost half his body, from the waist down. A quick pass of the transducer showed signs of blistering in his airway. His lungs sounded raspy, like sandpaper. "What's your name, buddy?"

Already confused from his injuries, he was even more surprised to see a human tending to him. *Garak*. Even telepathically, he sounded shaky.

I kept an eye on his vitals and started talking to him like I would any other patient. "Hi, Garak. I'm Mel. We're going to do our best here for you, okay? Try to relax." I felt for the handful of Reticulan probes in my trauma bag, but one look at his charbroiled groin made it clear their preferred delivery system wasn't going to work. His pulse was thready and his blood pressure was starting to fall precipitously. Even with the mask, O_2 saturation was barely hovering at eighty percent. Reticulans could tolerate lower sats than humans, but not that low for long.

I waved over a pair of Thuban orderlies. "This one's in respiratory distress. He needs to go upstairs right now," I said in a low voice. It wasn't my place to say, but the docs would probably have to amputate his legs as well. We exchanged knowing looks as they carried him away.

Every patient we saw suffered from some variation of the same injuries, it was only a matter of extent. The ones who were on the edge were sent upstairs, with a constant rotation of orderlies running for the elevators. In short order we'd probably filled half of their sick bay. We had a couple dozen Grays left in the hangar, all miserable but stable.

Another warning siren blared as the heavy-equipment lift began to descend. Another transport had arrived.

Burn injuries are the worst. Imagine what's happening to a steak on the grill or a chicken in the fryer; now imagine that's you. Third-degree burns are especially gruesome; that means the flesh has been cooked down through the fatty layers. Burns that deep over only one percent of a human body are considered severe, and it doesn't take much more for them to become life-threatening.

I stripped off my mask and wiped at my brow as the next drop ship was raised into the hangar. Clamshells opened, and more Thubans emerged carrying litters of what looked like roasted lobsters . . .

Oh. *Gliesans.* I know that lobster analogy sounds horribly callous, but dear God were they in bad shape. Their milky white exoskeletons had been turned red, with many of their limbs curled up at awkward, brittle angles. More than a few were missing eyestalks.

I can't explain why I felt so emotional at the sight of beings which had once triggered every imaginable insect phobia, plus a few I'd probably made up. A whole clan of them had put themselves at risk to drag me out of a deep hole in the ground, because I had done the same for their kind. All for simply doing my job.

I ran to the ship as more Gliesans were carried out into the hangar. A few random passes with my transducer over the first row of patients showed they were in fact still alive and stable, apparently in a self-induced torpor in reaction to trauma. The outsides of their shells were literally cooked, and all of them were spiking the rad meters. I looked to the other medics, who signaled they were all seeing the same thing.

I put my scanning gear away and spoke up to the group. "All right. Every one of these guys is going into oxygen therapy, *stat.*" They stared at me as their translators skipped over that last bit. "That means ASAP. *Right freaking now.*"

We all started picking up stretchers full of burned Gliesans and followed Chonk through an open door. It was a supply room, where he and a few Thuban mechanics had been busy clearing the equipment racks. It was perfect. We carefully stacked our litters along the empty shelves, with room left over. Two Gliesan medics scurried in behind us, and we shoved a crate full of those silver-plated bandages in behind them. A Thuban mechanic closed the hatch and began pressurizing the compartment until the medics inside signaled for him to stop.

Those little guys were tough, and I had high hopes for every one of them to recover. If only the rest of our runs could've been that easy.

The drop ships began to arrive with a regular cadence; I found out that they were all on the flight deck, waiting for their turns on the lifts. As soon as we'd finish offloading one wave, the next would arrive.

The hours went by in a blur. Check tags, take vitals, administer meds, move on to the next. This assembly line was interrupted by the occasional field amputation, a procedure with which the Thubans were distressingly efficient. *Combat medics*, I kept having to remind myself.

It was almost a relief when another shipload of Gliesan victims was unloaded, as they remained fairly straightforward. After a couple of hours our makeshift hyperbaric chambers were filled with them, most recovering quite well on their own. A Gliesan medic told me even their eyestalks would grow back over time.

A few didn't make it, too badly burned to survive. They were literally roasted in their shells. The stench made me queasy to the point of throwing up a couple of times—not that it was repulsive, quite the opposite. It was too much like the smell of stone bugs roasting on the grill at Wayside. I wondered how many Thubans would be swearing off that dish forever after today. I certainly was.

Every bed in our ward had been filled, all of them Reticulans. At that point, we were faced with the dreadful task of deciding which level 1 patients needed to give up their beds for new arrivals. If it didn't look like they'd make it, to the floor they went. It was an odd and depressing combination: Level 2 patients had already been relegated to sitting on the floors, lined two or three deep along the hangar walls. Now they were being joined by level 1's who were going to die. The Grays are highly disciplined beings, but even the most stoic must have recoiled at that thought. I could only imagine what they were saying to each other telepathically.

I followed Chonk into a storage room off the hangar, stripped away my mask, and collapsed beside him on the floor. We sat together in luxurious silence for several minutes. I might even have slept a little.

Chonk eventually nudged me back into reality. "How doing?"

"Tired," I whispered. "Very, very tired."

He handed over a bottle of electrolyte juice to jolt me awake. I downed it in one long gulp and rested my head against the wall.

"You strong. Do well. Has been long day."

I checked my watch. The first drop ship had arrived six hours ago, the Thuban cruiser was full, and there was still work to do. More ships would be coming. "It has. And we're not done yet."

"No," he said sadly. "Are not. Very bad."

"Any word from Bjorn?" I'd been too busy to keep in touch with him.

"More ships arriving. Second Th'u'ban cruiser. Med Corps hospital ship from capital, bring many with it. More transports, more beds."

"Good. Maybe someone else can take over." Not that I'd been doing much in that role since first getting our plan in motion. Bjorn must have been up to his eyeballs in their command center.

"Jarra came with. Is on-scene commander now. Needs status report."

That should have been a relief, but what was I going to tell her? *Thanks for coming, welcome to the shitshow.* Somehow I could sense her displeasure from here.

Chonk stood and helped me to my feet. I surprised him with a long, tight hug. "Thanks, my friend."

The control center was in much the same state as when we'd left it, but with a very tired Bjorn slouched behind an empty console. The Thuban commodore stalked the room with his claws clasped behind his back, watching the evacuation progress on the surrounding holoscreens.

He acknowledged us with a curt nod. Bjorn stood to meet us.

"How are conditions down below?"

"About what you'd expect," I said, before realizing he wouldn't have had any idea what to expect. He'd been attached to the Med Corps to be my case officer; the training was a side benefit. "It's under control," I finally said. "Overcrowded, but we're handling it. There's no room for any more patients, though."

"More relief is on the way. Transports from all over the Union are arriving. The commodore has them holding in rectilinear halo orbits, out of harm's way until we need them."

Not for the first time, I nodded as if I knew what he was talking about. It made more sense to see it depicted on screen. A whole daisy-chain of ships moved slowly in a wide oval around an empty point in space, far enough away that we could only see them as icons from their transponder beacons. It looked like a string of pearls, with individuals regularly breaking off to make their way toward what was left of Tanaan. The planet itself had become a boiling cauldron, barely held together by the collective gravity of its fragments.

"Where's the Med Corps? Chonk said we had a ship en route."

Bjorn swiped at his holoscreen, shifting the point of view. "The hospital ship is in a common orbit with us, offset one hundred twenty degrees ahead. The other Thuban cruiser is in the same orbit, one hundred twenty degrees behind. This gives us complete coverage of the planet with direct line-of-sight communication."

"Pick up any new distress calls, then?"

He shook his head sadly. "Not for several hours. We are moving into recovery operations. Jarra has requested a report."

I plopped into an empty seat beside him. "Sure. Let's talk."

"Excellent work, Melanie," Jarra said, though I couldn't shake a certain sense of displeasure from her. "You have given us cause to examine our response plans once this event is behind us."

That might take a while. Losing Tanaan had eliminated a third of the Union's supply of a crucial element. Interstellar travel was about to become a lot more expensive, and a lot less frequent.

"How long have you been on duty?"

Continuously, or just since we got here? Her slit mouth tipped into a tight frown. Damn it. She'd heard my thoughts. "It's been almost seven hours since the first evacuees arrived. We were evaluating the scene and putting plans together before that. Honestly, ma'am, I haven't thought about it."

On screen, I saw her turn to a subordinate and think orders at him. The room behind her was filled with more Grays. Tanaan was one of their worlds, and they'd taken this disaster personally. She turned back to face me. "Perhaps you should. It has been at least forty-two hours since your shift ended, though your proper time reference is no doubt a good deal less. We will make the necessary adjustments when you return. You are relieved. Jarra out."

The screen flashed blank.

I turned to Bjorn in confusion. "Am I in trouble? Because that sounds like I'm in trouble."

He laughed. "Perhaps. You missed your last two shifts."

I looked at my watch. "That can't be. I...aw, hell." *Friggin' Einstein, again.* "How fast were we going?"

"Enough to make you miss work twice, apparently."

Shift work was hard enough without your personal clock moving at a different rate than your boss's clock. She'd told me to help, and I hadn't taken that to mean staying in the hangar back at HQ. I rubbed at my forehead with the heels of my hands. "They can take it out of my pay."

Bjorn removed his earpiece ceremoniously and placed it on the console. "Come, let us find some food."

"That sounds—"

Melanie.

A ghostly voice at the back of my mind, like when you think someone has called your name but nobody's there. "Yes?"

It was more distinct this time. *Melanie.*

"Xeelix?"

Bjorn turned to me in surprise. I tapped a finger on my forehead, not knowing how else to indicate someone was thinking at me.

Yes. I am relieved you can hear me.

I closed my eyes in concentration. *Where are you? I wondered if you'd show up.*

I am on the surface, at the southern production control center.

I grabbed Bjorn and spun him back around to the open console, wildly gesturing for him to log back in. "Xeelix is down there," I whispered harshly. "Find him!"

You will not be able to locate me. I have lost my identification ring.

"He's lost his ID ring," I told Bjorn, who got to work trying to isolate Xeelix's personal signal. *Hang on, we're looking for it. Do you think it's close by?*

I am afraid it is gone, along with my right hand.

"What?" I blurted out. *Your hand—*

Severed by rockfall from an erupting vent. The surrounding area was consumed by lava flow not long thereafter. I made it to high ground. If you do isolate my ring, it has most likely been carried far from my location. Can you spare a transport?

Surrounded by molten rock and missing a hand, Xeelix still managed to be polite. "He asked us to send a ship," I told Bjorn. "What do we have?"

We grabbed Chonk and ran back down to the flight hangar. After a hurried conversation with a Thuban pilot, we clambered aboard a drop ship and were headed for the surface within minutes.

By now Tanaan had devolved into a loosely formed ball of molten rock interspersed with islands of solid ground. The poles had remained mostly intact, but they were increasingly being deformed by localized eruptions. With any useful signal from Xeelix's ring now long gone, our pilot flew us in a wide circle around the south polar complex.

"Xeelix said he was on high ground," I hollered at the pilot from my seat. The drop ship was loud, missing the swank interiors I'd become used to in favor of simple military functionality. Their machines hadn't been crafted with human-sized occupants in mind, and weren't particularly comfortable either. I held tight to the restraint bars, feeling like a toddler who'd snuck aboard a roller coaster and was seriously regretting her life decisions. "Look for hills, tall buildings, anything above the—"

There was that tickle in the back of my mind again. *Melanie.*

Yes! *We're here! Where are you?*

I see your vehicle. Tell the pilot I am off his left wing, and to maintain his turn rate. I am on top of a promontory, overlooking the complex.

"He's off your left wing!" I shouted. "He said to keep your turn rate."

Chonk relayed the command for me, and answered with the Thuban version of a thumbs-up.

Good. You are pointed almost directly at me. Stop turning and fly straight ahead.

"He says stop turning! Fly straight!"

Excellent. You are about half a kilometer away. Your pilot should perhaps slow down now.

Xeelix just might polite himself to death one of these days, but it wasn't going to be today if we could help it. I wriggled out from under the restraint bar and clambered up into the cockpit behind Chonk. I had to pull myself up to see outside, feeling even more like a toddler out of her depth. "He said we're almost on top of him, half a kilometer."

"Heard," Chonk said, and nodded toward the pilot who deftly manipulated a pair of control levers on either side of his seat. "Pilot thinks he see."

I stood on a railing behind Chonk's back for a better view, hoping I hadn't accidentally kicked something important, like an ejection seat. On a jagged outcropping overlooking what was left of the production buildings lay a small form in a tattered environment suit. That was our guy.

The pilot slowly pulled into a hover and opened the rear clamshell doors. I was about to jump out when Bjorn grabbed my arm. "Lower gravity, Melanie. You must move deliberately. Take it easy."

Right. Careful steps. I dropped in slow motion to the ground.

Xeelix propped himself up on his good arm, too weak to talk. *It is good to see you both.* He studied my face with those deep, penetrating eyes. *You look tired, Melanie.*

"Nice to see you too, Doc. And you look like shit." We lifted him together and carried him into the waiting drop ship. Chonk signaled the pilot, who closed up the door and began pulling away, leaving the decaying hell of Tanaan behind.

We laid Xeelix onto a gurney and I began cutting away his suit, while Bjorn fit a fresh breathing mask over his face and started taking vitals with the transducer.

I examined his arm. The point at which his hand was severed had been crudely cauterized. I shot him a questioning look.

I had to stop the bleeding, and had used up my tourniquets on others. There was no shortage of heat sources, thankfully.

"Thankfully," I repeated under my breath. He'd cauterized his own wound on a lava rock. My stomach turned at the thought.

The injuries extended well beyond where the hand had been severed, with ugly purple bruises spreading below his elbow. I ran the transducer over his arm to check internal pressure. I was worried about compartment syndrome, which was a danger in humans who'd suffered crush injuries. Reticulan anatomy was similar enough—if the fascia surrounding his muscles were stretched too much, it could cause enough swelling to stop blood flow. If left untreated, it could kill the underlying muscle tissue and nerve endings. Even with their advanced medicine, at that point the only treatment was amputation.

I know what you must do, Melanie. I can guide you. He pointed at his forearm. *Start your incision here. End it here, below the elbow joint.*

I pulled the plasma scalpel from my trauma bag and made small talk as I calibrated it, more to calm myself than Xeelix. He was unflappable, as usual. "I don't get it. How are you even here in the first place?"

With age comes enhanced telepathic sensitivities, and I am quite old, even by Reticulan standards. I sensed great trouble. When I learned of the first emergency signals, I arranged for transport. The crew did not elect to stay with me.

That was understandable, if maybe a bit cowardly. "So you stayed down here, made sure the survivors were evacuated."

For a time. Trust me, I did not intend to remain. I am sure the others thought I'd been lost to the eruption that caused this injury. It did not help that I was unconscious for some time. I do not blame them. Nor should you.

Fixing blame was the last thing on my mind now; it was time to fix Xeelix's arm before he lost it. Bjorn administered the pain meds, and I got to work.

☤ 33 ☤

It wasn't the prettiest incision I'd ever made, but it would do the trick. Relieve the pressure inside his arm enough to keep it alive, let the actual doctors do the rest. We flew him to the Med Corps hospital ship and ran him straight up to their trauma center, where a team of Gray docs waited. I gave my report to the attending, who was astonished that this unlikely human had performed field surgery on one of the Corps' most senior physicians without making matters worse. So, just another day that ends in "y."

We checked in with Jarra in the operations center, and filled her in on what that rogue Thuban drop ship had been up to. She was likewise astonished at our exploits, and even more so that Xeelix had been down on the surface this whole time without anyone knowing about it.

That could've been a much longer conversation, but she had other things on her plate. Namely, the ship which had suddenly appeared out of nowhere.

This one was nothing like the bulky Thuban battlewagons, or even the more stylish civilian transports. It was spectacular, a glittering jewel hanging in space, or a Christmas ornament the size of a small town.

It was ellipsoid, with its top half made of a transparent dome protecting what looked to be dense vegetation. It was a massive greenhouse, a conservatory floating in space.

The lower half was more functional, filled with whatever machinery was needed to make it function as a spaceship. A cluster of cylinders extended underneath like stalactites, with the largest of them beneath the ship's center. This one was filled with windows lit from within, which gave away the scale of the thing. Unless it was made for beings the size of small dogs, this ship was a beast.

Jarra stiffened. She seemed to anticipate what was coming next. One of the holoscreens flickered as its image shifted. An old man appeared against a background of cherry wood paneling, with what looked for all the world like an oriental tapestry hung behind him. His hair was slicked back, and he wore a gray wool suit with a garish floral necktie.

He was *human*.

"Jarra," he said.

"Gideon."

Bjorn winced as I squeezed his hand tight. *Gideon?*

"Can you tell me what's happened on Tanaan?"

"I was hoping you could tell me. Or rather, the science ministry. I am certain they have questions."

"I have a few of my own, though I wouldn't expect you to be knowledgeable about those matters."

Jarra clasped her hands behind her back, edgily working her long fingers. She looked pissed. "No, but I am curious. Though as you can see, we have many other concerns at this time."

"You're right about that. We were already en route to Tanaan when I heard about the accident. This is awful, simply awful."

Bjorn shot me a sideways glance, which I interpreted as Emissary for *bullshit*.

"We have the matter of survivors under control. All who could be evacuated are now aboard Union vessels, including many of your Gliesan contractors. You say you were already en route?"

Gideon shifted his weight. That's when I noticed he was leaning on a cane. "I was coming to evaluate the results of an ongoing research project. Tell me, when will my employees be free to leave?"

"Not for some time, though ultimately that is not up to me. They are all currently either in burn wards or undergoing treatment for radiation poisoning."

He made a *tsk* sound. "Terrible. A tragedy."

"Quite."

I'd heard enough, and was too tired to worry about stepping on anyone's toes. I moved closer to Jarra, making sure the man on screen could see me.

His mouth fell open, appropriately startled. He quickly composed himself. "Well, this is certainly a surprise! And who are you, young lady?"

"Melanie Mooney. From Earth, if you haven't figured that out."

An insincere smile crossed his lips, ending at his eyes. "North American. Midwest, if I gauge the accent correctly. Forgive me, but it's been some time since I've spoken with other humans."

"About eighty years, if I have my history right."

"The gal's done her homework. Yes, in Earth time. What brings you to the Union?"

"Recruited by the Medical Corps. And you?"

He ignored my question. "Med Corps, hmm? You a nurse?"

I shook my head. "Paramedic."

"Well, that *is* impressive. I suppose there's a lot of things you girls can do on Earth these days."

"Sure," I said acidly, getting my back up. "Some of us even work outside the home, become doctors. Lawyers. Even astronauts. It's all rather liberating." I threw in that last one just to get under his skin.

"Astronauts are a bit after my time, though it's an amusing notion given our surroundings. I'm sure you'll find the Medical Corps to be fascinating work. I've had many interactions with them myself," he said, lifting his arms and doing a slow pirouette. "As you can surely tell. Play your cards right and you'll have a long, healthy life here."

My eyes darted over to an image of the hellscape Tanaan had been turned into. "Is that what you've been doing here? Playing your cards?"

His eyes narrowed, signaling I needed to watch my tone. "All in legitimate business endeavors, young lady."

I glanced at Bjorn, who quirked an eyebrow. Exhaustion had depleted his normal reserve of diplomacy. "Any chance those 'endeavors' include monkeying around with zero-point energy?"

It was his turn to stiffen up. His calculated smile turned ice cold. "I'm not about to discuss my interests with you or anyone else here. They are between me and the science ministry."

That was as good as a "yes" by my reckoning. "And a few thousand innocents on Tanaan."

Gideon leaned forward on his cane, shaking a finger. "You're out of line, miss. The research I sponsor stands to benefit every race in the galaxy. There is nothing here that the Union isn't kept apprised of."

"Or maybe you only tell them what you want them to know."

"Unfortunate accidents are sometimes the price of progress. The workers on Tanaan knew the risks."

"You sure about that?"

"It's all spelled out in their contracts."

"What about industrial accidents that destroy entire planets? That kill and injure thousands? Is that in the contract, too?"

He was glowering now. "Do you know the sacrifices it took to build the first railroads, young lady? Power plants? Hell, to beat the Nazis for that matter? Or do they not teach history anymore on Earth?"

"I know there are great men, and not-so-great men that end up with a lot of money and power anyway. I'm guessing you're in the latter."

His cheeks flushed. "Jarra, get your human pet there under control. We're done here. Let me know when my employees are released for duty." With that, the screen went blank. Outside, the space around Gideon's yacht began rippling from the same kinds of gravity waves I'd only seen from inside Bjorn's ship. It soon disappeared, and the space where it had been returned to normal.

Jarra turned to face me. "We'll discuss this later. I believe you are off duty now."

It was a long trip back to the ring city. I spent my time on the hospital ship taking turns on shift rotation, though there weren't many emergent cases left to deal with. The Med Corps doctors had their hands full, so my duties mainly consisted of playing nurse, monitoring patient's vitals and administering meds. It was important work but a little boring, a reminder of why I'd chosen EMS in the first place.

Whenever possible, I'd visit Xeelix in his ward. Much of the time he was asleep as his body worked overtime to heal itself. The docs had cleaned up my incision but it still looked nasty. The muscle tissue remained exposed, protected beneath a sterilizing force field while a skin graft was grown in the lab from a batch of Reticulan stem cells.

It had to hurt like hell but he stubbornly refused any pain meds, protesting that they dulled his senses. With the sensory overload he'd had on Tanaan, I'd have thought he'd welcome having them dulled a bit. Personally, I was looking forward to dulling my own senses at Wayside when we got home.

Home. What a strange word for out here. Shared trials will do that for you.

I was sitting by Xeelix's bed when he awoke. "Hello, Melanie." His voice was weak.

"Don't strain yourself on my account."

"You have earned the privilege."

"As have you. Feel free to think at me."

His thin mouth curled up into a grin, or the closest he could manage. His voice was raspier than usual. "It helps to master your language if I vocalize instead of relying on the translator. Have you not noticed?"

I was taken aback at his gesture. "You're speaking English! That's not the chip in my head?"

"Ah. Then I was successful. I wondered if you were simply playing along with me."

"Never. I respect you too much. And thanks, by the way."

"It is I who owe you thanks. For rescuing me, and for teaching me."

"Teaching you? You're the reason I made it through training here. I was drinking from a fire hose in class and you broke it down into bits I could understand. Showed me how to pull it all together on runs."

He reached for me with his good arm and grasped my hand. "You possessed that ability when you arrived; we only needed to teach you the particulars. Remember why you were recruited."

I was still having trouble getting my head around that idea. Out of eight billion people on Earth, why had they chosen me? It was still hard to believe it had started with an accident, simply being in the right place at the right time.

There is something to that, of course. But your compassion and tenacity attracted our attention.

I tapped my forehead. "You're cheating."

He coughed. "My apologies. You must forgive me, I'm still rather weak. The old habits assert themselves."

"It's okay. But promise me you'll take it easy for a while."

"Of course." He fixed me with those deep black eyes, as if he could see right through me. It would always be a little unnerving, no matter how many Grays I might get to know. "I have learned a great deal from you, Melanie. I have always believed in your kind's potential. I also know there are many more like you, and they will be the ones who ultimately win over the Union. Not..."

"The ones like Gideon?"

"I suppose those personality types are unavoidable. Unfortunately, your kind possesses more than we typically encounter. It is one of those civilizational filters we discussed."

"I still don't understand why the Union puts up with him."

"Nor do I, though he largely resides outside of its influence now. I suspect after this misadventure, he will become even more estranged. You played no small role in that."

"You mean when I blew up at him? All I did was show my ass, and he barely gave up anything."

"It was enough. Trust me, Jarra will ensure the science ministry is fully informed. Small steps, Melanie. Small steps."

Weeks later, life had returned to normal. That is, normal for a medic in the Union. After a stint back in dispatch as "punishment" for missing two shifts in a row, I was finally back on ambulance duty. Whatever burr I'd planted under Jarra's saddle must have been forgiven, as I couldn't have asked for a better crew: Bjorn piloted, while Chonk worked with me in back.

Our first day together had come after a night of celebration at Wayside, but this time I'd been smart enough to pace myself. It had been a memorable evening, with plenty of *ka'vaa'ma'loi*, though none of us touched the stone bug burritos and we barely tolerated the smell from the grill. We elected to sit outside in the fresh air of the biodome.

Turns out it was all engineered for my benefit. Chonk led me to a patio crowded with Thubans, Reticulans, and a clan of Gliesans. Bjorn and Sven stood to one side with knowing smiles.

"What's this?"

Chonk unrolled a bolt of violet fabric from his waist pouch. "This for you. On behalf of all. Is Th'u'ban combat medic sash. You have proven worthy. Wear with pride."

I didn't know what to say, in fact I was a little weak-kneed.

Thubans beat their chests, Gliesans clicked their mandibles, and Reticulans regally bowed their heads as I slipped on the sash. It hung past my knees.

Bjorn placed a hand on my shoulder. "I believe you are one of us now," he said. "Welcome to the Galactic Union."

I'd heard that months before, from a faceless immigration clerk. Now it meant something. For the first time in too many years, I had a family again. I self-consciously wiped at my eyes. "Thank you, everyone. It's an honor, truly."

There was something of my own to give. I reached into my pocket and pulled out an old pin that I'd been keeping as a memento. It was the blue-and-white, six-pointed "Star of Life." The EMS pin. I handed it to Chonk.

"This is our shield. On behalf of . . . Earth." It sounded a little melodramatic, but it's hard not to be when you're surrounded by extraterrestrials. "You've proven yourself as well, Chonk." I finished by giving my friend a tight hug, and reached up on tiptoes to peck his cheek.

That's not weird. I was occasionally known to kiss my pet lizard. Deal with it, Earthlings.

We sat the next day aboard our good old Class III transport, waiting for the next call, with me fingering the sash now safely tucked away in my hip pocket and Chonk obsessively fidgeting with his human medic badge. He'd pounded it into the scales on his chest, and there it remained.

"How long you stay?" he asked.

I looked up in surprise. "How long? I just got here!"

"You once say human medics 'burn out.' Don't want you 'burn out.'"

"Me neither, buddy. I kind of like it here. It's a lot more interesting than picking up old ladies that fall on the sidewalk."

He considered that. "Happens much?"

"Too much."

We were interrupted by the warning siren and the beacons pulsing outside. Bjorn leaned in from the pilot's station, holding up a dispatch notice on his crystal. "I understand you'd like things to stay interesting? As your kind says, be careful what you wish for."

"What've we got?"

"An Eridani mother in labor, on a passenger transport passing our sector. The ship's physician is unfamiliar with her ... *unusual* needs. He's requesting assistance. Jarra thought we'd be the 'optimal crew' for this run, as she put it."

I hopped up to wave the door shut, then strapped myself in. "We'd better get moving if there's a mom in labor. Babies tend to make their own schedules." And I was anxious to deliver my first baby; human or otherwise it's the high point of any medic's career. "Eridani," I wondered. "They're the octopus-looking guys, right? Haven't had a run for one of them yet."

Chonk and Bjorn shared a look. "First time everything."

Enough screwing around. "I don't know what you guys think is so funny. How hard can it be?"